Praise for
Written in the Stars

"With perfectly woven vulnerability and playfulness, *Written in the Stars* is a riotous and heartfelt read. I was hooked from the very first page!"

—Christina Lauren, *New York Times* bestselling author of *In a Holidaze*

"*Written in the Stars* is everything I want from a rom-com: fun, whimsical, sexy. This modern *Pride and Prejudice* glitters with romance."

—Talia Hibbert, *USA Today* bestselling author of *Get a Life, Chloe Brown*

"*Written in the Stars* had me hooked from the first page. It's an adorable and heartfelt romance with everything I adore: a killer meet-cute, loads of cute banter, steamy love scenes, all the feels, and a happily ever after that left me in happy tears. I fell head over heels for Elle and Darcy's love story. Alexandria Bellefleur's debut will have readers seeing stars in the best way."

—Sarah Smith, author of *Faker* and *Simmer Down*

"A dazzling debut! The perfect combination of humor and heart really makes this book shine."

—Rachel Lacey, author of *Don't Cry for Me*

"*Written in the Stars* is what you might get if your favorite Instagram astrologer wrote you an adorable romance novel. Delightful, funny, and sweet, with just the right touch of woo-woo."

—Scarlett Peckham, *USA Today* bestselling author of *The Rakess*

Written in the Stars

Written in the Stars

A NOVEL

ALEXANDRIA BELLEFLEUR

AVON

An Imprint of HarperCollinsPublishers

WRITTEN IN THE STARS. Copyright © 2020 by Alexandria Bellefleur. All rights reserved. Printed in the United States of America. No part of this book may be used or reproduced in any manner whatsoever without written permission except in the case of brief quotations embodied in critical articles and reviews. For information, address HarperCollins Publishers, 195 Broadway, New York, NY 10007.

HarperCollins books may be purchased for educational, business, or sales promotional use. For information, please email the Special Markets Department at SPsales@harpercollins.com.

FIRST EDITION

Designed by Diahann Sturge

Title page image © Khaneeros / Shutterstock, Inc.

Emojis throughout © FOS_ICON / Shutterstock, Inc.

Library of Congress Cataloging-in-Publication Data has been applied for.

ISBN 978-0-06-300080-3

23 24 25 26 27 LBC 33 32 31 30 29

Written in the Stars

Chapter One

There was only so much chafing a girl could handle, and Elle Jones had reached her limit. Dodging strollers in front of Macy's splashy holiday window displays and hustling to make it to the restaurant on time had caused the creep of her lace to quicken until her brand-spankin'-new underwear functioned more like a belt than the boy shorts they were. She could practically taste her spring-fresh laundry detergent.

Tugging through her dress had been futile. Shimmying certainly hadn't done shit. Neither had casually leaning against the crosswalk pole and . . . gyrating? There was some hip action, but less *trying to grind this pole to bring home the bacon* and more *bear in the woods with an insidious itch*. Shoving her hand up her skirt had been a last resort, one with the unintended consequence of making it look like she was getting frisky with herself in front of Starbucks. The streets of Seattle had seen stranger things, but apparently not the dude leering from the passenger window of the mud-splattered Prius.

It was all because she'd chosen to wear *this* underwear, *new* underwear, *sexier* underwear than anything else wadded up in her dresser drawer. Not that she was *expecting* Brendon's sister to see her underwear, but what if the date went well?

What if? Wasn't that the million-dollar question, the spark of hope that kept her coming back for more time and time—*and time*—again? The butterflies in her stomach were a balm, each flutter of their wings soothing the sting of all those previous rejections and brush-offs until she could barely remember what it felt like when her phone didn't ring. When the spark just wasn't there.

First-date jitters? No, this feeling was *magic*, like glitter rushing through her veins. Maybe this dinner would go well. Maybe they'd hit it off. Maybe there would be a second date and a third and a fourth and—maybe this would be it, her last first date. Boom. End game. A *lifetime* of butterflies.

Wedgie-free, Elle stopped in front of the restaurant and breathed deep. Sweat darkened the powder blue cotton of her dress as she swiped her palms against her skirt, drying off her hands before reaching for the silver handle. She tugged and . . . the glass door barely budged, opening a fraction of an inch.

This restaurant was four-little-dollar-signs expensive, which begged the question: Were rich people seriously doing enough manual labor to have the muscle mass required to pry open these doors? Or were they ripped thanks to the personal trainers and private Pilates lessons they could afford? Elle pulled harder. Was there an access code? A buzzer she needed to press? Was she supposed to wave her credit card—with its admittedly dismal limit—in front of the door?

A hand with perfectly polished nails in the most boring

shade of blush fluttered in front of her face through the glass. She straightened and—oh sweet Saturn. No wonder this place was so popular, prices and impossible doors be damned. With long, copper-colored curls and even longer legs, the hostess was the sort of unfairly gorgeous that graced the covers of magazines, pretty to the point it made her eyes hurt. Of course, it didn't help that the glass reflected Elle's own slightly blurry face. Her dishwater-blond bangs had separated and her liner had smudged around her eyes, making her look less smoky-eye sexy and more sweaty raccoon. Talk about a smack to the self-esteem.

"You're supposed to push." The hostess's brown eyes darted down to the handle.

Elle pressed her palm to the glass. Featherlight, the door glided open smooth as butter. Despite the cool November air, her cheeks prickled with heat. Great going. At least her gaffe was only witnessed by herself and the hostess and not Brendon's sister. Now *that* would've been a difficult impression to come back from.

"Thanks. They should really consider putting up a sign. Or, you know, not putting a handle on a push door." She laughed and—okay, so it wasn't *funny*, but the hostess could've done the decent thing and pretended. Elle wasn't even asking for an enthusiastic chuckle, just the kind of under-your-breath puff of laughter that was polite because Elle *totally* had a point.

But no. The hostess gave her a tight smile, eyes scanning Elle's face before she glanced down at her phone and sighed.

So far, the service sucked.

Rather than push her luck and make a bigger fool out of

herself in front of the gorgeous hostess who'd rather futz around on her phone than do her job, Elle scanned the restaurant for someone who could be related to Brendon.

He hadn't said much about his sister. Upon overhearing Elle discuss the perils of dating not only as a woman, but a woman who liked other women, Brendon had gotten this adorable, wide-eyed, puppy-dog look of excitement and said, *You're gay? So's my sister, Darcy.* Bisexual, but yeah, Elle was all ears. His smile had gone crooked, dimples deepening as his eyes sparkled with mischief. *You know what? I think you two would really hit it off.*

And who was she to say no when she'd been ranting to Margot about her shoddy luck in the love department? Saying no would've been silly.

All Brendon had told her was that Darcy would meet her at Wild Ginger at seven o'clock and, not to worry, he'd take care of their reservations. Maybe she was waiting at the bar. There was a petite blonde sipping a pink martini and chatting with the bartender. It could be her, but Brendon was tall and had broad shoulders. Perhaps it was the—

"Excuse me."

She spun, facing the hostess who was no longer staring at her phone but instead looking at Elle, brows raised expectantly. "Uh-huh?"

God, pretty people made her stupid.

The hostess cleared her throat. "Are you meeting someone?"

At least now she wouldn't have to do the awkward thing and approach every lone woman in the joint. "Yeah, I am. Last name on the reservation should be Lowell."

Enviably full lips pursed as the woman's eyes narrowed minutely. "Elle?"

Hold on. "No, Darcy. Unless Brendon put my name on the reservation? With her last name? That's a little presumptuous, but okay." She snorted. "I've been on plenty of first dates and I've never had one go *that* well if you catch my drift."

"No, I mean *you* are Elle," the hostess spoke slowly. "*I* am Darcy."

Elle's heart thudded, skipping over one beat and quickening on the next. "Darcy . . . is you? You are Darcy?" So . . . not the hostess.

She nodded.

Of course this was Brendon's sister. This was just Elle's luck, and now that she knew, the resemblance was quite obvious. They were both tall and slender and unfairly attractive. Granted, Brendon's hair was darker, but it was definitely red, and they both had freckles. So many freckles it was like Darcy's skin was a peachy-cream sky covered in pale brown stars begging to be mapped out, connected into constellations. They spilled over her jaw and dotted her throat, disappearing under the collar of her green swing dress, leaving their path to Elle's *vivid* imagination.

Her toes curled, face flushing when Darcy's eyes dipped, mirroring her own unapologetic perusal. She bit back a grin. Maybe it was a good thing she'd worn this underwear after all.

"You're late."

Oof. Or not. "I am, and I'm really sorry about that. But there was—"

Darcy held up a hand, forcing Elle to swallow her excuse.

"It's fine. I've had a long day and I already settled my tab at the bar." She pointed over Elle's shoulder toward the door. "I was calling a Lyft."

"What? No." She was late, yeah, but only by a few minutes. Okay, fifteen, but that wasn't her fault. "I really am sorry. I wanted to text you, but my phone died and it was like mommy roller derby in front of Macy's. And let me tell you, those women are vicious with their strollers when there are sales at stake. *Vicious.* I swear to God, you'd think it was Black Friday. Can you believe they've already got Christmas decorations up? I've still got cobwebs and Jon Bone Jovi hanging in my apartment." Her face flamed at Darcy's puzzled frown. "He's, um, my apartment skeleton. We thought it'd be *humerus.* Because . . . anyway." She squared her shoulders and gave Darcy her most heartfelt smile. "I've been looking forward to tonight ever since your brother mentioned he thought we might hit it off. Let me buy you another drink?"

She held her breath as Darcy deliberated, fingers pressed to the space between her brows as if she was staving off a headache.

After an excruciating moment of silence where Elle struggled not to squirm, Darcy dropped her hand and offered a ghost of a smile. "One drink."

Once more with feeling. Elle bit the inside of her cheek and smiled. Beggars couldn't be choosers. Lack of enthusiasm aside, this was good. Promising. There was still a chance to make this right. She could do this. She could *totally* rally.

Darcy's shoes, a pair of towering red-soled pumps, click-clacked with every perfectly paced step across the restaurant.

Elle followed, fluffing her fringe with her fingers, quick and inconspicuous. Her first impression might've been lackluster, but that meant the only direction things could go was up.

"What are you drinking?" Elle plucked the drink menu off the table and— Oh sweet Saturn. Her wallet curled up into the fetal position.

"The Francois Carillon Chardonnay." Darcy flagged down a waiter with a twist of her wrist.

The Francois . . . Elle brought the menu closer to her face and nearly choked. Fifty-six dollars for a *glass* of wine? That couldn't be right. It had to be a typo, a misplaced decimal, maybe some trick of the candlelight playing off the gold gilded font. She double-checked to make sure she hadn't confused the price of a glass for a bottle, maybe a case, and . . . nope.

"What can I get you?" the waiter asked, and when Darcy finished relaying her order, he turned to Elle. "And you, miss?"

"Erm." She scanned the page, struggling not to cringe. Didn't this place believe in happy hour? Or hell, *happiness*? Making your rent? Shoot, her rent. That was due on Monday. "The Domaine De Pellehaut Merlot Blend?"

Not only did she butcher the pronunciation, she *hated* merlot. But nine dollars was plenty more palatable than *fifty-six*.

The waiter nodded and disappeared.

Salvage this date. A seemingly simple goal, only, all her wonderful, sparkling witticisms caught in her throat like a swallowed wad of gum when Darcy just *stared* at her. Candlelight transformed Darcy's light brown eyes into butterscotch and when Darcy glanced down at her phone, the light danced off the darkest, thickest lashes Elle had ever seen and—

"What mascara do you use?" Elle blurted.

Darcy flipped her phone over, screen side down, and looked up, brows furrowing as she met Elle's eyes. "My mascara? YSL."

"They're really pretty. Your eyes, I mean."

The crests of Darcy's cheeks turned an alluring shade of pink. "Thank you?"

Elle bit her lip and smoothed the napkin on her lap, smothering her grin at having taken Darcy by surprise. Only when she was no longer in danger of beaming like a loon did she lift her eyes and . . . Darcy was back to staring across the table, only this time there was something more than polite interest in her gaze.

For a moment, Elle couldn't breathe. All she could do was watch as Darcy's blush deepened, pink cheeks turning crimson.

The smooth column of Darcy's throat jerked as she swallowed. Her tongue darted out to wet her full bottom lip, drawing Elle's eye to a crescent-shaped freckle at her lip line, and dear God, she hadn't had anything to drink yet and already she was dizzy, though that might've had something to do with how her lungs refused to cooperate.

Magnetic. Elle couldn't look away because this was champagne bubbles on her tongue, the first plunge into a swimming pool on a scorcher of a day, that moment right before the bass drops in a killer song. Sparks, chemistry, whatever it was, this was the sort of *it's there or it's not* connection she'd been chasing.

Before she could find her voice, the waiter returned, tray in hand. First, he filled Darcy's glass from a miniature carafe, then poured a splash of red into Elle's. He waited, clearing his throat gently.

Was she seriously supposed to . . . sniff it? Sample it? And say what? God, just last week she and Margot had finished off a box of Franzia rosé. She'd guzzled the dregs from the wine bladder while Margot squeezed the bag. Elle's tastes weren't exactly what she'd call discerning.

She took a whiff, sipped, and hummed thoughtfully. Yuck. "Yep. That is definitely merlot. Thanks."

The waiter's lips twitched as he filled her glass with the rest of the wine. "I'll be back to take your order shortly."

Elle tucked her hair behind her ear, finger snagging on her hoop. Darcy's blush had mostly dissipated, but she gulped her wine, eyes looking everywhere but at Elle. That was fine; Darcy wouldn't be acting that way unless the moment had affected her, too.

"Brendon mentioned you work in . . . insurance? Is that right?"

Darcy swallowed and dipped her chin. "I'm an actuary."

"That sounds . . . interesting?"

Darcy actually chuckled. "I know, it sounds astonishingly dull, doesn't it?"

Leaning back in her chair, Elle grinned. "I'm not sure I even know what an actuary does."

"I help to establish accurate and fair pricing for insurance premiums by analyzing variables and trends in historical data. It's calculus, mostly." Darcy shrugged and set her wineglass on the table. "I enjoy it."

The word *calculus* gave Elle a violent flashback to undergrad. Math was not something that usually got her hot under the collar, even if she was decent at it. But if Darcy wanted to spend the evening discussing differentials and limits, Elle would happily listen to the smooth cadence of Darcy's voice.

"That's what's important." Elle crossed her legs beneath the table, her ankle brushing Darcy's briefly. "Life's too short to waste on something you don't enjoy. It's the best of both worlds when what you love also pays your bills."

Darcy smiled and a teensy dimple formed beside her mouth like a parenthesis for that special freckle. "What do you do?"

"Oh, Brendon didn't say?" For being the brains behind a *dating* app, Brendon was missing a few of the critical points of matchmaking. "I'm an astrologer. Margot—that's my roommate—and I, we're the voices behind Oh My Stars."

Darcy cocked her head, copper curls spilling over her shoulder.

"You know, the horoscope Twitter and Instagram account? We have a book coming out in six months, too."

Darcy shook her head. "I don't really do Twitter. Or Instagram. Social media at all for that matter."

Who didn't do social media? It was one thing to steer clear of Facebook, which had been infiltrated by older relatives, sure, but Twitter? Instagram?

"Well, we tweet advice interspersed with the occasional meme and joke. OTP wants us to consult on adding a birth chart element to the match system. It would allow users to evaluate compatibility, not only based on the fun elements OTP's already known for like their BuzzFeed-style personality quizzes and favorite ships and whatnot, but also the most pertinent planetary positions at the time of your birth." She pointed to Darcy's cell. "If you let me borrow your phone, I can pull up your chart really quick. All I need is your date, time, and location of birth."

Darcy's lips twitched. "I'm good."

"Do you not know your time of birth? Because most of the planets are slow moving enough that—well, I couldn't tell you about your ascendant or your houses, and your Moon could potentially be tricky, but we could still look at a few factors." Unless—oh crap, had she overstepped? Elle was so used to doing readings, not only for a living, but also analyzing the birth charts of friends and family, that asking was second nature. "If that's too personal, I completely understand."

Darcy plucked her glass by the stem and swirled her wine. "Sorry, I don't really believe in that stuff."

Elle frowned. "*Stuff*?"

Teeth sunk into her lower lip, Darcy looked like she was trying not to laugh. "The supposed link between astronomical phenomena and human behavior. Blaming your personality on the planets sounds a bit like a cop-out."

She'd heard this argument before. "It's not about *blaming* your personality on the planets; it's about understanding your-self and becoming aware of why you might be prone to certain behaviors and patterns. What people choose to do with that knowledge is up to them."

Darcy took a delicate swig of wine and set her glass aside. "Agree to disagree."

Elle bit the inside of her cheek. That was fine. She believed in it, and her five hundred *thousand* Twitter followers believed in it, too.

It *was* a bit of a bummer that she and Darcy weren't on the same page, but it was one topic. Granted, it was a topic near and dear to her heart, but it wasn't as if they came down on opposite ends of the political spectrum. She wouldn't press the issue . . . not on the first date. "At any rate, Margot and I are super excited to be a part of, *hopefully*, helping people find their soul mates."

Darcy snorted and not in that *I agree*, or *God, you're so funny* kind of way. It was a sardonic little puff, condescending when paired with the roll of her eyes. "You sound like my brother."

"Is that a bad thing?"

"It's a romantic notion." Darcy dropped her eyes, her expression shuttering.

Elle frowned. "And *that's* a bad thing?"

"It's silly. Soul mates. Your *one true pairing*." Darcy shook her head like it was ridiculous.

The butterflies quit fluttering, Elle's stomach souring, though that might've been the wine. What was Darcy even doing on this date if she wasn't looking for love, or at least the *chance* of love?

"I think it's nice," Elle argued. "If you don't believe in love, what's left to believe in?"

Darcy's tongue poked against the inside of her cheek. "Sweet in theory, but a bit starry-eyed, don't you think?"

Was that a dig *and* a quip about her profession? "I'd rather be starry-eyed than jaded."

Reaching for her wine, Elle's fingers skimmed the stem, her grip slipping. The glass teetered, tottered, swaying back and tipping forward. Her stomach rioted, mimicking the motion. In slo-mo, the red wine sloshed over the rim of the glass as the whole thing tumbled, merlot soaking into the linen tablecloth and splashing across the table, splattering Darcy's dress.

"Oh fuck." Elle scrambled for a napkin and stood, knees knocking into the table and—

Fifty-six dollars of wine toppled right over into Darcy's lap.

Elle froze, white cloth napkin poised to—what? Blot? Fuck, she'd better start waving it in surrender.

"I am *so* sorry." Heat crept up her throat, making her uncomfortably warm.

"It's—it's fine." Darcy shoved her chair back, legs squealing against the wood. The wine not soaked into her dress dribbled down her legs when she stood. "Excuse me."

Darcy shuffled off toward the back of the restaurant, where there was a sign pointing to the restroom.

Elle's pulse lurched in her throat and her eyes went damp as she set the now-empty glasses to rights. Fuck her life. She had *not* meant for that to happen. She wasn't usually clumsy, nowhere close, but Darcy had put her on the defensive.

Astrology was one thing—granted, an important thing—but not believing in *love*? How in the hell was she related to adorkable Brendon, *creator* of OTP? Brendon who rambled about Doctor Who and spoke with his hands and made "May the 4th Be With You" an official companywide holiday. Brendon who, in her two in-person meetings with OTP Inc., several lunches, and countless DMs, had displayed more verve for life in his pinkie than Darcy possessed in her whole, admittedly gorgeous, body. Elle had felt sparks, she absolutely had, but had Darcy? Apparently not if she could so easily scoff at the idea of true love.

Elle stuck her hand in the air and flagged down the waiter.

He frowned at the table. "Let me grab something to clean this up."

"Just . . . could you . . . I'm ready to leave." She handed him her card, forcing her fingers to release the plastic when he tugged.

One swipe of her Visa later, he returned, handing her the receipt folded around her card. Good. She didn't want to look at the bill right now, anyway. "Have a nice night."

Nice night, her butt. That ship had sailed and sunk and was now nothing but wreckage on the bottom of the ocean.

Time to cut her losses. As soon as Darcy came back, Elle would make her exit.

She crossed her legs and tried to ignore the twinge in her bladder. What was taking Darcy so long? Maybe she would hit the restroom first. If she ran into Darcy, she could kill two birds with one stone, making her good-bye brief before more damage could be done. Literally.

Decided, Elle stood and tossed her napkin on the table before heading to the restroom.

"—didn't even want to go on this date in the first place and now my dress is ruined, Annie."

Darcy faced the end of the hall, her back to Elle. Phone pressed to her ear, she paced slowly in front of the door to the ladies', one spindly stiletto placed perfectly in front of the toe of her other foot as if she were walking on a balance beam as she held her phone to her ear.

Elle's legs locked, trapped in the evolutionarily stupid choice between fight and flight. *Freeze.*

Darcy gave a dry laugh. "I don't see how that's relevant but, yes, she's pretty. I'm sure she's *loads* of fun, too. She's also a mess."

All she wanted to do was pee, but Darcy was *right there*, right in front of the restroom, blocking the hall, *roasting* her to this Annie person.

"What am I going to tell Brendon?" Darcy asked. "The truth, that we're total opposites. And I'm putting my foot down. This was the last date he's *ever* setting me up on."

Elle pressed her lips together and swallowed past the lump in her throat.

On second thought, she could hold it.

✧ ✧
✧

The air in the apartment was sticky with humidity and honey-suckle sweet. Thin wisps of steam floated out from beneath the bathroom door, filling the hall as Stevie Nicks's rasping voice flooded into the living room.

Elle flipped the lock and fell to her knees beside where Jon Bone Jovi hung from a double-knotted strand of monofilament tacked into the drywall. She crawled across the room, face-planting into the sofa with a groan. The blue afghan draped against the cushions smelled faintly like patchouli, and the lit-tle gold coins affixed to the fringes were cool against her cheek as she burrowed deeper, rubbing her nose into the well-loved fabric. Home sweet home.

The scent of honeysuckle grew stronger, more pungent as the whirl of the fan cut off, the bathroom door opened, steam spill-ing out like sweet smoke as the music cut off midverse.

Margot padded into the living room, leopard-print robe knotted around her waist and a towel wrapped around her head. Her footsteps faltered, her dark brown eyes turning into saucers behind her thick, black-rimmed glasses. Her mouth opened before she paused, sucking her bottom lip between her teeth. "How'd it go?"

"You know the public restrooms down by the market?" Elle kicked her shoes across the room, wincing when they left a dusty brown smudge against the baseboard by the breakfast nook slash Oh My Stars headquarters. Whoops.

"The one with doors so short you're forced to make awkward eye contact with the person in the next stall over?" Margot crossed the room and crouched beside her.

Elle nodded. "I lost my underwear inside."

Margot's jet-black brows rocketed to her hairline, disappearing into her turby-towel. "Explain, because my mind is going to some funky, debauched places."

"Gross, no. I had to pee." Her underwear—those impractical but pretty boy shorts—had been an unfortunate casualty, touching the grimy floor when she had squatted. "My underwear slipped and landed in a puddle of"—she wrinkled her nose—"something sticky."

There would be no coming back from that, the memory of them falling past her ankles onto the tile impossible to scrub away.

Margot's face screwed up, twisting in disgust. "The pair you just bought? The ones with the little bows on the side?"

"Yeah."

"Those were cute."

"Just not meant to be, I guess." Elle sniffed hard and buried her toes in the thick shag pile of the carpet. "They chafed like a bitch, anyway."

Margot's mouth opened only to shut, her lips tucking between her teeth. She cleared her throat. "I'm getting the sense your date didn't go well?"

A weak, watery laugh spilled from between Elle's lips, but she wasn't going to cry. No way, no how. Darcy Lowell did not deserve her tears. "What possibly gave you that idea?"

Without saying anything, Margot grabbed her hand and laced their fingers together, squeezing until the ache in Elle's joints surpassed the pressure in her chest.

"I've never met someone so gorgeous and yet so condescending in my life." Elle swallowed before her voice did something pathetic like crack. "Worst part was, I could've sworn we had . . . *something*. I felt a spark, you know?" She sighed, shoulders slumping. "Not that it matters. I didn't stand a chance, no matter the chemistry."

There were opposites and then there were *opposites*. Darcy didn't believe in astrology or soul mates and—what was it she had called her? A mess? Pretty, too, but a mess nonetheless. And fun. She couldn't forget that part.

This is fun, but . . .

You're so fun, Elle, but . . .

I had fun with you, but . . .

If Elle had a dollar for every time someone had used the word *fun* to reject her, she'd—no, it'd still suck no matter how many dollars she had.

Not that there was anything inherently wrong with being

fun—Elle *wanted* to be fun. But to be reduced to a good time was something else.

Couldn't she be fun *and* more? Couldn't a relationship? For that matter, shouldn't it?

Margot clicked her tongue against her teeth. "Fuck her, then. It's her loss, babe."

"You always say that."

"I always mean it."

Elle snorted. *Sure.* There were only so many times Margot could use that excuse before it lost its charm. Tonight, it rang hollow.

"You know what you need?" Margot grunted softly as she rolled to her knees and stood, plucking green carpet lint off her bare skin. "Tequila."

Margot made the best margaritas, tangy tequila-y perfection with a cheery rainbow salted rim. As much as Elle wanted to say yes, she couldn't. "I have to get up early. Breakfast with my mom tomorrow, remember?"

Waking up at the butt-crack of dawn and hauling herself over to the Eastside for their monthly mother-daughter breakfast was difficult enough without the added hangover.

Margot's lips twisted. "I'm guessing you still haven't told her about the deal with OTP?"

Elle snagged the bowl of dry cereal she'd left on the table this morning and sorted the minimarshmallows from the boring bits, placing them into groups of rainbows, moons, and balloons. She shrugged, avoiding Margot's hawklike stare.

"Elle." Margot pursed her lips.

Elle poured a handful of rainbow marshmallows into her mouth and munched. "The timing hasn't been right."

"I know the book deal announcement didn't go the way you'd hoped, but that doesn't mean your family won't be excited about this." Margot's grin was almost convincing, but it didn't quite reach the corners of her eyes. "Come on. This deal is *big*. If your family can't see that . . ."

Margot was right that the deal with OTP, the coolest dating app ever—for nerds, by nerds—was a BFD. The passion-project side hustle Margot and Elle had been working themselves to the bone over for years was about to become a full-time venture.

Elle should've been bursting at the seams to scream her good news at anyone who'd listen, but if history was anything to go by, telling Mom could go one of two ways. She would either have a million questions about what an *OTP* was and whether Elle had someone reliable checking over her contract and was she sure she didn't want to just get a nice, *normal* job with a steady paycheck and retirement benefits? Or she would smile blandly, her eyes glazing over as soon as Elle mentioned the words *dating app* and *astrological compatibility*. Then Mom would respond with *that's nice, Elle*.

She'd managed to earn a *that's really great, honey* when she'd told her family about the book deal. Only, her older sister, Jane, had followed with her own happy news that after a year of IVF, she and her husband were expecting twins. Obviously a bigger deal than Elle's news, but she was pretty sure her family had forgotten all about her book in the hubbub of Jane's announcement.

Playing second fiddle to her older sibling's achievements was the story of her life, but that didn't mean she was keen on suffering through another instance of hoping her family would *finally* take an interest in her life beyond polite tolerance of her *eccentricities.*

I'm sure she's loads of fun, too. She's also a mess.

Not just her family.

So what if Elle took her advice from the stars instead of the self-help section? Conventional was boring, but why was it impossible to find someone who liked the beat of her drum as much as she did?

Margot waved a hand in front of Elle's face. "Earth to Elle."

Elle forced a smile. "Sorry. I just had a bad night. It churned up some less than awesome feelings."

"Buck up, Buttercup." Margot stole one of Elle's marshmallow balloons. "Forget about Brendon's sister. She wasn't right for you, so just shake it off. You'll have better luck next time, okay?"

Elle opened her mouth but as soon her lips parted, a hazy, damp film clouded her vision. She had to swallow before she could speak. "How many more *next times* are there going to be, Mar? How many more first dates am I going to have to go on? How many times am I going to get my hopes up? I know I shouldn't . . . give up, but is it awful that I kind of want to . . . take a step back?"

Margot's dark eyes widened, probably because Elle was the optimist in their duo. She'd been called Pollyannaish a time or two, and whatever, she didn't care if people thought she was naively optimistic, but—maybe she *was* delusional. Maybe the beat of her own drum was best danced to alone.

"I think . . . I think you should do what feels right." Margot gave a definitive nod. "If you're feeling burned out and you want to take a hiatus from the dating scene? I say go for it. Your perfect person is out there somewhere, completely oblivious to the fact that their dream girl is sitting on the floor of her apartment right now, chowing down on Lucky Charms, commando. They can wait."

Elle tried to smile, but couldn't quite pull it off, not when the sting of rejection was so fresh. Not when she'd had such high hopes and had, for just a moment, felt a connection, the kind that couldn't be faked.

Maybe Margot was right. Maybe her perfect person was out there, but one thing was certain.

It wasn't Darcy.

—and that's when I said to my grandson, 'Johnathon, you're too talented to be working yourself to the bone for that chef. You should start your own restaurant.' And you know what? He did. Owns three food trucks. A real entrepreneur. Can you believe it?"

Mrs. Clarence's knobby, arthritic fingers trembled around the strap of her reusable grocery bag. Darcy had already snagged two of Mrs. Clarence's bags on the way into the elevator, but she went ahead and reached for the third, accepting a pat on the arm when her neighbor let her shoulder the weight of all three.

"That's nice, Mrs. Clarence." She tried not to wince when the strap of the heaviest bag bit into the thin skin of her inner elbow. "You must be very proud."

The older woman sighed. "Oh, I am. Now if only he could find a girl, a *nice* girl." Her shrewd eyes roved over Darcy from her head down to her feet. "Say, you're not seeing anyone, are you, Darcy dear?"

She gave Mrs. Clarence what hopefully came across as an appropriately apologetic smile instead of a grimace. "Sorry. Work has me busy."

Her elderly neighbor tutted, lips pursing in disapproval, *silent* disapproval. If only it were that easy to put her brother off.

Saved by the bell, the elevator dinged, spitting them out on the ninth floor. Mercifully, Mrs. Clarence was in apartment 901, the unit closest to the elevators.

Darcy lugged the bags the brief distance to the doorway, arms trembling under their weight as Mrs. Clarence took her time unlocking her door before ushering Darcy inside. She unloaded the bags into the kitchen, setting them down on the dining table beside Mrs. Clarence's Persian longhair, Princess. "You want me to unpack these?"

Stroking the purring cat between the ears, the older woman shook her head. "No, no. Just leave them here. I always appreciate your help, Darcy. You're a peach."

With a wave, Darcy departed down the hall, unlocking the door to her own apartment. As soon as she stepped inside, she placed her keys in the wooden bowl on the entry table and slumped against the door.

What a night.

Her favorite dress—vintage Oscar de la Renta that had once belonged to her late grandmother—was possibly ruined, the stomach-churning headache that had taken up residence smack between her eyes in the afternoon had only gotten worse as the day progressed, and for all that she loved Brendon, wrapping her hands around his neck and strangling him until his eyes bulged sounded like a fantastic idea right about now.

What had he been thinking? *Had* he been thinking? An astrologer? So what if Elle had been *unbelievably* pretty? They had nothing in common save for their mutual inability to keep their eyes off each other. Which could've been promising had Elle not been looking for her *soul mate*.

Darcy rolled her eyes.

She should've never agreed to Brendon's matchmaking in the first place, but he'd been so earnest and eager to see her get back up on the horse when she'd been ready to put the damn thing out to pasture. Saying yes had been easier than explaining why not . . . especially when Brendon had mentioned the reservation was at a restaurant she'd been dying to try ever since seeing the chef featured on Food Network. And so she'd reluctantly agreed. One date, a drink, some amazing food, and a bit of surface-level chitchat. She'd have *put herself out there* and Brendon would be appeased. What was the worst that could happen?

Come on, Darcy. You'll really like Clarissa.

Susanna's absolutely your type.

I think you'll hit it off with Veronica. I swear.

Really, Darce. I think Arden might be the one.

He hadn't stopped at just one date. Oh, no. One date had snowballed into weekly setups—*how* in God's name did he know so many single queer women?—and after three months of blind dates Darcy had officially reached her limit. Honestly, she'd reached her limit last month, but when she'd fessed up and told Brendon she didn't have the time or desire to pursue a serious relationship and he could cool it, he'd balked. *A few lackluster dates and you're throwing in the towel? Come on, she's perfect.*

No one was perfect.

Next time, she wasn't going to cave, wasn't going to simply roll her eyes and agree to some date just to get Brendon off her back. Not even if he pouted and played the baby brother card. Darcy was putting her foot down. She'd had enough of him projecting his own romantic notions of true love onto her. She wasn't looking for *the one*. Not anymore.

After stripping off her wine-soaked dress and setting it aside for dry cleaning—maybe they could work a miracle on the silk—Darcy stood in the kitchen, stomach rumbling.

Her eyes darted to the cabinet rather than the refrigerator. After a day like today, the peanut butter was *calling* to her.

Jar cradled in the crook of her elbow and bag of chocolate chips in one hand, a spoon in the other, Darcy curled up on the couch, leather groaning softly beneath her weight. At last. As soon as she fired up the DVR, she'd be in Whisper Cove, catching up on the antics of Nikolai and Gwendolyn, Carlos and Yvette, and the whole sordid Price family who had more skeletons in their collective closet than she had shoes.

Friday nights with her DVR, catching up on the week's episodes of *Whisper Cove*, were sacred. Sacred and *secret*. It was a silly show, ridiculous that she even enjoyed it, but it was called a guilty pleasure for a reason.

Three episodes in, Nikolai and Gwendolyn were about to kiss, a culmination of months of tension and chemistry sprinkled with tender moments. The distance between their faces shrunk as Nikolai reached out, thumb stroking the delicate curve of her cheek. Darcy's breath quickened as she inched closer to the edge of the cushion, bag of chocolate chips clenched in her fist. This was it, the moment—

A loud bang filled her apartment and her chocolate chips flew into the air as she jumped from the couch, heart hammering jackrabbit-fast against her sternum.

Someone was at the door.

Jesus. She rolled her eyes at her dramatics. It was only a knock, but she'd been swept up in the moment, oblivious to anything else. Ridiculous.

Tiptoeing over spilled chocolate chips, Darcy crossed toward the door, footsteps faltering at another thunderous rap of knuckles against wood.

"Darcy, open up."

Her eyes shut, her pulse slowing.

Brendon.

Her eyes snapped open.

Brendon.

Scrambling backward, she shut off the TV and then shoved the remote between the couch cushions, hiding the evidence of her date with the DVR. He banged against the door again, this time harder. For god's sake. She blew out her breath. "Coming!"

As soon as the door was open, Brendon shouldered his way past, eyes wide, frazzled, gaze bouncing around the living room before finally landing on her. "Are you okay?"

"Yes?" Aside from the near cardiac arrest.

Brendon shut his eyes and pressed a hand to his chest like

he was the one who'd been panicked. "I called you *four* times, Darce."

She lifted a shoulder. "Sorry. My phone was on silent."

For a reason. Brendon loved dissecting her dates like some sort of postgame interview. Tonight, she'd wanted to skip that. She didn't want to talk about it, definitely not what she did or didn't feel.

The furrow between his brows deepened as his gaze slipped down, noticing her pajamas. "Darcy."

"What?" She spun on her heel and returned to the living room, bending low to pick up her spilled chocolate chips before they wound up ground into her nice white carpet.

Brendon collapsed into the armchair, long legs splaying in front of him as he pinned her with a stare that knotted her stomach. "What was wrong with Elle?" He barely paused, didn't give her a chance to enumerate all their many, varied differences. "She's sweet, she's hilarious, she's—she's *fun*, Darcy. And God knows you could use some fun in your life."

The scoff bubbled up before she could stop it. "And what exactly is that supposed to mean?"

"It means what it sounds like." Brendon spread his arms wide, gesturing around them. "For one, it looks like West Elm and the Container Store had a baby and that baby vomited all over your apartment. *Neatly* vomited, because heaven forbid there be a *mess*."

That was a shitty non sequitur. "I like my apartment clean. I'm failing to see how my preference for organization somehow correlates with my ability to have fun."

"Look." Brendon ran his fingers through his hair, tugging

hard at the ends. He was in desperate need of a haircut. "I love you. If I didn't, I wouldn't waste my breath. God, Darcy, you're not even trying to have a life here in Seattle. All you do is stare at spreadsheets and numbers all day, you come home, you stare at spreadsheets some more, you eat out of color-coordinated Tupperware. And how could I forget?" He gestured to the TV. "You're invested in other people's *scripted* lives."

No. Heat crept up the back of her neck and wrapped around her throat. She needed to sit down. "Excuse me?"

Brendon's lips twitched. "You thought I didn't know about your thing for daytime soaps? Come on. I'm a lot of things, but oblivious isn't one of them."

"It's not a *thing.*" A thing would be writing *Days of Our Lives* fanfiction and she hadn't done that since college.

"What, did you think I'd judge you? Me? I'm the king of nerdy obsessions. Proud of it, mind you."

Darcy bit the inside of her lip to keep from smiling. "The king, huh? Awfully pretentious to crown yourself, isn't it?"

Not that it wasn't true, or that she wasn't proud. He was her baby brother. Gone were the days of shuttling him and his friends to summer STEM camp. Regardless of her feelings on love and dating apps, Brendon had turned his passion into an empire before he'd turned twenty-five. Of course, she was proud.

"Eh, I think the whole *nerd* bit balances it out." His self-effacing chuckle trailed off, his smile dropping. "Seriously, Darce, don't feed me that line about not being interested in a relationship. I'd respect that—I really would, I swear—if it weren't obviously a load of crap."

She opened her mouth to refute that, but he kept going.

"You sure as hell were interested in a serious relationship two years ago when you were *engaged*."

Her heart stuttered. "Don't go there."

"You refuse to talk about it, so maybe we need to go there." The way he winced *screamed* pity and she hated that. Hated it so much it made her stomach ache. "Not everyone's like Natasha."

Swallowing suddenly required effort. "I said, don't go there."

Brendon shook his head, jaw hard and expression fierce. "You're my sister, and you're also one of the greatest people I know, and you're . . . you're amazing, Darce. You've got so much to offer and there's someone out there for you, the *right* person for you. I know there is. I just . . . I don't want you to wind up alone and miserable because you're scared of getting your heart broken again."

Darcy blinked fast and crossed her arms, staring past Brendon at the iridescent oyster shell wall art over his shoulder.

Last she checked, she couldn't get her heart broken if she never put it on the line. That didn't make her scared, that made her realistic. Was she terrified of getting hit by a bus? No, but that didn't mean she had any intention of stepping out into traffic.

Brendon might've been a romantic idealist, and if that made him happy, great. More power to him. But she knew the truth. Life was not a fairy tale and she was not the exception.

Darcy's heart threw itself against her sternum as she gritted her teeth, pasting on the smile she'd perfected since . . . *since.* "I'm not scared. Don't be ridiculous."

Brendon cut his eyes, head tilting, studying her, so obviously appraising her for chinks in her armor. The muscles in her face twitched, smile wavering. *Shit.*

His answering smile was an infuriating mix of smug and sympathetic. "See, I think the reason you don't want to go on these dates is because you know, one of these days you're going to meet someone who makes you want to take that risk, and that terrifies you."

For some asinine reason that was entirely beyond comprehension, Elle's pretty heart-shaped face flashed through Darcy's mind. Her neck broke out into a damp sweat, her hair sticking to her clammy skin.

"I *said* I'm not scared." Her voice just had to go and crack. Salvaging what remained of her dignity, she cleared her throat and fixed him with a stern glare. "Or if I am, it's because I'm worried about your listening comprehension. Is your hearing okay?"

"Sure, Darce, whatever you say." Brendon rolled his eyes.

"I'm glad we understand each other."

"So if you're not afraid—"

"And I'm *not.*"

Brendon lifted his hands. "Then you won't have a problem with me signing us both up for speed dating next Saturday over in Kirkland. Eight o'clock. Goes for two hours, there's a nice break in the middle. Tapas, wine, mixing, mingling. You know, *fun.*"

"I can't." Her tongue traced the contours of her upper teeth. "I have . . . I have plans. I have, um . . ." *Saturday.* "My FSA study group is meeting that night."

It wasn't even a lie. She was one exam away from becoming a Fellow of the Society of Actuaries, the highest designation awarded by the SOA. Back in April, when she'd interviewed for the job with Devereaux and Horton Mutual Life, Mr. Stevens had made it clear she was guaranteed a promotion to a management role as soon as she passed this tenth and final exam.

So no, Brendon was wrong. It wasn't a matter of fear, it was about making a logical decision, one that centered her priorities. She refused to be like their mother, getting so wrapped up in a relationship that she lost herself in it, forgetting about everything else that mattered—her work, her passions, even her children. Yes, Darcy was over Natasha, but who was to say she'd be able to get over the next heartbreak, that something inside her wouldn't fracture irreparably? Better not to tempt fate than take that risk.

He cocked his head. "No worries. There's another speed-dating event on Tuesday. You know, for all the people who can't make it on Saturday because they have *plans.*"

Darcy set her hands on her hips. "Jesus, Brendon. Will you lay off already? Quit pressuring me to do things I don't want, okay?"

Brendon pressed his lips together and stared, eyes going wide as his jaw slid forward and back. She quickly looked away, having no interest in being on the receiving end of his stupid puppy-dog stare.

"You make it sound like I'm asking you to get a root canal."

Brendon huffed and pressed the heels of his hands into his eyes. "You've been in Seattle for six months and you have no friends, Darcy."

She cut her eyes. "I have friends, thank you very much." When all he did was stare blankly from the armchair, she insisted, "There's Annie—"

"Who lives across the country."

"And . . . and my coworkers. My FSA study group."

Brendon arched a brow. "Your *FSA study group*. Yeah, you guys sound really close."

She sniffed. "We *are*. There's Amanda and Lin and . . . and . . . M- . . . Mariel?"

"Was that a question?"

What a smartass. Darcy glared.

Brendon didn't even smirk. He just looked at her with pity and that was a million times worse than all his cajoling. "I know what happened in Philadelphia fucked you up—"

"It did *not*."

"Fucked you *over*," Brendon amended. "But you've got to let people in, Darcy. You've got to learn to trust people again. Put yourself out there, make some friends, meet *someone*. Please, Darce. Do it for me."

Do it for me. Fuck. He made it all sound so simple when it was anything but.

"Fine, Brendon. I'll work on it, okay?"

"You'll go to speed dating with me?" he pressed.

That wasn't what she meant, but Brendon wasn't going to stop until her calendar was full of cooking classes and book clubs and dates. So. Many. Dates. He'd keep setting her up until she was happily paired off.

Wait.

That was it.

Brendon wasn't going to stop until she was seeing someone, until he *thought* she was seeing someone.

"I can't. I didn't say anything because I didn't want to get your hopes up, but I'm seeing someone." There. She'd bought herself some time.

Except he frowned. "But you went out tonight. With Elle."

Elle. Damn it.

Unless . . . no. With a little finesse, she could absolutely work this angle.

"Right." Darcy nodded. "Elle. Maybe *seeing someone* is a bit premature, but she's . . . she's really something. She's pretty."

The furrow of Brendon's brow deepened, forehead wrinkling as he puzzled over what she wasn't saying. After a moment, his face cleared, his eyes doubling in size. "Hold the phone. You and *Elle?*"

She would *not* roll her eyes. "Me and Elle."

"You two hit it off?" he pressed.

Darcy bit her lip and stared hard at the jar of peanut butter on the coffee table as she considered the question, and her answer, carefully.

Scary thing was, they *had* hit it off. Not at first with Elle's tardiness, but there'd been a spark. For a moment. Until their *many* differences—and different desires—had become apparent. "Elle's not like anyone I've ever met. That's for sure."

Brendon laughed, drawing her focus back to his face. He grinned like it was the best news he'd heard all day, and for a moment her stomach panged, guilt corroding her insides. "You're seriously smitten, aren't you?"

"No, I'm—" Denial was instinctive, but she was supposed to be selling it. "We're obviously total opposites, but there's . . . something there. Potential."

"And here I thought with you being home early and already in pajamas that your date hadn't gone well." Brendon's crooked grin was sheepish, his eyes crinkling at the corners.

"Well, you know what happens when you assume." Darcy smiled, softening the gibe.

Brendon shrugged as if to concede the point and hunched forward, resting his elbows on his knees. "Tell me about it. Tonight."

To Brendon, every moment was a meet-cute waiting to happen, each first date he went on captured in his memory in case he found *the one* and needed to tell his future children about the night their mom and dad met.

She needed to sell it. Hard. Lucky for her, personality clashes and restaurant disasters were the stuff meet-cutes were made of.

"It's actually a funny story."

Brendon shook his head. "Don't leave me in suspense. I'm dying over here."

"Settle down." If her pause was overly long, it was only because she was gathering her thoughts. And okay, fine, she was milking it, but only a little. "I won't lie—at first, we got off on the wrong foot. Elle was late and you know I'm a stickler for punctuality."

He rolled his eyes.

"She offered to buy me a drink and she told me about her job, which she's *extremely* enthusiastic about. Even though I don't believe in astrology, that sort of passion is attractive."

Brendon waggled his brows.

"*Stop.*" She laughed.

"Sorry." Brendon grinned. "Didn't mean to interrupt. Keep going."

"Okay, let's see . . . we had wine." She smirked, not because what had happened was *funny* but because she couldn't wait for Brendon's reaction. "Or we would have, had she not spilled it all over me."

His eyes widened. "Get out."

"Eh." With a shrug, Darcy waved it off. "I'm sure my dry cleaner can work a miracle on the stain."

Fingers crossed.

"Details, Darce. Come on. Tell me about the *sparks.*" Brendon gestured for her to keep talking with an impatient wave of his hand.

"She said I have pretty eyes." Darcy hadn't meant to whisper, but it wound up being a more honest confession than she'd intended.

Her eyes were brown. Nothing was wrong with them, but no one ever complimented her eyes. They went for the obvious attributes—her hair, her legs, her breasts if they were being bold. But her eyes?

Ridiculous. If anyone had nice eyes it was Elle. Big and blue, *so* blue it was like staring off into the Puget Sound at midnight on a full moon.

"You're blushing."

She was *not*. Except, when she brought her hands to her cheeks, her face was hot, feverish beneath her fingertips. She cleared her throat. No, there'd be no more getting lost in Elle's eyes. Capsizing, more like.

"I don't like to kiss and tell."

Brendon's eyes went huge and round, his jaw dropping and it was only then she realized what she'd said, how it could be construed, *misconstrued*. Only . . . wasn't that the point? Make him believe there'd been sparks, enough chemistry to put him off her trail?

There *had* been sparks. Just none that she had any intention of acting on. Sparks either fizzled, or they caught fire and burned you. Badly. No, thank you.

Obfuscation wasn't *quite* the same as lying. Brendon could believe what he wanted. *Technically* she'd only embellished.

"When are you seeing her again?"

"I'm really busy this week." Brendon's face fell, so she hurried to add, "But I'm going to text her. We'll play it by ear."

Not that she enjoyed stretching the truth, especially not to Brendon, but it was sort of brilliant. Play it by ear, text when she could. If he asked, she'd make up an excuse about being busy, push it off, buy herself a little more time. She might even text Elle for real, just a quick thank-you for picking up the tab. That would be the polite thing to do, especially since she hadn't had the chance to thank her at the restaurant. By the time she'd made it back from the restroom, Elle had already left. A fact that should not have stung, and yet, for some inexplicable reason, had. Damp silk tickling the skin of her stomach, Darcy had frozen in front of the empty table. The sight of Elle's pink lip print on her empty wineglass but no Elle had felt like pressing on a bruise Darcy hadn't realized was there until she agitated it. Unsettled, Darcy had booked it out of the restaurant, wanting to put as much distance between herself and that feeling as possible.

The plan was perfect . . . as long as Brendon didn't actually *say* anything to Elle.

"Look." Darcy sat straighter, staring him down, or *up* as it was. He might've been taller, but she was his big sister and he'd be ill advised to forget. "No meddling, all right? Don't *say* anything to her. I don't want you messing this up."

"Me? Meddle?" Brendon held a hand up to his chest as if affronted.

"Brendon."

He rolled his eyes. "Geez, Darce, chill. I'm not going to say anything. It was honestly a stroke of luck that I overheard her talking about how difficult dating is. *Was*, I guess."

He shot her the world's most god-awful wink, both eyes closing. He'd have her married off within the year if he had his way.

"I mean it." She pinned him with a stare. "I've got this. Thank you, but you've done enough, okay?"

He shook his head. "You really like her, don't you?"

It didn't matter if she liked Elle. Chances were, they'd never see each other again. But if Darcy played her cards right, she could keep Brendon off her back—perhaps not indefinitely, but at least long enough to avoid several weeks of pointless speed dating.

Chapter Three

What Brunch Food Are You Based on Your Zodiac?

Aries—Spicy Chorizo Hash
Taurus—Monte Cristo Sandwich
Gemini—Chicken and Waffles
Cancer—Steel Cut Irish Oatmeal
Leo—Strawberries and Cream Stuffed French Toast
Virgo—Spinach and Egg White Omelet with Whole
Wheat Toast
Libra—2 Pancakes x 2 Eggs x 2 Slices of Bacon
Scorpio—Bottomless Bloody Mary
Sagittarius—Belgian Liege Waffles
Capricorn—Acai Chia Pudding Smoothie Bowl
Aquarius—Baked Egg Danish with Kimchi
and Bacon
Pisces—Giant Cinnamon Roll

Elle. *Elle*."

Elle tore her eyes from the *notes* app on her phone. Across the table, Mom stared at her, dark brows raised expectantly. Pen poised over a notepad, their waiter smiled tightly.

"Oh, shoot, sorry." Elle tossed her phone on the seat beside her and scooped the laminated menu off the table, scanning it quickly. Everything sounded delicious and the smells wafting from the kitchen weren't helping her make up her mind. Fresh brewed coffee. Maple syrup drizzled over banana nut pancakes. Sticky cinnamon rolls fresh out of the oven. *Bacon*. Oh man, bacon. She wanted it all, *right now*, her stomach unleashing a vicious grumble of agreement. She licked her lips. Hunger transformed Elle into an instant-gratification seeking Veruca Salt, albeit hopefully less bitchy. "Um, I'll have the cinnamon sugar crepes with raspberry jam and— Ooh, do you have whipped cream?"

The waiter nodded and scribbled down the order. "Sure."

"Elle." Mom pursed her lips, the *elevens* between her eyebrows deepening.

"Scratch the whipped cream?" She grinned, eyes darting between Mom who looked torn between amusement and exasperation, and the waiter who'd begun tapping the end of his pen against his pad.

"You're going to be in a carb coma all day, honey."

"Which is *why* I was ordering whipped cream. Dairy equals protein."

Mom rolled her eyes and reached for her green tea latte.

Elle shrugged at the waiter. "I'll have a side of scrambled eggs, too, please."

The waiter nodded and hurried off to the back of the crowded restaurant.

"How's Margot?"

"Good. She's been moderating this fic fest for rare pairs in one of her fanfiction groups and there were triple the number of entries than anticipated, but her new foray into rock-climbing seems to be helping with her stress. And her belay instructor is super cute, so." Elle grabbed her peppermint mocha and blew on it. "Yeah, she's good."

Tongue poking the inside of her cheek, Mom nodded slowly. "I understood most of that."

Elle sniffed theatrically and wiped away a fake tear. "I'm so proud."

"Cute." Mom took a sip of her latte before setting it aside. "It's funny that you mentioned rock-climbing, actually."

"Is it?"

"Lydia's boyfriend, Marcus, is an avid rock-climber. Loves hiking, too. He's gotten your sister into it."

"Lydia goes *hiking*? Our Lydia?" The idea of her sister in a pair of hiking boots was too much for Elle to wrap her head around. Lydia who refused to admit she sweated, instead referring to perspiration as *glistening*. Not that Elle was inclined to hit the gym, but come on. "Wait, back up. Lydia has a new boyfriend? Since when?"

When Mom's brows did the forehead equivalent of a shrug, Elle was in trouble. "Marcus isn't *new*. If you hadn't missed the past three family dinners, maybe you'd be up to speed."

Elle's molars clacked together. She'd heard similar iterations of the same chastisement on the phone. "I've been super swamped with—" The deal with OTP, but Mom didn't know that and Elle wasn't sure she was ready to broach that subject on the heels of hearing about Lydia's new—to her—boyfriend. "Life. I've been super swamped with life. Adulting. Bills, taxes, existential doom. You never told me it was such a drag."

Mom studied Elle, an inscrutable expression on her face. "How about you? Are you seeing anyone?"

Out of the frying pan and into the fire. Elle took a leisurely sip of her coffee and licked the lingering chocolate sauce from her bottom lip. "I see lots of people, Mom. I'm seeing you right now."

"Yes, dear, you're a smartass, I'm well aware." Mom set her elbows on the table and rested her chin on her laced hands. "That's not what I asked."

"Ouch. You need at least one of your kids to keep you on your toes and no one else is stepping up to the plate. I'm taking one for the team."

"How selfless of you." She smiled. "Now answer the question."

Elle sighed. "Yes. I go on dates. Loads of them. You know this."

"Dates. But nothing serious."

"Not for lack of trying," Elle muttered.

"Your father has a new manager working under him who is—"

"Mom, *Mom*." She dropped her head back against the booth and groaned.

If Mom finished that sentence, Elle would wind up saying yes—she never said no, not when there was a chance *this* date would be *the* date—even though the last person her parents had set her up with had worn khaki cargo shorts and spiffy Adidas dad-sneakers. He'd rambled about CSS and JavaScript, scoffed at her taste in movies, and his breath had smelled like pepperoni. They hadn't eaten anything with pepperoni. Her parents weren't *entirely* clueless in love seeing as they'd celebrated their thirty-fifth anniversary last June, but when it came to setting her up, they weren't exactly batting a thousand. Granted, neither was she.

"Craig is perfectly nice, Elle. I met him the other day when I brought your father lunch. He's bright and his desk is pristine." Mom leaned in. "He owns a handheld vacuum cleaner for keyboard crumbs and he keeps a photo of his mother beside his monitor. Adorable."

Elle cringed. Hard pass. "Thanks, but I think I'll take my chances on a dating app."

"At least tell me you're using the *good* ones. What's it called, *coffee and muffin?*" She shook her head, her perfectly highlighted bob swishing against the pearl studs in her ears. "*Fumble?*"

Elle covered her snort with a cough into her fist. "Yes, Mom. I've tried the *Cupid* one, too."

"Good, that's—" Her eyes narrowed, lips pulling to the side. "You're making fun of me."

"Just a little." Elle held up a hand, thumb and index finger almost touching. "Speaking of dating apps—"

Mom sighed. "Elle, you know I just want you to be happy"—Elle held her breath waiting for the inevitable but—"but sometimes I can't help but think you make life harder for yourself than it needs to be."

"What's that supposed to mean?"

Mom tilted her head to the side. "You could've finished grad school and *easily* gotten a job with—"

"Mom." Elle held up a hand, stomach already twisting at the way Mom's voice went strained. "How many times do we have to go over this?"

"Fine. You're right. That's in the past." Mom shrugged softly. "But look at how many people your father and I have set you up with because *you* said you wanted something serious. And you didn't like *any* of them?" She tsked. "I'm not claiming to be an expert, but I start to wonder if you're afraid of success when it seems like you're constantly setting yourself up for failure, honey."

Ouch.

Elle chewed on the inside of her cheek. Love, like all things, had come so easy for her older siblings. Jane and Daniel hadn't even been looking for love when they'd met Gabe and Mike. It was just like school. Elle had gotten good grades, yeah, but she'd had to work her butt off for them. Jane and Daniel had barely needed to study to get straight As.

Then again, Elle wasn't looking for easy. Elle wanted *right*. Would it have been nice if some of her dreams had been easier to achieve? Obviously, but she wished her family would understand that just because her path to success wasn't a straight line, and just because her definition of success was a little different, she wasn't automatically a failure.

"Look, I'm—"

Above the door, the bell chimed as someone darted inside to escape the downpour. Elle did a double take, recognizing the messy auburn hair and freckles—

"Shoot." Elle slumped in the booth. Her butt made an obnoxious noise against the leather as she slipped low, knees knocking into Mom's beneath the table.

"What in the world are you doing?" Mom stared at Elle as if she'd sprouted a second head.

Of all the breakfast joints in the greater Seattle area, Brendon Lowell just had to wander into Gilbert's at the same time she was grabbing brunch with her mother.

Elle liked Brendon. They were well on their way to becoming good friends. Any other day of the week, she'd have waved him over. Just not today, not when she was with Mom and *definitely* not after her disaster of a date with his sister. A date Elle never would've agreed to had she had even the slightest inkling it would've gone *that* wrong. Things with Brendon were bound to be awkward now, and all she could hope was that he would be decent enough to not let it affect their working relationship. The last thing Elle needed was for the shitty state of her love life to sour her career when years of her and Margot's hard work were finally paying off . . .

Peering past Mom's confused face, Elle spotted Brendon chatting with the host. Brendon clapped the man on the shoulder and walked toward the pastry case. Hallelujah, he must've been getting his order to go.

"Honey, what's gotten into you?" The corners of her eyes crinkled with concern.

Elle shook her head and gripped the edge of the table, heaving herself to sitting. "Nothing. Nothing, I'm just—"

It stood to reason that if she believed in *good* luck, and she absolutely did, there was also such a thing as *bad* luck. As evidenced when Brendon turned, hands tucked casually in the pockets of his stonewashed jeans.

Elle grabbed the menu and scrambled to unfold it. Once it formed a nice little cubby, she ducked behind it and rested her cheek against the table.

"Elizabeth Marie, what is wrong with you?"

The better question was what *wasn't* wrong with her.

"Elle?"

So much for that. Elle flicked her bangs out of her eyes and aimed a grin at Brendon who peered down at her with a bemused smile. "Brendon? Wow, hey! How are you?"

"I'm great." His smile brightened, bemusement transforming into amusement with a flash of his teeth. He pointed at his cheek. Brendon had dimples just like Darcy, but he was missing that stupid special freckle, the one Elle had wanted to kiss until the date had gone to hell in a handcart. "You've got a little something . . ."

Elle swiped a hand over her cheek, fingers coming back smudged brown with what she prayed was chocolate syrup. "Thanks. Um, what are you doing here?"

Getting food, most likely. *Brilliant, Elle.*

Brendon chuckled and jerked a thumb over his shoulder. "I live right down the street by the park. I drop by most mornings. They've got better coffee than the chain places, not so overroasted. What are *you* doing here? Don't you live downtown?"

A kick landed against her shin. *Ow.* Right, Mom was staring at her with wide eyes and a tight smile.

"I do, but my family doesn't." She gestured across the table.

"Brendon, this is my mom, Linda. Mom, this is my friend, Brendon."

Brendon's smile widened as he stuck out his hand. "It's nice to meet you."

"Likewise." Mom's eyes darted over to Elle as she shook Brendon's hand. "Always nice to meet a *friend* of Elle's."

Elle's eyes slipped shut at Mom's less-than-subtle suggestion.

Brendon, however, seemed to think the mix-up was *hilarious*. "Oh no, Elle and I are just friends. And business partners, too, I guess." His toothy smile went lopsided and Elle's stomach did an anatomically impossible nosedive, plummeting an unrealistic distance before threatening to drop out her butt. "Though I like to think our friendship supersedes that sort of thing."

"Right?" Elle chuckled nervously, avoiding Mom's questioning head tilt.

"Not that your daughter isn't amazing," Brendon continued, digging Elle's hole deeper. "But I'd have to fight my sister and I have full confidence Darcy could whoop my butt."

Hearing Darcy's name twisted Elle's already stressed stomach, her laughter taking on a frantic edge that had both Brendon and Mom staring at her funny. Elle shut the menu and fanned it in front of her, needing the breeze.

Had he not spoken with his sister?

"Elle?" With her brows lifted, the look on Mom's face brokered no argument.

She cleared her throat. "Right, sorry. Brendon's the creator of OTP. You know, the dating app?"

Brendon nodded. "The whole team is over the moon"—he dimpled—"to be working with Elle and Margot. Our algorithms are solid, but we're hoping that with their help, our success rate will break the forty percent threshold on relationships lasting longer than one month."

Based on Mom's frown, Brendon might as well have been speaking Klingon. "And you're—working for this company, Elle? Is this a salaried position?"

Elle's face flamed as she flashed an apologetic smile at Brendon. "*Mom*. We're consulting with OTP as independent contractors. It's . . . it's a big deal, okay?"

Mom's frown deepened, making Elle lose her appetite entirely. So much for that.

Her smile felt flimsy when she looked up at Brendon. "Margot and I are jazzed about it, too. We were just talking about it last night, how excited we are to hit the ground running."

Brendon stuck his hands in his pockets and rocked back on his heels. "Speaking of last night . . ."

Shit. Here it goes.

"Darcy made me promise not to say anything, but what she doesn't know won't hurt her, yeah?" He shot her a conspiratorial wink that under any other circumstance would have made her grin because he was absolute shit at winking, but in a totally endearing way because he either had no clue, or he knew and didn't care. Now, it just curdled the macchiato in her stomach.

"You talked to Darcy?" She swallowed, ignoring Mom's curious stare in favor of focusing on Brendon's face, studying it for any sign of what bombshell he was about to drop that he'd sworn himself to secrecy over. "About . . . about last night?"

"Oh yeah. She's . . ." Brendon trailed off, shaking his head, the expression on his face inscrutable. Her pulse tripped as she held her breath. Brendon ducked his chin, chuckling down at the table. "I've never seen her like this before."

What the hell? Elle wanted to grab him by the shoulders and shake him. What did that mean? Never seen her so *what*? "Oh?"

He lifted his head, smile still lovably lopsided. "She said you two really hit it off."

Elle's jaw dropped. *The fuck?* "She did?"

Brendon nodded. "She's . . . God, Elle, I mean it when I say I've never seen my sister so . . . so *smitten* before."

"Smitten," Elle echoed dumbly.

"Could you not tell?" Brendon laughed as if his sister's feelings were utterly obvious.

All she could do was shrug. "Darcy is . . . not the easiest to read."

Brendon nodded like he understood. "She keeps her cards close to her chest, that's for sure. But trust me when I say she had a great time."

Could've fooled her.

Either this was some gigantic misunderstanding, or Darcy had lied to her brother. But to what end? Elle had been the one who was late and had spilled wine all over the place, so why lie?

His smile fell. "You had a good time, didn't you?"

Ah, fudge.

Elle chanced a quick glance at Mom, who wasn't even pretending she wasn't listening, and tugged on her earlobe. "I—"

Almost cried on the way home?

Lost her new underwear in a public bathroom she was forced to use because she was too embarrassed to confront Darcy in the restaurant?

Had really hoped they'd hit it off and had been inordinately disappointed when the breath-snatching chemistry hadn't been *enough*?

Everything she could think to say seemed wrong.

The look on Brendon's face was so *hopeful*, like he honest to God believed his sister's happiness hinged on Elle. It didn't help that Mom was staring at her, that same hope reflected in her blue eyes.

Lying was something Elle avoided, but owning up to her part in last night's disaster date? Copping to spilled wine and lateness and head-butting over her job and hopes? Elle was tired of everyone looking at her like she was a mess when she was just trying her best.

"I just . . . I'm kind of speechless," she confessed, forcing out a laugh.

Mom looked at her strangely because if there was one thing anyone who knew Elle, *really* knew her, was aware of, it was that she was seldom at a loss for words.

"You sound like Darcy." Brendon's smile went sly as he leaned in, dropping his voice. "Until she finally spilled and told me all about your off-the-charts chemistry."

Not a misunderstanding, then. At least not one between Darcy and Brendon.

Torn between righteous indignation—because, *ha*, there *were* sparks, she *knew* it—and heavyhearted melancholy— because the confirmation of those sparks meant zilch—Elle chuckled nervously over the rim of her macchiato. "What can I say?"

Brendon, who continued to look a touch too smug, as if

his matchmaking skills were out of this world, looked at her expectantly, clearly waiting for her to finish her statement, but . . . what *could* she say? Darcy had put her in a pickle, a no-win situation.

Fortunately, the waiter swooped in, saving the moment from becoming too awkward when he dropped off their food. Regardless of how rude it was with Brendon still standing there, Elle promptly stuffed a forkful of crepe into her mouth. The cinnamon sugar melted on her tongue, not like butter, but like ash.

Blue eyes bright and smile poorly restrained, Mom looked inordinately pleased by this turn of events. Elle swallowed, wincing as her bite of crepe made a slow, dry descent, sticking thickly in her esophagus.

Brendon ran a hand through his hair. "Well, I should leave you two to your breakfast, but be on the lookout for a text from Darcy, okay? She said she'll be in touch."

For a moment, Elle's chest swelled with a strange surge of something that felt suspiciously like hope. Had *she* read the situation wrong? Maybe—

No.

There was no way. It just wasn't possible.

That didn't mean Elle didn't have questions. Darcy had some explaining to do. She owed Elle that much.

Elle pasted on a smile. "Not if I text her first."

Chapter Four

*S*team wafted off the top of Darcy's mug, tickling her nose as she brought the ceramic to her lips. Her eyes shut as she sipped then let out a contented sigh, her body sinking deeper into the couch cushion.

Bliss. Her apartment was silent, her coffee just this side of scalding, and she had nowhere she needed to be for the entire weekend. Two whole days where she could do what she wanted, when she wanted. No pointless dates or Brendon complaining she was behaving like a homebody.

Darcy cracked open an eye and glared at the coffee table. At her *phone*, which was dancing its way across the surface of her coffee table, vibrating noisily.

UNKNOWN NUMBER (11:24 A.M.): you have some explaining to do

Darcy wrinkled her nose and swiped at the screen, quickly tapping in her passcode with her thumb.

DARCY (11:26 A.M.): I think you have the wrong number.

After pressing send, Darcy spared a moment to consider what sort of explaining this person who was *certainly* not her had to do and to whom. Was it a lovers' spat? Some kid about to get a stern talking-to from a parent? Darcy set her phone down beside her. Not her problem.

Against her hip, her phone buzzed, the screen lighting up.

UNKNOWN NUMBER (11:29 A.M.): do i darcy?

What the hell? Darcy sat up, swiping at the screen.

DARCY (11:31 A.M.): Who is this?

She stared, watching those three little dots dance. In the meantime, she performed a quick mental inventory of who it could possibly be.

Brendon was saved into her phone alongside a truly awful photo of his sixteen-year-old self, crashed out on the couch, drooling, pizza sauce smeared on his chin. Her parents were saved, filed under their respective first names. She had Annie's number, and her boss never texted. *Never.* Then there was . . . well, that was it. Mostly. Aside from acquaintances who may or may not have had her number. Her texting sphere was small, selective. *Curated.* Darcy's lips tightened at the edges. Of course, there was always the chance it was— No. She'd blocked Natasha's number a long time ago.

UNKNOWN NUMBER (11:36 A.M.): your worst nightmare

Her grip tightened, fingers accidentally smashing the volume button on the side of her phone making the thing beep loudly in her fist. Darcy's pulse mimicked the surge, leaping in her throat. *What the actual fuck?*

Thumb trembling as it hovered over the keyboard, Darcy spared an instinctive glance at the front door, double-checking that it was locked. The dead bolt was bolted, the chain was latched, and she was apparently testing the limits of her ability to overreact. Between last night's door-pounding debacle with Brendon and this, she needed to get a grip, even if that text was creepy as hell.

Primed to block the number and move on with her life, another message appeared before she could pull the trigger.

UNKNOWN NUMBER (11:39 A.M.): ok that sounded kinda serial killer-ish

UNKNOWN NUMBER (11:39 A.M.): which im not

Because that's not exactly what some psycho with a butcher's knife would say.

UNKNOWN NUMBER (11:40 A.M.): which is totally what a serial killer would say

UNKNOWN NUMBER (11:40 A.M.): oops

At least they were a self-aware psycho.

UNKNOWN NUMBER (11:41 A.M.): it was supposed to be like im pissed at you and demand answers but not like im mouth breathing over your shoulder and wearing a hickey mask
UNKNOWN NUMBER (11:41 A.M.): *hockey
UNKNOWN NUMBER (11:42 A.M.): none of this is helping huh?
UNKNOWN NUMBER (11:42 A.M.): nvm

Darcy lifted her hand, resting her fingers along the notch at the base of her throat. Never mind? No, not never mind. This stranger thought *Darcy* had some explaining to do?

Staring blankly at the absurd conversation, it took the pre-installed wind chime ringtone to snap her out of her daze. **Unknown Number** was calling. Darcy's pulse sped. Should she answer or let it go to voice mail? She hated talking on the phone, even to Brendon. But could she really settle for a voice mail? What if they didn't leave one? On the third ring, the burn of curiosity bested her nerves. "Hello?"

Silence.

"*Hello?*" A spike of irritation made Darcy sit up straighter, her spine steeling. "Who is this?"

Hopefully, the *cut to the chase* was implied.

"Right. Hi. It's Elle. Jones. Elle Jones. We had drinks last night—"

"I know who you are." Darcy shut her eyes, and an image of Elle's pretty face appeared behind Darcy's lids. She wasn't easily forgotten.

Elle chuckled, but it lacked spirit, sounded stilted. "Right. I'm sure you're wondering why I'm calling. Aside from, you know, wanting to make sure you didn't think I was *actually* a serial killer."

Worst nightmare wasn't farfetched. Brendon *truly* knew how to pick them.

"Look, can you spare me the runaround and tell me what you want? I'm rather busy at the moment."

Her coffee was getting cold and microwaving it would be a cardinal sin. The sooner they wrapped this up, the sooner Darcy's life could return to business as usual.

A pause, followed by rustling loud enough for Darcy to yank the phone from her ear followed. "—because you'll never guess who I ran into this morning."

Darcy pinched the bridge of her nose. "Who?"

Elle chuckled dryly. "Your brother, and boy did he have some interesting things to say to me."

Elle had run into Brendon, big deal. It wasn't like—

The dots connected, the implication of this run-in clear. *Disastrously* clear.

"Fuck," she muttered.

"And this"—Elle gave a dramatic pause—"is where you have some explaining to do."

☆ ☆
☆

Darcy twisted the simple, platinum band around the middle finger of her right hand and stared at the front door.

What was supposed to be a peaceful, productive, bra-off morning was now inching its way into a stressful, inefficacious, bra-on afternoon. Any minute now, Elle would arrive, all because Brendon couldn't keep his big mouth shut.

Granted, somewhere buried in there, Darcy owned a bit of culpability in this, but it was Brendon who'd messed with her otherwise perfect plan for at *least* a month without meddling. She'd *told* him not to say anything to Elle, to not screw this up for her, but he'd outplayed her. Now, she'd have to explain this entire convoluted situation to Elle. Worst part was, she had no road map for this conversation, no game plan; what *she'd* say depended on what Brendon had said, *how much* Brendon had said, and how Elle had reacted.

All Darcy had going in her favor was that Brendon had yet to blow up her phone or come pounding down her door. Best-case scenario, this would be a brief, relatively painless conversation after which she and Elle could, once again, go their separate ways. With the caveat that Elle couldn't say anything to Brendon. Not yet, anyway. Worst-case scenario . . .

Darcy cracked her knuckles. *Painless* might be easier said than done. Already a headache bloomed between her eyes.

A rhythmic, five-note knock sounded against the front door. Darcy's heart tripped, stuttering out the couplet response. Game time. She stood, smoothing the wrinkles from her heather-blue lounge pants, and padded over to the door on bare feet. She took a deep breath and flipped the lock, yanking the door open like ripping off a Band-Aid.

Slouched against the doorframe, arms crossed over her chest, Elle glared up at Darcy with a withering stare. A stare made all the more disconcerting when Elle performed another one of those head-to-toe perusals of Darcy's body. Darcy went dizzy with the ferocity and speed of blood rising to the surface of her skin, her blush a beacon that no amount of affectation could conceal.

Elle's blue eyes swept back up Darcy's body and lingered on her face, stare penetrating. "You're shorter without your heels on."

Darcy sniffed. "That is how it works, yes."

Elle snorted and pressed off the door with her shoulder. Without waiting for an invitation, she slipped past Darcy through the doorway, their arms brushing.

Elle wore a soft, chunky blue cardigan that fell haphazardly from one shoulder, revealing a wide expanse of creamy skin and the jut of her collarbone. Darcy tore her eyes away and made herself focus on the imperfections, the way Elle's jeans were frayed and rain-soaked at the bottom and her Converse were scuffed and sure to leave tracks on the carpet.

"Could you—" Darcy's voice teetered on the verge of cracking. She cleared her throat and lifted her chin to stare down her nose. "Could you take your shoes off?"

Elle's brows lurched upward before she shrugged. "Fine. Figured you'd want me in and out, but yeah, I can get comfy."

Darcy rolled her eyes. Whether Elle was *comfy* wasn't her concern. "I don't want you making a mess of my carpet."

Elle's tongue poked against the inside of her cheek, her expression souring. Rather than argue, she bent at the waist and slipped her fingers behind the heel of one shoe, then the other, straightening to then step out of them. The move caused her sweater to slide farther down her arm, revealing more soft-looking skin and the subtle swell of her breasts. The chances of her wearing something under that sweater were looking slimmer by the second.

Leaving her shoes smack-dab in the center of the foyer, Elle traipsed farther into Darcy's apartment, brazenly surveying her surroundings. She studied the art on the wall with a curious tilt of her chin before moving on to finger the spines of the books on Darcy's shelf. Every so often, her whole face scrunched, occasionally accompanied by a stuck-out tongue that was *not* adorable.

Hanging back, Darcy swallowed down the lump of discomfort growing in her throat. Elle was a bright splash of color against the clean canvas of Darcy's apartment. Cobalt sweater, bleach-splattered jeans, and mismatched socks, one neon green and the other a soft periwinkle, with a pink chevron at her toes and a hole near the ankle.

Darcy tucked a strand of hair behind her ear. "By all means, make yourself at home."

Elle spun on her holey-sock-covered heel and narrowed her eyes. "Don't mind if I do," she said, before taking a seat and drawing both knees up to her chest, feet on Darcy's pristine sofa.

Darcy stayed standing, arms crossed, and chin raised.

"Nice place." Elle's eyes roved around the room, lingering on the neat stack of Darcy's FSA study guides before darting over to the fern—Darcy's singular pop of color—in the corner. Her brows furrowed. "Did you just move in?"

Darcy curled her tongue behind her teeth. "No."

"Huh." The fact that she was able to pack so much judgment into such a tiny word would've been impressive had Darcy not been one, slightly offended, and two, ready to get this conversation over with.

"You have questions." Darcy didn't bother asking. For all

that Elle had sprawled herself lazily across Darcy's sectional in an illusion of relaxation, her fingers twitched against her thighs, her feet shifting, toes curling and uncurling as her gaze bounced from one surface to another.

Elle wrapped her arms around her shins. "We're through with the small talk?"

"In the interest of time." Darcy dipped her chin. "Like I said, I'm busy."

Elle's too perceptive gaze darted from the lone, now-cold cup of coffee to Darcy, her eyes lingering on Darcy's lounge pants, then her hastily braided hair. "Right. Then in the interest of time, I'll get straight to it." Elle lifted her hips, wiggling her phone free from her back pocket. She made several swipes against the screen before clearing her throat. "Question one, what the fuck?"

Darcy shut her eyes and breathed deep for a count of four, held it for a count of seven, and exhaled for a count of eight. She'd have repeated the process had Elle's stare not been palpable, making the skin between Darcy's shoulder blades itch. "Can I expect question two to be more specific?"

Elle harrumphed and glanced down at the phone in her hand. "I don't know, let's see. Question two, how dare you?"

Darcy abandoned her yoga breathing and cut to the chase. "I'm sorry. Okay?"

Best to issue a broad-stroke apology because Darcy wasn't entirely sure what Brendon had said, only that Elle's reaction wasn't positive.

Elle's hand flopped down against the couch, her phone bouncing gently. "You're sorry. Sorry for what exactly?"

"For whatever has you all"—she waved her hand in Elle's general direction—"vexed."

Elle's shoulders shook with slow-building laughter. She leaned forward and dropped her head into her hands before letting out an aggrieved, muffled shriek. "Vexed." She lifted her head, face flushed pink. "God. Do you insert that stick up your ass every morning, or is it more like an IUD that lasts you five years?"

Her jaw dropped. "You know what—"

"No." Elle stood and sidestepped the coffee table, stalking toward Darcy. "I'm not finished. You want to know what has me all *vexed*? Let's see, maybe you're sorry for being rude last night? Poo-pooing what matters to me like my job? Ordering a fifty-six-dollar glass of wine? Talking smack about me to whoever the hell it was on the phone when you don't *know* me?" Elle took another step forward, fingers lifted as she aired her grievances. "Or maybe lying to your brother, huh? Telling him we hit it off when we obviously didn't? You put me in the position of having to choose between going along with *your* lie, a lie I can't for the life of me understand, or owning up to last night's disaster all on my own. So I don't know. Take your pick, Darcy."

Heat flooded Darcy's veins, creeping up her chest and neck, shame making her dizzy. Contradictory and ill-timed, a tendril of heat spread lower, settling beneath Darcy's belly button because anger turned the blue of Elle's irises into something fierce like a sea during a storm. Color settled high on her cheeks and her messy bun had come undone, strands of hair framing her heart-shaped face. For a moment, Darcy wondered what

Elle would look like, sweat dripping down that bare expanse of neck, her back bowing against Darcy's sheets. The temperature in Darcy's apartment climbed, her shirt sticking to sweat dotting the small of her back.

"I'm sorry." Darcy met Elle's glare, the ferocity of which was softened by a glossy dampness that replaced her urge to see Elle tangled up in sheets with the desire to wrap her up in something soft, a blanket, or Darcy's favorite duvet. How . . . utterly bizarre. Darcy cleared her throat. "I didn't mean— It wasn't my intention to be rude." Or upset her.

Elle sniffed loudly and crossed her arms, gaze sharpening once more. "Yeah. Well, you were, so . . ."

Her voice trailed off. An unspoken question. Why?

This was the part Darcy had been dreading down to her bones: explaining herself. Her behavior on the date. Why she'd led Brendon to believe she had any intention of seeing Elle again.

Part of Darcy was tempted not to bother. Wasn't an apology, a sincere one, enough?

Except if Darcy had any hope of salvaging her plan to get Brendon off her back, she'd have to share with Elle. Without an explanation, Elle had no reason not to go directly to Brendon and blab. Or at the very least, inadvertently contradict the carefully crafted picture Darcy had painted.

"Look." Darcy took a step closer and uncrossed her arms, posture relaxing from the defensive stance she'd adopted during Elle's outburst. "My brother is— I love him. But when he gets an idea in his head, he's like a dog with a bone. And he has this idea, misconstrued as it is, that I should be looking for love. That"—Darcy puffed out her cheeks, weighing the best words, the one's with the lowest probability of raising Elle's hackles—"I need to find my special someone. When a serious relationship is not on my radar. At the moment."

When it would be on her radar, *if*, Darcy wasn't sure.

Elle cocked her head, brow furrowing. "Why not?"

Something in her gut said Elle wouldn't be appeased with a simple *because*. Darcy sighed. "I'm busy? I'm studying for my final FSA exam. Once I pass, I'll have reached the highest designation awarded to actuaries by the governing body. The exams are rigorous and the pass rate is only forty percent. Studying takes up my scant amount of free time."

"So you're too busy right now? Tell him that."

As if she hadn't? "Brendon believes I should have a better work-life balance and he acts like it's his calling in life to make sure I do."

Elle shrugged. "He has a point."

Darcy knew how it sounded—too busy for dating, for friends, for any semblance of a social life. Yes, it was true she didn't have any friends in Seattle *yet*, but she was operating according to *her* schedule, not Brendon's. "I don't tell *him* how to run *his* business."

"Tell him you're just not interested."

If only it were that easy. Darcy had tried and it never worked. Brendon knew her too well, knew exactly what buttons to press to get his way. Darcy didn't feel like spilling to Elle that the reason Brendon pushed so hard was because he knew that once upon a time, she *had* wanted a relationship, marriage, family, the whole nine yards. Having the rug yanked out from under her wasn't something she'd been able to control, but how she chose to move on with the rest of her life was.

Darcy waved it off with a roll of her eyes and a scoff. "Easier said than done. You've met Brendon; he's a romantic, obsessed with happily-ever-after. He keeps setting me up on these dates, and when I try to back out, he acts wounded, like I'm giving up too easily. Last night had less to do with you and more to do with me finally reaching the end of my rope. I had a headache and all I wanted was to go home. You were a . . . casualty. Wrong place at the wrong time."

On a date with the wrong person.

Elle set her jaw. "Whatever. It's not like you're obligated to like me or anything."

It had nothing to do with liking Elle, or not. Had Elle not been looking for love, had she been fine with something less serious and more temporary, Darcy wouldn't have minded exploring what those heated glances could've led to. But Elle *was* looking for something serious and Darcy wasn't, so there was no use wasting time on *what-ifs* when they were inherently incompatible.

"I could've been nicer," Darcy admitted.

"True." Elle's lips quirked, her smile brief, a sun breaking through clouds. "I'm still missing something. Why lie and tell Brendon you wanted to see me again when you clearly don't?"

Not entirely true. Topic of conversation aside, talking with Elle wasn't awful. Granted, it would've been better had she been wearing less clothing. In which case, Darcy would've been happy to see a lot more of Elle. Often.

"Again, product of poor timing." Darcy lifted a shoulder and gave Elle a rueful smile. "Brendon came in here, guns blazing, talking about how I should sign up for speed dating and, to be honest, that sounds like my idea of hell. When my usual excuses—*reasons*—didn't work, I told him I was seeing someone. But then he wondered why I'd agreed to go out with you if I was seeing someone else."

Realization flickered in Elle's eyes. "So you told him it was me you hit it off with."

Darcy bit the edge of her lip and nodded.

For a moment, Elle was silent. Lips twisting to the side and brow furrowing, she finally asked, "What was your end game?"

"My what?"

"You know. How you saw this playing out. You tell Brendon we're seeing each other and then what was supposed to happen? Didn't you think he'd catch on eventually? Or, I don't know, ask me about you?"

Darcy scratched the side of her neck. She'd made a gamble, yes. She should've known better, but Brendon had given her no choice but to think fast on her feet. As a consequence, her plan had been riddled with holes. It could've worked, but she'd been thwarted by Brendon's absolute inability to keep his trap shut.

"For starters, I swore him to secrecy. I told him I didn't want him messing this up for me. I intended to capitalize on my *intention* to reach out to you and milk that for as long as I could before Brendon finally caught on. I didn't exactly lie, I omitted and let him fill in the blanks."

Elle gawked. "That's cunning."

"Like I said, I never lied," Darcy reiterated, keeping this conversation from getting further off track. "I stretched the truth."

"Stretched the truth? Are you kidding me?" Elle exhaled noisily through her nose, jaw ticking. "Look, what you choose to tell your brother, or not tell your brother, *whatever*, is your business. But whether you meant to or not, you pulled me into a narrative I'd very much like to be excluded from, *plus*, you put me in a pickle."

Swallowing a laugh at her phrasing, Darcy gave what she hoped was a carefully thoughtful stare. "I put you in a pickle?"

"Yes, a real gherkin of a situation."

How she managed to say that with a straight face was a mystery. Even Darcy couldn't keep from snorting at the word *gherkin* being used to sincerely describe one's state of being. "I didn't realize it would be such a big *dill*."

Elle rolled her shoulders back and glared daggers. "It isn't funny. I was at breakfast with my mom when your brother waltzed up and spilled your story. Told me you're *smitten*. Now my mom, and most likely my whole family, thinks I'm halfway to being in the first successful relationship I've ever had. I'm sure my mom's working on a cake as we speak. *Elle's finally got her shit together.* Let's bust out the confetti."

Darcy sobered. This was a different side of Elle than the starry-eyed soul-mate-seeking girl she'd met last night.

"I . . . *apologize*. Sincerely. I was remiss in assuming my brother could keep his mouth shut. But this isn't hopeless." Darcy licked her lips, shifting her weight from one foot to the other beneath Elle's stare. "Why don't you tell your mother Brendon was mistaken?"

Elle worried her bottom lip between her teeth, shoulders slumping. "Yeah, *sure*. That'll go great. And what am I supposed to say to your brother?"

"Maybe you could"—Darcy winced—"not say anything to Brendon? Yet."

Elle blinked those blue eyes of her balefully. "I'm sorry. Are you suggesting I lie to your brother? Your brother who happens to be my friend and brand-new business partner? Because that's what it sounds like."

The plan, the promising, practically brilliant plan, was slipping through Darcy's fingers. "I didn't say *lie*, I said don't say *anything*. There's a difference."

Elle stared.

"Look, I didn't mean to rope you into this, I swear, but maybe . . ." Floundering, Darcy was trying and failing to fill in the blank. *Maybe*s were flimsy, imprecise. She preferred *probabilities* and *proof* to *perhaps*. She met Elle's eyes and somehow in her stare, she found her answer. "If you look on the bright side, this could be beneficial to us both."

That was the sort of starry-eyed optimism that revved Elle's engine, right?

Elle's eyes narrowed. "How?"

Darcy knew how it would benefit her, but Elle's situation was a bit less defined. Vague, even.

"I'm at my wits' end with my brother's matchmaking," Darcy explained. "And you . . . you want your family to think you can hold down a relationship?"

"I—" Elle shut her mouth and frowned. "What I *want* is an actual relationship, one I don't have to fib about."

Each time Darcy felt like she was finally regaining her grip, the plan slipped further through her fingers.

"No one's saying you can't have that. This would only be for . . . a month, maybe two. Long enough for Brendon to think I'm trying."

Elle covered her face with her hands. Her fingers pressed into the skin beneath her brows, massaging the ridge of her eye sockets before she dropped her hands and pinned Darcy with a stare. "You want us to . . . to fake a relationship? Are you serious?"

Was it what Darcy wanted? No. Not even close. This had escalated into something she hadn't planned. This was decidedly more involved, requiring partnership when what she'd been aiming for was the soundness of singledom, Darcy Party of One. But she could adapt. She had no choice. "We can say we're spending time together. Getting to know each other, feeling things out. It doesn't have to be a *thing*. Just implied. We don't have to . . . define the relationship."

Elle's tongue poked against her cheek. "This sounds like a supremely stupid plan. Like, *awful*. And if I'm the one saying that?" Elle snorted.

"A month or two, Elle. All you have to do is tell Brendon we're talking and you will have done your good deed for the rest of the year. Then you can go back to trying to find your soul mate." Darcy fought against the urge to cringe.

"You seriously think your brother's going to buy that? No questions asked? Are we talking about the same guy?" Elle lifted a hand over her head. "About this tall, auburn hair, cute grin, shit at winking?"

Darcy sighed. She had a point. Brendon lived for details, *sappy* details, and if their stories didn't align? Brendon was bright, too bright to accept inconsistencies. He'd sniff out Darcy's lies and then she'd really be in hot water.

"That's a fair point," Darcy conceded. Not to mention, there was that pesky annual Christmas party of his. How was she supposed to act like she and Elle were together if they didn't go together? "There's an event or two I might need you to attend."

Elle's shoulders started to shake and it took Darcy a second to realize she was laughing. "Are you kidding me? You have some nerve, you know that?" She shook her head. "Why should I give a fuck about what you need?"

"I'd . . . I'd obviously return the favor." Darcy winced through the offer. "If that's what you want."

Elle blinked. "You're saying you'd come to something like . . . what, Thanksgiving? With my family?"

Oh Jesus. Darcy swallowed a groan. "I could do that."

"And you'd . . . act like you're *smitten*? Like the sun shines out of my ass?"

Darcy nodded. "Sure. Whatever."

What was one holiday? As long as she got Brendon off her back, she could suffer through a family Thanksgiving with Elle. How bad could it be?

Arms crossed, Elle nibbled on the corner of her lip, eyes staring off into space over Darcy's shoulder, going glassy. With a quick shake of her head, she snapped out of whatever thoughts were swimming around inside her head. "Darcy—"

"Please." The word popped out, reflexive. Anything to make Elle say yes. "Just . . . please, Elle."

Elle blinked, lips parting, pursing as she blew out her breath. "Fine."

Darcy's brows rose. "Fine?"

A muscle in Elle's jaw twitched. "I can't believe I'm saying this, but I'm in."

She slipped past, arms brushing even though there was plenty of room for her to pass. Maple syrup and spice filled Darcy's nose, making her mouth water. She swallowed and pivoted, watching as Elle shoved her feet back inside her shoes and opened the front door.

Fingers resting on the doorknob, Elle paused. "We can hammer out the details of this"—she made a face, lips twisting—"arrangement later." She glanced over her shoulder. "Put my number in your phone. I'll be in touch."

Chapter Five

*A*m I losing my mind, or did you just say you're going to fake a relationship with *Darcy Lowell*?"

Elle winced at the way Margot's voice went shrill. "You're perfectly sane."

Margot stared. "Are *you*?"

"I have my reasons, all right?"

"Name one."

"We haven't hammered out the details *yet*, but we agreed it's only for a month or two tops."

"That's not a reason, that's an excuse. You know what, I actually don't even know what that is, but it makes zero sense."

"Darcy put me in a real bind, okay? Lying to her brother who then blabbed at breakfast in front of my mom."

Margot slammed her laptop shut and tossed it on the cushion beside her. "So tell Darcy to go fuck herself."

"It's not that easy, Mar."

"You open your mouth and say it. *Fuck. You.*" Margot shook

her head. "Elle. *Elle*. This isn't what you want. This is the *opposite* of what you want."

A fake relationship *wasn't* what she wanted. What she'd told Darcy was true—Elle wanted a real relationship. And not just any relationship, but *the one*. Her end game. She wasn't picky, no matter what Mom said, but she was tired of going on first dates that never turned into second dates because either they were all wrong for her or she was wrong for them.

"You should've seen the look on my mom's face," Elle said. "Five minutes before that she was accusing me of being afraid of success, setting myself up for failure, and making life harder than it needs to be. In waltzes Brendon, talking about how his sister's crazy about me. I was caught between a rock and a hard place. What was I supposed to say?"

"I don't know. The truth, maybe?" Margot scowled. "Lying to your family isn't the way to get them to take you seriously. What you need to do is tell them if they don't like how you're living your life, they can go fuck themselves because it's not their life to live."

"Jesus, Margot. Is that your solution to everything? Just tell everyone I know to fuck off?"

Talk about oversimplification. Her family might get on her nerves, but she wasn't upset enough to burn bridges.

Margot drew a breath in and exhaled noisily before speaking. "It's better than lying. You're trying to find a short-term solution to a long-term problem. What are you going to do after your two months are up, hm?"

"When the time comes, I'll . . . I'll cross that bridge. Until then, I'm just . . ." Trying her best and hoping, like always, it would be good enough. "Making the most out of a weird situation."

Margot grabbed her laptop and shoved it inside her messenger bag, hauling the strap onto her shoulder. "Lying to your family's bad enough, Elle. Don't start lying to yourself, too."

What Rom-Com Are You Based on Your Zodiac Sign?

Aries—*Fools Rush In*
Taurus—*Sweet Home Alabama*
Gemini—*She's All That*
Cancer—*While You Were Sleeping*
Leo—*How to Lose a Guy in 10 Days*
Virgo—*The Proposal*
Libra—*Sleepless in Seattle*
Scorpio—*My Best Friend's Wedding*
Sagittarius—*The Holiday*
Capricorn—*Two Weeks Notice*
Aquarius—*Clueless*
Pisces—*Never Been Kissed*

"Whatcha lookin' at?"

Heart rocketing into her throat, Darcy smashed the back button on her phone and aimed a withering stare at Brendon over her shoulder. "Jesus. Could you try not sneaking up on me?"

"Boring." Brendon straightened from where he'd been crouched and rounded the table, dropping down into the chair opposite hers. "Besides, it's practically my birthright as a younger brother to give you hell."

"You're twenty-six."

He snagged a menu and ran his finger down the list of beverages. "Point being?"

"*Point being*, you should be above giving me grief on a daily basis. Don't you have more important things to worry about? Running a company? Being featured on *Forbes*'s Thirty Under Thirty list?"

Flipping the menu over, Brendon shrugged. "Are you done deflecting? Can we discuss the fact that you were scrolling Oh My Stars?"

"I was *not*." Darcy slipped her phone behind the salt and pepper shakers as if moving it out of sight might further refute Brendon's accusation. Based on the way his smile grew even as he studied the menu, it did not. "I was . . . okay, fine, I was *glancing*. It doesn't mean I believe in any of it. It's ridiculous. How does my astrological sign correlate in any capacity to my preference for rom-coms? It doesn't. I don't even like *Two Weeks Notice*."

Brendon gaped at her. "Blasphemy. It's got Sandra Bullock and Hugh Grant. Rom-com royalty. Don't let me catch you saying that sort of thing again or else I'll sit on you and force you through a remedial rom-com marathon."

She took a sip of her sparkling water and mock-shivered. "Oh, the horror."

"I, for one, think it's *cu-te*"—he drew out the word, turning it into two obnoxious syllables—"you're reading Oh My

Stars. Taking an interest in your partner's job and hobbies is important, Darce."

Spare her the touchy-feely mumbo-jumbo, *please*. For starters, she wasn't relationship illiterate, and two, there was nothing cute about it. Elle was not her partner. Partner in crime perhaps, but Darcy's perusal of Elle's Twitter account had nothing to do with caring about astrology and everything to do with preparedness. Like studying for an exam. Clearly, all this astrological malarkey meant something to Elle. If Darcy wanted to sell this relationship, she needed to understand what made Elle tick. If such a thing could even be pinpointed. So far, the verdict was out, the inner workings of one Elle Jones less of a neat little package to be unwrapped and more like a clown car full of increasingly random and terrifyingly endearing quirks.

Darcy took a sip of water. "Right. I was doing—that."

The waitress swung by the table, dropping off her coffee before taking Brendon's drink order. As soon as she was gone, Brendon leaned in, resting his elbows on the table, and gave her his best shit-eating grin.

"Speaking of Elle."

Darcy took a long, slow sip of her coffee and stared at him over the rim. "What about Elle?"

He rolled his eyes. "Darcy."

She smoothed the linen napkin on her lap and cocked her head. "All right. Should I start with how you did the one thing I *expressly* asked you not to? Not even twelve hours after you promised you wouldn't go blabbing to Elle, what did you do? You ran your mouth, in front of her *mother* no less. You told her I was *smitten*, Brendon. Do you know how mortified I was when Elle told me?"

She had been, just not for the reasons he might think.

"She tattled?" Brendon had the decency to look sheepish for a whole two seconds before his expression shifted into a gloating smirk. "Come on. Tell me this won't make for the greatest toast at your wedding one day."

Wedding. It was almost Pavlovian how the word inspired a visceral reaction, chills racing down her spine, a cold sweat breaking out along the nape of her neck, her molars clacking together. "Slow the fuck down, Brendon. Elle and I aren't getting married."

How she managed to string together complete sentences when her throat was narrower than her coffee's stir straw astounded her. She counted it as no small miracle that she could even say the word *married* at the moment.

Brendon snagged her cup of coffee, taking a sip before his whole face screwed up at the taste. And he called her a snob.

"You don't know that."

She did. But she couldn't say that. Not without calling her own bluff.

"Quit trying to marry me off like I'm some Regency spinster in one of your favorite Austen novels."

"Your name *is* Darcy."

"And I might be a single woman in possession of a good fortune, but I'm not in want of a wife." Once upon a time, she'd wanted that. Look how it had gone. No, thank you. "You're putting the cart in front of the horse. Elle and I aren't even officially together. We're testing the waters. Getting to know each other. Don't get your hopes up, is what I'm saying."

The waitress dropped off Brendon's Arnold Palmer and took their orders—salmon salad for Brendon and steak carpaccio for Darcy.

What with how Brendon was going around telling everyone, Elle included, that she was *smitten*—God, she detested that word—she'd oversold herself. This, walking it back, was all part of the plan. Make Brendon think she was trying with Elle, putting her heart out there, eradicating any and all belief on his part that she was scared to fall in love. But she had to hold back just enough to make their eventual split believable. It was a balancing act, appearing cautiously optimistic without making excessive promises.

"I can't believe you right now."

Darcy's head snapped up. "Excuse me?"

Brendon slouched in his chair. "You've got this great thing started with Elle, you're in the midst of the magical time at the beginning of a relationship when you're supposed to be on cloud nine thinking anything's possible, and yet here you are, being a total downer."

"Brendon—"

"No." Brendon shoved his chair back, metal legs squealing, and sat up straight, leaning his elbows on the table. "You're self-sabotaging right now, Darce. I know it isn't always easy to break the habit, not with—with what's happened, but you've got to stop seeing a dead end around every corner or else you're going to turn it into a self-fulfilling prophecy. And the only person you're going to have to blame is yourself."

Darcy traced the rim of her coffee cup with her pointer finger, pausing to rid the porcelain of her red lipstick smudge. If she was avoiding Brendon's eyes, it was completely coincidental. "I'm not self-sabotaging. I'm getting to know Elle and she's—she's more than I bargained for," Darcy conceded, letting Brendon make of that what he wanted.

Never before had Darcy ever seen someone's face look quite so much like the human equivalent of the heart-eyes emoji. Like drippy ice cream on a hot summer's day, Brendon melted in his chair, shoulders slumping as his whole face screwed up, lips pressed together to no doubt keep from *awing*. "Darcy."

Darcy had to bite the tip of her tongue to maintain her glare. "I swear on all that's holy, if you so much as make a single joke right now or butcher a playground nursery rhyme about trees and kissing and baby carriages, I'll let myself into your apartment and use your comic book collection as kindling. Capiche?"

He had to know she was all bark and no bite, but still, Brendon gave a full body shudder. "Got it." Brendon thanked the waitress when she dropped off his salad. Fork poised to dig in, Brendon paused, stare going serious and sincere. "I'm happy you're happy."

Her stomach twisted itself into a pretzel. "Thanks, Brendon."

"You know," he said, picking the tomatoes off his salad and tossing them on her plate. "You do kind of owe me for introducing you to Elle."

She owed him something all right.

"You know how you could make it up to me?"

She arched a brow. "How?"

Brendon dimpled. "This Saturday, eight o'clock. You, Elle, me, and Cherry. Double date. Say yes."

Darcy shut her eyes. "I'm sorry, did you say *Cherry*?"

When she opened her eyes, the corner of Brendon's mouth twitched. "She's sweet."

She was choosing to ignore the innuendo wrapped up in that statement because *gross*. "Brendon, I don't know if that's—"

"Please, Darce," he begged. "Say yes. Please say yes. Please, please, please with a cherry on—"

"*Jesus*, all right!" She lifted her hands in concession. Anything to make him *stop* before he finished that sentence.

Brendon's entire countenance shifted, posture relaxing into his usual laissez-faire, long-limbed slouch. He grinned, looking pleased at having pushed the right buttons to get his way. "Thank you. You and Elle, me and Cherry. We're gonna have a blast."

Chapter Six

DARCY (4:57 P.M.): I think we need to discuss the details of this arrangement sooner as opposed to later.

ELLE (5:08 P.M.): how come?

ELLE (5:09 P.M.): i mean that's fine

ELLE (5:09 P.M.): jw if there was a reason

ELLE (5:09 P.M.): something i should know

Elle wasn't keen on being kept out of the loop again anytime soon.

DARCY (5:16 P.M.): My brother has invited us on a double date this Saturday. And by invite, I mean strong-armed me into agreeing. In the interest of selling this, I believe it would be best to have our ducks in a row ahead of time.

Elle had already had several stress dreams about Brendon finding out this was all a ruse and hating her for it. In her last dream, she had been on a trashy tabloid talk show. Brendon had forced her to undergo a lie-detector test and after she'd failed, he'd torn up the contract negotiations between OTP and Oh My Stars before storming off the set. In the audience, her entire family had booed. Darcy had been conspicuously absent.

It was just a dream—Elle didn't really believe the deal with OTP was predicated or somehow tied to the success of her relationship with Darcy—but Darcy had a point. She didn't know Darcy's birth date or . . . well, *anything* about her beside the fact that she was an actuary and workaholic. They needed to get to know each other better before this double date or else it'd look like the sham it was.

ELLE (5:20 P.M.): what are we doing?

ELLE (5:20 P.M.): on the double date i mean

DARCY (5:24 P.M.): I didn't ask. Is it relevant?

Elle rolled her eyes. Looks like she'd have to ask Brendon.

ELLE (5:25 P.M.): okay np

ELLE (5:26 P.M.): you free tonight?

ELLE (5:26 P.M.): say 7?

ELLE (5:26 P.M.): we can rendezvous at your place since i know where you live

DARCY (5:33 P.M.): That's fine.

Elle tucked her phone inside her messenger bag and slipped the strap over her shoulder. It was—she peeked at the Kit-Cat

clock that hung crooked on the wall beside the microwave—
ten to six. Just enough time to stop by Safeway before darting
over to Darcy's posh Queen Anne apartment.

Hopping off the barstool, Elle glanced at Margot who continued to click away at her keyboard, pausing every now and
again to glare menacingly at the screen. "I'm headed out. I
guess I'll see you later if you're still awake."

She made it halfway to the front door—the whole two steps
it took—when Margot sighed. "Elle, wait."

Elle bit the inside of her cheek and braced herself for another
dig at what she was doing with Darcy. "Yeah?"

Margot set her computer aside and rested her elbows on her
knees, fingers laced loosely together in front of her. "When I
said you were making an epic mistake the other night, I was
out of line. I'm . . . I'm sorry."

Elle shut her mouth. Apologies from Margot were rare. Just
as rare as the arguments between them. "You don't have to—"

"No, I do." Margot blew out a breath, the thick fringe of her
bangs parting like a curtain. "I'm pissed off, okay? On your
behalf. And I know you think because Darcy apologized that
it's fine now, but sometimes sorry isn't good enough, Elle. The
last thing I want to do is harsh your vibe or rain on your pa-
rade, but I take no shit on your behalf. I haven't since the day
we moved into the dorms freshman year and you demanded
we stay up all night bonding over burnt microwave popcorn
because you, and I quote, *have a feeling we're supposed to be best
friends*. I'm not going to start now."

Elle wasn't sure whether she was supposed to laugh or cry.

Caught in a state of flux, she did both at the same time. She swiped at her face, no doubt smearing eyeliner all over the place. But the pressure inside her chest that had taken up residence during her sort-of tiff with Margot deflated, leaving room for her heart to swell. "Margot. That was nine years ago."

"Stop crying." Margot sniffed, her expression shifting into a put-off frown. "You're going to make me cry. I *hate* crying. Don't hate me, but please hear me out?"

It would take an utterly uncharacteristic move on Margot's part, like murdering someone, to make Elle hate her. Even then, Elle would at least ask why before passing judgment.

"You were really upset the other night. I know you were trying to put on a brave face, but it was obvious Darcy hurt you. Worse than you let on. Now you're agreeing to fake a relationship with her? Because of your family? Elle, if they can't see how amazing you are . . . this isn't worth it."

Elle ground the toe of her boot into the rug, tracing the singe mark in the paisley pattern from the Birthday Sparkler Incident of 2017.

"I don't really know what I'm doing," she admitted. The lump inside her throat grew, forcing her to swallow to keep her voice from cracking. "I'm just tired of falling short, Mar."

Margot's face crumpled. "Elle—"

She jerked her chin and sniffed hard, blinking away the film of tears blurring her vision. She smiled and shrugged. "If I can get my family to take me seriously about *one* thing, see that I have my life together in a way that makes sense to them, maybe they'll come around to the rest."

Margot shook her head. "So you're throwing in the towel?

You're going to be like Lydia now? Dating the sorts of people your parents want and shrinking yourself down to be palatable to people who don't *get* you? Who don't even try?"

No. *God* no. Elle wasn't going to actually compromise who she was or how she lived her life. No, this was a blip on Elle's radar, a pit stop, a means to an end. Elle wasn't settling. She just wanted her parents to be proud of her for who she was. If she had to speak their language for a brief bit of time, what was the harm? "No way. This is fake. I just want them to understand I'm not the letdown they think I am. Maybe hearing how awesome I am from someone else, someone like Darcy who's the sort of person who satisfies their whole *nine-to-five I'm a serious adult* vibe, will help."

Margot stuck out her tongue, eyes rolling. "Boring, you mean?"

Elle shrugged. "Besides, it's cuffing season and Lydia's got a boyfriend. Jane's got Gabe and Daniel has Mike and I'm just— *Elle.* I'm not exactly jazzed about spending another holiday alone as the black sheep of the family."

"*Just Elle* is pretty great." Margot smiled. "But I get it. I mean, I might not be in your shoes, but I understand where you're coming from. I just want you to remember that you deserve someone you don't have to fake it with." Both her brows rose. "And I mean that in all ways."

Elle cracked a smile. "Thanks."

"But seriously, have you thought about what you're going to do when your two months are up? How are you going to spin your breakup that doesn't make you look like you can't hold down a relationship?"

Elle grimaced. That would be counterintuitive. "I'm thinking we'll split because of some crucial but faultless incompatibility like . . . I don't know, I want kids but she doesn't."

Breakups happened all the time. There didn't need to be culpability. It could be a mature split that in no way served as a blight on Elle's character.

"*Does* she want kids?"

"I don't know."

Margot frowned. "Don't you think that's something you should probably discuss before you start making plans? Kids might be excessive, but *things*? Her favorite color. Food allergies. I don't know."

She nodded. "I'm headed to her place now, actually. We're going to get to know each other so we can make this whole thing a little more believable."

Margot worried her lip. She wasn't entirely sold, Elle could tell, but something was better than nothing.

Elle gave one last shrug. "It's not ideal, but it's better than nothing, I guess? It's like hiring an escort but better because it's beneficial for the both of us and on the bright side, I don't have to pay."

"You getting some other perks out of this you failed to mention?" Margot waggled her brows.

Her face warmed. "I don't think it's like that."

"Something else you might want to hammer out, yeah?" Margot's smile flattened into something tense. "Just watch your back. I don't want you getting hurt."

"It's not like Darcy can hurt my feelings any worse than she already has. I know she doesn't like me, so what's the worst that could happen?"

✩ ✩
✩

Elle shifted the bags from her left arm to the right and tried—subsequently failing—to smother her smile when Darcy opened the door, this time wearing a camel-colored pencil skirt that hugged her hips, and a polka-dotted pussy-bow blouse in off-white that Darcy would probably dub something fancy like eggshell or mascarpone. On anyone else it would've been very *blah*, but the fall of Darcy's copper hair over one shoulder and her curves made it less boring and more librarian chic. Never before had Elle met someone so pretty that it pissed her off.

Darcy shifted her weight from one foot to the other, hips cocking, emphasizing the crescent curve of her waist. She side-eyed the bags looped over Elle's arm, looking equal parts intrigued and distrustful. "Hello."

Elle lifted the bags. "I come bearing libations and craft supplies."

Darcy's brows rocketed to her hairline. "*Craft supplies?*"

Sliding past Darcy into the apartment, Elle bit back a grin. Score one for her for managing to knock Darcy off-kilter. "Mm-hmm. I figured we could hammer out the details of this arrangement and share some facts about ourselves."

Elle set the bags on the floor beside the coffee table. From the first bag she withdrew two notebooks, one black and the other white, and a twelve pack of gel pens. "Facts we can write down in these handy notebooks. I brought gel pens in case you want to color code anything. Because if there's one thing you should know about me—okay, there are a lot of things you should know about me. But right now, it's important to know I don't have much Virgo in my chart. I mean, there's Jupiter and it's retrograde and my seventh house is in Virgo, but that's a whole other story." And too much to unpack in one night. "However, I aspire to Virgo-level detail orientation and I do it through color-coordinated crafts. Got it?"

That was an ultrasimplification, but it was doubtful Darcy wanted details. Elle believed in astrology, believed the cosmos controlled more than met the eye and *that* was what Darcy needed to know if this was going to work, if this fake relationship of theirs would ever fool a single soul. She needed to know it, and inside it might make her roll her eyes and despair at how *silly* Elle was, but outwardly Darcy needed to not scoff at it. Even if this entire charade was pretend, Darcy needed to respect Elle's beliefs. Respect *Elle*, or no dice.

Elle held her breath as Darcy frowned thoughtfully. "Okay, got it. May I ask a question?"

"Absolutely." Elle gestured for Darcy to go on. "There's no such thing as a stupid question. There's a definite learning curve to this."

Darcy nodded. "All right. If your Jupiter is . . . in Virgo?" Elle nodded. "Where's your Uranus?"

"My Uranus is in Capri—" Elle froze. "*Wow.*"

Darcy's dimples deepened as she smiled impishly. "Sorry, it was just *right there*. You probably get that a lot."

"From frat boys and five-year-olds, not . . ." She trailed off, gesturing up and down in Darcy's general direction with her free hand. "People like you."

"People like me?" Darcy's brows rose and fell. "Like me how?"

People who drank fifty-six-dollar glasses of wine and wore tight little pencil skirts and Christian Louboutin heels and worked as actuaries. Insufferable know-it-alls with cunning sensibilities and kissable little moon-shaped freckles. People with eyes like burnt caramel and full lips that looked candy-apple sweet. People who . . . who . . .

Elle waved the notebooks in the air. "I don't know. Which is why I'm here. I figured, we'd drink a little wine, play twenty questions, jot down our notes, and get to know each other a little. Make this charade a little more believable, if not truthful. Or close enough to assuage my conscience."

Darcy did that thing where she stared, brown eyes studying Elle from across the living room. It was only a look and yet it made Elle feel weirdly naked.

"If you think it's silly, we can—"

"No." Darcy shook her head and stepped closer, nudging the remaining bag with a stocking-covered toe. *Stockings. Fuck.* Elle sunk her teeth into her bottom lip. Pantyhose were the bane of her existence—if she so much as tried to put on a pair, she'd immediately get a run—but on Darcy . . . Elle tore her eyes away and feigned interest in ripping open the cardboard pen packaging. Darcy went on, "It's not silly. No doubt Brendon will dig for details. It's important for us to be on the same page. Good idea."

Good idea. Between the hot librarian getup, complete with pantyhose, and the kernel of praise, Elle had a flashback to when her pretty fifth-grade teacher put gold stars on all her best work.

"You mentioned wine?" Darcy prodded when Elle remained mute, silenced by the awkward fantasy playing out inside her head. A fantasy replete with *bow chicka wow wow* seventies porn music and slo-mo swishing hair.

"Wine! Yes, wine." Crouching on her knees, Elle set the notebooks aside so she could grab the— "Ta da! Wine."

Nose wrinkled and lips parted in revulsion, Darcy looked at the box of Franzia rosé in Elle's hands like it was a personal affront. "What the fuck is that?"

"Wine," Elle chirped. "My favorite wine. That merlot I drank the other night? Disgusting. I don't care how fancy a wine is or about trendy cocktails; I like drinks that actually taste yummy. If it comes in frozen slushie form, even better."

Darcy's frown deepened as she digested that little factoid. "Must it come in a *box*?"

Said box in hand, Elle made a beeline for the kitchen. Glasses, glasses, where would Darcy keep her—bingo. Near the sink, logical. Darcy's middle name. "All my favorite foods come in boxes. Wine. Cereal. Takeout." Elle smushed the cardboard seal into the box and plucked out the nozzle. She filled both glasses with rosé before passing one to a circumspect Darcy. "Here's to—"

Elle raised her glass in the air, momentum splashing wine against the back of her wrist, a dribble splattering against Darcy's floor, a pale pink puddle forming atop the crisp white tile.

"Here's to not spilling." Darcy gave a deadpan stare before dropping her eyes to the puddle and arching a brow, a silent command to clean it up. She left the kitchen, shaking her head, hips and hair swaying.

Elle took a swallow of the sweet wine and sighed. "Cheers."

☆
☆
☆

Glass of rosé in hand, Elle settled in, getting comfortable on the floor in front of the coffee table. She lifted her glass, taking a generous swig, and set it down, cracking open the spine of her notebook. "All right. Let's get to know each other, shall we?"

"Do you mind putting that on a coaster?" Darcy gestured to the stack of white Carrara marble coasters.

Elle snagged a coaster, then reached for a pen. "Fact number one—compulsive about coaster usage."

Darcy huffed softly and took a sip of wine, ignoring the notebook on the couch cushion beside her. "I'm not compulsive."

Elle clicked the end of her pen. "What are you then? I mean, tell me something about you. Where are you from, where'd you go to school, any pets? Greatest wish, biggest dream? How about any super sordid secrets I should know?"

Darcy swirled the wine in her glass out of habit, obviously, because even Elle knew swirling Franzia was pretty pointless even if it did look posh. "I don't think you need to know all that if we've only known each other a week."

Elle doodled a smiling flower in the margin of the paper. "What do *you* talk about on first dates? Successful ones."

"I was born in San Francisco," Darcy offered up, not *quite* answering her question. "But I grew up across the Bay in Marin County."

Elle reached for the green gel pen and wrote that down. "California, huh? That must've been nice."

The left corner of Darcy's mouth quirked upward. "It was."

Elle waited for Darcy to say something else, keep going, add an anecdote, *anything*. When she simply stared into her glass of pink wine, Elle bit back a sigh. "All right. So you were born in San Francisco and obviously you've got a younger brother. Any other siblings?" When Darcy simply shook her head, Elle grabbed her glass and took another swig. Coaxing details out of her was like pulling teeth. "How about the rest of your family?"

Darcy's teeth sunk into her lower lip for a brief moment before she tipped her glass up, polishing it off in one swallow. Impressive. "We had—*have* a small family. It's just Brendon, my mother, father, and me. My grandmother—my mother's mom—passed away five years ago."

Elle dropped her pen midsentence and stared at Darcy. "I'm sorry. Were you close?"

"My grandmother?" Darcy's brows rose.

Elle nodded.

"We were." The platinum band on Darcy's middle finger tapped against the stem of her empty wineglass. "My, uh, my father traveled a lot, for work. My mother hated how often Dad was away, so Brendon and I spent the summers at my grandmother's house so my mom could go with him on his business trips." Darcy pressed her lips together. "The summer before my junior year of high school, my parents divorced. We—my mother, Brendon, and I—moved in with my grandma. I loved living there." Darcy tucked her hair behind her ears. "And that's probably way more than you need to know after a week of dating—*fake* dating—me."

She could take a hint. "All right. Hometown, family, when'd you move here? *Why'd* you move here?"

"Six months ago." Darcy spun the stem of her glass between her fingers. An elegant move that Elle wouldn't have been able to pull off without dropping or spilling. "I moved from Philadelphia where I majored in actuarial science at Fox Business School at Temple University before working at a midsize life insurance company. As for why I moved . . ." Darcy pursed her lips and shrugged. "It was time for a change."

"Time for a change," Elle repeated. "That's not, like, code for *I committed a crime and now I'm on the lam*, is it?"

Darcy cocked one brow, lips curling. "If I told you, I'd have to kill you."

A shiver raced up Elle's spine at the look in Darcy's low-lidded eyes and the way her voice had gone teasing, mischievous. *Evasive*. Elle sat up straighter and smiled. "Seriously. What brought you to Seattle?"

Darcy's lips flattened, eyes darting off toward the wall of windows on the far side of the room. "There wasn't much opportunity for growth at the company I was with and . . . and I went through a breakup and unfortunately, other than my best friend, Annie, most of our friends were mutual, our friend groups intermingled, so my social life stagnated." Her throat jerked as she swallowed. "It really was time for a change." She turned, eyes narrowed slightly and chin lifted. "And that's *definitely* more than you need to know after a week of fake dating me."

A breakup. Interesting, but Elle wouldn't pry. It was none of her business. "So you packed up and moved across the country for a fresh start. That's cool. Like spring cleaning for the soul."

Darcy cracked a smile. "I moved in the spring, so that's a surprisingly accurate metaphor."

"What can I say, I'm full of surprises."

Darcy chuckled. "I'm getting that."

Elle bit down on the inside of her cheek to keep from grinning.

"How about you?" Darcy gestured to Elle with her empty wineglass.

"What about me?"

"You know. Your story. Where you're from, your family, that sort of thing?"

"Oh." Right, she'd gotten so wrapped up in learning about Darcy, who until now had been a closed book, that she'd forgotten they were both supposed to be sharing. "Um, born in Seattle on February twenty-second but I grew up in Bellevue. I've got two older siblings, Jane and Daniel. They're both married. And I've got a younger sister, too, Lydia. Jane has a three-year-old, Ryland, and she's expecting twins."

"Big family." Darcy pulled a face and Elle couldn't tell if it was overwhelm or wistfulness that made Darcy's mouth twist and her eyes widen. "Are your parents still together?"

She nodded. "They're wildly in love with each other. My dad still buys her flowers every Friday."

Darcy smiled. "That's sweet."

It was, but talking about it was doing stupid, painful things to Elle's insides. "That's the gist of my immediate family, but I can give you a better briefing closer to Thanksgiving, okay?"

✿ ✿
✿

Darcy nodded and reached for her pen, black, unlike the glittery eyesore-color Elle had selected. She jotted down the basics she'd gleaned thus far. "Fair enough. Born and raised in Seattle—did you go to school here?"

Elle tugged on her ear. "I did. I went to UW. That's where I met Margot. We roomed together freshman year and when we were unpacking, I noticed she owned a bunch of books on astrology. I'd been studying it since high school, and as soon as I got my driver's license, I applied for a part-time job at Wishing Well Books, a metaphysical bookstore not far from where I live now. On the weekends and over the summers, when I wasn't working the register and stocking shelves, the owner kind of took me under her wing, like an apprenticeship. Margot and I bonded over it and we started Oh My Stars the next year. We didn't really get any traction until a couple years ago when we got a job writing the astrology column for *The Stranger*. Our following grew, one of our posts went viral, and we pretty much blew up."

If someone had asked Darcy two weeks ago whether she was curious about what went into being a social media astrologer, she'd have unequivocally answered no. Now, after acquainting herself with Oh My Stars's Twitter account, she'd have to say she was . . . but only from the standpoint that she didn't like not understanding things. "And now you make memes for a living?"

Elle threw her head back and laughed. "No. I mean, kind of? It's way more than that."

"So what do you *do*? What's a day in the life of Elle look like?"

Elle shrugged. "Wake up, caffeinate, check email and social media accounts. That takes an hour or two. Margot and I handle most aspects of the business fifty-fifty, but we each have our strengths. Having majored in communications, Margot tends to handle website maintenance and our social accounts and I take on more of the readings because I have more experience there. In between appointments we do live Q and A's, and in our spare time we make content because, yeah, memes get us retweets and followers, which in turn grows our audience. But that's not where we make money. Not really."

Darcy tried not to frown. "How do you make money? If you don't mind me asking."

Elle leaned back on her elbows, reclining on the rug. "We make a tiny bit from advertisements and paid sponsorships, but only if it's a product or service we can get behind, like astro-themed apparel we'd actually wear or zodiac-inspired perfume that really smells good and aligns with your birth chart."

How a scent aligned with a person's *birth chart* was a mystery, but Darcy didn't want to interrupt.

"Our book, which is an astrological primer and guide to compatibility, is up for preorder, but most of our income comes from giving chart readings. We offer thirty-minute and hour-long phone sessions where we review a client's birth chart and break it down or, depending on how much they know, we might touch on a specific topic they want answers on, like their Saturn return. If a client's local and would rather meet in person, we have a deal with the bookstore I used to work at so we can use their back room. Occasionally I'll spend the day there and take walk-ins. We also have subscription plans where clients pay monthly or annually for shorter, check-in text sessions where they can ask any burning questions they might have about transits or retrogrades. That sort of thing."

"People actually pay for that?" Darcy winced as soon as the words were out of her mouth. "Sorry, that was rude of me. I just meant . . . isn't something like that, one and done? You have your chart read and you're set? If you believe in . . . that."

If Elle was offended, it didn't show. Her head tilted to the side, a smile playing at the edges of her lips. Darcy cast a forlorn glance at her glass, wishing it were full, even if the wine was too sweet.

"The planets aren't static and neither are we. It's good to check in with the stars and, if nothing else, it's time spent on self-reflection." Elle's toes curled in the soft pile of the rug, her hot pink toenail polish catching the light. "As for readings as a whole, don't knock it until you've tried it."

Darcy set her wineglass aside.

"Have you ever worked for a company that had you fill out an MBTI questionnaire? INFJ? ENTP? Or enneagram?" Elle asked.

Only every company Darcy had ever worked for, internships included. "And?"

"Tons of people consider MBTI pseudoscience and it has known issues with validity and repeatability. But people dig it because it gives them a way to describe themselves and what they value. How they function."

Darcy had never been one to care about those four-letter designations. Half the time, her answers changed depending on her mood, the time of day, whether she'd eaten, and how much sleep she'd gotten.

"It's why we're obsessed with personality quizzes. Yeah, there are think pieces about how it makes us narcissistic, but we're not. We're freaked out and confused. Existential angst is legit. We like to feel *seen* so we cling to meaning where we can find it even if it's as basic as what your favorite item at the Cheesecake Factory says about you."

Darcy laughed. "My favorite item at the Cheesecake Factory is not a reflection of some deeper facet of my personality. I don't even *like* the Cheesecake Factory. The menu is the size of a novel and they use blue-cheese-stuffed olives in their dirty vodka martinis. Not to mention, the decor is confused. Greco-Roman meets Egyptian meets Eye of Sauron. The whole place is bullshit. I'd rather go to a Medieval Times dinner show. It might be kitsch, but at least it's consistent."

"Like that doesn't speak volumes right there." Elle tapped her pen against her teeth, smiling broadly. "What I'm saying is, we're all just trying to understand ourselves and each other and what it all means. Why it matters. Astrology gives us a language for that. It helps us practice empathy. Which makes us less shitty." Elle kicked a foot out, knocking Darcy's ankle. Darcy froze at the unexpected contact. "Come on. What time were you born?"

"I don't know."

"How do you not know your time of birth?"

"I just don't," she deflected. She knew *exactly* what time she was born at, but she had already told Elle more about herself than she'd planned.

Elle stared hard at Darcy's face, and Darcy willed her eye not to— *Damn it*. She twitched. Elle threw her pen down and bear-crawled across the room. She heaved herself up onto the couch. "You're so lying right now. You don't want to tell me."

Darcy puffed out her cheeks and closed her eyes. "Eleven minutes past noon."

Elle grabbed her phone and swiped against the screen, tapping values into text boxes, before staring at what looked like a wheel divided into wedges of varying sizes. "Hm."

Darcy's fingers covered hers, concealing the screen. "Stop. This is . . . strange."

Elle's tongue darted out, wetting her bottom lip. "I thought you didn't believe in it."

Darcy's grip loosened, her fingers sweeping against the back of Elle's hand and ghosting over the thin skin of Elle's wrist. Darcy dropped her hands back to her lap. "I don't." But Elle did. "Fine. Whatever. Read my chart."

Elle spent a moment studying Darcy's chart. "Interesting."

Darcy huffed. "You can't say something's interesting and not explain."

Elle looked up, smirking. "What happened to not believing in it?"

"I *don't*." With another aggrieved sigh, Darcy pointed impatiently at Elle's phone. "But you do. And you're clearly passing judgments on me based on these beliefs of yours. So go on. Tell me something about myself."

"It's not about passing judgments. It's about empathy, remember?" Thumb swiping down, Elle scrolled back to the top of the page. "All right. Let's see. You're a Capricorn sun, Pisces moon, and Taurus rising."

None of that made a lick of sense.

"Your sun symbolizes your ego, your sense of self. Capricorn's an earth sign. You're realistic, reserved, probably a little circumspect. Not known for taking risks. But you're responsible, so kudos there. Your rising, or ascendant, is the sign that was rising in the eastern horizon at the time of your birth. It often dictates people's first impression of you, more so even than your sun sign. Taurus means you might be stubborn and resistant to change, but you're probably loyal and dependable. Also, you likely crave stability and creature comforts like quality clothing and good food. Considering those placements together, no wonder you're a skeptic," Elle ribbed her gently.

Darcy rolled her eyes.

"Now, this Pisces moon is interesting. Your moon represents your inner self; it's representative of how you deal with and express your emotions. You're imaginative, compassionate, and occasionally value an escape from reality."

Darcy scratched the side of her neck, refusing to so much as glance at the television where she had two days' worth of soaps recorded.

Elle licked her lips. "You've got a Capricorn stellium, meaning you've got four or more planets in that sign. Big Capricorn Energy, basically. I won't bore you with them all, but you've got Venus in Capricorn meaning you're likely cautious when it comes to love and value goal-oriented partners. You take love seriously, you understand it takes commitment and devotion to make a relationship last. You yearn for the right person to share your life with."

Darcy scoffed, shaking her head. She gathered her hair off her neck and tossed it over her left shoulder. God, she was about to burst into flames she was so hot.

"Your Mercury is in Aquarius, so you might value intellectual debates and even contradicting the opinions of others for kicks."

"Now you're just trying to give me shit."

Elle leaned in, shoving her phone in Darcy's face. "It's all right here. Written in the stars. I'm merely an interpreter."

"Well, are you finished interpreting?"

Elle gave an exaggerated eye roll and stretched across the gap between the couch and the coffee table to set her phone aside. Precariously balanced on her knees, straightening made her sway. The couch cushion dipped and sank under their combined weights, forcing them even closer together, so close Elle was practically in Darcy's lap. She must've realized it at the same time as Darcy because her eyes widened, gaze dropping suddenly to where her hand gripped Darcy's thigh for balance. Darcy's skirt had bunched, riding high and exposing the thick lace band of her stockings. Elle's cheeks pinked and her breath caught, fingers twitching. An inch higher and it would be her skin Elle touched instead of nylon.

Elle lifted her head, catching Darcy staring.

Around them, the air crackled, Darcy's whole body tingling from her scalp to her soles. She shivered as Elle leaned a little closer, close enough to feel the heat radiating off her, her wine-sweet breath warm as it puffed against Darcy's face. *Too close.* Darcy wasn't supposed to be getting close to anyone.

Darcy stood quickly, wobbling briefly before steadying herself on the edge of the couch. "Do you want more wine?" Without waiting for Elle's answer, she strode off in the direction of the kitchen, both their glasses in hand.

Darcy rested her forehead against the stainless-steel door of her fridge and breathed deep. Get a grip. Clearly there was chemistry at play, but as satisfying as giving in would be in the moment, the consequences would be catastrophic. Elle was looking for love and Darcy wasn't. End of story.

After filling both glasses from the black plastic pour spout on the atrocious box of wine, Darcy took a healthy swallow from hers and returned to the living room, uncertain of whether she'd have to let Elle down gently.

"Enough about astrology," Elle said, taking her glass from Darcy with a smile. "We should probably talk about selling this."

The tension between Darcy's shoulders subsided. They were on the same page then. "More than we have already?"

Elle made a soft noise in the back of her throat. "I mean, the logistics of it all."

Darcy liked logistics. Logistics were safe. They could talk about that. "Okay."

"We've got our double date on Saturday. Then Thanksgiving at my parents' and Brendon's Christmas party. Is that it?"

Is that it? As if it weren't already too much. "Unless Brendon springs something else on us, which is entirely in the realm of possibility." Darcy paused. "That's only one event of yours. Not exactly equitable."

Elle laughed under her breath. "You haven't met my family. But Thanksgiving is an all-day thing anyway, it's like a two-for-one. No worries."

Yes, worries. "If you say so."

Elle pulled a loose thread on the bottom of her sweater. "In terms of *selling it* . . . what exactly are you comfortable with?"

"Comfortable with?"

"You know." Elle huffed. "There's more to making everyone think we're dating than knowing each other's middle names and where we went to school." Her tongue darted out, wetting her bottom lip. "Like, being comfortable with a certain degree of . . . familiarity. Hand holding, touching—"

"Fine." Darcy clutched her wine, thigh burning with the ghost of Elle's touch. "That's . . . fine."

Elle's forehead wrinkled. "Fine? You're good with—"

"Anything." A dizzying wave of heat crashed over her as her mind caught up to her mouth. It had been how long exactly since she'd gotten laid? Too long apparently. Darcy coughed. "Whatever it takes to sell it."

"Okay." Elle worried the corner of her bottom lip for a moment before gathering up the gel pens scattered across the coffee table. "Well. That's all I had. Unless there was something you wanted to add?"

Right. There was something. She'd made a mental list. If she could just remember, stop getting distracted by— "Actually yes. I was thinking it would be a good idea if we set a termination date."

Elle straightened from where she'd been hunched over the bags of craft supplies. "Sorry, a what?"

Darcy tugged at the hem of her skirt before primly crossing her legs at the ankles, knees slanted to the side. "A termination date, the day on which a contract ends and a deal expires. We should set one."

Elle nodded. "When were you thinking?"

Darcy grabbed her phone off the table and several swipes later, she presented Elle with a screen showing her calendar. Her phone shook faintly in her hand, hopefully not enough for Elle to notice. "Today's November fifth. Why don't we keep it simple? December thirty-first?"

Elle resembled a bobblehead, nodding briskly and for too long. "Sure."

"I know neither of us asked for this," Darcy added. "I'm sure we'll both be glad when we don't have to keep pretending."

God knew she would. This was all more involved than she'd anticipated. Getting to know Elle, being in close proximity with her. It was too much, made it hard for her to think, made her want things she had no business craving with Elle.

The new year couldn't come soon enough.

Chapter Seven

ELLE (7:15 P.M.): about this double date

ELLE (7:15 P.M.): your sister forgot to ask what we're doing

ELLE (7:16 P.M.): so what's the 411?

BRENDON (7:20 P.M.): You know the Seattle Underground? Entrance is in Pioneer Square?

ELLE (7:22 P.M.): i know of it yeah

BRENDON (7:24 P.M.): There's an escape room. I thought it'd be fun. Race against time, you know?

BRENDON (7:25 P.M.): Then drinks? Trivia and drinks? Thoughts?

ELLE (7:27 P.M.): an escape room?!?

ELLE (7:27 P.M.): ive always wanted to do one!

ELLE (7:28 P.M.): and yes to trivia and drinks

BRENDON (7:30 P.M.): Sweet!

BRENDON (7:32 P.M.): Btw! Contracts are moving along on HR's end. You should have a final draft in your inbox early next week.

ELLE (7:33 P.M.): 😃 yesssss

ELLE (7:34 P.M.): cant wait!

ELLE (7:35 P.M.): and thats perfect timing because mercury wont be retrograde yet

ELLE (7:35 P.M.): and youre not supposed to sign contracts during retrograde

BRENDON (7:36 P.M.): See, even the universe is jizzed about us working together.

BRENDON (7:37 P.M.): FML. Jazzed. Sorry. 😔

ELLE (7:38 P.M.): 🤣

✩ ✩
✩

Be honest. How do I look?" Elle gave a twirl, the hem of her dress flouncing against her thighs as she spun, ending with a spirited flourish of her fingers.

On the couch, legs tucked beneath her, Margot cocked her head, expression inscrutable. "Honest, you said?"

Elle dropped her arms and sighed. "You don't like it."

Margot sucked her lips between her teeth. "It's not that I don't like it, I do. You look like a punk rock Rainbow Brite."

Huh. Margot's comparison wasn't off the mark. She'd paired her favorite navy dress from ModCloth, the one with the rainbow unicorn print, with the black rainbow patent Doc Martens she'd snagged on sale at Buffalo Exchange. Shoes that would hopefully be perfect for traipsing around in Seattle's Underground. But, without a doubt, the most critical part of her outfit wasn't the shoes, but instead was her comfortable undies. She was ready for whatever the universe hurled her way, including but not limited to chafing calamities.

Thirty minutes after waving good-bye to Margot, who again assured Elle she looked fine, she stepped inside the heated interior of the Underground's tour office and spotted Darcy's red hair over by the will call window. Right on time.

"Boo." Elle poked Darcy in the side before leaning against the ticket counter.

Darcy's throat jerked, her eyes dipping to take Elle in from head to toe. "*Wow.*"

Elle's knees went weak so she decided to work with her body's reaction rather than against it. Dipping at the knee, she gave a mock-curtsy, tugging at one side of the hem of her dress. "I'm choosing to interpret that as a compliment, Buttercup."

Darcy wrinkled her nose. "*Buttercup?*"

"Baby? Sweetheart? My moon and stars?" The amount of pleasure Elle took in Darcy's deepening look of disgust was second to none. "We forgot to think up pet names."

"Let's not." Darcy thanked the attendant when they slid a stack of tickets beneath the plexiglass divider. "We're trying to sell it to my brother, not make him think I've had a personality transplant."

"Where *is* Brendon?" Elle craned her neck, searching the crowd for Brendon's tall frame and mop of auburn hair.

"Searching for his date." Darcy gestured to an empty bench against the wall beside the posted sign that said TOURS START HERE. "She thought we were meeting at the bar first."

Elle followed as Darcy led the way across the room and tried not to stare. Darcy wore dark, high-waisted, figure-hugging jeans tucked into a pair of brown riding boots that made their height difference a little less disparate, and her green sweater brought out the honey-colored flecks in her eyes. Not that Elle cared about Darcy's eyes or that the color she wore complemented them. It was a passing observation, that was all. The sky was blue. The grass was green. Darcy was beautiful. Universally acknowledged truths.

Darcy's butt barely touched the bench before she stood back up. "There they are." She pointed across the room to the doubled-doored entrance before quickly spinning back around to face Elle. The corners of her mouth puckered, her nostrils flaring delicately. "Okay, here's the plan. If Brendon starts digging for details, let me do the talking."

"That's a terrible plan, baby."

"It's a *great* plan, and don't call me baby."

"I'm not going mute to make you happy. *I'll* look like the one who's had a personality transplant. Besides, we have a game plan. We discussed it. You don't get to pick the game *and* make all the rules, Darcy."

Elle had agreed to fake a relationship, but she refused to be anyone other than exactly who she was, not for her family, not for the people they set her up with, and definitely not for Darcy. If the idea of being coupled up with her was so objectionable that a few pet names got Darcy huffy, she should've thought twice before fibbing to her brother.

Darcy shot a quick glance over her shoulder and frowned. "Fine. Try not to oversell it and don't offer up information unless Brendon asks."

Before Elle could respond, Brendon spotted them through

the crowd, waving and making his way over with a leggy brunette who was rocking the hell out of a pair of four-inch candy-apple red stilettos. Drool-worthy, but not exactly the right attire for heading underground.

"Hey, glad you could make it." Brendon wrapped Darcy in a bear hug before giving Elle a quick, enthusiastic squeeze. "Guys, this is Cherry. Cherry, this is my sister, Darcy, and her girlfriend, Elle."

Girlfriend, huh? Elle glanced at Darcy. She looked like she was about to argue but thought better of it, instead reaching out and resting a slightly stiff hand against the small of Elle's back. Elle leaned into the touch and aimed a dazzling smile up at Darcy. That wasn't so hard, was it?

"It's nice to meet you." Cherry nodded, slipping her fingers around Brendon's elbow. "Cute dress."

"Thanks." Elle tugged at the skirt. "It has pockets."

A man with a thick handlebar mustache approached. "Lowell party of four for the escape room?"

Brendon stepped forward and patted his pockets. "Yeah, I've got the tickets—wait."

"I have them. You asked me to pick them up from will call, remember?" Darcy passed them to the man whose nametag read *Jim*. He gave the stack a cursory glance before tucking them away inside the inner pocket of his blazer. "Follow me and mind the stairs." He sighed heavily, mustache twitching when he caught sight of Cherry's heels. "Terrain gets a touch uneven."

Down a rickety set of wooden stairs, the man led them into a hall, lit by several flickering incandescent bulbs. The air was cool and damp and a little musty, earthy even. Moss—or maybe that was mildew—grew on the gray brick walls, concentrated around the grout lines. Somewhere, a pipe was leaking, the steady *drip, drip* lending to the overall vibe of abandoned decay.

"Ever been to the Underground before?" Jim asked.

Everyone shook their heads.

"Quick bit of history before I give you the backstory for your one-of-a-kind escape room experience. In 1889, thirty-one blocks were destroyed in the Great Seattle Fire. The buildings were rebuilt and the streets were regraded a couple stories higher than what was previously street level, a strategic decision to prevent flooding from Elliott Bay."

Jim gestured around them to where the hall branched to the left and right. "Seattle Underground, as we now know it, is a network of passageways that existed at ground level prior to the regrade. For a time, pedestrians and business owners continued to use these underground sidewalks, but that all changed in 1907 when the city condemned the Underground out of fear of the bubonic plague. As a result, portions of the Underground were left to deteriorate. Opium dens, speakeasies, gambling halls, brothels, and doss houses cropped up, operating in the literal shadows of society, right beneath everyone's feet."

If the walls down here could talk, she could only imagine the sorts of seedy, scary stories they'd tell.

"Which brings us to your escape room." Jim set off down the hall to the left at a quick clip, waving for them to follow. When Cherry stumbled on a loose cobblestone, Darcy rolled her eyes.

"Is there a theme? Or are we just trapped in the Underground trying to escape?" Elle asked.

Jim smoothed his mustache with a finger. "Is there a theme? she asks." He stopped in front of a nondescript door, wooden and without windows or special markings. "The year is 1908. Each of you were unfortunate enough to lose family during the reconstruction that followed the Great Fire, prompting you to seek closure by communing with your loved ones via a séance."

Ever the skeptic, Darcy snorted.

Elle couldn't pass up the opportunity to tease. "Psst. Your Capricorn is showing."

"Shh." Darcy's cheeks turned pink in the dim, flickering light of the Underground. "That doesn't even make sense."

"You're cute when you blush," Elle blurted.

Brendon grinned, looking awfully smug as he rocked back on his heels. Darcy simply stared, blush deepening to the point where her freckles disappeared.

The room was cool and drafty but still, Elle's whole body flushed at her failed brain-to-mouth filter.

Jim continued his spiel, "You were referred to a spiritualist by the name of Madame LeFeaux who operates out of one of the illustrious gambling halls in Seattle's Underground. Under the cover of dark, you convene. Madame LeFeaux begins to conduct the séance, and a foreboding chill settles over the already cool space, an impossible breeze blowing through the enclosed room extinguishing the lights. Someone shrieks." Jim's pale blue eyes bounced between the three women. Elle narrowed her eyes at the assumption.

"Me." Brendon pointed at his chest. "I'd totally scream."

Darcy smiled fondly at her brother.

"Out of nowhere, the lights return. You blink, eyes readjusting, and note that Madame LeFeaux is missing."

"Perhaps because she was a con artist," Darcy muttered. *Such a skeptic.*

"You're trapped inside the séance room and the spirits Madame LeFeaux called upon are angry to have been disturbed. You'll have one hour to find the key that opens the door—the *proper* door—that will lead you out of the Underground and to safety. But be careful—there are other doors. Choose wisely, or you won't reach the street, but instead one of the dangerous, illegally run gambling halls. And if you don't escape within an hour?" Jim arched a bushy white brow and let the question hang for a moment, building the suspense. He turned the knob on the door and ushered them inside. "You'll be at the mercy of the spirits who grow stronger by the second."

Inside the simple, stone-walled room was a large round table covered in a floor-length tablecloth. A crystal ball sat atop its surface. Several chairs were overturned, further setting the scene. Against one of the walls rested a mirror, sturdy and with an ornately carved wood frame.

"Remember." Jim paused dramatically. This was so campy it hurt. Elle *loved* it. "Whether you're a skeptic or a believer, there's more than smoke and mirrors at play. Good luck, and your time starts . . . now."

Jim shut the door, locking them inside.

For a moment, they were silent, soaking in their surroundings. The room was austere, all stone and hard surfaces, and yet, starting was a little overwhelming. Especially with the giant red timer mounted to the wall, counting down the seconds, reminding them what was at stake even if it wasn't *real*.

"So." Brendon rocked back on his heels, neck craning to survey the ceiling. "Anyone have any idea where to start?"

Darcy pointed at the table where the crystal ball sat on a three-legged pewter stand. "There."

Not a bad idea.

There was nothing special about the crystal ball, nothing Elle could see at least. Nothing other than the fact that it wasn't perfectly smooth, was more of a nonagon than a sphere, and its stand was glued to the tablecloth. The tablecloth was unadorned and glued to the center of the table, too. Lifting its edges revealed nothing but a smooth, wooden surface. Huffing softly, Elle dropped to her knees.

"What are you doing?" Darcy demanded, stepping closer.

"Call it a hunch." Elle peeked up at Darcy from beneath her lashes.

"I think Elle has the right idea. You two go low, and Cherry and I'll search high, yeah?"

Darcy set her purse on the floor beside the door before dropping to her knees beside Elle. She lowered her voice, "What was that about?"

"What was *what* about?"

"I look cute when I blush?" Darcy narrowed her eyes.

"Well, it's the truth," Elle admitted, sweeping the floor with her hands.

Darcy scoffed dismissively, effectively brushing aside Elle's compliment and making her feel like a complete and total fool for bothering to be nice.

"I know it's *such* a hardship, but at least try to pretend you like me. That's the whole point, isn't it?"

Elle ducked her head beneath the tablecloth, squinting into the dusty darkness. She sneezed twice back to back and sniffled. Smitten, her ass. If Darcy didn't step it up, Brendon was sure to catch on and that was the *last* thing Elle needed. Maybe this hadn't been her idea, but she'd committed. If this thing fell apart? Brendon would think her a total liar. *Not* the best way to begin a business partnership.

Using her hands as eyes, Elle felt along the legs of the table, searching for something that stood out, something *different*, anything that could be a clue. On the other side of the table, she could hear Darcy shuffling around, but she couldn't see her, couldn't see anything.

"It's not," Darcy whispered.

"It's not what?" Her nose tingled as she staved off another sneeze.

"A hardship. Liking you . . . pretending . . . this—" Darcy sighed heavily. "You took me by surprise, okay?"

Suddenly there was a hand on the bare skin of Elle's thigh where the hem of her skirt met her leg. Elle's breath caught and a sharp gasp escaped Darcy's lips, no doubt realizing what she was touching, *where* she was touching. Only, Darcy didn't immediately move her hand. Instead her fingers twitched and Elle heard her swallow in the darkness, her breath quickening. Elle held so still she nearly shook as Darcy's touch lingered, frozen, before Darcy finally yanked her hand away as if she'd been burned. If the rest of Elle's body was as scorching as her face, it was no wonder.

Surprise was right. If it hadn't been for Darcy's muttered, "Fuck," Elle might've wondered if she'd imagined the whole thing.

"Hey, keep it PG under there," Brendon joked, making Darcy groan.

Elle shook off the shock and snickered, though her pulse still raced, her skin tingling where Darcy had touched. "Nothing about me is PG, Brendon."

Brendon laughed. "Not trying to ruin the mood, but we're down to fifty minutes."

Elle changed trajectory, tracing her fingers along the bottom of the table above her head. Her thumb raked over a rough notch, an inconsistency in the wood.

"I found something." Elle scrambled out from under the table and blinked, eyesight adjusting. She whipped back the tablecloth as a neon-red-faced Darcy straightened, brushing invisible dust from her knees. Their eyes met and Darcy's lips turned up at the corners, making Elle's pulse leap.

Pressing that lever had ejected a secret compartment from the side of the table. Nestled inside was a ring of skeleton keys and beside them, an old deck of cards, weathered with fraying edges. Not just any deck of cards. A deck of *tarot* cards.

Brendon pumped a fist in the air. "Hell yes. We're rocking this."

Ever the realist, Darcy's gaze locked on the timer. "What now?"

"We could try the keys?" Cherry suggested.

Brendon shook his head, grimacing softly. "We don't know which door is right."

And there were half a dozen keys, each marked with a different number. *Eight, twenty-six, thirty-four, forty-two, fifty-five, ninety.*

Elle flipped through the deck. There was nothing special about it. All the Major and Minor Arcana were present.

"Um, I think I found something."

Across the room, Cherry had lifted a corner of the rug with the toe of her pump, revealing a series of symbols written on the stone floor in ominous red paint.

Brendon cocked his head. "Are those hieroglyphs?"

Elle bounced on her toes. It was like she was in *Indiana Jones*, or better yet, *The Mummy*. This was *too* cool.

"Okay, so we've got a code to crack." Darcy set her hands on her hips, a furrow forming between her brows as her gaze darted between the hieroglyphs and the timer.

Cherry stuck her hand in her purse and pulled out her phone. "Can't we google it?"

"No!" Darcy and Brendon shouted in tandem.

Darcy glared. "That's cheating. We're going to win this and we're going to do it fair and square."

Brendon nodded. "There's got to be a codex somewhere. Do you see any of these symbols on those cards?"

A *codex*. Elle covered her mouth, concealing her smile. Brendon and Darcy took this shit seriously and Elle loved that they did. An image of Darcy with a wide-brimmed, high-crowned fedora, a leather jacket, and a whip flitted through Elle's head.

"Elle?" Brendon stared at her expectantly.

What? Oh. *Right.* Elle shuffled through the deck. No dice. "Nope."

Darcy cracked her knuckles. "Check every surface. We're down to forty-five minutes."

Twenty minutes later, every chair had been overturned, the tablecloth examined, and the rug lifted and flipped. Darcy ran her fingers through her hair, tugging at the roots. "*God*. This is bullshit."

Claiming her feet hurt, Cherry had taken a seat on the floor, checking out of the game and engrossing herself in her phone.

Brendon shot his date a look full of exasperation and scraped a palm over his jaw. "There's got to be something we're missing. Something obvious."

He was right. The clue had to be staring them dead in the face. Mocking them for missing it. Twenty-four minutes remained. Elle refused to lose hope.

"Come on, guys, we can do this. Let's take a closer look at these glyphs." Elle dropped to her knees, wincing as the stone floor bit into her bare skin. Sighing, Darcy stood beside her, the soft, lived-in denim of her jeans brushing against Elle's arm, making Elle shiver. Elle swallowed hard and stared down at the floor.

The first symbol was a five-pointed star. Then there was a pharaoh? Lying on its side. Dead? A mummy? Elle bit back a sigh. Next was a crescent. The moon? And after that was—

"*Oh*. Oh!" Scrambling to stand, Elle rushed over to the table and swiped the tarot cards, quickly flipping through the deck.

Hot on her heels, Darcy asked, "What is it? Did you find something?"

It was so obvious it hurt. "The cards are the codex, after all.

The symbols themselves aren't on the cards, but they represent some of the Major Arcana."

Darcy blinked. "What does that mean?"

Elle splayed the cards out on the table so that Darcy, and Brendon who'd joined them, could look over her shoulder. "That first symbol on the floor is a star." Elle pushed the cards around until she found the Star card, separating it from the rest. "Next is a mummy." She rifled around until she found Death. "There's a moon. And a set of scales." Scales . . . scales . . . "Temperance!" She frowned at the last symbol. "I have no freaking idea what that wheelie thing's supposed to be."

Brendon's eyes narrowed before he shuffled the cards out, clearly looking for something. "A cart of some sort?"

Brendon was brilliant. Elle crowed and slapped a card down on the table. "The Chariot."

Darcy's face lit up. "This is . . . great job, Elle."

Elle bit the inside of her cheek to keep from smiling stupidly.

Across the room, Cherry coughed. "Hey, guys? There's something happening."

Something was right. Smoky fog, the kind from dry ice, drifted into the room from beneath the doors. *Uh-oh.*

"Heads in the game, guys." Darcy snapped her fingers. "What are we supposed to do with the cards?"

She was right. There had to be something about the cards, something Elle was— *Wait.* "These numbers are wrong."

"What do you mean?" Darcy crowded closer to Elle, so close the delicate scent of her shampoo tickled Elle's nose. Rosemary and lavender, earthy and sweet. Elle wanted to bury her face in Darcy's hair and breathe deep.

Elle bit down on the inside of her cheek. The air down here was getting to her. "The Major Arcana all have a numerological association. The Star is seventeen." She flicked the top of the card. "This has a five written on it."

Brendon read off the other numbers in the sequence corresponding to the glyphs on the ground. "Eight, thirteen . . . hey, Darce, you're good with numbers maybe you should—"

"Gimme." Darcy snagged the cards from Brendon. Several seconds later, Darcy laughed. "Twenty-one, thirty-four." She tossed the cards back on the table and crossed her arms over her chest. "It's the Fibonacci sequence. Next comes fifty-five."

Elle could've totally kissed her, aside from the obvious reasons why that was a bad idea. Though they were supposed to be selling it . . . no. Bad, Elle. "You're brilliant."

Darcy smirked and *shit*. Elle changed her mind. Being bad sounded like the best idea she'd ever had.

Brendon held up the brass skeleton key etched with the number *fifty-five*. "Can I just pause and say teamwork makes the dream work?"

Darcy hiked a thumb over her shoulder at the door marked *fifty-five*. "You want to get this show on the road and win this thing?"

"Please," Cherry groaned. "I'm dying for a drink."

The whole group, save Elle, migrated toward the door. Something didn't *feel* right. It was too easy.

"Wait." Three sets of eyes landed on her, expressions expectant. Elle tugged on the lobe of her ear. "I don't think that's the right door."

Darcy set her hands on her hips. "It's got the number fifty-five on it and it matches the key. I'm not wrong about the Fibonacci sequence."

Elle wasn't suggesting she was wrong. Not about that. "I think that's the right key, but we never solved a clue for the door."

"We don't need to." Darcy shook her head, eyes narrowing. "It matches the key."

Elle chewed on the inside of her cheek. Her gut niggled. "I don't know. It makes too much sense."

Darcy looked at Elle like she'd lost her mind. "How can something make too much sense?"

Brendon lowered his arm, holding the key at his side.

Elle didn't know how to put into words her intuition, this sense of something being off. "It doesn't *feel* right."

Darcy's brow pinched, her jaw setting.

Elle stared, willing Darcy to understand with every fiber of her being. "Trust me."

She was asking a lot, she knew, asking Darcy not only to trust her, but her nebulous, indescribable intuition. Nothing solid, nothing *real*, not in the *seeing is believing* sense.

Darcy glanced at the clock. "All right. Go with your gut, Elle. Just *hurry*."

Four minutes was how long she had to figure out what about that door didn't feel right. Heart racing, Elle rushed back to the table, double-checking for something, anything, a sign that her gut wasn't leading her—and the rest of the group—astray.

Nothing. There was nothing she hadn't touched, turned over. The fog thickened around their feet, rising to their knees. Elle turned, facing the mirror, catching a glimpse of Darcy's tight-lipped reflection. Elle's stomach twisted.

Above her head, the clock counted down from two minutes.

Fuck. She couldn't see anything on the floor, her vision tunneling. Not to mention, the smoke was too thick, practically opaque, and the—

Smoke.

What had Jim said? Elle tugged on her earring. She'd been so excited to get started that she'd stopped paying attention. "Jim said something. Before he locked the door. Something about smoke and mirrors."

Face slackening, Darcy's lips parted. "The mirror. Go to the mirror."

They both made it there at the same time, right as the clock hit seconds.

"What do we do?" Darcy ran her fingers along the mirror's edge.

"Do *something*," Brendon urged.

Elle swallowed down her nerves and gripped the edge of the mirror. This couldn't just be a prop, it *couldn't*. Wait. *Prop.* Propped against the wall, *angled* against the wall . . .

It was a long shot. "Let's try tilting it."

Forty-five seconds.

Together, she and Darcy hauled the mirror forward to where a barely perceptible chalk line was drawn far enough away from the wall for them to angle it back, careful not to drop it. At sixty degrees, the reflection of the overhead light bounced off the stationary crystal ball and pinged across the room, a beam of light landing on the second door, the one *not* marked with the number fifty-five.

"Holy shit." Brendon laughed and jogged over to the lit door, key held out in front of him like a baton. He slipped it inside the lock, turned the knob, and threw the door open. Confetti and a dozen brightly colored balloons rained down over their heads as the buzzer squawked.

They did it.

They won.

Mirth bubbled up inside Elle like an overflowing champagne fountain, laughter spilling from her lips.

Darcy plucked a blue balloon out of the air and spiked it at Brendon, shrieking when he caught it and rubbed it across her head, static making her strands stick up wildly, confetti catching in her curls.

Through the rising fog and falling confetti, Darcy caught Elle's eye and beamed.

☆ ☆
☆

"To Elle!" Brendon hoisted his beer in the air. "For going with her gut."

Darcy clinked her glass of wine against her brother's bottle and nodded, smile small and conciliatory. But that was fine. There were still bright gold flecks of confetti stuck in her mussed hair. It was the closest Elle had ever seen Darcy to being a *mess*, and she liked it. A little too much. "To Elle."

Elle laughed and lifted her candy cane cocktail, complete with peppermint stick garnish, acquiescing to the praise. She sipped through the straw, face scrunching at the shock of rum. Surprisingly strong for being half-priced on trivia night.

That same gut feeling that had driven her to search harder

urged her to lift her head. Across the table, Darcy was staring, bottom lip trapped between her front teeth.

Elle chewed on her swizzle stick straw, failing epically when she tried not to smile.

Feedback from the bar's audio system filled the room, rowdy gripes following. At the front of the room near the bar, a man with a full ginger beard and a shiny bald head gave a rueful wince before tapping the mic. "Sorry 'bout that folks. Who's ready for some trivia?"

"Cherry's been outside for a while," Darcy pointed out. "Doesn't take that long to smoke a cigarette. Vape. Whatever." Darcy waved her hand.

Brendon grimaced, one hand reaching back to grip his neck. "Yeah. She texted me. Apparently, she ran into a friend and . . . she's not feeling it, I guess."

Darcy's eyes flashed, jaw dropping. "She *left*. Without saying good-bye?"

Blink and miss it, Darcy glanced across the table, the nostrils of her pert nose flaring.

Elle stiffened. Was that meant to be a comparison, a dig at how Elle had dipped during their date while Darcy was in the bathroom? Because if so, it was apples and oranges. Unfair because the situations couldn't have been more different. Brendon was sweet and thoughtful and fun. Darcy had been rigid and skeptical and downright rude.

And it hadn't been a matter of *not feeling it* when Elle had left, bladder screaming, ego battered, and hopes crushed. She'd felt it, that spark, but Darcy had done everything in her power to douse it. Sparks hadn't mattered, not when Darcy's beliefs, or lack thereof, made them incompatible. You could bring a horse to water, but you couldn't make it drink.

Oblivious to the thread of tension connecting her and Darcy, Brendon shrugged affably, lips quirking. "Wasn't meant to be."

He was a better sport about it than she'd been, that was for sure.

"Onward and upward." Elle gave him a nod. "If she couldn't see how awesome you are, she didn't deserve to revel in your awesomeness."

Brendon laughed and Darcy shot Elle a curious glance, one Elle couldn't quite parse. Darcy patted her brother on the arm. "You'll, um, you'll find her. Your . . . *person.*"

Lips pinched together, Brendon met Elle's eyes. They burst out laughing.

Darcy shifted on her barstool, arms crossing over her chest.

Brendon threw an arm around Darcy's shoulders. "Thanks, Darce." He pressed a quick kiss to the crown of her head. "Got to say, I'm starting to think my person is something of a unicorn."

"Ooh, now that could be a problem," Elle joked. "Unicorns are only attracted to virgins." She waggled her brows and reached for her drink.

Darcy did a poor job of muffling her laughter with a cough. "Now that would be ironic."

"*Darcy*," he warned, face flushing. "Don't you dare."

She waved him off. "It's not embarrassing."

"It's *humiliating*," Brendon grumbled over the lip of his bottle. "And I told you that in confidence. *Drunken* confidence."

Darcy turned, focusing on Elle. "Brendon didn't lose his virginity until he was twenty because he was saving himself for my best friend, Annie, who he had the *biggest* crush on for practically his entire childhood. For years, he was convinced that they were destined to be together." When Brendon's head thudded against the table, Darcy snickered. "That's what you get for telling her I was smitten."

Brendon lifted his head and glared. "You're making me sound pathetic. Besmirching my good name."

"Good name?" Elle teased.

Brendon gasped. "*Elle*. I thought we were friends." He shook his head. "I see how it is. You've picked a side. My own sister turning my friends against me."

"Oh please. Besides, Annie thought you were cute." Darcy pinched his cheek before smacking him lightly.

"You're cruel, Darce. After everything I've done for you"—he gestured to Elle—"and *this* is how to repay me? By mocking me?"

Another burst of feedback filtered over the speakers followed by the first question.

Between Elle's knowledge of the physical sciences, Brendon's knowledge of the tech industry, their shared knowledge of pop culture, and Darcy's knowledge of everything from seventeenth-century painters to fashion designers to baseball, they answered nearly every question correctly, tying them for the lead with two other teams.

Elle had reached the fun stage of tipsiness where the lights in the bar were bright and the tip of her nose was numb, when the emcee cleared his throat to ask the final question.

Elle sucked the dregs of her cocktail through the straw as Darcy gripped the pencil in her hand, teeth sunk into her bottom lip.

"The 1999 Emmy for Outstanding Lead Actress in a Drama Series went to Susan Lucci for playing what character on the ABC daytime drama *All My Children*?"

Several things happened in quick succession.

The bar fell silent, save for several exasperated groans filtering through the crowd.

Standing so fast he knocked his chair over, Brendon dropped to one knee and pointed at Darcy.

All eyes in the bar on her, Darcy froze. "Get up," she hissed. A pink, mottled flush crept up her neck.

Brendon tilted his head, gaze narrowing. "Darcy."

She shut her eyes, mumbled something beneath her breath, then scribbled something on the paper before flinging it at Brendon, their designated runner who flailed his way to the front of the bar, panting as he reached the bewildered emcee.

They were the only team to submit an answer, the question stumping everyone.

Everyone except Darcy, who stared down at the table, lips pinched and face red, wringing her hands together anxiously atop the table.

The emcee shook his head and brought the microphone to his mouth. "Erica Kane was correct. Table three for the win!"

It took a split second for Elle to realize the exultant scream was coming from her own mouth. Darcy Lowell, gorgeous tight-ass with a head for numbers and no room for Elle's frivolity, watched *soap operas*?

Elle's feet moved disconnected from her brain. Before she knew it, she had rounded the table and was throwing her arms around Darcy's neck, wrapping her up in an eager hug that pressed their bodies together.

Darcy tensed in Elle's arms, body rigid as a board. Elle held her breath and was primed to let go, when Darcy *finally* returned Elle's embrace. For all that her wit was cutting, her tongue barbed, and her jaw a pretty knife's-edge cliff, hugging Darcy was anything but sharp. From the lavender-scented silk of her hair against Elle's cheek to the swell of her breasts pressed against Elle, Darcy's hug was all softness and the last thing Elle wanted was to let go.

Houston, she had a problem.

Chapter Eight

Don't think about it became Darcy's mantra as she followed her brother out of the pub and onto the sidewalk, Elle floating along at her side. Every other step, Elle would sway into Darcy, arms bumping, the backs of their hands, their fingers, brushing.

Don't think about it.

It could've gone worse, this double date. Sure, Elle had delighted in watching Darcy squirm with each pet name uttered, but there'd been no giant blowup. No fights or spilled wine or ruined silk dresses or sudden disappearances that made Darcy's chest ache. They'd managed to set aside their differences, their distinctly different ways of looking at the world, in order to come together and solve the puzzle, winning the escape room. Brendon was right. Teamwork really had made the dream work even if she had, at first, been reluctant to trust something as imprecise as Elle's *gut*.

They'd escaped the room, won trivia, and as far as Darcy

could tell, Brendon was none the wiser that this thing with Elle was all an act. All in all, the night had been a success.

Save for the part where Elle's bright, twinkling laughter made Darcy dizzy. Or how the look of unadulterated joy on Elle's face when those balloons and that annoying confetti had rained down on them made Darcy feel like someone had punched her in the gut, then chopped her off at the knees.

But she wasn't thinking about that. No. She wasn't going to think about how smooth Elle's skin, her thigh, had felt beneath that table, how she'd wanted to stay hidden by the tablecloth. She wasn't going to think about how Elle's breath had tickled her neck during that hug or how Elle's lip had brushed her jaw as she lowered back down from where she'd risen up on her tippy-toes and flung her arms around Darcy's neck.

No, Darcy wasn't going to give oxygen to that . . . that *spark*. If she breathed life into it, it would grow and that—

Darcy curled her toes inside her boots, nails biting into the palms of her hands. She *definitely* wasn't going to think about what might transpire if she let that happen because it was pointless. Elle was technicolor chaos and the feelings she inspired in Darcy were a hazard straight out of Pandora's box. Treacherous and *confusing* and better kept under lock and key. Darcy didn't need disorder in her life.

Elle stopped walking and jerked her chin to the right. "Hey, so, I'm this way."

She opened her mouth to say good night, when Brendon frowned and shook his head. "Where's your place?"

Elle shoved her hands in the pockets of her crazy dress, the navy color complementing her skin—the rest of her, too—perfectly. She practically glowed. "It's just up Second to Union till it turns to Pike and then up to Belmont." A breeze blew past, ruffling Elle's bangs and making her shiver. "Not far."

Darcy hadn't lived in the city for long, but she knew it was a trek to Capitol Hill, over a mile. It was after eleven, dark, and the temperatures were dropping, not quite below freezing but enough to make her breath fog. Elle wasn't even wearing a jacket. Walking—and by herself no less—wasn't smart.

"We'll split an Uber," she suggested, thankful when Brendon nodded.

Elle didn't look sold. "Isn't that out of the way? You're in Queen Anne and Brendon's over on the Eastside so—"

"I drove." Brendon tucked his hands in his pockets and rocked back on his heels. "I left my car in Darcy's parking garage and took advantage of the guest space. Free parking."

Elle appeared a bit more convinced, the frown between her brows softening. "Okay. Thanks."

Within five minutes, their Uber arrived, a blue Prius with a back seat nowhere near big enough for the three of them, so Brendon called shotgun, as if they'd have chosen any other configuration.

Wrinkling her nose at the smell of old takeout and musty gym clothes, Darcy slipped inside the back seat, shuffling over to make room. Elle sat, hands tucking around the back of her skirt as she swung her legs inside the vehicle, those strange, sparkling combat boots catching the streetlight and turning the black patent leather into an oil slick against Elle's pale skin.

Skin bare all the way to where the hem of Elle's dress brushed against her thighs.

Don't think about it.

Face prickling with heat, Darcy tore her eyes away and stared resolutely out the window. The lights from bars and late-night eateries blurred past, stoplights reflecting off puddles on the ground and turning the city into a neon nightscape, still nowhere near as colorful as the girl sitting beside her.

Techno-pop blasted through the speakers and beneath her, the electric engine purred, the combined beat rumbling through her body and sinking into her bones, making her aware of her heartbeat. It was beating too fast, faster even when the driver made a right at the light and the tire rolled over the curb, jostling them until Darcy, once again, nearly had a lapful of Elle.

Elle steadied herself with a hand on Darcy's thigh. *Don't think about it* didn't do shit when those fingers with their chipped blue polish relaxed enough to slide down to where Darcy's hand was gripping her own knee, knuckles white.

Don't think about it. Don't think about it. Don't think about it.

All Darcy could do was think about it. About how Elle's hand was soft, the spaces between her fingers warm as she wiggled them between Darcy's until they were holding hands in the back of the dark car while Brendon sat in the front, unable to even see them.

She tried to swallow, but her mouth was too dry.

Darcy stared at their hands, her fingers longer, making Elle's hand look tiny. Elle was a force, a larger-than-life hurricane of a human; her hands were too small, too delicate for someone who'd come crashing her way into Darcy's life with all the finesse of a wrecking ball.

The car braked a touch too fast and Darcy's stomach swooped as if she'd rocketed down Space Mountain.

Darcy wasn't a thrill seeker and she didn't like roller coasters. The probability of being injured on one had been estimated at one in twenty-four million. Slim, but certainly higher than sitting home and reading a book. Growing up, she'd tolerated them, mostly for Brendon's sake.

Surprisingly, what she disliked wasn't the drop, but the moments before, when the rickety boxcar would creep up the metal track, higher and higher, her heart crawling into her throat as she gripped the bar in front of her for dear life. As if clutching a silly metal rod would spare her in the event of an emergency, total disaster. Those anxious moments right before the plunge, when all those worst-case scenarios would flit through her head, but getting off the ride wasn't an option. Stuck, knowing what would come next, dreading it and being able to do nothing, Darcy hated being out of control, at the mercy of *chance*.

That's what this moment, blazing through yellow lights past a blur of people stumbling from bars, and holding on to Elle's hand felt like. Darcy had gotten on this ride and now she couldn't climb off. Not yet.

The car stopped at the curb of a dingy, but not-unsafe-looking building, and Darcy's anxiety continued to mount, her palms starting to sweat. Elle squeezed Darcy's fingers and it felt like she had a stranglehold on Darcy's pounding heart. "This is me."

"Right." Darcy tried to smile in case Brendon was watching. "Good night."

A cough came from the front seat. Brendon *was* watching, one brow quirked.

Darcy rolled her eyes. "I'll walk you to the door."

The car idled at the curb as Elle finally let go of Darcy's hand so they could climb out of the back seat. Without Elle's fingers twined with hers, Darcy didn't know what to do with her hands and she was suddenly absurdly aware of them, of all her limbs and where they existed in space. Tuck them in her pockets? No, her jeans were too tight, her pockets tiny. She settled on crossing her arms, fingers gripping her biceps as she followed Elle up the steps to the entrance of her building.

Elle reached behind her neck, freeing the clasp of her necklace. From inside the neckline of her dress she withdrew two keys, both hanging from a simple silver chain.

Don't think about it.

"I was thinking." Elle tapped the spiky silver teeth of one of those keys against her bottom lip. The metal had to be warm from resting against her skin all night.

"Oh, no," Darcy joked, trying to regain her footing.

Elle kicked Darcy's shin lightly, and the corners of her eyes crinkled. "I had fun tonight."

So had Darcy, only the words, a simple *so did I* stuck in her throat when the light from the streetlamp hit Elle's eyes. Her eyes *weren't* just blue, but gray, too, silvery striations winding out from a storm cloud center that hugged her pupils.

"We should kiss," Darcy blurted.

Elle's eyes doubled in size.

Darcy knew better, knew that kissing Elle was a terrible idea. It couldn't lead to anything, Darcy wouldn't *let* it lead to anything. And yet something inside her, some tiny, illogical part of her rebelled at the idea of never getting a taste of Elle. Even though that's all it would be. One taste.

The overwhelmingly rational part of her needed to explain, to justify this, apply logic to an altogether illogical desire. "My brother's probably watching."

Elle wrinkled her nose. "Is that supposed to make me want to kiss you?"

No, but that made this less dangerous. The odds of getting injured on a roller coaster were slim. They were well-designed, tested. There were seat belts and safety precautions in place. As far as risks went, it was *safe*. This was a safe risk because if this was all fake, there was no chance of Darcy falling.

She laughed, the sound warbling in her throat. "I mean, he's probably expecting it."

Elle dropped her eyes to the ground, to the small bit of space between them. Her tongue darted out, wetting her already shiny bottom lip, licking off some of her gloss. Darcy was dying to taste her. "Right. Sure. You should—" Elle cleared her throat and lifted her head, eyes sparkling under the amber glow of the streetlight. "You should really sell it then."

Darcy stopped thinking about Brendon and stepped closer to Elle, erasing the distance between them. She lifted a hand, commanding it not to shake as she set it on the dip of Elle's waist, drawing her in until their knees knocked gently.

Don't think.

If she were lucky, the kiss would be terrible and she'd never want to do it again. The unsettling burning in her chest would fizzle out and all would be restored to normal, the world righted, back on its axis.

Leaning in, she brushed her lips against Elle's and it was like striking a match, that spark she'd refused to acknowledge catching flame with the slightest friction of lips on lips.

It was mutual, it had to be, because Elle gasped, lips parting and turning what was supposed to be a *fucking stage kiss* into a frenetic exploration, wild and charged. Suddenly Elle's fingers, those fingers that had touched the spines of all of Darcy's books and left smudge marks on her coffee table, were buried in Darcy's hair, pulling her closer and keeping her there.

Darcy stumbled, vertigo making her head spin, and backed Elle into the wall beside the building's door. Had it not been for Elle's hands in her hair and the snug press of their bodies, Darcy might've crumbled at the hot, wet drag of Elle's tongue against the edge of her bottom lip. Still, a shiver skittered down Darcy's spine, her knees weakening.

Darcy tilted her hips into Elle, triggering an intense pulse inside her. Something snapped, want overriding everything else. She pressed Elle firmly against the wall and tasted the blunt edges of Elle's teeth, dipped her tongue deeper, traced the roof of Elle's mouth and dropped her hands, palming Elle's hips when Elle shivered and melted. Sweet; Elle's lips tasted like strawberries and her tongue like peppermint. Darcy wanted more, was suddenly greedy for a taste of—

Reality crashed down on her in the form of someone laying on a car horn. Elle rolled her lips together, eyes flitting away.

Darcy turned, glaring at the car where her brother was hanging out the window, grinning stupidly.

"Get a room." He winked. *Tried* to wink.

Brendon was getting fucking socks for Christmas. Boring, black, argyle ones.

Darcy turned back to Elle who was chewing on the corner of her lip. Darcy's stomach flipped, not because the world had righted itself and the sudden adjustment was jarring. No, everything had gone pear-shaped, worse than before because now that she'd had a taste of Elle, she wanted another.

Chapter Nine

$\mathcal{D}$arcy wasn't good at this, gift-giving. Not under normal circumstances and this was anything but normal.

What were you supposed to give someone you were fake dating, someone you weren't supposed to like, but were finding yourself increasingly—and worryingly—fond of? Someone you couldn't get out of your head no matter how hard you threw yourself into work, someone whose laugh you couldn't quit hearing inside your head, whose lips you could swear you could still taste, even days later? Darcy was pretty sure *Cosmo* didn't offer a gift guide for the niche category of fake girlfriends. Go figure.

Whatever it was, the gift needed to say *congratulations* without being over the top, and it needed to be something Elle would actually appreciate. An interesting challenge because as a general rule, Darcy usually refused to gift anything that she, herself, didn't like. But Elle's taste was so . . . *distinct* that Darcy needed to think outside the box.

Which was why she was standing in the middle of Northwest Beer and Spirits staring not at the prized Napa cabernets, but at the—she repressed a shiver—boxed wines.

A five-liter box of Franzia sunset blush cost eighteen dollars and twenty-eight cents. The box proclaimed there were thirty-four glasses inside, making each five-ounce glass approximately fifty-four cents. *Fifty-four cents.* Less than a dollar for a glass of wine.

Darcy frowned at the box. Her wallet liked those numbers, but something about paying that little for wine felt . . . unreal. Like someone was going to pop out from the other side of the shelf and shove a camera in her face and tell her she'd been punked before slapping her with a fifty-dollar bill.

Darcy depressed the handle and lifted, cardboard cutting into her fingers. Maybe it was cheaper than dirt, but it was heavy as lead. Couldn't they at least try to make the design a bit more ergonomic? She'd have paid five more dollars for better packaging alone.

Inside her coat, her phone buzzed. If that wasn't an excuse to set the box down, she didn't know what was.

Annie.

Darcy swiped and lifted the phone to her ear. "Hey, Annie."

A horn honked in the background, followed by muffled cursing. "Darce! How are things?"

She nudged the box of wine with her toe. Where to start? She hadn't spoken to Annie since talking her ear off about the mess she'd gotten herself into, lying to Brendon. "Things are . . . complicated."

"Complicated. Hmm," Annie said. "That wouldn't have

something to do with a certain cute blonde? Tiny thing with huge eyes that she has just for you?"

"What's that supposed to mean?"

Another horn honked, meshing with the sound of Annie's laughter. "Brendon posted pics from your date the other night. Elle is all googly-eyed over you in them and you're just as bad. When you're looking at her, she's looking away. And vice versa. It's cute."

Darcy's stomach lurched, pulse pirouetting. "It's fake."

"*Sure.*" Annie was probably rolling her eyes. "When's the next time you're going to see her?"

Darcy glanced at the box by her feet. "Seeing as I'm currently buying her a box of wine, I'd say soon."

"Wait. Slow down. Back the fuck up." Annie sighed. "*Ich spreche mit meinem freund.*"

"Are you speaking *German*?"

"I'm in Berlin. Business trip. Did I forget to mention that?" The better question was since when did Annie speak German. "Sorry. My cabdriver thought I was talking to him. You were saying?"

"It's nothing. Brendon told me the deal with Oh My Stars was finalized this morning and then he asked if the two of us had plans to celebrate and I didn't know what to say and Brendon looked at me like I had dropped the ball. Like I was, I don't know, being a bad girlfriend. So I'm buying Elle a box of wine because it's her favorite. You know. To congratulate her."

Annie didn't say anything for so long that Darcy glanced at the screen, checking if the call had been disconnected. "Huh. Okay. That's. Hm."

"That was a lot of noise for managing to say *nothing*."

"I was emoting, you bitch. Read between the lines."

"If you have something to say, *say it*."

Annie laughed. "Is your brother going to be there when you gift Elle with this *box of wine*?"

"You sound like a snob, Annie."

Like the drama queen she was, Annie gasped. "Said the pot to the kettle. Stop avoiding my questions."

"No." She leaned against the aisle endcap. "Brendon's not going to be there. What's your point?"

"Just interesting is all. What's the point of giving Elle a gift if your brother isn't there to see it? Unless you *like her*."

"I—"

She did. She liked Elle. She just didn't know what it meant or if it meant anything. It was the last thing she wanted to think about, but of course, because her brain was a fucking traitor, that kiss was *all* she could think about. That kiss. Elle's smile. The way her eyes had shone beneath the streetlights. Her *laugh*.

Brendon might've planted the seed that brought her to this liquor store, but she *wanted* to see Elle.

Annie gasped. "Oh my god. You're shitting me. You like her? *Elle*? The girl who spilled wine all over your favorite dress and believes in *one twu wuv*?" She giggled. "This is perfect. You realize that, right? You're starring in your own romantic comedy, Darcy. Next thing you know, there's only going to be one bed at the B&B and you'll have to huddle for warmth beneath one tiny blanket and—"

"*Stop.*" Darcy pinched the bridge of her nose. "*Annie.*"

"You just whined at me." Annie cackled. "Oh my god. I'm dead. You're so fucked. I love it."

She was right. Darcy was well and truly fucked.

"I hate you."

"You love me."

"You had the audacity to compare my life to a romantic comedy." Darcy scoffed. "You sound like Brendon."

Annie said, "Speaking of your brother. You didn't tell me he'd gotten so cute."

Kill her now. "Don't be gross, Annie. That's my little brother you're talking about."

"I *know.*" Annie said something else to the driver in German, too fast for Darcy to catch. "He was always adorable, but now he's—"

"Stop. Do not pass go and whatever you do, do not finish that sentence." Darcy shivered.

"I'm just saying! Objectively. He rarely posts pictures of himself and when he does, they're these shoddy cropped selfies with the worst lighting and half the time he's got his thumb partway over the camera. You'd think with limbs as long as his he'd get his whole self in the frame, but no. He posted that group picture of you guys and it was a shock. Little Brendon grew up nice, is all I'm saying."

Darcy sniffed. "Brendon is handsome, yes. Of course, he is. He's *my* brother."

Annie chuckled. "Okay, okay. No more drooling over your little bro. Got it."

Gross. "Thank you."

For a moment, Annie was silent. "How are you really doing, Darcy?"

Darcy sucked on her lower lip, shrugging even though Annie wasn't there to see. "I'm all right."

"Darcy."

She dropped her chin. "I'm confused."

Annie's sigh was soft. "I didn't mean to laugh. Not if you're not laughing, too."

Friends since fifth grade, Annie had been there through it all—Darcy's parents' divorce, moving away to the same college, the death of her grandmother, new jobs, new relationships, *failed* relationships. Annie had packed up most of Darcy's apartment, the apartment she'd shared with Natasha, just so she wouldn't have to deal with it. Annie might tease, but if anyone could imagine how confused Darcy felt, it was her.

"I know you didn't. It's fine. It's— I just need to calm down. I'm blowing everything out of proportion."

She'd give Elle her wine and get out, go home, and put her head down. With eight weeks until the FSA exam, she needed to focus. Not on how Elle tasted or how her laugh made Darcy's chest throb, but on studying. Just yesterday, her boss had asked how her exam prep was going before dropping the bomb that her coworker Jeremy was *also* scheduled to take his final FSA exam in January. Mr. Stevens wanted to give the promotion to Darcy since Jeremy had only been at the company four months to Darcy's six, but if she didn't pass . . .

She'd pass.

More of Annie's rapid-fire German came through. Darcy eyed the wine at her feet. "Look, Annie, I should let you go. Call me later, okay? When you're not in a cab."

"Wait. Darcy? I'm not going to be like your brother and pressure you to put yourself out there if you're not ready, but life's short. Carpe diem."

✫ ✫
✫

What Holiday Activity Are You Based on Your Zodiac Sign?

Aries—Snowball Fight
Taurus—Baking Cookies
Gemini—Ski Trip
Cancer—Holiday Movie Binge
Leo—Caroling
Virgo—Secret Santa Gift Exchange
Libra—Volunteering
Scorpio—Photo Session with Santa
Sagittarius—Santa Pub Crawl
Capricorn—Christmas Tree Decorating
Aquarius—Shopping at the Holiday Market
Pisces—Ice Skating

Elle's foot was asleep, her toes tingling, full of pins and needles as soon as she put her weight on it. Whoever was at the door knocked again. "Just a sec!"

It was closer to a minute by the time she hobbled across the room and opened the door. Darcy stood in front of her apartment cradling a box of wine wrapped in a hot pink bow. Elle blinked. She was seeing things. She had to be.

Only, Darcy cleared her throat, hefting the box of wine upward. *Not* a figment of her imagination. "Hello."

"Hello," she echoed. "Sorry, um, come in."

Elle stepped back, letting Darcy pass. She stopped just shy of the kitchen entrance, barely far enough inside for Elle to shut the door.

"Here." Darcy thrust the box of wine into Elle's arms. "I brought this for you."

Elle hugged the box, the satin bow cool against the inside of her wrist. "Thank you?"

"As a congratulations. For finalizing your deal." Darcy tucked her hair behind her ear and shrugged. She was wearing another pencil skirt, this one navy, and it hugged her hips perfectly. Elle's mouth went dry. "My brother told me."

"So you bought me a box of wine?"

"Yes?"

Elle chuckled. "Color me surprised, is all. Didn't it pain you to purchase boxed wine?"

Darcy crossed her arms over her chest. "Well, you like it, so."

Elle bit down on her lip, something inside her chest squeezing hot and tight. "You didn't have to do that, but thank you. Do you want to come in? Have a glass?"

Darcy's pert nose wrinkled, a line forming along the bridge. "I've got to get back home. Study for my FSA exam. I just wanted to drop that off and . . ."

"And?"

See her?

Kiss her again?

Elle held her breath.

"And congratulate you."

Of course.

Not that Elle wasn't thrilled—not to mention relieved—the deal was official, but she'd hoped Darcy showing up meant maybe their kiss had changed things for her. That Darcy had felt the way the earth had shifted beneath their feet, too. That it was something more.

Maybe not.

And yet, Darcy lingered in the entryway.

"Right." Darcy cleared her throat before pointing at the box of wine. "I didn't know if you wanted to post that online or something. Because Brendon follows you."

Elle's stomach sank. Of course this was about selling it to Brendon. That was what their deal was all about. How silly of her to think otherwise. "Sure. Good idea."

Darcy's jaw clenched, her chin lifting, eyes going hard, determined. "Look, Elle—"

An unholy grumble came from Darcy's stomach, so loud and vicious that Elle's eyes widened. Darcy's face turned red, her eyes slipping shut, her lips rolling inward and flattening.

Elle's fingers itched to trace the blush, feel the heat of Darcy's cheeks against the pads of her fingertips. "Hungry?"

"*Clearly.*" Darcy snorted. "I should go before my stomach cannibalizes itself."

"Sexy." Elle leaned her shoulder against the wall and shifted the box of wine, her biceps beginning to burn. "Or you could stay. I've got—"

She performed a quick mental inventory of the contents of her fridge. Salsa. Juice. Freezer-burned breakfast sandwiches. "Or we could go out?"

Darcy's lips twisted in genuine-looking remorse. "I can't. I've got—"

"To eat, yeah? We could do that together." When Darcy didn't immediately fire back a no, Elle pressed on. "I could Instagram a picture of us there. Better than posting a picture of a boring box of wine. And I could brief you on Thanksgiving. Tell you what to expect."

Darcy dropped her chin and chuckled. "I'm too hungry to cook."

"Is that a yes?"

She nodded. "Sure. Why not?"

☆ ☆
☆

It was only four blocks to Katsu Burger, a little hole in the wall joint that served the best Japanese deep-fried burgers Elle had ever tasted. It wasn't fancy by any stretch of the imagination, but the food was fantastic, inexpensive, the service was stellar, and it wasn't too rowdy, a combination not easy to find on this part of Broadway.

Elle jerked a thumb over her shoulder. "You want to snag a table while I order for us?"

Darcy stared at the sprawling menu on the wall with rounded eyes. "I don't have any idea what I want."

"Just go sit down. I know what's good." Elle shooed her off. "Seriously. Trust me."

"Nothing with dairy, all right?"

"Roger that."

Inching her way toward the bank of empty tables, Darcy shot her one final wary glance that made Elle roll her eyes.

After placing their order, Elle wiggled her way through the maze of tables until she reached the one Darcy had claimed in the far back corner. She collapsed into the seat across from Darcy and performed a quick double take at the state of the table. "What the—"

The salt and pepper shakers, bottle of hot sauce, both bottles of soy sauce, *and* the napkin holder had been moved toward the center of the table, dividing Darcy's table space from Elle's. Like a moat, only without the water.

Darcy smirked. "I happen to like this outfit."

"What does that have to do with—" Oh. *Oh.* Her face heated, an undeniable blush creeping up her neck. "*One* accident and you're taking precautionary measures?"

"Twice," Darcy argued. "You spilled in my kitchen, too."

"Once is an instance, twice is merely a coincidence. *Three* times is a pattern." Elle winced. "But I really am sorry about that. It was . . . ugh." The shame of that moment returned, the memory of spilling first her glass of wine and then knocking the table and spilling Darcy's wine as fresh as if it had just happened. Elle dropped her face into her hands and groaned. "Not a great first impression."

"Not like mine was much better." Elle lifted her head to find Darcy looking contrite, lips tugged to the side. "Hindsight makes it seem trivial. It's just— I was wearing my favorite dress. It belonged to my grandmother. So."

Elle's stomach plummeted. "Did it come out? The wine stain?"

Darcy lifted her eyes and offered a small smile. "It did. My dry cleaner is a miracle worker."

Elle breathed a sigh of relief, shoulders slumping. Thank God.

"Two sake bombs?"

Elle glanced up, smiling at the waitress who held a tray with two beers, two shots of sake, and two pairs of chopsticks. "Thanks."

Darcy glowered at her from across the table. "*Sake bombs?*"

All right, so maybe it wasn't the *best* choice, but it didn't have to be messy. You could chug neatly . . . if you set your mind to it . . .

Shrugging, Elle unwrapped her chopsticks and set them across the top of her pint glass, wide enough apart to balance the shot. It appeared Darcy needed a little cajoling when all she did was cross her arms and stare. "Come on. It's fun. You pound the table, pound your drink, and try to finish first." She wiggled her brows. "You aren't *scared*, are you? Worried you won't win?"

Eyes narrowed, Darcy snatched her chopsticks off the table and placed them across her glass. She reached for her sake, hand hovering in the air over the shot glass, and then changed course, finger reaching for the topmost button on her blouse. Brown eyes meeting Elle's across the table, the corner of Darcy's mouth twitched as she undid the pearl buttons of her blouse one by one.

Elle's mouth went dry. "What are you doing?"

Darcy's nimble fingers reached the middle of her chest, revealing a strip of nude lace. A camisole. "As I said, I'm fond of this outfit. If you're going to all but dare me to drink with you, I'm not keen on ruining this top."

Elle tore her eyes from Darcy's cleavage and fiddled with the chopsticks atop her beer. "Ah. Good plan. I, uh, like the way you think."

Darcy chuckled lowly and untucked her blouse, sliding it down her arms before hanging it over the back of the chair beside her. "I've never done one of these before. Do we go on three?"

"Sake bombs?" Elle goggled. What did Darcy do in college if not attend a copious amount of cheesy *around the world* parties featuring alcohol from other countries? Study? Elle lifted her shot of sake to demonstrate. "Okay. You balance the sake atop the chopsticks, like so. Then you count to three, preferably in Japanese. Ichi, ni, san, then you shout *sake* and bang the table with your fists. The shot falls into the beer and you chug it."

Darcy shut her eyes and groaned quietly. "Are you serious?"

Elle chuckled. "You don't *have* to."

Darcy rolled her shoulders back, posture perfecting, and when she opened her eyes, her gaze was steely and determined. Elle wiggled in her seat. *Piece of cake.*

"Ready?"

"As I'll ever be," Darcy muttered.

"Okay. Ichi, ni, san . . . sake!" Elle banged the table, her chuckle mingling with Darcy's bright bark of laughter as they both tipped back their glasses. Elle squeezed her eyes shut and opened her throat, swallowing as much of the bitter beer as quickly as possible. Foamy, slightly too warm beer dribbled down her chin, sliding down the front of her throat as her eyes and lungs burned, the latter demanding she take a breath. Just a little more.

The slam of glass against the Formica tabletop made her open her eyes. Cheeks pink and lips and chin wet, Darcy grinned, panting, all breathless and smug.

Elle lowered her pint glass, an inch of foamy beer left in the bottom. "What the fuck."

Darcy threw her head back and laughed. *Fuck*. A tiny drop of beer trailed down her throat and Elle wanted to lick it off, taste Darcy's skin. Her back teeth clacked together.

"What do I win?"

Elle snorted and polished off the remainder of her beer. "Bragging rights? I don't know. Was there something you wanted?"

Either the beer was hitting her hard, or Elle was imagining the way Darcy's eyes darkened.

Darcy shrugged and sniffed, tossing her hair over one deliciously freckled shoulder. "I'll think about it."

So would she.

"You're full of surprises, you know that?"

Darcy cocked her head, frowning softly. "What's that supposed to mean?"

"What it sounds like." Elle ripped the paper of her chopstick wrapper down the middle. "You're a beer-chugging champ and you watch soap operas? Or at least know enough about them to answer a trivia question that stumped everybody else."

Darcy's expression shuttered, her eyes blanking before dropping to the table. "What about it?"

Elle didn't mean anything by it, definitely no offense. "Nothing. It's just . . . unexpected. I think it's cool."

Darcy scoffed. "Sure."

"I *do*. Why would I bullshit you? Seriously, what do I have to get out of being anything other than perfectly honest?"

Darcy appeared to weigh her words, the furrow between her brows softening. "Oh."

"*Oh*," Elle teased.

"Most people make fun of them. The plots are contrived and . . . people die and come back to life for crying out loud, but my grandmother was obsessed." Darcy's smile went soft and nostalgic, her voice quieting, "During the summers, and then after we moved into her house, I'd watch with her. It was our thing. Every day at one o'clock we'd bring lemonade and little tea sandwiches into the living room and watch *Whisper Cove* and then *Days of Our Lives*. Every day."

"Sounds nice," Elle said, shredding the paper of her chopstick wrapper so she wouldn't do something ridiculous like reach for Darcy's hand.

"I know they're silly," Darcy said, sounding like she still thought she needed to justify her interests. Temper it by distancing herself from them emotionally.

"It's not silly. Not if you enjoy it. And even then, silly's not a bad thing."

There were far worse things to be.

"Brendon said something similar."

"I knew I liked him for a reason." Elle grinned. "He sounds like a great brother."

Darcy's smile became achingly fond, her eyes creasing at the corners. "He is. Overbearing at times . . ."

"I'm sure he means well."

"Yeah, well, he forgets that it's not his job to take care of me. It's the other way around."

Elle brushed the mangled shreds of paper into a pile and pushed her empty beer glass to the right, clearing a space for her to rest her elbows. "Can I ask you a question?"

Darcy's brows rose. "You can ask."

The *doesn't mean I'll answer* was heavily implied.

"You and Brendon . . . sometimes you talk about him like you raised him."

The corners of Darcy's mouth pinched, her throat jerking as she swallowed. She dropped her gaze to the table and traced a gouge in the surface with her finger. "I— It's nothing so extreme as that. I told you our parents divorced. It was the summer before my junior year of high school. Our mother was awarded custody; Dad didn't ask for it since he traveled two weeks out of the month. But . . ." Her jaw shifted to the side, her finger pressing against the scraped table so hard her fingertip turned white. "My mother didn't handle their split well at all. She was heartbroken by it and so, she sort of . . . checked out."

What did that *mean*?

Darcy saved Elle the trouble of figuring out a polite way

to ask. "She slept all day, stayed up till all hours of the night. Stopped leaving the house, hardly even left her room. Someone needed to step up, so I drove Brendon to school and picked him up and took him to his after-school activities. No one starved on my watch. But I wasn't exactly thinking about paying the mortgage, and apparently neither was my mother, so a few months later the house was foreclosed on and we moved in with my grandmother."

"Junior year of high school . . . you were—"

"Sixteen." Darcy dipped her chin. "Brendon was twelve."

Jesus. "Did your mom ever—"

Get better sounded stupid.

"Grandma helped her find a job. Forced her to, actually. If that's what you mean. She was a photographer, did portraits, weddings, senior photos, that sort of thing, but when I was born, she quit working so she could take care of me and then, when I was a little older, so she could travel with my father. Later, after the divorce, she switched to travel photography, which lets her float wherever she wants whenever she wants, which she prefers." Darcy shrugged, the strap of her camisole sliding off her shoulder. "We've never been close."

"At least you've got Brendon."

A waiter stopped beside their table holding a tray topped with two gargantuan burgers. "Two Mt. Fuji burgers?"

"What the fuck," Darcy whispered once the waiter was gone. "*Elle.*"

Elle stared at her own triple-stacked burger with wide eyes. "I didn't think they would be *this* big."

"What *is* this?" Darcy poked the top bun of her burger, her nose scrunching adorably.

"Um, beef katsu, chicken katsu, pork katsu, egg, bacon, pickles, tomato, cabbage, wasabi mayo, and a few other sauces I can't remember. I had them leave the cheese off yours." Elle snagged a wad of napkins from the holder in the center of the table. She had a feeling she was going to need them.

"How do I even begin to eat this?" Darcy muttered. "Don't we get silverware?"

Elle gasped. "Eating a burger with a fork and knife is a *crime*. You just have to dive in. Shove it in your face and hope most of it winds up in your mouth."

"Do you have a lot of experience with that?"

"I usually order the Tokyo Classic, which is only one—" Darcy's words caught up to her. "*Wow.*"

Darcy's lips twitched into a grin that showed off her perfect teeth. "It was practically *begging* to be said. Come on."

Elle snorted and wrapped her hands around the ginormous burger in front of her. She could barely get her mouth around it, wound up with an unbalanced bite of bun and cabbage, but she had to start somewhere.

Darcy, on the other hand, examined her burger with narrowed eyes before smushing the whole thing down with her palm until it was half its original size. She lifted it to her mouth and took an inelegant bite, wasabi mayo and tonkatsu sauce dripping down her chin as she groaned, eyes rolling back as the flavor combo hit her taste buds.

Elle buried her smile in her burger. "Scale of one to ten, what do you think?"

Darcy wiped her chin and looked thoughtful. "Solid nine point two. You?"

"An eleven, easy."

"You said scale of one to ten."

"It's a hyperbole. Sometimes coloring inside the lines just doesn't cut it. Like when you're two hundred percent certain about something. Haven't you ever felt that?"

Darcy stared for so long that Elle squirmed. "It's a burger. I don't think it's that deep."

Elle snorted and took another bite.

"What about you?"

Elle finished chewing before she asked, "What about me?"

Darcy set her burger down and reached for another napkin. "Are you close with any of your siblings?"

That was . . . relative. "I'm closest with Daniel, probably. There's only two years between us, which helps. But these days, he and Jane have the most in common." Elle reached for her water and took a fortifying sip. "I don't butt heads with Jane or anything, we're just on entirely different wavelengths. But she lets me babysit my nephew, so she's at least deemed me trustworthy enough to watch a toddler."

Darcy smiled around her straw. "Why do I get the feeling you're surprisingly good with kids?"

Elle scoffed. "*Surprisingly*? Excuse you, Ryland is lucky to have me as an aunt. Maybe I can't cook, but I make mean macaroni art and I do voices for all the characters in his books."

Last-minute requests to watch Ryland were the norm, because as far as Jane was concerned, since Elle *worked* from home, her schedule was flexible. The only reason she didn't complain was because she enjoyed it.

"What about your other sister?"

"Lydia?" Elle shrugged. "We're like oil and water. She idolizes Jane and figured out a long time ago that the easiest way to get our parents' approval was to do everything by the book, but even then, it's hard to compete with Jane and Daniel because anything you do? They did it first and they probably did it better. They were honor students, on ASB, Daniel was president of the GSA, both did a million sports, and now they've got great jobs and families of their own. Brace yourself for Lydia to be a bit of a brat because she has it in her head that the best way to make herself look good is to point out my flaws."

Darcy frowned. "Your parents don't approve of what you do?"

Approve. If only. "They've sort of stalled in the *grudging acceptance* phase where we mostly don't talk about the fact that I don't have a nice, stable job with a pension plan, not that those really exist anymore. Mom makes the occasional comment about what I do and how she wishes I would settle down with one of the nice, boring people they've set me up with. I'll occasionally catch Jane looking at me like I'm some sort of weird puzzle from another planet she's trying to solve, but mostly everyone just ignores me." *Shit.* Elle grimaced. "I mean, they don't *ignore* me. The things that matter to me don't really rate for them."

The furrow between Darcy's brows deepened. "But you wish it did. Matter to them."

"Well, sure." *Of course.* "But, unlike Lydia, I decided a long time ago that I wasn't going to change who I was just to suit someone else."

"Where do I fit into all this? On Thanksgiving?"

Right. *Thanksgiving.* That was the reason they were here, not to get to know each other better *just because.*

"Act like you like me?" Elle gave an awkward laugh, avoiding Darcy's eyes. "You've got the sort of job and vibe that screams *I've got my shit together,* so if my family thinks you're into me and hears you talk about how awesome you think I am, maybe they'll see me in a different light without me having to, you know, *do* anything."

Darcy nodded. "I can do that."

Elle's chest squeezed, wishing Darcy didn't have to *act* like she liked her.

"Anything else I should know, or is it more of a learn-as-you-go thing?"

Ha. Elle was still learning how to navigate the waters of formal family dinners.

"If it's any consolation, you'll probably fit in with my family better than me."

☆ ☆
☆

Despite the conventional wisdom that said no one had any business eating something larger than their head, they both managed to polish off their burgers and a shared order of nori fries.

Back on the street, Elle crossed her arms against the chill

and smiled at Darcy who'd been smart enough to wear a coat. Elle had been too caught off guard by Darcy's unexpected visit to think to grab her jacket. "Well. This was fun."

Darcy nodded. "It was. Thanks for the food. Are you sure you won't let me pay for mine?"

Elle waved her off. "My treat."

She wasn't sure if they were standing there on the street corner because the light was red, or for some other reason. "All right. Well—"

"I'll walk with you," Darcy blurted. "It's nice out."

It was *freezing*, but okay. Elle wouldn't argue. The company was nice.

Elle led them two blocks south, pausing at the corner of Pike and Broadway, waiting for the light. She peeked around the corner, checking for oncoming traffic. The neon sign hanging in the window on the next block caught her eye. She grabbed Darcy's wrist and tugged her in the new direction.

"What? Where are we going? Your apartment's that way."

"Change of plans," she said, stopping in front of a store with the sign ONE MAN'S TRASH. The *T* in trash was burned out, turning the store into ONE MAN'S RASH, which made Elle chuckle under her breath. "This is my favorite thrift store."

"And we're here because . . . ?" Darcy goggled at the window display of half-dressed mannequins posed to look as if they were having an orgy.

"I forgot about my favorite Thanksgiving tradition. It's the only thing my family does that's *odd*, if you can even call it that." Elle reached for the handle on the front door, eager to step inside out of the cold. "We all wear the tackiest ugly

Christmas sweaters we can find. We've been doing it for years. You *have* to wear one."

Darcy didn't argue, though she did pull a face, lips twisting like she was beginning to regret this whole plan, if she didn't already.

The inside of the store smelled like fabric softener and Lysol, and beneath that, mothballs and body odor, which Elle tried hard to ignore. Detouring past the front display of puffer jackets, Elle tugged Darcy deeper into the store where they kept their funkier offerings.

"Jesus." Darcy tugged on a poofy, crinoline prom dress shoved between an old D.A.R.E shirt and a leather motorcycle jacket. "There's no rhyme or reason to any of this. How do you find anything in here?"

"You don't. Not really. Stuff tends to find you."

"Like that doesn't sound ominous." Darcy set the dress back on the rack. The bar holding the hangers made a low creak before the entire rack collapsed in on itself. "Shit."

Darcy bent down, reaching to clean up the mess. Something green and sparkly in the pile caught Elle's eye. "Wait, hold up."

She grabbed the item in question, sure enough, a sweater. And not just any sweater, but a delightfully hideous knitted monstrosity with a sequined Grinch.

Darcy recoiled, elbow knocking into the rack of shoes. "Ow. *No.* Absolutely not. Not even if you paid me."

Elle gave her what she hoped was a convincing pout, pulling out all the stops, widening her eyes and jutting out her bottom lip. "I told you—things find you in here."

"Nope." Darcy shook her head. "That is *odious*."

"All the better! It's supposed to be ugly."

"Ugly is an understatement, Elle. It offends me."

Elle thrust the sweater at Darcy, who shrieked and backed away. "Just try it on."

Darcy paled. "*Try it on?* Are you fucking kidding me? I don't know where that's been or who wore it. I'm not buying it, but if I did, you bet your ass I'd wash it first."

"*Gah.*" Elle dropped her head back and groaned. "Oh my god. Don't be such a *grinch* about it. You can wear your camisole. You'll be fine."

With a huff, Darcy snatched the sweater from Elle and stomped off in the direction of the dressing room, grumbling nonsense under her breath.

Lingering outside the curtain of the dressing stall, Elle waited, snickering as Darcy muttered to herself about *fucking sweaters* and how she *better not get bedbugs or something* and *Elle better be happy*.

Happy was an understatement. When Darcy flung the curtain aside and stepped out of the dressing room, Elle doubled over. Darcy was drowning in the three-sizes-too-big sweater that nearly hung down to her knees. When she lifted her arm to flip Elle off, the sweater slipped over her hand and the excess fabric made it look like she had wings. That didn't even account for the atrocity that was the sparkling Grinch whose eyes lined up rather perfectly with Darcy's chest.

Darcy scratched the base of her throat, her expression twisting, eyes going wide. "I'm itching. Why am I itching?"

"It's probably psychological." Elle shrugged. "Or you've

gotten so used to wearing fancy fabrics that polyblend gives you hives?"

"*Ugh.*" Darcy whipped the sweater over her head, her hair sticking up from the static. The strap of camisole slipped down her arm again, the strap of her bra following it down. Elle swallowed thickly. "You happy?" Darcy asked.

"Hmm. Oh!" Elle nodded. "I will be if you buy it."

Darcy threw the sweater on the floor and reached for her blouse. "It's *awful.*"

"It's amazing. You *have* to wear it."

"You wear it if you love it so much."

Elle already had a sweater. "It found you, Darcy. It's *fate.*"

Darcy sighed. "Everyone's going to be wearing one?"

"You'll stick out like a sore thumb if you don't."

Darcy's eyes flickered between Elle's pouting face and the sweater pooled on the floor.

"*Please.* It's a tradition."

Her shoulders dropped. "Fine. But I'm washing it first."

Elle couldn't help it. She stepped forward and threw her arms around Darcy, hugging her tight. "Thank you."

Like the first time she hugged her, Darcy stiffened. But this time, she relaxed into the embrace sooner, her own arms wrapping around Elle's waist. She had to have felt the forceful thud of Elle's heart, kicking against her chest, their bodies pressed together.

Darcy was the first to pull away, leaning back, her hands slipping, fingers brushing the small of Elle's back as she dropped her arms. Their faces were close, so close Elle could've leaned in and pressed her lips to Darcy's. She teetered on her feet, knees faltering at the soft smile Darcy sent her. "It's . . . it's fine. It's just a sweater."

It wasn't just about the sweater, but Elle didn't say that for fear of saying too much. Instead she stepped back and pointed at the rack of recent arrivals. "I'm going to look around for a minute, if you don't mind?"

Darcy nodded and began doing up the row of tiny pearl buttons on her blouse.

Elle's favorite thing about One Man's Trash was that they offered a little bit of everything. Looking for antique silverware? Suits that looked like they were straight out of *Saturday Night Fever*? They had housewares, costumes, knickknacks, a little something for everyone.

Darcy caught up with Elle just as she was salivating over a letterman-style jacket, only instead of being for a school or team, it had a gigantic embroidered cartoon Samantha from *Bewitched* on the back.

"Brendon and I used to watch that when we were little." Darcy bit her lip. "When we spent summers at Grandma's, she'd let us build pillow forts in the living room and stay up late to watch *Bewitched* and *I Dream of Jeannie* on TV Land until we crashed on the floor."

Elle traced the stitching and smiled. "When I was a kid, I was convinced I was a witch and that the rest of my family were mere mortals and that was why I was different. Never could wiggle my nose like Samantha." Elle smiled. "You've got a very Samantha-ish nose, you know that?"

Darcy cupped her fingers around the tip of her nose, forehead wrinkling. "What's that supposed to mean?"

"Why do you always think what I say has some double meaning? It's a compliment. It means I—" *Like your face.* "I think you've got a cute nose."

It felt like someone had cranked the heat in the store up to a million degrees, like Elle was standing on the surface of the sun instead of wearing an impractical T-shirt in the middle of November. She ignored the flush climbing up the sides of her throat and stared at Darcy from the corner of her eye, watching as an identical blush crept up Darcy's jaw.

"Oh." Darcy cleared her throat. "Thanks."

Elle bit the inside of her cheek and hummed, flipping the tag on the jacket so she could see the price. Her brows rocketed to her hairline. *Never mind.*

Moving down the aisle, Elle stopped in front of a case of creepy dolls that Darcy refused to look at because she'd *seen enough horror movies to know how that goes, thank you very much.* When Elle paused to peruse the vintage hair accessories, Darcy slipped off to buy her sweater.

Casting one last forlorn glance to the back of the store where the *Bewitched* jacket was tucked away, Elle made her way to the front of the store, meeting Darcy by the door.

Bracing herself for the cold, Elle crossed her arms tight across her body and ducked her chin as she stepped onto the sidewalk. Warm fingers gently seized her by the elbow, keeping her from going far.

"Here." Darcy shoved a bundle of fabric at her, pressing it to her chest.

It was the jacket, the one she'd wanted terribly, the one that cost ninety dollars. Too much. Elle's heart climbed its way up her chest, settling inside her throat, an immovable lump that made it hard to swallow. "Darcy—"

"You're always forgetting to wear a jacket. I start to wonder if you even own one." Darcy stared at a spot over Elle's shoulder.

She clutched the jacket to her chest reverently, words failing her.

"It's really nothing," Darcy said. "You bought my dinner. And paid for our drinks that first night. Consider it an additional congratulations for closing your deal with OTP."

Darcy sniffed softly, the move making her nose twitch. All Elle would be able to think about each time she wore the jacket was Darcy's pert little nose wrinkling.

The box of wine wasn't nothing and *this*, this was definitely not *nothing*. It was *something*, Elle just didn't know what. But she liked it, liked that Darcy had thought about her, had gone out of her way to do something kind just because. Despite what she'd said, what they both had said, not once all evening did Darcy press Elle to commemorate the night with a photo she could post so Brendon would see them together. Elle didn't know what any of it meant, only that it felt like this thing between them had shifted.

Elle slid the jacket over her arms and pushed the sleeves up over her wrists. A perfect fit.

"And you liked it. So."

There was that word again. *So*. Imagining what came after that teeny tiny word was too tempting.

So tempting that later that night, as Elle lay in bed, staring up at the glow-in-the-dark stars stuck to her ceiling, the ones that brought her joy no matter how silly some people might think them, she let herself hope that something real could come from this fake arrangement.

☆ ☆
☆

"—and the engineers want to know how the planets could be represented visually. Like, with emojis. I was thinking eggplant and peach beside Mars since that's most strongly representative of action and sex drive. And a smoochy face and diamond ring next to Venus for values and— Elle? *Elle.*"

Elle blinked, tearing her eyes away from where she'd zoned out staring at the purple beaded curtain that partitioned off the private room inside Wishing Well Books from the public portion of the bookstore. Elle had had an in-person reading scheduled at five thirty and another at eight, so Margot had tagged along so they could get some prep work done for OTP between her appointments. "Sorry. Eggplants." She frowned. "When did we start talking about dicks?"

Margot snorted and chucked her pen at Elle. "Let me guess, daydreaming about"—she swooned, draping herself over the arm of her chair—"Darcy."

"*Stop.*" Elle lobbed the pen back at Margot where it left a fuchsia streak across her arm. Elle opened her mouth to argue, but paused. Anything she would've said to the contrary would've been a bald-faced lie. "Okay, yeah, I was."

While Margot still wasn't pleased with the circumstances

that had thrown Darcy and Elle together, or how Darcy had behaved on their blind date, Margot had taken the stance that if Elle was happy, she was happy for her.

"Of course you were." Margot set her notebook on the table between them beside the sage, cypress, and lemongrass scented pillar candle whose flame flickered softly in the dimly lit room. "What was it this time? The kiss? The jacket? The wine? Her *nose*?"

"All of the above?" Elle shot Margot a subdued smile and shrugged. "I just . . . I want her to like me. Is that silly? You probably think I'm being ridiculous."

"Do I think you're ridiculous for wanting the girl you like to like you back?" Margot tsked. "Of course not, Elle. I'm worried you might be playing with fire, but if you think this thing with Darcy, whatever it is"—Margot rolled her eyes—"is worth your time, then I support you. Although, speaking of time, have you given any more thought to how this is supposed to end?"

"I don't know." Elle plucked at a loose thread on the hem of her sweater, avoiding Margot's too-perceptive stare. "Who's to say this has to end?"

When Margot said nothing, Elle lifted her eyes, flinching at the way Margot's entire face, from her furrowed brow to her pinched lips, screamed pity. "Elle—"

"*Maybe*," Elle tacked on. "Maybe it won't end. Maybe she'll . . . we'll . . . ." She sank down in her chair with a sigh. "Just because it started out fake doesn't mean it can't become real, right?"

Margot shrugged. "Sure, Elle. Anything's possible."

Right. "Thanks. I didn't mean to get us off track. What were you saying? Engineers and emojis?"

Margot snatched her notebook off the table and slid her glasses up the bridge of her nose. Back to business. "We've got to pick a sampling of placements because, according to the team, the rest of the chart won't be accessible unless users go premium."

Fair enough. OTP had to make money somehow, and as far as incentives went, access to the rest of a match's chart would be a solid draw for users to upgrade. Curiosity was an incredibly powerful motivator. Didn't Elle know it.

"All right. Sample . . . Sun's a given so I'd say . . . Moon, Rising, Mars, and Venus. Shoot, Mercury's important, too."

Without a complete chart, it was difficult to determine compatibility. But most people who hadn't studied astrology extensively—and to be honest, few had, despite the absurd number of astrology accounts cropping up claiming to know what they were talking about—wouldn't be able to parse out the nuances of a natal chart.

Behind the scenes, she and Margot were working with engineers at OTP to fine-tune the algorithms behind matching in a way that considered a more thorough approach to synastry. Most users didn't need the nitty-gritty. And if they wanted it? They'd have to pay.

Margot twirled her earring between her fingers and frowned thoughtfully. "I'm right there with you about Mercury. So much of communication isn't what we say, but how we say it."

Wasn't that the truth. And not only when talking face-to-face, either. It was as important in text, which mattered more than ever. One too many exclamation points and you'd sound too eager. Whether you chose *lol*, *rofl*, or *haha* said something about you, about the conversation. How you spelled the word *okay* mattered, each iteration distinct in tone. *K*, of course, was in a league of its own, and if there was a period behind it? Chances were, things were not, in fact, *okay*.

But not everyone was aces at that, understanding how what they said mattered or how it might be perceived. How a single reply could sink a conversation or how a joke gone wrong could get you blocked. Or ignored. Ghosted.

Texting was a minefield of miscommunication and uncertainty, especially since everyone had unique styles of—

"Margot, you are a genius." Elle lurched over the table and kissed the side of Margot's head.

"What?" Margot's eyes widened behind her lenses. "What did I say?"

"OTP's chat feature. You know how OTP already does an awesome job of encouraging dialogue? Like when a conversation lags and no one texts for two hours, you get a notification with a helpful hint from the person's profile? 'Jenna enjoys watching *Euphoria*. Why don't you ask her about the latest episode?'"

Margot nodded.

"What if we pitch it to Brendon and the rest of the team that, in addition to those helpful profile convo starters, if users upgrade to premium, they'll get guidance on how best to communicate with their matches based on what sign their Mercury is in?"

"So premium users would basically be getting us as virtual dating assistants?"

"When you put it like that . . ." Elle winced jokingly.

For whatever reason, it was easier to solve other people's problems than her own.

A slow smile tugged at the corner of Margot's mouth. "This is amazing, Elle. Not only would we potentially be able to increase the number of conversations that lead to first dates, but encouraging users to continue to text through the app versus their regular messaging platform would increase retention, which increases revenue from ads. Brendon's going to eat this up with a spoon."

Elle snatched her phone, itching to tell him before he heard along with the engineers during their next meeting.

ELLE: mar and i have the coolest idea about the apps chat feature. youre gonna have kittens

On second thought, he'd have kittens and then demand to meet up for coffee to talk about their idea ASAP because *impatience* was Brendon's middle name. That conversation would undoubtedly somehow segue into a chat about how things were going with Darcy and no. Elle's headspace was wacky enough when she was on her own; adding Brendon's interference into the mix would only convolute her already tangled web of feelings. Elle pressed the back button, deleting the message. Maybe, for now, avoidance while letting Margot run interference was the smartest solution.

While Margot jotted down a few notes for their next meeting with OTP, Elle started a new list for Oh My Stars based on *How the Zodiac Signs Text*.

As soon as she was finished, she flipped over to her own text messages, rereading the last messages she and Darcy had exchanged earlier that morning.

ELLE (3:14 A.M.): do you think hotel california inspired season five of american horror story?

ELLE (3:19 A.M.): the whole checking out but never leaving part

DARCY (5:32 A.M.): Why were you listening to Hotel California at three in the morning?

ELLE (7:58 A.M.): because that's the best time of day to listen to the eagles

ELLE (7:59 A.M.): obvi

DARCY (8:07 A.M.): You know the song isn't actually about a hotel, right?

DARCY: (8:09 A.M.): It's about disillusionment and the American Dream.

ELLE (8:16 A.M.): wooow

ELLE (8:16 A.M.): what song are you gonna ruin for me next darcy?

ELLE (8:17 A.M.): you're beautiful? time of your life? every breath you take?

DARCY (8:20 A.M.): Just a suggestion, but maybe you should google those.

They had extremely different styles of texting, Darcy using proper punctuation and full sentences whereas Elle couldn't be bothered. She could try, but so far it hadn't seemed to hinder their communication, or her success rate. Darcy always responded, even if she wasn't as instantaneous with her responses as Elle was. The way Darcy texted made it possible for Elle to imagine Darcy actually speaking her response, her sense of humor—often dry, sometimes dirty—shining through.

Margot was still engrossed in her notes, so Elle opened a new message.

ELLE (4:16 P.M.): favorite movie

ELLE (4:16 P.M.): go

DARCY (4:19 P.M.): Just one? That's too difficult.

ELLE (4:20 P.M.): fine

ELLE (4:20 P.M.): action comedy rom-com and idk drama?

DARCY (4:25 P.M.): Comedy would be History of the World Part One. Action . . . God, I don't know. The Mummy, maybe? Rom-com . . . America's Sweethearts. Drama would have to be Dead Poets Society.

ELLE (4:26 P.M.): the mummy?!?

ELLE (4:26 P.M.): i credit that movie for my bisexual awakening

She waited, watching the little dots dance up and down, up and down . . .

DARCY (4:28 P.M.): Oh?

ELLE (4:29 P.M.): yeah

ELLE (4:30 P.M.): did I want to be evelyn or did i want to ride off into the sunset with her?

ELLE (4:30 P.M.): both obviously

DARCY (4:32 P.M.): So you came out after watching The Mummy?

ELLE (4:33 P.M.): no

ELLE (4:33 P.M.): it actually took me a while to figure things out

ELLE (4:34 P.M.): i tried to heterotextualize my feelings for a while

ELLE (4:34 P.M.): in retrospect idk why

ELLE (4:35 P.M.): all part of the process i guess

DARCY (4:37 P.M.): You what?

It took her a second to figure out what had confused Darcy.

ELLE (4:39 P.M.): apply hetero context to a super not straight situation

ELLE (4:40 P.M.): hetero + contextualize = heterotextualize

DARCY (4:42 P.M.): Huh. New word. Thanks for broadening my horizons.

Elle bit the inside of her cheek to keep from laughing.

ELLE (4:43 P.M.): i made it up

ELLE (4:43 P.M.): but you're welcome

DARCY (4:45 P.M.): 😊 Of course.

DARCY (4:49 P.M.): So when'd you stop? Heterotextualizing?

Elle chuckled as she typed.

ELLE (4:50 P.M.): shortly after I tried to heterotextualize my friend going down on me at a theater cast party when I was in high school

ELLE (4:51 P.M.): just gals being pals

ELLE (4:52 P.M.): the mental leaps and bounds were like, acrobatic

DARCY (4:53 P.M.): You're lucky you didn't pull something.

Cheeky. Elle could be bold, too.

ELLE (4:55 P.M.): it was good head. I might've strained something. I can't remember

A minute later, her phone rang. Stomach fluttering, Elle swiped at the screen as soon as she saw the *Da*— appear on the screen.

"I was kidding. I didn't *really* pull a muscle when she went down on me, I just—"

"Elle?"

Elle cringed so hard she was going to need to see a chiropractor. "*Mom?*"

Margot recoiled in sympathy, sucking in a soft gasp through her teeth.

Mom cleared her throat awkwardly through the line. "I'm guessing you were expecting a different call."

Sweet Saturn, Mary, and Joseph. *Da*— as in Dad and Mom, the house phone. Kill her now. "Um, can we pretend that didn't happen?"

"Pretend what didn't happen?" Mom asked.

"Right, good." Elle coughed. "You rang."

"I did. I hadn't heard from you in a while."

"I guess I didn't have much worth reporting." Aside from

finalizing the deal with OTP. Nothing to write home about. But she could try. "Except—"

"I wanted to make sure you were still coming to Thanksgiving."

"Why wouldn't I?" It was Thanksgiving. Obviously, she'd be there.

"I wasn't suggesting you wouldn't come, Elle. It was a question."

Arguing wasn't worth it. "Right. I'll be there."

"Good. Lydia's bringing Marcus over on Thursday and Jane and Gabe will obviously be there with Ryland. Daniel and Mike are getting in on Wednesday so that makes nine—"

"I'm bringing Darcy," Elle blurted.

Mom paused. "Who?"

"You met her brother, Brendon? At breakfast a couple weeks ago?"

Several seconds ticked by before Mom made a hum of recognition. "*Oh*, right. The actuary?"

Mom had a terrible habit of reducing everyone to their professions. Jane, the pharmacologist. Daniel, the software engineer. Lydia, the dental student. She could only imagine what Mom referred to her as. *Elle, the disappointment.*

"Yeah, she's an actuary."

"You're still seeing her?"

"I'm still seeing her."

"It's been a few weeks."

"You sound surprised."

"Honestly, Elle, can you blame me?"

Elle pressed her lips together, damming up the words inside her throat, none of them right.

Mom prattled on, oblivious to Elle's plight. "Ten for dinner. I'll need to come up with another side dish. I wish you would have told me you were bringing her sooner. But I guess you couldn't have known, could you?"

After another two more minutes of back and forth, Elle managed to end the call.

Margot whistled through her teeth. "That sounded fun."

"So much fun. Can't you tell how overjoyed I am right now?"

Margot snorted.

Elle only hoped that phone call wasn't a sign of what she had to look forward to at Thanksgiving.

Chapter Ten

$\mathcal{D}$arcy sipped her coffee and stared at the *check engine* light on Elle's dash, biting her tongue. When Elle forgot to flip off her blinker after merging onto I-90, Darcy couldn't help herself. "Your turn signal's on."

Elle made a soft noise of acknowledgment and flipped it off. "Sorry. I'm a little out of it. Didn't sleep much last night."

Neither had Darcy.

She had been up until two studying. *Trying* to study. Between practice sets, her mind had drifted, thoughts occupied with Elle. How soft her lips had been when they'd kissed. How she'd tasted like strawberries and how she'd made a tiny sound, no more than a catch in the back of her throat when Darcy had bit down on her lip. The way Elle's absurdly blue eyes lit up when she smiled. The bright peal of her laughter when Darcy made a truly awful joke. How she'd clutched the jacket Darcy had bought her—a purchase fueled by the desire to put another smile on Elle's face—with the sort of reverence most people reserved for precious, priceless finds they planned on cherishing.

Elle might not have had on the jacket, but she *was* wearing a truly out-of-this-world Christmas sweater. *Truly.* Colorful bauble planets with sequined rings popped against the black knit, but it was the addition of *actual* light-up stars operated by a battery pack tucked against Elle's back that set the sweater apart. Darcy fingered the hem of her atrocious Grinch sweater that she'd only purchased because it made Elle smile. She felt a little less out of place than when she'd tried it on.

Thumbs tapping absently against the scuffed leather of the steering wheel, Elle pulled alongside the curb in front of a pale green bilevel house in a quiet, older-looking neighborhood. All the homes looked like they'd been built in the fifties, maybe sixties, but had been well-kept, the lawns manicured and the stoops swept free of leaves. In the driveway, there was an ostentatious green sports car parked alongside a white Honda CR-V and a silver Tesla.

"This is it," Elle said, hands clenching around the wheel. "Home sweet home."

"It's nice." Darcy rested her fingers on the handle, cracking the door. Elle continued to stare through the window, teeth worrying her bottom lip. Darcy wanted to reach out, tug it free. She cleared her throat. "Are we heading in?"

Elle relaxed her grip on the wheel and nodded. "Yeah. Probably should. It looks like everyone else is already here."

Darcy wouldn't say it, definitely not when Elle looked like she'd rather be anywhere else but here, but she was oddly looking forward to a family Thanksgiving even if it wasn't *her* family and even if this *thing* between her and Elle was contrived. The last official family Thanksgiving Darcy had had was five years ago when Grandma was still alive. Even then, the family was broken up and small—just Grandma, Mom, Brendon, and her. Now, Mom spent every holiday other than Christmas gallivanting off to some foreign country, a ski lodge or a sunny escape like Bali, with her flavor of the week, leaving her and Brendon to fend for themselves. Nothing new. It was the sort of behavior she'd learned to expect from Mom—frivolous, self-centered, careless. Brendon had learned to shrug it off; Thanksgiving was never his favorite holiday anyway, no matter how hard Darcy had tried to make it something they could celebrate together even if it was just the two of them. If there weren't costumes involved or some tie-in to a movie franchise, Brendon wasn't interested. At least, for some reason, he still liked Christmas.

Darcy followed Elle up the brick steps. The closer they came to the front door, the slower Elle's steps became, like she was marching off to the executioner's block and not her childhood home. On the landing, Elle spun on her heel, nearly knocking into Darcy who was right behind her. Her lips pulled back from her teeth in a grimace. "Look, Darcy—"

The front door opened, stopping Elle from finishing what she'd been trying to say. "Elle, you made it."

This must have been Elle's mom. The woman opening the door had the same blue eyes, the same tiny cleft in her chin. Fine lines appeared beside the corners of her eyes when she smiled and reached for Elle, hands curling around her shoulders, tugging her in for a brief hug before drawing back, her eyes darting over Elle's face, before she caught sight of Darcy over her shoulder. "You must be Darcy. It's so good to meet you. Call me Linda."

Darcy slid the strap of her brown leather hobo bag down her

arm and withdrew the bottle of wine she'd packed as a hostess gift. "Likewise. Thank you so much for having me. I wasn't sure what kind of wine you like, so I brought my favorite."

Linda's eyebrows lifted high on her forehead. "Why don't I take this to the kitchen and open it up?"

Elle goggled. "Mom, it's barely after noon."

"And?" Linda waved for them to follow as she slipped inside the house.

"How come when I day drink on holidays, it's all 'Elle, be reasonable. Tequila's not a breakfast food.' Or, 'Elle, take that onesie off. You're scaring the kids.' But now you're all, *it's five o'clock somewhere*. What gives?"

Linda ignored her.

"Mom."

"I'm sorry." Linda didn't even look over her shoulder. "I thought that was rhetorical."

Elle frowned sharply as Linda disappeared around the corner, a dismissal if Darcy had ever seen one.

She snagged Elle by the elbow. "You own a onesie?"

"A unicorn onesie, yes. What's your point?"

Darcy tried not to wince when the itchy polyblend of her sweater scratched her shoulders. "Sounds cute."

Laughter drifted down the hall.

"Come on. Let's go meet my family." Fingers tangling with hers, Elle tugged her down the hall, stopping in the entry of a spacious living room, the walls painted a soothing shade of pale olive. The conversation cut off, all eyes on them.

Lifting a hand, Elle was nearly bowled over by the force of a tiny shouting boy. "Aunt Elle!"

Voices blended together into one synchronous, "Hey, Elle," and six sets of eyes quickly turned to Darcy, studying her with looks ranging from openly curious to shrewd.

Elle coughed lightly, hand drifting down to rest on her nephew's head. "Everyone, this is Darcy. Darcy, this is . . . well, everyone."

"I'm Ryland." Elle's nephew peeked up from where he was hugging Elle's knees. He lifted a hand, thumb and pinky folded against his palm. "I'm three."

Darcy dropped to a crouch and grinned. "My name's Darcy. I'm almost *thirty*."

Ryland's eyes rounded comically.

Chuckles came from the couch. "Come on, Rye. Give your aunt some space."

Elle's nephew scampered off toward where a mess of Legos lay scattered by the dining room table.

"I'm Jane, and this is my husband, Gabe." Elle's oldest sister waved, her other hand resting atop a noticeable baby bump stretching the limits of her garish red-and-green sweater that matched her husband's.

"Daniel." Elle's brother stood and offered his hand and a warm smile. He jerked a thumb over his shoulder to the guy holding a chubby dachshund. "That's the love of my life. And then there's my husband, Mike."

Mike rolled his eyes. "Always good to know where I stand. The dog's Penny, by the way."

Darcy shook his hand and nodded. "Nice to meet you both. And Penny."

From the far end of the sofa, dressed in a blue-and-cream

snowflake-embroidered sweater that was festive but not *ugly*, waved a girl who had the same chin but darker hair than Elle. "I'm Lydia. And this is my—" She glanced up adoringly at the guy with a blond high fade wearing a basic gray crewneck sweater whose side she was tucked against. He returned her smile, tapping her on the tip of the nose. "Marcus."

He tipped his chin in a greeting before addressing Elle. "Lyds has told me a lot about you."

Elle stiffened, her grip on Darcy's forearm tightening minutely. She gave an awkward chuckle. "All good things, I hope."

The corner of Marcus's mouth lifted in a not-quite smile.

Jane cleared her throat and patted the couch. "Come sit. Tell us how you've been."

Darcy took a seat beside Elle on the one open cushion. Elle tapped her fingers against her thighs, prompting Darcy to grab a hand to keep her from openly fidgeting. The gesture earned her a quick squeeze.

"I've been good. Actually, I've been—"

"I've got your wine, Darcy." Linda returned to the living room, a glass in each hand.

"What about me?" Elle frowned.

Linda took a sip from her glass and sat in the armchair closest to the fire. "Did you want some? You should've asked."

Elle's frown deepened, expression clearing when a tall man with gray hair and smile lines stepped into the room. "Dad."

When she stood, Darcy quickly followed suit.

"Elle-belle." He leaned over the coffee table, planting a kiss on her forehead. "And this must be Darcy who we've all been dying to meet."

Darcy wasn't so sure about the *dying to meet her* bit, but she smiled anyway. "It's nice to meet you, sir."

He batted at the air, chuckling softly. "Sir, bah! Call me Simon." His hazel eyes darted back to Elle as he held out a bottle of hard cider. "Got you covered, kid."

Elle smiled. "Thanks, Dad."

Simon perched on the arm of the chair beside his wife. "So. Darcy. Tell us a little about yourself."

Inside, Darcy groaned. She loathed the spotlight, but she'd been to enough corporate retreats over the last eight years that she had a neat elevator speech at the ready. "Sure. I recently moved to town from Philadelphia, though I'm originally from San Francisco. And I work at Deveraux and Horton Mutual Life as an associate actuary, although I'm currently preparing for my final exam to become an FSA."

Simon whistled. "Impressive."

This wasn't supposed to be about impressing Elle's family. Tangentially, perhaps, if it reflected good on Elle. "Not as impressive as Elle's work."

Across the room, Linda smiled politely. "How about your family? I believe I met your brother. Any other siblings?"

Elle sank into the couch, fingers sliding against Darcy's palm as she attempted to withdraw her hand. Darcy squeezed her fingers, holding firm. "Other than my father who lives in Toronto and my mother who still lives in California, it's just me and Brendon. He's *extremely* excited to be working with Elle."

"Right." Linda's smile tightened. "The *dating app.*"

Darcy bit the side of her tongue to keep from pulling a face at the way Elle's mother made *dating app* sound like a dirty word.

"What dating app?" Daniel asked, leaning forward, elbows on his knees.

"One True Pairing," she said.

His brows rose. "You're working for OTP?"

Elle cleared her throat, sitting up straight. "*With*. Um." She scratched the side of her neck, eyes darting around the room. A soft flush spread up her throat, deepening at her cheeks. "Margot and I, we're consulting with OTP to add synastry, or astrological compatibility, to the app's matching algorithm. It's, um, it's pretty cool, I guess."

Pretty cool. I guess. Darcy would have to be oblivious not to notice how Elle shrank in on herself, couching her words and understating her success. She was no expert, but she couldn't help but wonder if Elle subconsciously downplayed her achievements to soften the blow when her family did the same.

Despite the furrow of his brow, Daniel smiled. "Well, congrats, sis."

Linda nodded absently. "That sounds like a neat opportunity for you, Elle. I'm sure it'll be a . . . fun job. Right up your alley."

A neat opportunity. Darcy's jaw ticked, her ability to tolerate bullshit slim, her ability to tolerate condescension worse.

Could they not have *tried* to appear authentically enthused? Darcy might not have believed in astrology—most of it honestly went over her head, talk of houses and returns and interceptions—but she listened when Elle spoke about it because it may not have mattered to her but it sure as hell mattered to Elle. How could they not see that? How could they not care? At the very least, Darcy understood what a fucking fantastic opportunity this was. Neat, her ass.

Still gripping Elle's hand fiercely, Darcy sat up straighter. "Elle's being modest. The deal with my brother's company is quite frankly, massive. The dating app industry, as a whole, is oversaturated, and while OTP does a fantastic job of offering a unique user experience, it was brilliant of my brother to look to a rapidly growing, yet still young industry like astrology." Darcy reached for her wine and took a fortifying sip. "Did you know venture capitalists have invested over two *billion* dollars in astrology apps because they're popular with Gen Z and Millennial women? That means there's money to be made. There are *thousands* of social media astrology accounts and yet Oh My Stars has more followers on Twitter and Instagram than any of their competitors, so you might not believe in it, plenty of people might not, but a huge number do." Darcy shrugged. "And like I said, my brother's brilliant. He wouldn't take a chance on just anyone, let alone sign a deal this big."

Linda's eyes, suddenly wide, darted between her and Elle. "How big?"

Elle's face had turned the prettiest shade of petal pink, her eyes huge and glassy as she stared at Darcy for a long moment, finally looking at her mother. "Um. *Big.*"

"Damn, get that bread, sis," Daniel joked.

"Bread?" Dad frowned thoughtfully. "I thought it was bacon? What's next, *get that guacamole*?"

Daniel laughed. "Dough, Dad."

While Elle's family argued over the etymology of bread as a stand-in for money, Jane insisting it dated back to Cockney slang, Elle leaned in, lips brushing against the shell of Darcy's ear as she dropped her voice to a whisper. "Two billion dollars, huh?"

Darcy rolled her eyes, but *Jesus*. Elle's breath against Darcy's skin did outrageous things to her pulse. "I did my research."

Elle had no idea how many nights Darcy had stayed up, scouring Oh My Stars's various social media accounts and reading articles from the *New York Times* on venture capital and astrology apps. It had started as a means of making sure she had her *i*'s dotted and *t*'s crossed if Brendon seemed suspicious about the veracity of her dating Elle. After that kiss, that *fucking* kiss, it had been her way of gaining insight into Elle's mind. Because perhaps if she understood astrology, she'd understand Elle, and if she understood Elle perhaps, she'd be able to untangle what it was about her that she couldn't shake.

Why she was so in knots over this impossible woman who had her head in the clouds and wore her heart on her sleeve. A woman with the world's least refined palate and an inability to sit properly in a chair like a normal person. Darcy should've wanted as far away from her as earthly possible and yet her laugh was infectious and made something warm bloom inside Darcy's chest like stubborn wildflowers poking up through cracks in the pavement, growing where they didn't belong. And the way she looked at Darcy with those dark blue eyes made Darcy feel *seen* like Elle wasn't looking at her but into her and it was raw and uncomfortable and yet—

That she'd tacked on the word *yet* should've sent warning bells off inside her head. Darcy wasn't looking to be seen. Not like that. Not now. She had an FSA exam to pass, a career to focus on. The only place Darcy had any business being *seen* was in the mirror each morning as she got ready for work, and yet every free moment—even moments that weren't free—Darcy spent thinking about Elle. About that kiss. About the sorts of things Darcy could do to put a smile on her face. About—

Something smacked the side of Elle's head. A bottle cap. Across the room, with his sock-covered feet propped on the coffee table, Daniel grinned. "Quit making out."

Elle plucked the cap off the floor and flicked it back at him. "We weren't making out, you douche canoe."

"*Elle.*" Jane widened her eyes and tilted her head toward the dining room where Ryland was building a tower out of Legos, none the wiser.

"Oh, come on."

"Last month after you babysat, Ryland asked me what a"—she dropped her voice—"twatwaffle was and if his could have chocolate chips."

Darcy pinched her lips together, eyes watering and shoulders shaking as she leaned into Elle who was stifling her laughter—poorly—by biting her knuckles.

"Twatwaffle?" Daniel cackled. "That's fucking inspired, Elle."

"*Language.*" Linda glared briefly at Elle before turning to Daniel, lips curved downward in apparent disappointment. "I expect this sort of thing from your sister, but honestly, Daniel?"

"What's that supposed to mean?" Elle asked, frowning sharply.

Linda shut her eyes. "Elizabeth—"

"*Ahem.* Not that this isn't totally *riveting.*" Lydia unfolded herself from the couch and stood, tugging Marcus up with her. "But while we're talking about good news, Marcus and I have an announcement we'd like to make."

Beside her, Elle stiffened.

"Oh my god," Linda breathed, clasping her hands in front of her chest.

Elle's little sister reached inside her sweater and withdrew a long chain from around her neck. Dangling from its length was an impressively sized princess-cut diamond engagement ring. Lydia bounced on her toes, beaming from ear to ear. "Marcus proposed and I said yes, *obviously*. I'm engaged!"

Darcy swallowed her groan, not that anyone would've heard it over the din of Elle's family jumping to their feet to wrap Lydia in hugs and congratulate the newly engaged happy couple.

She didn't want to think the worst of Elle's little sister, but seriously? Of all the times to announce her engagement, did it have to be right on the heels of Elle finally getting her moment in the spotlight? Finally being seen for the bright, successful, enterprising woman she was? She'd argue the timing was circumspect if not for the fact that Lydia did, in fact, have a ring.

"*Elle.*" Linda jerked her head at Lydia pointedly.

"Right, *shit*. I mean, sorry. Congratulations, sis. That's—" Her eyes shut for just a moment. When she opened them, she offered Lydia a genuine smile. "I'm really happy for you."

Lydia had slipped the ring on her finger. She twisted it slightly, adjusting it so it sat right. "Thanks, Elle." She chuckled. "Who knows, maybe you'll be next?"

Elle tugged her fingers free from Darcy's grip and Darcy immediately missed the warmth of her skin.

Her laughter sounded forced, fake. "Ha. Maybe."

An hour later, from the head of the table, Mom lifted her glass of wine in the air and looked at Lydia with a glowing smile. God, what Elle wouldn't give to have Mom look at her like that, just once. "A quick toast. To Lydi-bee. Your father and I are so proud of you and we couldn't be happier for you and for Marcus as you embark on this exciting journey together. We love you, Lydia."

Lydia wiped beneath her eyes as everyone, Elle included, saluted them, drinks raised. As soon as she could, Elle gulped her cider, trying to wash out the bitter taste that had taken up residence in the back of her mouth. Envy never failed to make Elle feel guilty; it just wasn't who she was, wasn't an emotion she felt at home in, but there was a part of her, a secret part tucked away, buried so deep she didn't even let on to Margot, that was worried it was who she was becoming. That her feelings of inadequacy were mutating into something ugly. *Resentment.*

She was happy for Lydia, but that didn't make this any easier. Sitting and smiling and nodding politely as everyone congratulated her loudly, Elle's own accomplishments once again taking a back seat. God. Not even the back seat because then, at least, she'd be included. There was no room for Elle in the car.

Making matters worse was that Darcy had seen it all unfold, had a painfully intimate front-row seat. And that comment Lydia had made about Elle being next to get married? Fuck her life. Lydia couldn't have known Darcy and Elle's relationship was fake; Darcy had done a commendable job of playing the role of besotted girlfriend. An *achingly* good job, so good Elle almost felt like this was real, which was almost worse because added to the brewing resentment was an unhealthy dose of yearning. Tugged in too many directions, Elle felt sick, stomach queasy.

She had agreed to go along with this fake-dating sham in hopes that her family might take her seriously if they saw her in a different light, if they saw she had one part of her life going according to a plan they could get behind. So far, her stock had barely risen in their eyes even with Darcy talking her up. Adding insult to injury, she and Darcy were scheduled to "break up" in a little over a month.

Where would that leave her? Back where she started or worse? Maybe her family would think her an even bigger mess. She'd hoped to paint the breakup as mutual and faultless, but knowing her luck, her family would find her culpable no matter what she said.

Mom clapped her hands and scooted her chair forward. "All right, everyone. Dig in."

Serving dishes were passed around the table from person to person until everyone had a plateful of Thanksgiving's best dishes. A minute later, Marcus's expression soured.

Lydia was quick to rest her hand on his shoulder. "What's wrong?"

"Um, I think there's something wrong with the turkey."

A concerned frown quickly replaced Mom's immediate look of startled displeasure. "What is it? Underdone?"

His jaw shifted, tongue rolling against his cheeks. "Tastes like soap? Did you wash it?"

Mom was a lot of things, but domestic goddess wasn't one of them. Dad cooked 364 days of the year, but for some reason, Mom had claimed Thanksgiving as her own, ruling the kitchen with an iron fist and refusing to surrender even as much as a side dish or dessert to anyone. Her efforts were met with varying degrees of success they were all forced to grin and bear. Elle couldn't quite wrap her head around why Mom would wash a turkey—don't ask, don't tell was Elle's Turkey Day motto—but in comparison to 2008's corn and giblet pudding, a little dish soap was mild.

Jane took a bite and after swallowing, said, sounding surprised, "It's cilantro, yeah?"

"Cilantro lime." Mom nodded. "I always go with sage and thyme, so I thought I'd try a new recipe. Brighten the meal up a bit."

Marcus shook his head, a contrite smile crossing his face. "Sorry. I've got a thing with cilantro. Tastes weird to me. No offense."

Mom waved him off. "You're fine, Marcus. I'll remember that for next time."

Lydia took a bite of her turkey and then hummed, eyes flaring. She finished chewing and smiled broadly. "You know, Elle, you're a little like cilantro."

Elle set her fork down. She didn't want to put the cart in front of the horse, but she had a sneaking suspicion Lydia hadn't said that because of Elle's ability to add flavor to a meal. "What's that supposed to mean?"

A pucker appeared between Lydia's brows. "You know. People tend to either love cilantro or . . ." She winced. "It was supposed to be a joke because you're . . ." She wiggled her head. "Never mind."

The bitter taste in the back of Elle's mouth returned with a vengeance. "Because I'm *what*, Lydia?"

"Relax, Elle," Mom chided from the head of the table. "I think what your sister was trying to say is that your interests tend to be a tad peculiar is all."

"Quirky." Lydia nodded, smiling placidly like she hadn't just called her a fucking weirdo.

Elle tossed her napkin beside her plate. She didn't have much of an appetite. "What exactly is *peculiar* about my interests?"

"All I was trying to say is, your interests are *unique*. For people who aren't used to your . . . new age philosophy, it can take some time to get used to. Crystals and chakras and relying on advice that might as well be printed in the *Farmer's Almanac*. Elle. You're—*they're*—an acquired taste. I think that's all your sister meant."

An acquired taste.

All Elle could hear was *hard to swallow* and *unpalatable*.

She could sign all the book deals and consulting contracts with Fortune 500 companies, have all her ducks in order, but because she didn't live her life exactly the way Mom wanted, take the right jobs, date the people Mom set her up with, *settle* for safe, she'd always fall short.

"An acquired taste." Elle sucked her bottom lip between her teeth to keep it from doing something stupid like quivering. "Nothing I do is ever going to be good enough, is it?"

Dad's fork clattered against his plate and Jane gasped, the final noise before a collective hush descended over the room.

"*Elizabeth*," Mom stage-whispered. "What on earth—"

"Come *on*, Mom. It's not even an elephant in the room anymore, it's . . . it's writing on the wall. Because I don't have your job or Dad's, follow in your footsteps, do everything exactly the way you want, everything according to *your* plan, *your* schedule, I'm *peculiar*."

Dad coughed into his fist. "Elle-belle, no one ever said you had to have the same job as me or your mother. Look at Jane, she's—"

"Perfect." Elle nodded. "And can do no wrong. Old news. I wasn't being literal; I meant the sort of job you have. In an office or a hospital, somewhere I report to a manager and put family photos up in a cubicle and drink tepid coffee in a break-room and make insignificant small talk with coworkers who probably also hate their jobs. You want me to fit myself in a box and I just . . . I don't. I'm not like that."

Mom stared from the head of the table, hands clenched around her cutlery. One deep breath later, she said, "Only because you don't *try*. Six years of college and grad school and you threw it all away—all that effort, all that money, all that time—so you could have fun becoming a social media sensation? What's going to happen to you when the next big thing comes along, Elle? When Instagram and Twitter are obsolete and people have moved on from this pseudoscientific astrology fad to something else? You could've been a chemical engineer or a climatologist or worked for NASA had you wanted, but—"

"But I didn't!" Elle's eyelids were hot and a sour knot had

formed inside her throat, bile and bitter indignation creeping up her esophagus, the resentment she'd buried for years
beneath layers of defensive humor and nonchalance clawing
its way to the surface. "That's my point. That wasn't what *I*
wanted. I wasn't happy."

Mom pressed her fingers to the space between her eyes and
gave a weary sigh. "It's Thanksgiving. The whole family is together. Your sister just announced her engagement. Could we
not make a scene?" Her gaze darted to Darcy who was looking
at Elle, eyes wide and jaw clenched.

Inside her head, Elle's pulse beat too loud.

A scene. Of course. Adding insult to injury, she was also a
train wreck. *A mess.* Darcy wasn't looking for a relationship,
but if she were? What did Elle even have to offer? Not even her
own family thought she was good enough.

Her face was hot and her legs weak and her thoughts went
disjointed, a scattershot inside her brain of colors and isolated
words, desires and aches. She swallowed twice, her tongue
thick, curling strangely around her words as she stood, arms
hanging limply at her sides, fingertips tingling as the fight
drained from her, replaced with bone-deep lethargy. "I'm going
to get another drink and take a minute. So I don't, you know,
make another scene."

"Elle," Darcy called out, but Elle kept moving.

Left foot. Right foot. One foot in front of the other until she
escaped down the hall to the kitchen with its clean counters and
bright white cabinets. Elle ducked her chin and ran her fingers
over the jingle bells affixed to her sweater. Blues and reds and
greens. Orange and pink planets set against a starry sky. It looked

like a box of crayons threw up on her and she *loved* this sweater but no one else did. She'd discovered it in the bottom of a half-off bin at a thrift store in the middle of April, someone having cleared out their closet and tossed it. Deemed it unworthy.

But Elle had loved it enough to take it home.

Elle loved herself, but what a feeling it must be, being loved by someone else exactly as you are, quirks and warts and all. She wouldn't know.

Santa's knit face blurred before her eyes. Over the ringing in her ears, footsteps approached down the hall, getting closer, the loose floorboard near the kitchen door squeaking. *Shoot.* Elle swiped a hand over her face, mopping her tears with her sleeve.

Darcy ducked her head around the corner, eyes flaring when she spotted Elle. Elle who undoubtedly looked like a wreck, face streaked with salty tears and . . . she looked at the sleeve of her sweater. Plum-colored eyeliner smeared the wool. What else was new. Elle was the definition of an ugly crier, her complexion going splotchy and her eyes swelling like she was having an allergic reaction, her body trying to shove her emotions out violently through her tear ducts. Of course, Darcy was there to bear witness to another shade of Elle in all her messy glory.

"So. Your family kind of sucks," Darcy said, plainly.

Elle snorted, but her nose was stuffed so it came out like an awkward honk.

"It's no big deal." She forced a laugh. "If you think about it, it's stupid. I don't know why I'm so upset. Cilantro, I mean . . . shit. Saying I taste like soap to a vocal minority of the population, that's— It's ridiculous."

It didn't *feel* ridiculous.

Darcy's shoulders rose as she stared hard at Elle. Elle crossed her arms, hugging herself tight, and shifted her weight from one foot to the other, briefly lifting one leg to scratch the back of her knee with her opposite toe.

Darcy took a careful step toward her, then another and another until she was close enough that Elle could count the freckles on her nose. Only there were too many, countless others spreading out along Darcy's cheeks, spilling down her jaw. Of course, there was that special freckle shaped like the moon beside Darcy's mouth, the one bracketed by her dimple.

She was so busy trying in vain to count Darcy's freckles, to remember what the freckle at the corner of her mouth had tasted like when they'd kissed, that it wasn't until Darcy's thumb brushed the skin beneath Elle's right eye that Elle even realized Darcy had reached out to touch her.

"For what it's worth," Darcy said, her right hand joining the left to wipe away the tears and liner from beneath Elle's eyes. "I like cilantro."

Elle blinked, thoughts jamming because there were too many of them competing for space inside her brain. Overriding everything was the fact that Darcy was cradling Elle's face in her hands and staring into Elle's eyes, her perfect teeth sunk into the swell of her lower lip, so sharp her lip had turned white from the pressure.

When Darcy released her lip, the flesh plumped, turning red. Her hands slipped lower, thumbs no longer grazing the thin, delicate skin beneath Elle's eyes, but the side of her jaw, her fingers curling around the back of Elle's neck. "And when we kissed? I really liked how you taste."

Warmth seeped from Elle's chest down into her stomach like she'd taken a shot of tequila. It spread lower, heat settling between her thighs. Her thoughts turned syrupy slow and candy sweet as Darcy leaned in, erasing the distance between them inch by torturous inch.

This was really happening and it couldn't be for show because it was just the two of them inside the kitchen, their faces growing closer together. Elle could taste the sharp, fruity, warmth of Darcy's breath and her chest started to ache, arms and legs and the muscles in her stomach quivering, all but vibrating from keeping still. Waiting . . . waiting . . . Anticipation was the sweetest torture as Darcy exhaled, lips curling in delight at the whimper that clawed its way up Elle's throat when Darcy's nose brushed hers, Darcy's nails—

"There you two— *Whoops.*"

Elle stepped back, hip knocking into the counter, sending a frisson of pain radiating from her hip bone all the way up her side. A pink flush crept up Darcy's jaw as she stepped away, ducking her chin and staring at the floor.

Frozen in the doorway, Dad smiled sheepishly. "Right. Just coming to make sure you were okay, Elle-belle."

"Fine, Dad." At least her voice had barely shook. "We'll be out in a minute."

He coughed lightly, feet already carrying him backward through the door.

A moment passed, Elle weighing words that would do her feelings justice. She wanted to chase after the moment, snatch it back, crawl inside that bubble where she and Darcy breathed the same air, but she didn't know how to revive it.

Darcy opened her mouth and a sudden pulse of panic clawed its way up Elle's throat not knowing what Darcy was going to say but terrified it would erase the progress they'd made.

"What are you doing this weekend?" Elle blurted.

Darcy shut her mouth, lashes fluttering. "Why?"

Elle swallowed and took a leap of faith. "Do you want to do something? With me?"

That moment was gone. But they could make a new moment. Several moments. If Darcy wanted. If this, Darcy following her into the kitchen, and saying what she had, meant what Elle hoped it did.

Darcy's lips drew to the side. "Not with your family, right?"

"Definitely not." Elle laughed, relieved beyond belief that Darcy hadn't immediately said no.

"And not with my brother?"

Darcy was flirting and there was no one around for her to fool, no one to convince that this was anything but exactly what it was. Something real.

Elle shook her head and boldly reached out, brushing a strand of hair out of Darcy's face before it could fall into her eyes. "Just me."

Hopefully *just Elle* would be enough.

The smirk on Darcy's face grew, spreading, transforming into a genuine smile, the sight of which made Elle's stomach explode in a spray of butterfly wings. "I'd like that."

Chapter Eleven

*A*re you sure we're allowed to be here?" Darcy whispered, following Elle up a long, narrow flight of stairs sandwiched between two stone walls.

The step beneath Elle's right foot creaked when she turned, one hand resting on the railing, the other clutching her phone, which served as their flashlight, illuminating the otherwise pitch-black stairway.

"No." A scant amount of light rebounded off the stone wall casting shadows across Elle's face. Darcy couldn't see her mouth, but the lilt to Elle's voice hinted at a smile. "We're actually *not* allowed to be here."

"Elle."

"Come on." Fingers caressed the inside of Darcy's wrist making her shiver. "Break the rules with me, Darcy."

Little did she know Darcy was already breaking all sorts of rules. Rules of Darcy's own making.

Darcy should've known Elle had a reason for refusing to answer any of her questions about where they were going and what

Elle had planned for their . . . date? It *felt* like a date, had all the trappings of one. Darcy's stomach had been in tangles all day, thinking about it. Her focus had been shot, her ability to get work done dismal. Rather than accomplish any studying, Darcy had performed an unreliable risk assessment of her own. Answer? If she had to ask whether it was a date, her risk was too high. Even knowing that, all she could think about was Elle, seeing Elle, what it meant and how it terrified her and how, despite the risk, she'd been unable to bring herself to cancel.

Dress warm and be ready by eleven was all Elle had said. At first Darcy had thought Elle meant eleven in the morning because what reasonable person planned a date for eleven at night? But according to Elle, the best adventures happened after dark.

Elle jiggled the knob on the door, hips and ass shaking in the cutest victory dance when the door opened revealing a round, moonlit room. "Ta-da! Welcome to the Jacobsen Observatory, the second-oldest building on campus." Arms outstretched above her, fingers lifted toward the domed ceiling, Elle spun in a dizzying circle, her black skirt flouncing out around her tight-covered thighs. She was wearing the jacket Darcy had bought her.

Feigning interest in the building's architecture, Darcy turned, pressing her fingers to one of the stones in front of her, hiding her smile in the shadows. "How'd you find this place?"

As covertly as possible, she peeked over her shoulder, watching as Elle dropped her arms, her smile dimming. Subtle, but Darcy noticed. She wasn't sure when it had happened, but she noticed everything about Elle. How she tugged on her ear when she was anxious. Her bad habit of biting her bottom lip, a bad habit Darcy liked very much. *Too* much. She'd never been jealous of someone else's *teeth* before, but Elle could bite that lip whenever, and there was something patently unfair that Darcy wasn't allowed the privilege of doing the same.

Losing it. Darcy was absolutely losing it, losing her head, losing her grip, losing it all over Elle. She had sneaked up on Darcy and now here she was, jealous of Elle's fucking teeth. God help her.

"Come on." Elle tilted her head toward one of the arched French windows.

Darcy breathed deep, lungs swelling, burning before she exhaled and followed where Elle led.

Like the door, the window wasn't locked, opening with ease when Elle pressed against the latch. She threw her right leg over the sill, straddling the ledge, then shimmied out the window, dropping onto the balcony that wrapped around half of the turret-shaped building. Elle held out a hand. Resting her fingers in Elle's warm palm, Darcy stepped over the edge and into the cool, night air, her hair whipping in the breeze.

Above them, bright, winking stars twinkled against an inky blue canvas, the view expansive and impressive and it made Darcy's breath catch in her throat. "*Oh.*"

Elle tugged, dragging Darcy eagerly over to the stone railing. "Life would be a lot better if we all spent a little more time staring at the stars." Loose strands of blond hair caught the moonlight, creating a haloed glow around her when she turned her face up to the sky. "It's beautiful, isn't it?"

"Yes." Darcy wasn't looking at the sky.

"You see that cluster of stars right there?" Elle pointed, drawing Darcy's attention to a grouping to the right. "Right"—she grabbed Darcy's hand and lifted it toward the sky, tracing a pattern in the stars—"there. That's the Big Dipper. If you follow those stars—the vertical ones on the end—straight up, you reach Polaris, also known as the North Star. It's a constant, never moves. If you're ever lost, you can always find true north, as long as you can spot that star."

Elle let go of Darcy's hand and placed her palms flat against the railing. Hyperaware of where her limbs existed in space now that Elle was near but no longer touching her, Darcy's hand hovered awkwardly at her side, her fingers tingling as she flexed them.

"I know about this place because I was an astronomy major." Elle's lips quirked. "The last person I told that to assumed I was some ditz who confused astronomy with astrology and was in for a rude awakening." She huffed out a laugh. "Shockingly, not true."

Darcy hadn't thought it was. "People are assholes."

"They can be." Elle's earrings, dangling azure baubles shaped like planets, skimmed her jaw. She cleared her throat and tilted her head to the side, meeting Darcy's eyes, her lips crooking. "I got into grad school and got my master's in astronomy with an emphasis in cosmology."

Her teeth scraped against the swell of her bottom lip making the muscles in Darcy's stomach quiver and clench. It was Elle's lip Darcy was jealous of now, the desire for Elle to sink her teeth into *Darcy's* lip fierce, consuming.

"I was working toward my PhD. It was a six-year program, the first two geared toward coursework for your master's, and the rest was teaching, research, writing your dissertation, and preparing for what comes next, whatever that was. I was stuck teaching this intro course that was full of freshmen looking for an easy A and staying up until all hours working on my thesis, and it all just hit me that it wasn't what I wanted but I kept plugging along because what else was I supposed to do? Then Oh My Stars—it was Margot's and my side hustle at the time—took off when we got a job writing horoscopes for *The Stranger*. Grad school had zapped the magic out of learning, but Oh My Stars was something I was excited about, the thing that got me out of bed each morning. I woke up the next day and decided I wasn't going to let anyone take the stars from me so I quit the program."

"I'm guessing your family didn't take it well?" Darcy arched a brow.

Elle ducked her head, chuckling in that self-deprecating way people tend to when what they're saying means more to them than they're letting on, than they want you to know. "My family was . . . I want to say concerned, but I think they were *horrified*. They sat me down for an intervention. Everyone thought I was burned out or having a quarter-life crisis. Mom thought I'd lost my mind."

Elle leaned her elbows on the railing and rested her chin in her hands. "I don't . . . I don't expect them to agree, or even completely understand, but I wish they'd respect it. My choices. *Me*. I wish I didn't have to be so . . . so *serious* in order for them to take me seriously. Does that make sense?"

Mom liked to joke that Darcy had been born serious, but

that wasn't true. She knew how to have fun; her interests just leaned toward quiet, individual pursuits. Reading. Crossword puzzles. Yoga instead of team sports. Even her more whimsical hobbies—watching soap operas and TV Land—put her firmly in the camp of *millennial grandma*.

That didn't mean she didn't understand how Elle felt. "Fewer than a third of actuaries are women and even that's five times higher than it was a decade or so ago. It's not the same. I'm not trying to say—" She sighed. "My job is conventional. It's garden variety. No one thinks you're peculiar when you say you're an actuary. *Boring*, maybe."

Elle chuckled softly.

"But I've had people assume I'm an administrative assistant. If they know I'm an actuary, they assume I'm a career associate—which there's nothing wrong with, don't get me wrong—but they balk at the idea of me reaching FSA designation. Why would I take all those tests? Aren't I happy being an associate? The pay's good, but—"

"You want more than that," Elle said.

She nodded. "I want more than that."

"I know why I want more, but how about you? Is it proving that you can? That you can be the best? Or I assume the pay *is* better . . ."

It was, but that wasn't why. Or it wasn't only why.

How much did she want to tell Elle? She *didn't* want to talk about it. Simply churning up the memories in turn churned up her stomach until she was queasy. But Elle had been so open, so honest, let herself be vulnerable. Darcy owed the same, and a tiny part of her wanted Elle to know. Know her.

"I told you about my parents." Darcy rubbed the hollow of her throat. "About how my mother quit working when I was born. My father made enough that he was able to support the family on one income, so even when we got older, she didn't go back to work because she didn't need to. She had hobbies and volunteering to fill up her time, and over the summer, she went with my father when he traveled for business. She didn't like that he was gone so often, or . . . she didn't like that she didn't know what he was doing, she didn't trust him, and seeing as the reason for their divorce was that he left her for his twenty-four-year-old personal assistant, I suppose her worries weren't unfounded."

"Shit," Elle muttered.

"Yeah, it was. It was shit." A gust of wind blew, bitter sharp air biting at the tip of Darcy's nose and messing up her hair. She brushed her curls out of her face and sighed. It wasn't like she'd never told anyone this story. Annie knew all the dirty details; Natasha, too. Maybe that's why it was so hard to talk about. Not because the words were unfamiliar on her tongue, but because she'd hoped that Natasha knowing this, knowing how she felt about the mistrust and disloyalty and how it had wrecked her mother, would've been decent enough not to break Darcy's heart. To be decent enough not to repeat history, in a sense.

Darcy bit the inside of her cheek, the sting of her teeth sinking into the tender flesh of her mouth enough to quell the tears making the stars twinkle and blur. "Mom got custody and child support and a lump sum alimony, but she didn't have the best money management skills, so it was gone in no time.

And she hadn't worked in over sixteen years so she had trouble finding a job and getting back on her feet. Having seen her go through that, I promised myself I'd never put myself in the same position. I liked numbers and I was good at math, it made sense. I wanted a job with benefits, a job that paid well. And I was going to be good at it, the best at what I do, so I'd always have job security. I wanted a job that would never just disappear or where I'd become obsolete."

Mom might've had Grandma to fall back on, but Darcy didn't. She only had herself.

"Anyway. That's why."

With a wry twist of her lips, Elle shook her head. "You must think I'm crazy. You have the sort of job my mom would love me to have. You want stable and secure and I want—it's *not* the opposite, not like Mom thinks. I'm not throwing my life away or trying to self-destruct, I just wanted the right fit. But she's not wrong. There isn't job security. All our followers could disappear tomorrow or a platform could, *poof*, become old news. Or maybe our book bombs or I mess something up some other way." The forward curl of her shoulders was subtle as Elle drew in on herself. "That would suck, don't get me wrong, but I'd rather fail at something I love than succeed at something I don't."

"You're not going to fail." Lifting her head, Darcy glanced up at the sky, at the stars, her eyes catching on the one Elle had pointed out. Polaris. "Despite whatever your family thinks, you're . . . you're brilliant at what you do. Not to sound conceited by affiliation, but my brother wouldn't have wanted to work with you if you aren't the best."

"Yeah?" Elle's teeth were frustrating Darcy again, sunk into her bottom lip. "You think?"

"I know." Darcy nodded. "And for what it's worth, I take you seriously."

Elle rolled her eyes. "Sure. Thanks."

"I mean it." Darcy gripped the railing and rocked back on her heels. "What I said at Thanksgiving . . . I did do research. Some of what you said about astrology made sense and I wanted to know more. It wasn't for the sake of selling it, Elle. I didn't say it because of that. I meant what I said."

Elle turned her head, meeting Darcy's eyes. "I never actually thanked you for saying what you did. For defending me. For whatever reason you did."

It hadn't even been a question, sticking up for her. Elle who wanted terribly for the world to be full of love and understanding, or at the very least, for her own family to understand.

In retrospect, the impulse terrified Darcy. Protecting Elle had been practically instinctive, but protecting her meant she cared and Darcy wasn't supposed to care. Not about Elle, not about her hopes and dreams, certainly not how she might factor into them. Or how Elle might factor into hers.

Darcy turned, gazing pointedly at the building behind them. "You still come here. Even though you dropped out. It's not a reminder? A sore spot for you?"

Elle's throat jerked, her lips pressed together. "No, it's the opposite. When I've had a crappy week, I come out here and look at the stars and I remember being six years old and watching my first meteor shower on a family camping trip and feeling awe like I'd never felt before. Stars shooting through the sky, it was like . . . it *was* magic. Carl Sagan said we're made of *star stuff* and it's true, you know? Stars, the really big ones, don't just make carbon and oxygen but they keep burning and burning and burning and that burning produces alpha elements like nitrogen and sulfur, neon and magnesium all the way up to iron. It's called supernova nucleosynthesis. Say that five times fast." Elle laughed and Darcy's chest ached as if something inside her was stretching, making space. Growing pains.

"Eventually, when those massive stars reach the end of their lives, they go out with a bang, a supernova so bright, so beautiful it drowns out all the other stars. And when they do, they throw out all those elements they created. That's what we're made of. We've got calcium in our bones and iron in our blood and nitrogen in our DNA . . . and all of that? It comes from those stars." Elle's eyes glistened, sparkling as bright as the stars she spoke of as she blinked and pointed up at the sky. "We are literally made of stardust."

Moonlight danced off the tips of Elle's pale blond eyelashes and made her eyes twinkle. If anyone was made of star stuff, it was her.

"No matter how old I got or how much everyone told me I needed to *get real* or *be practical* I never stopped wishing on stars or dreaming impossible dreams." A watery laugh spilled from Elle's lips. She shook her head and sniffed, clearing her throat. "Sorry. Whether you take me seriously or not, I know you think it's silly. Astrology and magic and soul mates."

"It's not. I think it's nice," Darcy whispered. "That you still believe in all that."

That Elle woke up every morning and hoped for the best instead of anticipating the worst.

"But you don't, right? Believe in that? Soul mates?"

Darcy gripped the ledge like the safety bar of a roller coaster, her knuckles going white and the bones in her hands aching as she swayed on weak knees. Elle tucked her hair behind her ears and turned her head, blue eyes meeting Darcy's and for a moment, one tenuous moment, Darcy forgot how to breathe.

She couldn't speak, didn't know what she'd say even if she could. Instead, Darcy let go of the railing and reached for Elle, resting her hand on Elle's waist, thumb stroking her through the fabric. Elle lifted her chin, stars reflecting in her eyes, and the curve of her lips dared Darcy to take a chance, a leap of faith. Jump.

Lips covering Elle's and fingers bunching in Elle's hot pink sweater, Darcy threw herself off the cliff's edge and let herself fall. Not to Earth, but toward Elle. Elle, who was magnetic and made it sound like nothing was impossible. That even gravity could be defied if Darcy simply *believed*. That even if she didn't defy gravity, she could fall anyway and it would be okay because Elle would give Darcy a soft place to land. That Darcy could trust Elle with every fragile inch of herself.

What started slow and soft, a tentative exploration, turned desperate when Elle sucked Darcy's lower lip into her mouth, teeth scraping her flesh. Darcy crushed herself closer, hands circling Elle's neck, her fingers raking through the soft strands at her nape as she rocked her hips into Elle's.

Now that she'd given herself permission to want, to want Elle, she wanted everything, wanted it all with an unbridled urgency. Tearing her mouth from Elle's, she sucked in a gasp of air, lungs filling as she dragged her lips down Elle's cheek, skimming the soft, silky skin of her neck where her pulse beat wildly, an echo to Darcy's own. Tongue darting out to taste the salty sweetness of sweat dotting Elle's throat, Darcy let her hands drift, explore, sliding from Elle's waist down to her hips, around, fingers cupping her ass and squeezing, anything she could do to bring her closer, make her gasp, make her pulse dance harder under Darcy's lips.

The sexiest mewl slipped from Elle's lips when Darcy sucked on the lobe of Elle's ear and tugged, teeth scraping her skin. The sound went straight to Darcy's core, making her ache.

"I— *Fuck*, Darcy." Elle shivered in Darcy's arms, body going tense, then pliant, sagging against the railing at her back.

Fuck, *yes*. Darcy slotted her leg between Elle's and rocked against her, delighting in the way Elle moaned, the sound vibrating against Darcy's lips, and traveling all the way down to her curling toes.

She wanted more. Wanted more of Elle's noises, more of Elle's lips against hers, hers against Elle's, the feel of Elle beneath her hands and between her thighs. She wanted to strip off the rest of Elle's layers and lay her bare, physically, the way Elle had been brave enough to bare her soul beneath this clear, starry sky. She wanted all of Elle—the good, the bad, the messy.

Elle's fingers, the ones that had crept under the cashmere of Darcy's sweater, her nails raking against the sensitive skin above the waistline of Darcy's jeans, pressed, pushing Darcy away.

Darcy stumbled backward, heart pounding. "Sorry."

"Shut up." Elle panted. Her fingers, those fingers that had pulled Darcy closer then pushed her away, slipped around the belt loops of Darcy's jeans, keeping her from fleeing farther. "You're just . . . *ugh*." Elle's head dropped back on her neck as she groaned, thumbs stroking the thin, sensitive skin over Darcy's hip bones. "You're impossible, you know that?"

The laugh bubbled up inside Darcy's throat unbidden. "Me? *I'm* the impossible one?"

"I dream about impossible things, remember?" Elle grazed a nail against the skin beneath Darcy's navel, making Darcy shiver. Elle's smile was somehow both wicked and sweet. "Come home with me."

Chapter Twelve

Please don't let Margot be awake. Please don't let Margot be awake.

It had occurred to Elle, as they pulled into the lot behind her building, that she should've suggested they go back to Darcy's. Darcy had no roommates, but Elle had blurted out the invitation and could hardly walk it back without fear of it coming across like she was walking it *all* back.

Which was absolutely not the case. Nowhere close, not now, when this nebulous relationship between them had finally started to take shape and become something real.

Twisting the key, Elle pushed the front door open and peered into the dark living room. All the lights were off, save the pineapple-shaped light on the breakfast bar, the one they always kept on in the evenings, no matter what.

Breathing a sigh of relief at her luck, Elle stepped farther into the apartment, waving Darcy in after her.

Darcy had been here before, but only once, and she hadn't stepped beyond the threshold. Now, her eyes made a curious sweep around Elle's Cracker Jack box–size living room. Every now and then she'd pause, alighting on various knickknacks scattered on surfaces, precious memories and mementos Elle and Margot had collected. Turnabout was fair play and all; Elle had definitely taken her sweet time getting acquainted with Darcy's spartan furnishings.

Elle's apartment was decidedly more colorful. And cluttered. A sushi-shaped pushpin holder rested precariously near the edge of the breakfast bar. Photos inside bright, Pantone-colored frames hung crooked on the walls and a cloud-shaped storm glass sat on the windowsill, small dots in the liquid foretelling foggy weather. A floor-to-ceiling tapestry of the zodiac wheel took up most of the wall beside the couch. Shoes were piled beside the breakfast bar, mostly hers, save for a pair of boots that belonged to Margot. Smack-dab in the center of the floor sat one lone sock, and Elle couldn't remember for the life of her how or why it had ended up there.

"I'm guessing you didn't just move in," Darcy said, smirking over shoulder.

"Ha ha." Elle smiled. "No. I've lived here . . . four years? Five?"

"With Margot?" Darcy asked.

Elle nodded. "With Margot."

Darcy's eyes darted around the space. She flicked the bobblehead astronaut on the bookshelf and arched a brow. "Where *is* Margot?"

Elle jerked a thumb over her shoulder. "Her room, probably."

Her stomach somersaulted when Darcy nodded and stepped toward her, thumbs tucked inside her front pockets. Casual, graceful, Darcy's footsteps didn't even wobble at she put one foot in front of the other, stopping about a foot away from Elle. "And your room is . . . ?"

Elle tugged at the lobe of her ear. "Also, down the hall. Not to be confused with the bathroom. Not that my bedroom looks like a bathroom. Just that you'd be in for a rude awakening if you somehow managed to confuse the two. Basically, everything's down the hall. It's small. My apartment."

"Can I see it?" Darcy asked, hand reaching up and tucking her hair behind her ear.

Elle toyed with the rings on her Neptune earrings. "My room?"

Taking one step closer, so close there was nowhere else for Elle to go, so close their toes bumped, Darcy set her hand on Elle's hip and nodded.

"Sure," Elle breathed. She covered Darcy's hand with hers, slotting their fingers together, and tugged, leading Darcy down the hall to the last door on the right. Feeling along the wall for the switch, she flipped the lights. Not the regular ones that were too bright, gross fluorescents that turned everything in the room an unflattering shade of blue and made her hair look green, but the strands of twinkling fairy lights she'd tacked up along the walls. They bathed the room in a warm, champagne glow bright enough to see, but dim enough to set a certain ambiance. Flattering as candles, but less dangerous. Mood lighting at its safest, not to mention cheapest. That, and hopefully they'd keep Darcy from spotting the mountain of laundry between Elle's desk and dresser that she had yet to fold.

Her concern was for nothing. Darcy didn't look around, definitely didn't judge. She was looking straight at Elle, lids low, her lower lip captured between her teeth.

Elle gripped her sleeve, rubbing the fabric between her fingers and her palm. "So. My room."

Darcy reached out and ran her hands up Elle's arms, over her shoulders, until her fingers rested on either side of Elle's neck. Beneath Darcy's fingertips, Elle's pulse pounded in an unmistakable display of nerves.

Not just nerves. Elle wanted her so badly her fingertips pulsed with the need to touch Darcy, skin burning with the desire to be touched in turn, but she didn't want to mess this up. *This*, whatever it was they were doing that Elle didn't know for sure, didn't want to risk asking because what if she didn't like the answer and—

"Hey." Darcy's thumb brushed along the underside of Elle's jaw, a gentle graze that made Elle shiver. "What are you thinking?"

What was she thinking? God, what *wasn't* Elle thinking? A flurry of half-formed thoughts zipped through her mind. What she wanted, what she hoped . . . so much hope her bones ached, her body too small, almost bursting with holding it inside. Her skin was too tight, hot, itchy, and she wanted to strip it off, strip herself down, let Darcy see the full shape of her heart, messy and imperfect and with a space carved out, a space she'd been aching to fill for so long but no one ever fit, their angles too sharp, too rough, puzzle pieces never lining up right with hers. Elle had been waiting, waiting for the right person to come along who fit inside the space, that space inside her heart carved out just for them. For her person, not a *perfect* person, but a person perfect for *her*.

A person she hoped just might be Darcy.

Elle turned her head and brushed her lips along the inside of Darcy's wrist. "You know, hoping I'm wearing cute underwear."

Laughter sputtered from Darcy's mouth, warm and bright, replacing the anxious swirl in Elle's stomach with a giddy sort of levity.

"I should be the judge of that, don't you think?" Hands still cupping Elle's jaw, cradling her face with a delicacy no one had ever treated her with, Darcy leaned closer until their noses brushed once, twice—

Patience wasn't a virtue Elle possessed. Surging up on her toes, she pressed her lips fully against Darcy's, smiling into the kiss, her stomach erupting in a kaleidoscope of butterflies when Darcy smiled, too.

Hands sliding back to tangle in Elle's hair, Darcy swept her tongue against the seam of Elle's lips. Elle opened, moaning softly when Darcy flicked the tip of Elle's tongue with hers, tasting, teasing.

The kiss was dizzying, her knees going stupidly weak stupidly fast. Screw sports cars, Elle had zero to sixty down pat. Fingers knotting in the hem of Darcy's cashmere sweater, Elle gripped her tight, swaying into her. She groaned when Darcy's tongue traced the roof of her mouth, sending tingles down her spine, her nipples pebbling against the wool of her sweater.

Gasping for air, Elle tore her mouth away and panted. "Can I take this off?"

Elle already felt bare, stripped down to hope and bones and the pulse inside her veins, raw from sharing on the astronomy tower and inviting Darcy over. It was only fair to strip Darcy down a little, too.

Darcy's head bobbed as she lifted her arms into the air, letting Elle tug the sweater up and over her head.

Gah. Darcy's bra was black, all delicate, sheer lace and thin straps that contrasted heavenly against her peaches and cream skin. A flush worked its way up her chest, skin mottling in sunset shades of pink and red, dark orange freckles dotting the swells of her breasts. Elle bit down on a whimper and dropped the sweater to the floor, hands hanging limply at her sides.

"Freckles and dimples and . . . damn it, Darcy." Elle panted. "You're so gorgeous you make my head hurt."

Her heart, too, in the best way. A good ache, the best ache. Anticipation married to a promise, satisfaction guaranteed, only a matter of time.

Darcy threw her head back and laughed, the move highlighting the long, elegant line of her throat. More skin Elle wanted to trace, taste, freckles she wanted to connect in constellations she'd never get tired of exploring, the freckle beside Darcy's mouth, Elle's favorite, the one she'd always come back to. Her new North Star.

"Dimples? They're caused by having a shorter than normal zygomaticus major muscle. It's a facial flaw."

Oh, please. "A sexy flaw."

Cheeks pink and eyes bright, Darcy reached one finger out,

curling it beneath the low V-neck of Elle's sweater. Her finger brushed Elle's bare skin right over her heart. "Fair's fair."

Elle reached for the hem of her sweater and yanked it over her head, freezing when the fabric snagged hard on her earring. *Perfect.* "Um. I'm stuck. Could you . . . ?"

Hands reached up the neck of Elle's troublesome fluffy sweater. Gently, Darcy freed Elle, then helped her tug the sweater the rest of the way over her head.

Hair mussed and bangs falling in her eyes, Elle blinked, flushing hotter as Darcy's eyes dipped, staring unapologetically.

Pupils blown wide, Darcy lifted her eyes. Her tongue, bubblegum pink and just as sweet, darted out, licking her lips. "May I?"

Yes, yes. A thousand times, yes. Elle nodded so fast her head spun.

Fingers danced up Elle's side, forcing her to bite back a giggle at the way it tickled, Darcy's touch too soft. The laughter stuck in her throat, transforming into a moan when Darcy cupped the small, braless swell of her breast, her thumb sweeping against her nipple, featherlight.

Her knees trembled and her back arched sharply into Darcy's touch. Her brain forgot how to make words entirely when Darcy dropped her head, lips skimming the skin stretched over her collarbone, and lower, trailing down Elle's chest, pressing wet kisses to her skin that led to the peak of her right breast. Darcy's lips wrapped around Elle's nipple, sucking gently, tugging with her teeth until Elle's skin went taut, pebbling. Darcy drew back and blew, the sudden rush of cool air against Elle's sensitive skin making her gasp and reach out, fingers tangling in Darcy's red hair.

One of Darcy's hands slipped lower, slid beneath Elle's skirt and between her thighs, cupping Elle over her leggings and damp underwear and pressing, rubbing with the heel of her hand, making Elle clench and mewl.

Before Elle could get any real relief, Darcy straightened and walked them both backward until Elle's knees hit the side of her unmade bed. Elle fell, bouncing against her mattress and sinking into the mess of soft blankets.

Darcy tumbled down after her, hands braced on either side of Elle, bracketing her head. She skimmed her nose against Elle's, breath fanning her mouth, making Elle's tender, kiss-swollen lips tingle. Eyes dark and lids heavy, those long, enviable lashes that had first caught Elle's eye on their disastrous blind date swept against the thin skin beneath Darcy's eyes as she blinked, throat jerking as she swallowed.

"Do you have any idea how long I've been dying to taste you?" Rhetorical, it had to be, the way Darcy's tongue darted out from between red lips turning the question into a confession. "It's all I can think about. Tell me I can. Please."

Fingers twisting in the sheets beneath her, Elle arched her back, pushing up into Darcy. The ache between her thighs intensified. "Fuck. Yes."

A relieved sigh slipped from between Darcy's lips as if she'd thought Elle might say no. As if there were a universe where Elle would *ever* tell her no.

Darcy slipped lower, lips skimming the hollow of Elle's throat, the space between her breasts, her hands ghosting over Elle's ribs, down her waist, her hip, along the curve of her thigh, goose-flesh prickling in the wake of Darcy's touch. Fingers tucking beneath the band of Elle's skirt and the leggings underneath, Darcy tugged, yanking the fabric over Elle's hips and thighs, down her calves and over her feet, her mismatched socks sliding off with them, inside out. Flung across the room and forgotten.

Naked save for the bright blue lace boy shorts hugging her hips—not as sexy as that unfortunate pair she'd lost after their first date, but close—Elle tried not to squirm. The room was warm, but a shiver skittered down her spine at the look in Darcy's eyes. A look that ignited a want inside Elle that made her dizzy with desperation even though she was lying down. "*Darcy.*"

Blinking fast, Darcy leaned over Elle, lips trailing a hot path down her torso, tongue dipping inside Elle's navel, making her squirm, hips dancing. Those kisses trailed lower, lips brushing the elastic band of Elle's underwear, teeth snapping the fabric before her fingers dipped beneath the waistband, tucking and curling. "Okay?"

Elle's back bowed, hips arching off the bed in silent invitation. Silently pleading for Darcy to *please* get her naked and do dirty things to her, things that would leave her boneless and breathless and blissed out beyond belief.

Taking the hint, Darcy inched Elle's underwear over her ass and down her legs. She shimmied between Elle's thighs, lowering herself to the bed, lying on her stomach against the mattress. Warm lips caressed Elle's inner thigh, laying down teasing kisses, Darcy's tongue darting out every so often to trace shapes on Elle's skin. Darcy gently nipped the crease of

Elle's thigh, a pleasant sting that drew a needy whimper from Elle's lips. One hand hooked Elle's right knee over Darcy's shoulder, spreading her legs, opening her wide.

Elle held her breath, chest growing tight as Darcy's breath ghosted over where Elle ached.

"Oh my god." Her neck arched against the bed at the first broad swipe of Darcy's tongue against her.

Darcy's breath was hot, her lips even hotter as she kissed Elle, openmouthed and eager, her tongue sliding through Elle's wetness, lapping at her entrance. Another desperate groan spilled from Elle's lips when Darcy wiggled her tongue, slipping inside Elle, her hands reaching down to cup Elle's ass, holding her to Darcy's mouth.

Elle scrunched her eyes shut, fingers clenching the sheets so hard she nearly tore them off the corner of the bed as Darcy licked a path from Elle's entrance all the way to her clit, two slender fingers replacing her tongue. Elle was so slippery with arousal that those fingers sank inside with ease, curling, pressing hard against Elle's front wall, making her thighs tremble and her tummy harden.

In a blink of an eye, those clever fingers of Darcy's slipped out of Elle, making her whimper at the loss. "*God . . . I—*"

Darcy leaned up on one elbow and brought her hand to her mouth, plump red lips enveloping her glistening fingers. Her lashes fluttered, lids lowering on a moan before they flickered open. Intense, brown eyes stared up at Elle, Darcy's lips curling in a devilish smile around her digits, a smile that made everything south of Elle's navel go painfully tight.

Slick with spit, Darcy slipped her fingers back inside Elle, adding another, Elle's walls gripping Darcy tightly. Trembling, Elle's back bowed, neck arching when Darcy splayed one hand against Elle's belly holding her down as she lapped at her clit, soft licks interspersed with openmouthed kisses.

Letting go of the sheets, Elle threaded the fingers of her right hand in Darcy's silky-soft hair. On a whim, she glanced down, breath catching in her throat at the sight of Darcy's brown eyes locked on her face.

Between that stare and the perfect feel of Darcy's mouth, Elle tipped over the edge, back bowing against the mattress, one hand clutching Darcy's head to her sex, the muscles in her thighs shaking as she came apart in slow, trembling convulsions that stole the breath from her lungs and made her chest burn.

A weak whimper fell from Elle's lips as she tugged even more weakly at Darcy's hair. Fingers pressing firmer than before, Darcy didn't back off, didn't let up even when Elle thrashed against the covers, just this side of too sensitive. Elle had barely recovered from her first orgasm when Darcy wrenched another from her, teeth scraping gently against Elle's sensitive clit.

An explosion of color flared against the black of her vision, a supernova bursting behind closed lids. Her back arched, a cry spilling from her lips, loud and unrestrained, nearly sobbing as Darcy licked her through it, the hand holding her down gently stroking the sweat-slick skin of her stomach.

Fingers untwining from Darcy's hair, Elle let her hand flop down against the bed. Darcy pressed a kiss in parting to Elle's clit and sat back on her haunches, a grin curling her mouth, lips shiny and chin wet, those dark eyes of her gleaming.

Fuck. Elle stared up at the ceiling, at where the stars stuck to her ceiling shone weakly, pale green light competing with the strands of fairy lights illuminating the room in a dim champagne glow. Her heartbeat slowed to something approaching normal, as her brain returned to her body, no longer rocketed to somewhere outside the stratosphere.

Darcy prowled up Elle's body, all lean muscles and mouthwatering curves. She was still only half naked, though the flimsy lace bra she wore did a poor job of concealing much of anything, the taut pucker of her dusky pink nipples visible beneath. Leaning over Elle, hands braced on either side of her head, Darcy dropped, nose nudging Elle's. "Good?"

Boneless and muscles composed of jelly, all Elle could manage was a weak laugh.

"I'll take that as a yes." Darcy grazed her nose against Elle's, lips brushing. Elle parted hers lazily, letting Darcy slip her tongue inside Elle's mouth. A moan slipped from her lips at the taste of herself on Darcy's tongue, warm musk and salty, tangy sweetness. *Fuck.* Elle opened wider, hands clutching the back of Darcy's neck, tugging her close, wanting another taste of herself on Darcy's lips.

Straddling Elle's thigh, Darcy's hips began to rock, riding her desperately.

Elle slid her fingers down the gentle curve of Darcy's stomach to pop the button on her jeans. The sound of the zipper lowering was loud in the otherwise silent room, but nothing compared to the gasp Darcy made when Elle slipped her fingers inside Darcy's undone jeans, fingers rubbing Darcy's clit through her underwear.

"Shit," Darcy swore, scrambling backward and tearing the denim down her thighs.

Of course, her underwear matched. Crisp black lines curved around her hips, a triangle of barely there lace covering her core, red curls trimmed neat beneath.

Elle's heart skipped several beats before crashing against her sternum. "Come here," she whispered, hands reaching for Darcy.

Darcy crawled back up the bed, legs straddling Elle's hips. Her hair spilled over one shoulder and down her back in a cascade of copper curls that Elle wanted to sink her hands into, so she did. Short nails scraping against Darcy's scalp, she drew her closer, close enough to kiss.

The hand not tangled in Darcy's hair slipped down her side, tracing the sinful curve of her waist and paving a path lower, fingers plucking at the thin band of Darcy's underwear, snapping it gently against her skin.

Hips circling, Darcy groaned into Elle's mouth, rocking against Elle's thigh.

Taking the hint, Elle slipped her fingers beneath the crotch of Darcy underwear and ran her finger along Darcy's slit. Sinking two fingers inside, Elle let her thumb brush against Darcy's swollen clit, lips curling in satisfaction when Darcy whimpered against Elle's mouth and circled her hips.

"Harder," Darcy whispered against Elle's lips. "Please."

Elle crooked her fingers, applying more pressure to the raised patch of nerves inside Darcy's slick heat, and thumbed her clit faster. "Like this?"

Darcy threw her head back, long hair tickling the tops of Elle's thighs as she straightened, riding Elle's hand. It gave Elle a perfect view of where her fingers disappeared, sinking inside Darcy's tight, wet heat. Shiny arousal slid down the back of her hand as Darcy rose and fell, fucking herself on Elle's fingers, starting slow and moving fast, desperate, soft cries spilling from Darcy's lips as Elle moved her thumb faster, harder, determined to make Darcy come as hard as she'd made Elle.

Gorgeous, Darcy was so unbelievably gorgeous. Sweat broke out along her neck and the space between her breasts. Leaning up on her left elbow, Elle tugged at the cup of Darcy's bra until it slipped, and closed her lips around Darcy's nipple, sucking hard, teeth grazing the pebbled flesh and making Darcy keen, thighs shaking as she came hard around Elle's fingers.

Stroking her through the aftershocks, Elle tried to gauge whether Darcy could keep going, whether she wanted Elle to get her off again. When Darcy reached a hand down, weakly pressing at Elle's wrist, Elle stopped, fingers sliding out of Darcy and splaying limply on the bed beside her.

Darcy rolled to the side, collapsing against the mattress, chest heaving, her legs tangled up with Elle's. Her skin was flushed, her bra and panties askew, and a slight sheen of sweat covered her skin from her hairline all the way down to her navel, which rose and fell, jumping in time with her pulse.

Elle licked her lips, suddenly parched. Reaching over to her nightstand, she unscrewed the lid on her bottle of water and drank deep, gasping lightly after she finished. Pivoting, she turned, bottle in hand, and stared at Darcy's wrecked form.

Hair sticking to her forehead and splayed against the pillow in a fiery halo, Darcy panted lightly, chest heaving and air whistling from between shiny red lips. Debauched, Darcy looked like Elle felt—a beautiful mess.

"You want some?" Elle swung the bottle by its neck, biting the inside of her cheek when Darcy snatched it and arched up, throat working as she chugged deeply until not even a drop remained.

"Sorry." Darcy laughed, collapsing back against the pillows. "If you wanted more of that."

Not a big deal. Elle tossed the bottle back on the nightstand where it rolled, landing against the floor. She'd pick it up later.

With a sigh, Elle lowered herself back down to the bed, muscles finally sinking into the mattress as she gave herself permission to go from person to amorphous puddle of goo. Or she did once she flipped over to her side, facing Darcy, who appeared to have finally caught her breath.

Reaching out, Elle rested a jittery hand on the dip of Darcy's waist and waited for her to roll away or say something that would cement the fact that Elle was never this lucky. But that didn't happen. Elle waited another beat for good measure, then paved a path from Darcy's ribs down to her hip, delighting in the way her clumsy touch managed to make Darcy shiver and burrow closer.

Kicking the covers free, Elle reached down and tugged the sheet over them both, cocooning them inside her warm, if not slightly small bed and slid closer, close enough for their knees to knock.

"Stay?" Elle whispered.

Darcy pressed her lips together, her eyes flickering over Elle's face, searchingly. Elle held her breath, hoping that maybe fate and the universe had conspired and decided she had waited long enough. That she could have everything she wanted and then some.

A dimple appeared in Darcy's cheek, bracketing Elle's favorite freckle as her eyes softened. "I can do that."

Chapter Thirteen

Whoever gave the sun permission to shine that bright needed to take several seats.

Elle scrunched her eyes shut against the midmorning sun streaming through the window beside her bed. Even then, a warm orange glow penetrated her lids, forcing her to burrow into the pillow. With an east-facing bedroom, she seriously needed to invest in some blackout curtains. The legit kind, not the ones she'd bought on sale off Amazon from a third-party seller that had one promising review that she was now ninety-nine percent certain had been written by the seller themselves.

Hadn't the sun gotten the memo that it was the weekend? That Elle had nowhere she needed to be, nothing she needed to do except laze around in bed and—

Bed.

Darcy. Elle had had sex with Darcy. Great sex, too.

Elle smothered her grin against her pillow.

Now with an incentive to face the day, Elle flipped over.

The other half of her bed was empty, the sheets pulled up to the pillow and tucked neatly beneath.

A quick glance revealed that Darcy's clothes were no longer lying on the floor, no longer tossed haphazardly across the room. Darcy was gone.

Pain bloomed between her ribs, jagged and sharp like someone had jabbed a knife into her side and wiggled until the blade found its mark. No good-bye, nothing.

People liked to say the definition of insanity was doing the same thing over and over again, expecting different results. Maybe Elle was crazy for expecting this time to have been different, for Darcy to be different. Maybe she'd lost her mind for assuming something real could come from a fake relationship, but last night had *felt* real. Standing up on the observatory and baring her soul to Darcy, Elle had felt seen in a way she never had before. Seen like there was something inside her Darcy recognized.

There was no word that existed in the English language that meant the opposite of *lonely*. Some came closer than others, but nothing did justice to the feeling of someone looking into your eyes and connecting with you on a soul-deep level.

A connection was what Elle craved. To see and be seen, then to take that one step further and for someone, for Darcy, to like what they saw enough to want to stick around and see more.

But Darcy hadn't stayed. For whatever reason, a reason Elle would probably never know because there was only so much rejection she could handle, so much battering her heart could take before the hope of something better could no longer sustain her. She'd confronted Darcy once before, but that had been *before*. When there'd been significantly less at stake. Darcy hadn't known Elle then; the rejection had barely been personal. To confront Darcy now, to demand to know why she'd left, why Elle hadn't been worth staying for . . . if Elle had to ask, wasn't it obvious?

No, she could take a hint.

Clutching the sheet to her bare chest, Elle bit down hard on the inside of her cheek. Vision blurring, Elle shut her eyes and sniffed hard because she didn't want to cry. Crying sucked.

She sniffed again. Someone in the building was cooking pancakes. At least it smelled like pancakes. Buttery, vanilla-sweet heaven. Either that, or her brain was self-soothing similar to how cats purred, manufacturing her favorite smells where there were none. Was that a sign of an impending stroke? A seizure? WebMD would tell her she had a tumor or some fatal one-in-a-million neurological condition.

Elle sniffed again. No, the smell was unmistakable, stronger each time she took a whiff.

She threw back the covers and rifled through her mountain of unfolded clothing, plucking a robe out from the bottom of the stack. Tying the sash tight, Elle stepped out into the hall to investigate further.

Margot was sitting at the breakfast bar and—

Darcy was in the kitchen, in *her* kitchen, wearing one of Elle's shirts, and she was cooking. There were pans and bowls and a spatula—since when did they own a spatula—and the whole apartment smelled like pancakes because Darcy Lowell was cooking inside Elle's apartment.

Darcy had stayed.

Because she couldn't just *stand* there, Elle cleared her throat, body flushing with warmth at the way Darcy's smile lit up her whole face when she looked at Elle. "Morning."

Darcy wrinkled her nose in that adorable way of hers that Elle loved, before turning and fiddling with one of the knobs on the stove. "Barely. It's after eleven."

They hadn't made it back to Elle's apartment until after one, hadn't fallen asleep until easily after two. Not such an egregious lie-in, all facts considered.

Margot spun on her stool, eyes widening as she mouthed the words *Oh my god*.

Elle tugged on the sleeve of her robe, bare toes curling into the carpet. Oh my god was right.

Margot shut her laptop and hopped down off the stool. "All right. I'm off. Don't have too much fun." She waggled her brows.

"Where you going? It's Saturday."

"Interestingly enough, I'm going rock-climbing with your"— she turned, pointing finger guns at Darcy—"brother."

Darcy's lips pulled to the side. "Oh?"

"Settle down. I won't say anything incriminating." Margot paused in the doorway. "Speed dating didn't go the way he planned, apparently, so he's got it in his head that maybe he needs to join a gym or something. Meet someone out in the wild. I offered to take him rock-climbing. I'll be back in a few hours." Margot slipped through the door. "Don't do anything I wouldn't do!"

Knotting her fingers in the sash of her robe, Elle stepped into the kitchen. "You're cooking?"

That Darcy hadn't left was a relief. Pancakes? Those were promising.

Darcy tucked her hair behind her ear. "It was either that or order in from Postmates and I don't know what's good in this neighborhood."

Elle stepped into the kitchen and sidled up beside Darcy, peeking into the bowl of batter. "Um, everything? It's Capitol Hill." At the sight of a short stack of pancakes sitting on a plate, Elle's mouth watered. "How are you even making pancakes? We don't have flour. Or eggs. Or milk. Or . . . whatever else you need for pancakes."

Reaching around her, Darcy grabbed a box of pancake mix. The corner was dented and there was a fifty-percent-off sticker slapped across the first half of the brand name. "I found this in the back of your pantry. The best-by date was last month, but I figured it's probably safe."

"I'm not concerned." Bracing her hands on the edge of the counter, Elle heaved herself onto the tile surface, narrowly avoiding putting her butt in the batter bowl. Once settled, she hooked a foot around the back of Darcy's knee, drawing her close. "You met Margot."

Darcy's fingers crept up the inside of Elle's thigh. When she reached the hem of Elle's robe, she walked her fingers backward, down toward Elle's knee. Elle blew out the breath she'd been holding. Such a tease. "I met Margot."

"And?"

Darcy tossed her hair over her shoulder and laughed. "And what? She's nice. A little scary." Darcy retrieved the spatula and flipped the pancake bubbling away in the pan with an expert flick of her wrist. The underside was the perfect shade of golden brown. "She made me pinky promise not to break your heart."

Elle shut her eyes. Damn it, Margot. Way to be the opposite of chill. "She was kidding."

Darcy turned, glancing over her shoulder. There was a hickey on her neck, a bruise in the shape of Elle's mouth, the sight of which made Elle flush from head to toe. "She sounded serious to me."

"Did she say what she'd do if you did?" Elle tore a piece off her pancake and popped it in her mouth. "Break my heart, I mean."

Darcy laughed, the sound light and bright. "I didn't ask."

The simple way Darcy said that, as if that outcome were unlikely, not worth worrying over, put a stupid smile on Elle's face. Leaning back against the cabinets behind her, Elle swished her feet, limbs weightless, gravity nothing in the face of the buoyant force swelling inside her chest.

"Anything else I should be aware of? You know, any torrid secrets Margot might've let slip?"

"Do you *have* any torrid secrets?"

"Depends on what you consider *torrid*, I guess," Elle joked. For the most part, she was an open book. But even the parts of herself she didn't broadcast she'd revealed to Darcy.

Darcy reached for the bowl and spooned a perfect pancake's worth of batter into the pan. Bubbles appeared around its edges. "We had a good conversation, actually. Margot's funny when she's not threatening me."

"A good conversation about what?" Elle didn't want to come out and ask if they'd talked about her, but she was dying to know what she'd missed. She could always ask Margot later, but she wanted to hear it from Darcy.

Facing the stove, her back toward Elle, Darcy shrugged. Her hair reached the top of her waist and Elle wanted to bury her fingers in it. "She was reading when I came in here, so I asked what. We talked about fanfiction."

"Fanfiction?" Had she heard that right? "Really?"

Darcy's shoulders stiffened. "What's wrong with that?"

Elle frowned at Darcy's defensive tone and brushed the crumbs off her leg. "Nothing. Margot writes it. She even admins a couple Facebook groups."

"She told me." With another flick of her wrist, Darcy added a pancake to the stack, replacing the one Elle had snagged. "Margot made it sound more mainstream than when I—"

Record scratch. "When you?"

Darcy glanced over her shoulder, not meeting Elle's eyes, but peeking in her general direction. "Nothing."

Like that would work on her. "When you what? When you—" *No fucking way.* "Darcy Lowell. Do you read fanfiction? Oh my god, what fandom? Do you *write* it? Is it smutty? *Please* tell me it's smutty. What's your—"

Darcy held up a hand. Her entire face was neon, her freckles blending into her flush. "I'm *not* telling you the name of anything I wrote. Margot already tried that."

This was too good to be true. *Darcy. Wrote. Fanfiction. Mind blown.*

"Come on. Don't I get"—*girlfriend* hovered on the tip of her tongue—"'I've seen you naked' privileges?"

Darcy arched a copper brow. "Seeing me naked *is* a privilege."

Elle slipped off the counter and sidled up behind Darcy. Gently, Elle brushed the hair off Darcy's neck and around her shoulder before leaning in to brush her lips against the knob at the top of Darcy's spine. When Darcy shivered, Elle grinned. "Lucky me."

Darcy reached out and flipped off the heat to the front burner. "Promise not to laugh?"

Hands drifting and delighting in the way her touch seemed to drive Darcy to distraction, Elle let her fingers dip beneath the hem of Darcy's borrowed shirt, teasing the skin over her hip bones. "Cross my heart."

"I mean it. No laughing or I'll leave."

Elle forced her face into the most earnest expression of sincerity she could muster and waited.

Darcy nibbled on her lip. "When I was in college, I wrote *Days of Our Lives* fanfiction."

Soap opera fanfiction. Elle beamed. "*Darcy.*"

"*Ugh.*" Darcy scrunched up her nose. "I told you not to laugh!"

Elle snagged Darcy by the wrist before she could turn away. "I'm not laughing. I swear. I'm smiling because I think it's cool and if it's something that makes you happy, well . . ." She shrugged. "It makes me happy for you."

Lips pressed together and eyes still averted, Darcy appeared to weigh the veracity of Elle's words. After a moment, the tension in her body bled away, shoulders dropping from where she'd had them hiked up to her ears. "Margot's not well versed on the *Days'* fandom, but she says there's this site that does a great job of archiving fics and keeping everything organized. She wanted my email so she can send me an invitation. Archive of Our Own?" Darcy shrugged. "Apparently the filters for searching for fics are unparalleled, but there's still a bit of a learning curve. She offered to show me the ropes. Give me a tour of the site. In case I want to get back into it. Reading, maybe writing."

Without even thinking, Elle brushed her fingers along Darcy's skin. "You should do it. You should *absolutely* do it."

"Well, I don't exactly have the luxury of loads of free time at the moment." Darcy rested a hand on Elle's arm, just beneath her shoulder. Her thumb made tiny circles against Elle's skin, tiny circles that summoned goose bumps. "Perhaps after I pass this last exam, I might consider it. If it's not too weird."

Darcy was barking up the wrong tree, seeking reassurances that her hobbies weren't odd. Or maybe the right tree. Elle wasn't quite sure. One thing stood out—Darcy didn't have the luxury of free time and yet she was here. She was here with Elle. That had to mean something, something big and undefined. As of *yet*, undefined. She smiled and shrugged. "I say you should go for it. Embrace the weird, Darcy."

Darcy slid her hands up Elle's neck, burying them in her hair. Tipping Elle's head back and leaning in, Darcy smiled and murmured against Elle's lips, the touch tickling, "Embrace the weird, huh?"

Before Elle could answer, Darcy covered Elle's mouth with hers, kissing her quiet.

Atop the counter, beside the bowl of batter, something buzzed. And kept buzzing. Darcy's phone.

Elle drew back and reached for it, wanting it to shut up so

they could keep kissing. She'd pass the phone to Darcy so she could—

Darcy had a fancy calendar widget Elle had never seen before, something that took organization to the next level. The current month and the next were visible from her lock screen. A notification near the top, *Finish C.E. Report*, wasn't what caught Elle's eye as much as the highlighted green text on December thirty-first. *EDT.*

Eastern Daylight Time? Eau De Toilette? Estimated Departure Time?

No, something about that acronym niggled in the back of Elle's mind. It meant something else.

Effective Date of Termination.

Termination Date. The agreed-upon end of their arrangement.

Elle's heart sank into her stomach like a lead weight.

Last night had felt real. *This* felt real, kissing Darcy and eating pancakes and sharing secrets. But what did Elle know? Not what did she *feel*, but actual irrefutable facts.

Nothing. Darcy had said nothing. She'd kissed Elle instead of answering her question last night, about whether Darcy believed in soul mates, whether that had changed. And maybe her not asking Margot what would happen if she broke Elle's heart had less to do with Darcy being optimistic about their relationship, and more about Darcy not believing they had one.

"Is everything okay?" Darcy's eyes darted to her phone clasped loosely inside Elle's hand.

Elle wasn't sure what to say. Elle wasn't sure of anything.

Chapter Fourteen

$\mathcal{D}$arcy's heart crept inside her throat, making it impossible to swallow.

Elle had gone pale, her face draining of color, that pretty flush on her cheeks fading as she stared down at Darcy's phone.

"Elle," she repeated, stepping closer and resting a hand on Elle's bare knee. Elle jerked and lifted her head, eyes going wide.

"Sorry." Elle shook her head and all but tossed the phone at Darcy. She tucked both sides of her peacock-print robe between her thighs, gaze dropping to her covered lap. "You, um, had a calendar notification. Didn't mean to snoop or . . . whatever."

Darcy's phone synced to her Outlook account; on any given day, she would have at least half a dozen calendar notifications. Meetings, appointments, lunch with Brendon, basic task reminders. Big or small, Darcy liked to be prepared, liked to know in advance exactly what her week looked like down to the hour. None of that was any reason for Elle to have suddenly gotten—

Darcy's eyes dipped down to the glaring green text, the only color on her calendar. *EDT*. No wonder Elle was upset.

It would be a lie to say the date hadn't been looming in the periphery of her mind. At first, after getting Elle to agree to go along with her ploy to get Brendon off her back, Darcy had counted down the days until she could drop the act. Until she could ditch Elle and go back to business as usual as intended. But that had been *before*, before she'd gotten to know Elle. Before Elle had crawled under her skin, burrowed even deeper. Somewhere along the way, when exactly she wasn't sure, in the back of the cab probably, it had stopped being an act. The attraction had been there since day one, but feelings . . . feelings Darcy hadn't counted on. Definitely not *these* feelings, a particular set of emotions Darcy had long ago tried to bury.

Deleting the reminder was instinctive. She wanted that ostentatious green text gone, wanted to rewind the moment and erase that look off Elle's face. Go back to how things had been before, before that terrible little notification had burst their bubble and injected reality into the fantasy world Darcy had immersed herself.

The moment remained fractured. Elle picked at a fraying thread on her robe with unsteady fingers, refusing to make eye contact.

Darcy needed to say something. She had never considered herself particularly skilled at this, verbalizing her emotions. Not because she struggled with eloquence but because she'd attempt to rationalize her feelings to the point of talking herself out of sharing them. In the past year, Darcy had done everything in her power to disconnect herself from them— most of them—altogether.

Two impulses warred within her, churning her stomach, turning her gut into a battlefield. There was the desire to tell Elle that she hadn't expected any of this, but here she was. Completely upside down, but Elle was a bright star lighting up the dark, keeping her from feeling entirely lost, entirely alone in this. That yes, this had started out as a fake relationship, but now these feelings felt anything but fake.

Darcy's tongue stuck to the roof of her mouth, words clogging in her throat, overpowered by the second impulse, the desire to never talk about why she hadn't wanted a relationship and was so resistant to Brendon's matchmaking, the reason that went beyond being busy. Most of the time she did everything in her power not to *think* about it. Saying it was out of the question.

There had to be a balance between saying something and revealing everything. She needed to find that happy medium, find it *now*, because the look on Elle's face was growing grimmer by the second.

"Brendon." *Fuck.* Her tongue really had adhered to the roof of her mouth. She swallowed and tried again. "Brendon's Christmas party. Do you . . . do you want to go with me?"

Her heart beat against her sternum like an angry kickdrum when Elle frowned. "I already said yes. That was part of our deal, wasn't it? You go to Thanksgiving with me and I go to the Christmas party and whatever else I needed to. To convince your brother."

Darcy was bad at this, rusty at sharing how she felt. She hated being bad at things, hated not knowing what she was doing, obvious in her ineptitude. She huffed, despising how her cheeks went hot, her feelings splashed across her face.

"I know that. *Obviously*, I know that. I meant." Darcy took a deep, shuddering breath in and stepped closer into the space between Elle's knees. "Do you . . . do you *want* to go? Forget the deal. Do you still want to go with me?"

Elle's head snapped up. "What?"

That her voice was barely above a whisper emboldened Darcy, made her heart beat harder, so hard it was as if it were trying to bust out of her chest and fling itself at Elle.

"I said, forget the deal, Elle." Darcy rested a hand on the outside of Elle's leg, gripped the warm skin of her thigh. Her pinkie grazed the soft, thin fold behind Elle's knee and she could've sworn she felt Elle's pulse jump. "That's not why I want you to go. Not anymore."

Elle's tongue darted out from between her lips. She blinked twice and her shoulders rose and fell on a sigh, breath pancake-sweet. "Why?"

Because she couldn't stop thinking about her. Because she'd had plans, very specific plans not to enter into a relationship, but Elle made her second-guess every last one. Elle made her want things she wasn't supposed to want, not right now, not for God knows how long. Until she was ready? Darcy didn't know when that time would come but here Elle was. And Darcy was right here, too. Wanting and hoping and being terrified of it all but not willing to let Elle go.

"I don't know what I'm doing, Elle." Immediately, Darcy lifted a hand, clutching her neck. Her throat wasn't the only thing left raw by that confession.

Elle's lip popped free from her teeth, her mouth falling open. She could do this. She could be brave, be as brave as Elle. "I don't know what I'm doing, but this doesn't have anything to do with Brendon. Not anymore. I'm . . . I'm not ready for this to be over." Darcy didn't want to wake up to a world where Elle didn't text her, where there wasn't the promise of seeing Elle again, of hearing her laugh. Being the reason for it. "I'm not ready to say good-bye."

Not in one month or two. Maybe not ever.

Behind her, the refrigerator hummed. Elle was disconcertingly quiet as she stared at Darcy, eyes wide and mouth agape. A fresh wave of heat crept up Darcy's jaw as she waited for Elle to say something. Anything to put her out of her misery.

"Oh my god," Elle muttered. "You like me?"

What kind of question was that? That it was even a question at all was absurd, the most absurd thing to ever come from Elle's mouth and that was truly saying something considering the number of strange, unfiltered thoughts she shared.

Wasn't it obvious? Written all over her face? "You sound surprised."

Elle made a noise somewhere between a laugh and a scoff and kicked at Darcy's leg, missing by a mile. "I *am* surprised."

"Really." Darcy gave Elle her best deadpan stare. "That thing I did with my tongue last night didn't clue you in?"

Her words had the desired effect. Elle's face turned scarlet as she shut her eyes and laughed. Fighting her own smile would've been futile, and in keeping with the theme of the morning, Darcy wasn't in the mood to deny herself. When it came to Elle, Darcy truly was a hedonist.

Elle gave a tiny shrug after she'd calmed down. "But you never actually said it and . . . I don't know. Plenty of people have hookups where they don't particularly know the other person, let alone like them."

She wasn't wrong, but that's not what this was. Darcy had had hookups like Elle had described, and this was nothing like that. Not even close.

"This is different. This is—" Approaching a line she wasn't ready to cross. "I don't cook breakfast for just anyone, you know."

Or spend the night. Or talk about her mother. Or share her fondest memories. *Sharing*, period, was something Darcy seldom did these days.

"Lucky me," Elle said, reaching for the plate of pancakes. She snagged two off the top and brandished the plate in Darcy's direction with a wrist wiggle. "Care to partake in the fruits of your labor? They're extra yummy." As if to make her point, Elle stuffed half the pancake in her mouth. "*Sweriously.*"

Darcy bit the inside of her cheek and took the plate from Elle, setting it down beside the stove. Then she grabbed Elle by the hips and pulled, yanking her near the edge of the counter. She stepped into the cradle formed by her thighs and brushed her lips along Elle's jaw, humming in satisfaction when Elle shivered in her arms. "I don't want pancakes."

Chapter Fifteen

December 5

MARGOT (9:43 P.M.): <link>

DARCY (9:55 P.M.): Is there a reason you sent me a compilation video of Greatest Soap Opera Slaps of All Time?

MARGOT (10:02 P.M.): Elle and I are watching soap operas on YouTube and I fell down the rabbit hole.

DARCY (10:03 P.M.): Oh god.

MARGOT (10:04 P.M.): You ever watch Passions?

ELLE (10:05 P.M.): omg there's a soap with a witch Darcy

ELLE (10:05 P.M.): her name is *Tabitha* omg

ELLE (10:06 P.M.): this is the best

DARCY (10:10 P.M.): There's a crossover connection with Bewitched, actually. Tabitha claims to be the daughter of a witch named Samantha and a mortal named Darrin.

In a later season, she has a daughter who she names Endora. Dr. Bombay makes a few appearances which suggests that Passions and Bewitched exist in the same universe.

ELLE (10:11 P.M.): #obsessed

MARGOT (10:11 P.M.): Elle just made a weird choking noise and keeps muttering oh my god.

DARCY (10:12 P.M.): Did you try turning her off and turning her on again?

MARGOT (10:12 P.M.): Jesus. Nerd.

MARGOT (10:12 P.M.): You're as bad as your brother.

MARGOT (10:13 P.M.): You're just closeted. A closeted nerd.

MARGOT (10:14 P.M.): Btw turning Elle on is your job. Ugh.

DARCY (10:43 P.M.): Was I supposed to sort by kudos or hits on AO3? I can't remember.

MARGOT (10:47 P.M.): Kudos if you're looking for quality. You strike me as the type who's picky about her word porn.

DARCY (10:48 P.M.): 😳 Excuse me for being concerned about proper grammar and punctuation.

MARGOT (10:49 P.M.): You're excused. Elle's texting must drive you up the wall.

DARCY (10:52 P.M.): It's fine. I don't mind.

ELLE (10:54 P.M.): awwwww

ELLE (10:54 P.M.): you dont mind my texting shorthand

ELLE (10:55 P.M.): wud u still lik me if i typed lik this

ELLE (10:58 P.M.): darcy?

ELLE (11:03 P.M.): DARRRRRCCY

MARGOT (11:05 P.M.): Idea! You should write a Passions x Bewitched crossover fic. I'll beta it for you.

MARGOT (11:06 P.M.): You'll get like 2 kudos and 6 hits because there's no audience for something that niche, but I'll love it and so will Elle.

DARCY (11:08 P.M.): Maybe.

ELLE (11:10 P.M.): you should do it!

ELLE: (11:11 P.M.): 11:11 make a wish!

ELLE (11:13 P.M.): <attached selfie of Elle pouting>

ELLE (11:13 P.M.): Please do it.

DARCY (11:15 P.M.): Fine. Only because you said please and used proper punctuation.

ELLE (11:16 P.M.): 🙌 🎉 🍑 🍑 ♣ ♣ ♣

DARCY (11:18 P.M.): Good night. 😊

ELLE (11:19 P.M.): 😘

DARCY (11:28 P.M.): 🙂

✫ ✫
✫

December 6

ANNIE (2:43 P.M.): Elle requested to follow me on Instagram. Should I accept?

DARCY (2:56 P.M.): I don't care.

ANNIE (2:58 P.M.): Just wondering if it was crossing a line or something.

ANNIE (2:58 P.M.): Since, you know. It's fake.

ANNIE (3:01 P.M.): You didn't tell me Elle was so pretty. She's freaking adorable. That group shot your brother posted didn't do her justice.

DARCY (3:06 P.M.): About that. It's not fake.

ANNIE (3:10 P.M.): Wait. What?!

DARCY (3:15 P.M.): It's not fake. It's complicated.

ANNIE (3:20 P.M.): Oh my god. You had sex. You slept with her.

ANNIE (3:21 P.M.): I fucking knew it.

ANNIE (3:24 P.M.): It was good, yeah? It must've been.

ANNIE (3:29 P.M.): <link>

DARCY (3:32 P.M.): Did you really just send me a link to Baby Got Back?

DARCY (3:34 P.M.): I rue the day I ever got a cell phone. I'm at work and everyone I know keeps texting me. I forgot I had my volume on and I tried to play that video and now my coworkers are staring at me like I'm a freak.

ANNIE (3:39 P.M.): 😂

DARCY (3:40 P.M.): Annie!

ANNIE (3:43 P.M.): Oh boo hoo. You have friends who like talking to you. People care about you. Your coworkers know you listen to music other than fucking Chopin. Wah. Poor Darcy. 😭

DARCY (3:46 P.M.): It's a hard knock life.

ANNIE (3:47 P.M.): Oh fuck you very much.

☆ ☆
☆

December 9

ELLE (2:08 P.M.): so annie and i were discussing your aesthetic earlier this morning and we think 70s style jumpsuits should be your new thing

ELLE (2:08 P.M.): you have the height to pull them off

ELLE (2:09 P.M.): granted going to the bathroom might be a bitch but you'll look sexy while you struggle

DARCY (4:15 P.M.): Since when do you talk to Annie? Let alone about me?

ELLE (4:27 P.M.): annie and i go waaaaay back to last tuesday

ELLE (4:28 P.M.): catch up

ELLE (4:29 P.M.): jumpsuits yay or nay?

DARCY (4:31 P.M.): May . . . be?

ELLE (4:32 P.M.): 😂

☆ ☆
☆

Darcy!"

She tore her eyes from the *Passions* x *Bewitched* fanfic she was drafting in Google Docs on her phone and searched for the source of her name. There, sitting on one of the couches in the center of her apartment's lobby, was Gillian. *Her mother.* What was she doing in Seattle, let alone her apartment building?

"Mom?" Darcy crossed the lobby, stopping in front of her

mother who clasped her arms with cold fingers and buffed a
kiss across each of her cheeks. Darcy's nose wrinkled at the
cloying scent of nicotine and Yves Saint Laurent Opium that
clung to Mom's hair, so pungent Darcy could taste it. "What
are you doing here?"

The colorful enamel bangles on Mom's left wrist jingled as
she released Darcy. "Have you done something different with
your hair?"

"No?"

"Huh." Mom laughed. "It looks different. Good, but different. You look great."

"So do you." Darcy raked her eyes over Mom's outfit.
It was Darcy's style, but the yellow floral maxi and brown
leather jacket looked nice on Mom. "But you didn't answer
my question."

One hand on Darcy's back, Mom silently ushered her in the
direction of the elevator. "Why don't we head upstairs?"

Darcy held her tongue until after the elevator spit them out
on the ninth floor. "So. What brings you to Seattle?"

"Your brother's Christmas party is next weekend." Mom
surveyed Darcy's apartment for the first time with a specula-
tive tilt of her head. Her wall art received an interested hum,
her furniture a none-too-subtle frown.

"Does he know you're already here?"

Mom gave a quiet huff of laughter and plucked a book off
the shelf, scanning the cover before placing it back out of order.
When Elle had touched Darcy's things, at least she'd put them
back where they belonged. "I would imagine he does, seeing as
I'm staying in his guest room."

Why was she just now hearing about this? Brendon hadn't said anything at their lunch yesterday. "When did you get into town?"

Mom chuckled. "God, Darcy, what's with the third degree?"

It wasn't every Tuesday that Mom showed up at her apartment unannounced, but when she did, it spelled trouble. As much as Darcy wanted to believe this was nothing more than a surprise visit, that maybe Mom wanted to catch up, see how Darcy was settling into a new city, ignoring history would be foolish. Mom didn't check in and she didn't stop by for the hell of it. She made time for Darcy when she needed something— occasionally a place to stay for a night's layover, quick cash when her latest ex screwed her over, most often someone to dump her emotional baggage on.

Every time, Darcy vowed to put a stop to the cycle and every time, she caved. Annie—because she couldn't talk to Brendon, not about this—encouraged her to establish clear boundaries or else one day she'd snap from the pressure. It wasn't healthy and it wasn't fair, but what in life was? She had learned the meaning of resiliency when she managed to muscle through, shoulder a little more of Mom's baggage.

She ran her fingers over the waist of her skirt, fidgeting with the tuck of her blouse. "You want a drink, Mom?"

Darcy escaped to the kitchen, assuming the answer would be yes.

"Since when do *you* drink boxed wine?" So much for an escape. Mom stood in the doorway, frowning.

And apparently, she was the one who asked too many questions?

Turning, Darcy reached inside the cabinet and grabbed two glasses. She snagged the bottle of red closest to her and tugged on the cork, quickly filling both glasses before adding an extra splash to hers for good measure.

"It's not mine." She offered Mom a glass and slipped past, leaving the kitchen. "A friend left it here."

"A friend?" Mom asked, aiming for nonchalance and missing by a landslide.

Taking a generous sip, Darcy set her glass down on a coaster and sat on the far end of the sofa closest to the window. "Yes, Mom. I have friends."

Mom perched herself on the other end of the couch, pinching her glass tightly by the stem. "Well, go on. I want to hear about this *friend* of yours."

Her brow wiggle passed suggestive, entering into lewd territory.

Darcy acted like she hadn't spoken. "So. You're staying with Brendon."

Mom hauled her purse onto her lap and rifled through the inner pocket. "No hard feelings, I hope. I called him to pick me up from the airport and he offered his guest room, so . . ."

With a crow of satisfaction, she withdrew a cigarette and lighter from her purse.

"You can't smoke in here," Darcy said.

Cigarette hanging from the side of her mouth, Mom waved Darcy off. "Oh what? Like your landlord's ever going to find out if I—"

"I don't want you smoking in here." Yes, it was a building policy, but it was also a Darcy policy. One she wouldn't budge on.

Mom tugged the cigarette from her mouth and gestured to the wall of windows. "What if I crack a window?"

Jesus. "We're on the ninth floor. The windows are floor to ceiling; they don't open."

With a huff, Mom threw the cig and lighter back into her purse, which she then tossed on the floor. "Okay, *Mom.* Jeez, I never raised you to be such a tight-ass."

Darcy bit the tip of her tongue, swallowing her retort. Mom had barely raised Darcy at all.

"So you're here for Brendon's Christmas party. You must be planning to fly home around the same time as Brendon and me."

"About that." Mom tucked one leg up on the couch, turning to face Darcy.

Ah, the *but.* It had only been a matter of time, a matter of how long Mom was going to beat around the bush before she came out with the real reason why she was here. Not only in town, but at Darcy's apartment, on her couch, guzzling her wine down like it was water, and gripping the stem of her glass so hard Darcy worried it would break.

"I was thinking we'd have Christmas here this year," Mom said. "Save you and Brendon the trip."

"We already have tickets."

Mom opened her mouth only to pause. She took a deep breath and smiled tightly on the exhale. "Your brother canceled those."

Darcy's brow furrowed. "He didn't say anything."

"I asked him not to." She scooted closer, sliding across the cushions. "I wanted to tell you myself. Preferably in person."

Darcy's pulse stuttered then sped. "Is everything okay? You're not—"

Mom rested a hand on top of hers. "Everything's fine. God, you worry too much." She reached up, poking the space between Darcy's brows. "It's gonna give you wrinkles one of these days."

Darcy batted her fingers away. She worried for good reason. "Then what is it? Why aren't we having Christmas in San Francisco?"

"Well, that would be hard to do," she said, "seeing as I'm selling the house."

"You're selling Grandma's house?" Darcy's voice nearly cracked, so she coughed.

Mom squeezed her fingers. "It's just a house, Darcy. A house your grandmother hasn't lived in for years. A house, quite frankly, you haven't lived in for years, either."

It wasn't just a house. The three-story Victorian with its steeped, gabled roof and bright, stained glass and broad bay window was full of memories. It was weekends spent baking scones and slathering them with homemade strawberry jam and afternoons curled up on the sofa watching soaps with Grandma. It was creaking stairs and an ornate bannister Brendon had broken his arm sliding down when he was eleven. It was summer nights on the porch swing under a blanket and slumber parties with Annie.

To Mom it was a house, but to Darcy it was home.

Darcy twisted the platinum band on her middle finger. "*Why*? Do you need money because I can—"

"It's just time for a change."

"What if you rented it? That way if you change your mind—"

"I won't change my mind." Mom gave a sardonic laugh, lips twisting in a way that said there was more to this story than she was letting on. "I'm selling it. I'm moving. End of story."

"Fine." It wasn't, but what else was Darcy supposed to say? It wasn't her house, and while she had a nice nest egg put away, it wasn't enough to buy a house in San Francisco.

"Darcy, baby, you're not usually this sentimental." Mom patted her on the arm.

Darcy covered her flinch by reaching for her wine. "I said, it's fine."

Mom heaved a sigh. "Your brother and I are planning on looking at houses this weekend."

Darcy's head snapped to the side. "Here? You're planning on moving here?"

"Well, I don't know where exactly." Her head waffled side to side. "Mercer Island, maybe. Somewhere close to the water. Doesn't it remind you of the Bay?"

Something did *not* compute. "If you're looking for something that reminds you of the Bay why are you moving?"

Mom pressed her fingers between her brows. "Darcy. Can I not want to move closer to my children?"

Darcy stared.

"Fine." Mom dropped her hand and sighed. "Kenny and I broke up."

Of fucking course this was about a guy. When *wasn't* it about Mom's latest flavor? "Ah."

"Yes, *ah*." Mom huffed. "And where did he decide to move to? He's renting an apartment two blocks away. I see him all the time." She reached for her wine and nearly drained it. "I'm sure you of all people can understand what I mean when I say I need distance."

Mom had effectively backed Darcy into a corner. Because what could she say? She'd packed up her life and moved all the way to Seattle after . . . after she'd broken off her engagement with Natasha. Been *forced* to break off her engagement. It wasn't so much a choice as an act of self-preservation. She wasn't going to go through with it, not knowing what she did. And staying in Philadelphia had been too hard, her life there too integrated with Natasha's to make for an easy break. It had been messy, their group of friends entirely assimilated. Darcy hadn't just wanted a fresh start, she'd needed one.

"Sure." Darcy nodded. "I get it."

Except she had learned her lesson, whereas Mom clearly hadn't. She bounced from relationship to relationship, building her life around whoever she was seeing. She didn't know how to just *be*, let alone be alone and so she'd move on to the next guy until the pattern repeated itself and she wound up with a broken heart. Again.

The corners of Mom's mouth lifted. "I thought you would." Her veneer of happiness was flimsy at best, her smile not reaching her eyes. "Brendon and I are going house hunting this Saturday, then we're grabbing drinks and a show at Can Can. You should come with us. You could use a little fun in your life."

She might not begrudge Mom her attempt at a fresh start,

but house hunting with her? *Drinks?* Darcy could already feel a tension headache forming at the base of her skull. "We'll see. I might have plans."

"Plans?" Mom wiggled her brows. "With a friend?"

Darcy reached under her chignon and jabbed her fingers into the space where her head met her neck. "Yes, Mom. A friend."

"The same friend who leaves cheap wine in your kitchen?"

A strange surge of protectiveness rose up in Darcy's chest. "Honestly, Mother?"

"You *mothered* me." Mom stared, dark eyes wide. She lifted a hand, lightly stroking the front of her throat. "Brendon told me you were seeing someone and that it was serious but I couldn't believe it. Looks like I owe him twenty bucks."

She wouldn't quit. Darcy clenched her teeth until her molars creaked. "Brendon doesn't know what he's talking about."

"So it isn't serious?" Mom pressed.

"Why do you *care?*"

Mom's eyes widened. "Darcy, I'm your *mom.*"

"Yeah, well, you could try acting like it." The words were out of her mouth before she could stop them. "Mom—"

"No." She sniffed and smiled tightly, eyes wet with tears unshed. "It's nice to know what you really think. You're always so tight-lipped with your feelings around me. Tight-lipped, tight-ass." Mom scoffed out a laugh. "It's fine."

The barb barely stung, the slick feeling of guilt swimming in Darcy's stomach winning out. She meant what she'd said, but that didn't mean she wouldn't undo it, press rewind if she could. "Look, me and Elle . . . it's complicated, okay?"

"Complicated?" Mom's brows flew to her hairline. "Darcy,

baby. That doesn't sound good. Haven't you had enough of *complicated*?"

Her spine stiffened. *This* wasn't like *that*, and she had enough with Brendon meddling. She didn't need Mom nosing in, too. "That wasn't an invitation to give your two cents."

"Not the answer to my question. But I can take a hint." Mom stood and reached inside her purse, withdrawing her cigarette and lighter. "I'll get out of your hair, but just let me say this. Your brother . . . he's like a rubber band. He's got an immense capacity to love and his highs are high, his lows low, but he always snaps back. His heart is elastic. You and I, we're more alike than you want to believe. But it's true.

"When we feel things, we feel them deeply, all the way to our bones. We don't snap back like your brother, and our hearts aren't made of elastic. They're breakable, and once broken, it's difficult to piece them back together." She lifted her head and stared at Darcy with wide, shiny eyes. Darcy wasn't good with tears, not hers, not anyone's. Definitely not Mom's. She was all too familiar with those.

Darcy found it hard to swallow. "Mom—"

"I know. You don't want to talk about Natasha any more than I want to talk about your father, and I understand that. I do. You were ready to spend the rest of your life with her and that's no small thing. Natasha broke your heart and while I'm sure Elle's nice—Brendon seems to think she is—do you have any business getting involved in something that's *complicated* this soon after you've put yourself back together, Darcy?"

Cold settled in Darcy's chest, her stomach heavy and hard.

"Which isn't to say you should spend the rest of your life

alone." Mom waved her hand, dismissing the thought. "Life is short and you deserve to have fun. But you're sensible, far more sensible than me and for that I'm thankful. I'm only suggesting that our hearts can lie. You have a good head on your shoulders, baby. Use it."

Natasha had checked all her boxes, was all the things Darcy thought she wanted. They'd made sense together. She was a safe, sensible choice and Darcy had been ready to spend the rest of their lives together. It had never, for one second, crossed Darcy's mind to fear that sort of betrayal before it happened, before she saw it with her own eyes. Even knowing what Mom had gone through, learning that Dad had cheated on her during those long business trips, and how Mom had drunkenly told her love was a lie more times than she could count, Darcy hadn't believed it could happen to her until the day it did.

Was she right? Were they more alike than Darcy wanted to believe? Here she was, supposed to be dedicating her time to passing this FSA exam and instead she was carving out time, carving out a space in her life, for Elle, free-spirited Elle who couldn't have been less like Natasha if she tried. Elle was all she could think about half the time and it was more than just *fun*, it was—

God. It was times like these, Darcy would do anything to have just five minutes to talk to Grandma. She'd give it to Darcy straight, tell her if she was behaving irrationally, if she was in danger of losing her head. Grandma had been the only person to get Mom back on some semblance of a track in life and Darcy, for all she tried, couldn't do the same, not alone. It was too much, the weight of it crushing.

But Grandma wasn't here and soon her house would be gone, too.

Darcy's nails bit into her skin when she crossed her arms. "While I appreciate the concern, it's unnecessary." She crossed the room in the direction of the door, hoping Mom would get the hint. "Since we're doing Christmas at Brendon's this year, did you at least pack Grandma's ornaments?"

Mom frowned, cigarette poised halfway to her mouth. "Those old things? Darcy, they were falling apart. I donated everything in the boxes in the basement. They *reeked* of mothballs."

Darcy's heart seized. They weren't *old*, they were one of a kind. Delicate lace angels and hand-carved nutcrackers. Felt trees and mercury glass globes. They were *tradition* and *family* and Mom had tossed them out without a second thought.

Darcy opened the door with sweaty fingers and stepped aside.

"You're not upset with me, are you?" Mom rested a hand on Darcy's shoulder as she passed by, her cigarette tickling her neck.

"I'm—" Darcy shook her head. "Good night, Mom."

As soon as the door was shut, Darcy pressed her back against it, sinking slowly to the floor.

Talking to Mom was like speaking to a brick wall and expecting it to understand, to *empathize*. But Darcy needed to talk to *someone* or else she was going to go crazy.

Who? Normally she could talk to Brendon about anything— *almost* anything—but certainly not this. Annie was still in Berlin, working on behalf of her company, an independent human resources consulting firm, to facilitate a corporate merger. It was just after seven, which meant it was the middle of night there. Then there was—

No one. She'd done an admirable job of accomplishing what she'd set out to do—isolate herself. Before this moment, she'd never realized what a lonely job it was, protecting a fragile heart.

Darcy clutched her phone, staring at her contacts. No. *Not* no one. She had the phone pressed to her ear before she could second-guess herself.

"'ello," Elle's voice came through the line, so vibrant and happy it made Darcy ache inside. "Darcy?"

She sniffed as quietly as she could, covering the receiver. "Hey." Her voice quivered, but held, flimsy but unbroken.

The line was quiet, the sound of Elle's breathing a near-silent whistle. "What's up? Let me guess, can't stop thinking about me, can you?"

Darcy laughed, the edges of her self-control fraying, thinning, split in too many directions. Elle had no idea how right she was. "Something like that."

"You know, this is the first time you've called me."

Darcy took a shallow breath. "I hate talking on the phone."

Elle chuckled. "And yet you called? You could've texted."

She scrunched her eyes shut. "I hate talking on the phone but I—"

Wanted to talk to you. Elle was the exception to so many rules it made her head spin.

"Darcy?"

"Sorry." She had to clear her throat. "I just— My mom's here."

She could hear Elle shift, fabric, a blanket maybe, rustle. "Right now?"

"No, I mean, *yes*. She's in town, but she was at my apartment. She just left, but she'll be here through Christmas. She's, um, she's selling my grandmother's house. No questions, just like that. She's selling the house and she got rid of the Christmas decorations and . . . and I just wanted to . . ."

She trailed off, not because she didn't know what she wanted but because she did. She knew what she wanted but she didn't have the slightest idea anymore what she needed. If they were one and the same or polar opposites.

Elle cursed quietly beneath her breath. "God, Darcy. Are you okay?"

"I'm—" It was there, on the tip of her tongue. *Fine*. Darcy always had to be fine, always had to be okay, because if she wasn't, who would be? She always had to hold it together, be strong, keep her chin up. But she wasn't. She was anything but fine. "Not really."

Two words and she split straight down the middle, her voice breaking and her chest cracking open, all the feelings she'd kept compartmentalized, carefully tucked inside boxes set neatly on a shelf deep within herself, spilled out. Messy overflowing feelings seeped out in the most inopportune places, eyes leaking and nose running. *Fuck*.

"Darcy—"

"Sorry," she said, hating how her voice quivered. "I didn't mean to call and dump all over you."

"You didn't." Elle sounded sincere, vehement even, her voice a firm contrast to Darcy's weak *everything*. "You didn't dump all over me. I swear."

Nice of Elle to say that, but it wasn't true.

"Still." Darcy swiped a hand across her face, the heel of her hand coming back smeared with mascara and smudges of brown and cream eyeshadow mixed with her concealer. "It's getting late. I just couldn't talk to Brendon about this and I—" She needed to stop. She had no business making herself more vulnerable than she already was and especially not to someone like Elle, someone who Darcy had no guarantee would be a permanent fixture in her life. She'd make herself vulnerable, crack herself open, and . . . then what? "You know, I should let you go. I should . . ." Darcy scrunched her eyes shut, shoulders bunching by her ears because this was awkward as hell. "Bye."

"Wait, Darcy, don't—"

Darcy pressed end and let her phone fall against the floor, her head knocking against the door with a muted thud.

Ears ringing, Darcy played over everything she'd said, her memory unfortunately practically perfect. Mortification set in, her skin itching and stomach churning.

Perhaps Elle would pretend this hadn't happened. Perhaps they could act like Darcy hadn't called and gone all soppy, spilling her guts all over the place. Perhaps Darcy could change her name and number and move to a small village in the south of France. She could eat enough butter and wine that the humiliation wouldn't matter.

Changing her identity might take some time, but she could get a jump start on the wine. Rolling to her knees, Darcy stood and filled a fresh glass with the cheap, cloyingly sweet boxed rosé because it made her think of Elle and apparently, unbeknownst to her until nearly her thirtieth year on this planet, Darcy was a masochist. The more you know.

☆ ☆
☆

Sitting in the middle of her kitchen, pencil skirt hiked up around her waist for comfort, Darcy polished off her second glass and was reaching for her third when someone knocked on her front door.

Brendon. Darcy shut her eyes. Mom had probably blabbed to him about how poorly Darcy had taken the news. Now she was going to have to do damage control, smoothing over her emotions, sweeping them under the rug. Prove to Brendon that she was fine, that while she wished Mom wasn't selling the house, it hadn't affected her in whatever way Mom claimed.

Ready as she'd ever be, Darcy adjusted her skirt and reached for the knob. As soon as she opened the door, she was greeted with a face-full of plastic pine needles.

"Sorry! Shit, it's slipping. Let me just . . ." The branches pressed against Darcy's face moved, revealing a harried-looking Elle. Blond hair fell free from the messy bun at her nape, and sweat glistened at her temples, her breath coming out in haggard little puffs. "You mind if I . . . ?"

Darcy clutched the—tree? bush?—and let Elle step past. Arms wrapped around a bursting cardboard box, the flaps flipped up and bent to the sides because the contents were brimming over the top, Elle waddled in the direction of the windowed wall where she bent and set the box down with a grunt. "*Fuck*, that was heavy."

Darcy kicked the door shut, plastic pine needles biting into the skin of her biceps. "What is all this?"

Elle's eyes bounced between the box at her feet and Darcy. "It's a good thing you called me when you did. One Man's Trash is only open until eight on weekdays. I managed to slip in right before they closed." She nudged the misshapen box with the toe of her boot. "It was kind of slim pickings this far in the season, so the ornaments are . . . *eclectic*."

Darcy set the tree down beside the box and stared blankly at Elle's haul, trying and failing to make sense of what this was.

"As for the tree." Elle winced. "There were only two, but the other was ginormous. Like, couldn't fit my arms around it even if I tried . . . which, okay I did try. It didn't work. I could actually carry this one and fit it in the back of the Uber I took here. It's a little"—Elle shut one eye and stared at the pile of disassembled branches—"like a shrub. But I think it has a certain charm. A je ne sais quoi, you know?"

Darcy pressed her knuckles to her mouth. "But . . . why?"

Elle scuffed her toe against the floor, then seemed to think better of it, quickly toeing her way out of her boots, hobbling when she nearly toppled over. Her pajama bottoms—Christ, she was wearing *PJs*—were too long, tucked halfway under her fuzzy-socked feet. Darcy's stomach swooped and then disappeared altogether.

"You said your mom got rid of your grandma's holiday decorations, so I just thought . . ." Elle shrugged. "I guess I didn't do much actual thinking. You could've already had a tree and ornaments, or Brendon might've, but I wanted to make sure you had *something*. I know the tree is kind of ugly, and none of the ornaments match but if—"

"It's perfect," Darcy whispered. Her eyes stung, her sinuses burning with each rapid, tear-stifling blink. "It's really perfect."

Too perfect. *Scary* perfect because nothing this good could last forever. It never did.

Elle's smile didn't just light up her face, it lit up the whole room. "Yeah?"

Darcy stepped over the tree and grabbed both of Elle's hands in hers. Elle's fingers were frozen, so Darcy laced them with hers and drew her closer. Elle slid forward, her pajamas gliding against the hardwood, their toes bumping. Darcy used Elle's forward momentum to her advantage, ducking her chin and stealing a kiss, lingering. Just a little more, for a little while longer.

Chapter Sixteen

I think it looks . . . nice."

Elle cocked her head, studying the tree, not that there was much tree to study. The branches were twiggy and the needles sparse. None of the ornaments matched—a glittery Barbie-pink Jeep hung beside a camouflage snowflake, and several branches down a cranberry-filled snow globe bumped up against a felt stocking and a hideous papier-mâché elf. But at least the tree had come prestrung with lights, none of which were burned out.

Darcy must've pressed a button on the switch because the amber-colored lights flickered, and suddenly, the room was bathed in a rainbow of colors. Pink and teal and orange and violet bulbs winked from the branches like little colorful pin-pricks of light.

"That's—"

Darcy threw her head back and laughed. "I love it."

For someone who had a seemingly bottomless well of hope to draw from, Elle was *hopeless* when it came to Darcy. Hopeless in that there was no cure for how she felt. Hopeless in that, each time Darcy laughed as if taken by surprise by her own joy, Elle's insides turned to marshmallow fluff. Hopeless in that she wanted to make Darcy laugh so often that the novelty of elation would wear off, but that it might never lose its appeal. Elle was hopeless and she didn't *want* a cure.

She tugged on Darcy's sleeve, yanking hard as she knelt in front of the tree. "Come on. Get down here."

Without so much as a single gripe, Darcy lowered herself to the floor and looked at Elle with one brow raised as if to say *now what*?

Leading by example, Elle scooted backward toward the tree and then lay flat when she had just enough clearance to do so without bumping her head. Wiggling beneath the lowest branches was a precarious feat, but she did so without knocking a single ornament.

Staring up at the brightly lit branches didn't quite have the same appeal as it did when she was a kid, probably because these branches were relatively bare, but it was still nice. Especially when she scrunched her eyes and the lights twinkled like stars. Even nicer when Darcy joined, snuggling close and tangling their fingers together.

"Didn't they do this on *Grey's Anatomy*?" Darcy whispered.

Elle huffed softly. "Yeah, but I did it first. I used to make Jane and Daniel crawl under the tree with me. Drove Mom crazy because we'd ruffle up the tree skirt and get pine needles all over the place."

"Brendon and I never crawled *under* the tree, but I remember trying to climb *up* it once."

Elle sputtered. "*What?*"

"Well, we forgot the star on top." Darcy's shoulder bumped against hers when she shrugged. "I guess I saw it as a wrong I needed to right and Brendon was smaller so I sort of . . . shoved him up there."

"Was he okay?"

"Of course." Darcy sniffed. "I'd never let him fall. Besides, Grandma caught us when he was barely off the ground."

Elle laughed, stomach muscles burning at the mental image of a little Darcy shoving Brendon up a Christmas tree to place the topper. Plastic pine needles from the lowest branch tickled her nose, a renegade needle managing to go *up* her nose. A suspicious burn built in her sinuses and *no*. It would be the worst if she—

Elle sneezed, catching a face and mouthful of pine needles. On second thought . . . "Maybe if we're going to talk, we shouldn't do it under the tree."

Darcy hummed her agreement and wiggled out from beneath the tree first. When they were both free and clear and leaning against the sectional, she bumped Elle gently with her elbow. "Thanks. Not for encouraging me to climb under a secondhand tree that could be full of, I don't know, bedbugs, but—"

"Oh my god. Lighten up, it doesn't have—"

Darcy pressed a finger to Elle's lips. She was smiling. "I'm kidding. About the bedbugs, not my appreciation. It means a lot that you came, let alone *thought* to bring the tree and decorations, and then to actually do it?" She shook her head, but didn't drop her hand. Instead, she traced the bow of Elle's mouth with the pad of her fingertip, so gently Elle could feel the delicate friction of each ridge and whirl in Darcy's finger-print.

Elle shivered and kissed the tip of Darcy's finger because she could.

Breath speeding and eyes darkening, her pupils widening—or maybe that was just a trick of the light—Darcy dropped her hand, not to her lap, but to Elle's knee. Warmth from her palm sank through the flannel of Elle's pajamas. "I, um, I hope I didn't mess up any plans you might've had."

"Plans," Elle echoed, eyes dropping to her pajamas. She hadn't bothered to throw on more than a jacket—*the* jacket—after Darcy had hung up. She hadn't seen the point, not when it had felt like time was of the essence. That Darcy needed her, needed her right then. "I was just messing around, making memes. I wasn't busy."

"Can I see?"

"Seriously?"

Darcy simply stared, waiting.

Elle fished out her phone, the LED light flashing with a notification. Another text from Daniel and two missed calls from Mom. Her chest went tight as she ignored them both and opened the note she'd made, the one she'd finished in the Uber on the way over. She passed it to Darcy, watching, lip trapped between her teeth as Darcy read down the list.

The Zodiac Signs as Christmas Songs

Aries—"Jingle Bell Rock"
Taurus—"The Twelve Days of Christmas"

Gemini—"Merry Christmas, Happy Holidays"
Cancer—"I'll Be Home for Christmas"
Leo—"All I Want for Christmas Is You"
Virgo—"The Christmas Song"
Libra—"Walking in a Winter Wonderland"
Scorpio—"Baby, It's Cold Outside"
Sagittarius—"Santa Baby"
Capricorn—"White Christmas"
Aquarius—"Do They Know It's Christmas"
Pisces—"Last Christmas"

"'White Christmas.' Are you kidding me?"

"What's wrong with 'White Christmas'? Everyone loves that song. It means you wrap your Christmas presents with the precision of one of Santa's elves. Or Martha Stewart. And you probably buy into charming, old-fashioned traditions like mailing handwritten Christmas cards and roasting chestnuts or something. Whereas Margot and I hide a pickle in a plastic tree and I take the fairy lights off my wall and repurpose them for a month."

"Well. Not everyone loves that song. *I* don't."

"How? It's about snow."

"Exactly." Darcy nodded. "And I hate snow."

Elle covered her mouth. "*What*? How? Why? Darcy, who hurt you?"

Darcy wrinkled her nose. "Have you ever spent thirty minutes scraping ice off your windshield?"

"That's ice, not snow. Snow is pretty."

She stuck out her tongue. "Oh please. For all of ten minutes before it turns into gray sludge that refreezes into black ice that's responsible for twenty-four percent of weather-related vehicle crashes, injuring over seventy-five thousand and killing nearly nine hundred annually."

That was depressing and yet, something about Darcy's ability to rattle off random statistics—morbid as they were—was oddly hot. Disconcerting competence porn. "Bah fucking humbug. I'll change your song." Elle snatched her phone back. "How do you feel about 'You're a Mean One, Mr. Grinch'?"

"Funny." Darcy's face didn't so much as twitch, but her eyes had a bright twinkle that belied her deadpan expression. "I'm not a grinch because I don't like snow. San Francisco *never* gets snow, or at least it hasn't in my lifetime, and the weather's rather temperate. The year I moved to Philadelphia, we had four snowstorms in the span of one month. And it was freezing." Darcy shivered as if just thinking about it gave her a chill. "I hate being cold."

Elle leaned into her side. "Is that why you're always trying to get me to wear a jacket?"

"Not that I don't like seeing your bare skin, but it makes me cold just looking at you." Darcy smiled, looking at Elle from the corner of her eye. "You can keep 'White Christmas.' I *do* like traditions, especially holiday traditions." She stared at the tree with its oddly colored lights, her throat jerking on a hard swallow. "I know ornaments are just . . . *things*. Twine and felt and glass and—it feels a little ridiculous to be upset about Mom getting rid of them, but I am."

Elle's attachment to material items had always been more fleeting, her most precious keepsakes few and far between and more likely to be photos than anything else. But that didn't mean she didn't understand. "They were . . . physical embodiments of memories. It's not ridiculous to be upset, Darcy. Whatever you feel is justified, okay?"

Darcy nodded. "That's exactly it. It's the memories. Those ornaments were all one of a kind and priceless and we even had these fragile glass balls with each of our names written on them in gold paint. It's a wonder they never broke." She huffed. "Came close, though."

"Climbing the tree?"

Darcy shook her head. "No, it's silly."

So far, all of Darcy's most silly secrets and stories had been revelations. "Tell me."

Darcy licked her lips. "I was . . . twelve? I think I was twelve, or maybe I was about to be. Brendon was either seven or eight. We had this tradition where we'd bake cookies with Grandma. Always thumbprint cookies and we used homemade jam. Strictly strawberry." Darcy's lips curled in a smile. "We'd set out the cookies and a glass of milk beside the fireplace for Santa. Dad would slip downstairs and drink the milk and eat a few cookies. Until that year, when I was twelve, Dad was gone on business. He was flying in that night, Christmas Eve. I didn't believe in Santa anymore, but Brendon still did, so I lay in bed waiting for Dad to come home so he could drink the milk and eat the cookies but eleven o'clock became midnight became one then two then three and he still wasn't home. I guess his flight got delayed."

"Did he make it in time? For Christmas?"

Darcy shook her head, a forlorn smile on her face like she

was remembering the disappointment. "For Christmas, but not to be Santa." She choked out a laugh. "*I* was Santa that year. After three o'clock, I snuck down the stairs, extracareful to not make any noise since I swear to God, every step creaked. I inhaled six cookies and then I reached for the milk only to remember we put dairy milk out because Dad's not lactose intolerant, but I am."

Her eyes widened, seeing where this was going. "*No.*"

Darcy grimaced. "I didn't know what to do. I was twelve and trying to be sneaky. I grabbed the glass and was going to head into the kitchen and pour it down the drain when I thought I heard someone on the stairs. I panicked, chugged the milk, and ducked behind the tree. One of those glass ornaments fell, but in the best twist of fate, it hit my slipper, which cushioned the landing. I hid there for at least twenty minutes before sneaking back upstairs. Brendon was fast asleep and none the wiser. And I lay in bed with stomach cramps for the rest of the night." Darcy's smile went fond and her voice dropped to a whisper. "But Brendon believed in Santa for another year, which was all I cared about."

Elle could picture it perfectly. A too young Darcy sneaking around behind Brendon's back. She was still doing it, still taking care of him, even now.

Elle bit the inside of her cheek to get a handle on herself. "You really love him, don't you?" She laughed. "I mean, duh. Of course, you do. I just meant, I love my brother and sisters, and as contentious as things between us can get, I know they love me, too. But I can't imagine any of them going out of their way to do anything like that for me."

Darcy shrugged. "I learned about Santa too soon when I was six and realized Santa used the exact same gift tags as Mom and Dad. I wanted Brendon to believe as long as possible. With Dad gone half the time and Mom either traveling with him or being obvious about how she wished she was, it wasn't much, but it felt like the least I could do."

There was nothing small about it. Darcy didn't do the bare minimum, she went above and beyond, more than any sister should feel obligated. Driving him to school, fixing him dinner, making sure he believed in magic for just a little while longer.

Darcy glanced at Elle and squeezed her knee, smiling softly before turning back to the twinkling Christmas tree. It was a quick look, but in that brief moment when their eyes met, something rearranged itself inside Elle's chest, all her *maybes* becoming *certainties*, her anxious musings about what this was and what it meant, resolved.

Darcy was sitting there, lips pursed so prettily, completely lost in thought, oblivious to how the earth was teeter-tottering under Elle, shifting and turning and spinning her around like those nauseating teacups at Disney she rode each time she visited without fail, because apparently, her memory was a fickle friend.

But Elle wouldn't forget this, her ass falling asleep from sitting on Darcy's floor, her heart stuttering and speeding, mind spinning, and her stomach swooping.

She swallowed, her mouth suddenly dry. "You take care of your brother. You take care of everyone. Who . . . who takes care of you?"

All she could think about was the night she'd sat on her floor beside Margot after that disaster date. Hopeless and raw, and so damn tired. How she'd decided to pack it in, take a break, quit looking for love and let it find her.

Boy, had it ever.

Something like panic flashed in Darcy's eyes, a fleeting, frantic flicker. She shook her head slowly, shoulders sagging, mouth opening and shutting before a desperate laugh that sounded almost like a sob burst from between her lips. "You're doing a pretty good job of it."

No one had ever said that to her before. Elle had never been put in the position of caring for someone, not really, not beyond a weekend of babysitting. Margot was too headstrong for it, and no one else trusted Elle enough to let her take care of them.

Stomach jittering like it had the first time she'd seen a meteor shower, watched while celestial debris fell from the sky, Elle reached out, cupping Darcy's jaw. She turned Darcy's face toward her and leaned in, brushing a kiss against her mouth that immediately made her stomach drop like she was one of those stars, falling, falling, *gone*.

Quitting grad school and pouring herself, heart and soul, into Oh My Stars hadn't been easy. Making that leap into the unknown had been *terrifying*, but it had always felt right, because she wasn't one to settle. She wanted *more*. This, kissing Darcy beside the rainbow lights of a Christmas tree with more heart than pine needles, was the closest Elle had ever come to experiencing real magic, the kind that sparkled inside her veins and electrified her from the ends of her hair to the tips of her toes.

Hands drifting, Elle sneaked her thumbs beneath the fabric of Darcy's untucked blouse, needing skin, needing more. She traced her nails over the thin skin on Darcy's hip bones, making her suck in a quiet breath.

Darcy drew back, lashes fluttering as her gaze immediately dropped to Elle's mouth like she already missed kissing her. Maybe Elle was giving that look more credence, maybe it was just a look, nothing more, nothing less, but speculating made her heart pound.

"Elle, I—" For a moment, Darcy looked utterly and completely lost and all the more terrified for it. She blinked twice, her breath shuddering from between parted lips that twitched into a smile. "We should go to my room." Darcy reached out, fingers tracing the plains of Elle's face, each brush of her fingers driving Elle's need for her up a notch. She wanted her touch, wanted Darcy to touch her everywhere.

"Oh yeah?" Elle let her fingers drift to the hem of Darcy's skirt. "What for?"

Fingers brushing the soft skin of Darcy's inner thighs as she slid the fabric up her legs, Elle bit the inside of her cheek to keep from smiling when Darcy practically panted. *Skin*. Now Elle was biting her cheek for a whole other reason. Darcy was wearing stockings, the band of her lace only going so far.

Eyes slipping shut, Darcy's tongue darted out to wet her bottom lip. "*Elle*."

She leaned in to Elle's touch, hips pressing into Elle's hand like she was trying to get closer. Elle slipped her hand higher, fingers dipping inside Darcy's underwear and through her curls until she found her clit.

Darcy let loose the softest, greediest little moan as her nails bit into Elle's arm, her hips rocking against Elle's hand, squirming. Darcy slipped down until she was no longer resting against the couch but instead splayed against the rug. She glanced up at Elle from beneath heavy lids and thick, dark lashes, and the hungry look in her eyes robbed Elle of the air inside her lungs.

"Kiss me," Darcy panted and used her grip on Elle's arm to pull her down to the floor on top of her. She kept her there with both arms banded around Elle's shoulders.

Leaning in, she nipped the swell of Darcy's lower lip. Ghosting her mouth over Darcy's chin, Elle slipped lower, trailing kisses down her throat, tongue darting out every so often to taste the silk of her skin. When her lips reached Darcy's neckline, Elle sat up on her knees and grabbed the hem of Darcy's blouse.

Darcy leaned up and helped her strip it off. Once her top was gone, Elle took a minute to appreciate all the new skin on display. Her bra was pink and polka-dotted and sheer. Her nipples pebbled against the fabric, begging for attention.

Elle ducked her head and laved her tongue against Darcy's right nipple through the delicate lace, teeth closing around it and biting gently, then harder when Darcy's hand flew to the back of Elle's head, fingers tangling in her hair and holding her there, encouraging her with little whimpers. Drawing back a bit, Elle blew against the pebbled flesh, grinning when Darcy's hips bucked, her back arching.

"*Elle*, God." Darcy's groan verged on praise, nails raking against Elle's scalp and sending tingles down her spine. "Your mouth. You're killing me."

Darcy's head pressed back against the rug, her hair splayed out around her, the copper a stark contrast against the plush, white sheepskin. Her back curved, bowing sinfully, her hips arching up off the floor the best they could with Elle straddling her thighs.

Skimming her lips down Darcy's stomach, Elle fumbled for the zipper on Darcy's skirt, finding it tucked away against the side of her hip. She lowered it, the sound of the zipper's teeth loud, making the moment feel a little more charged. Her fingers slid beneath the waist of the skirt, and tugged, yanking the stretchy wool over Darcy's ass and down her thighs. Darcy wiggled, helping Elle slide the tight fabric off the rest of the way, down her calves and over her slender feet, her polished toes visible through her thin stockings.

Fuck. Darcy was . . . pretty beyond belief would be putting it lightly.

She wore a black garter belt, suspenders attached to the flesh-tone stockings ending midthigh. Elle swallowed and traced a finger beneath the thin, satin suspender, snapping it gently, the subtle sting, or maybe just the sound, making Darcy gasp.

Darcy was apparently impatient because one of her hands slipped between her legs, touching herself over her underwear.

"No." Elle batted her hand away and leaned in, kissing the skin where Darcy's leg met her body. "I'm taking care of you, remember?"

Darcy's breath sped, rasping between her lips, and she dropped her hand to the floor.

Elle sucked at the skin on Darcy's inner thigh until her muscles quivered and a sharp gasp slipped from her lips. "*Elle.*"

She stared at the skin she'd turned bright red. As far as un-expected turn-ons went, she had not expected the bright red bloom of a love bite on Darcy's thigh to get her hot. But the thought of Darcy walking around the rest of the week with a mouth-shaped bruise—*Elle's* mouth-shaped bruise—beneath her pristine dresses and perfectly tailored pants was undeniably sexy. Their little secret, proof that Darcy might looked pulled together, but Elle had the ability to unravel her at the seams and turn her into something soft and messy to be taken care of, too.

Darcy wiggled against the floor and keened softly, hips arch-ing up off the floor.

Tearing her eyes away from the mark she'd left on Darcy's skin, Elle kissed her way up Darcy's thigh and over, lips skim-ming the edge of Darcy's underwear. Tapping Darcy's hip so she'd raise her hips, Elle tugged the fabric over her ass and down her thighs, letting Darcy kick them off the rest of the way. She got comfortable between Darcy's legs, reaching out, thumbs parting her folds. Darcy was soaked, glistening with arousal, her thighs sticky damp when she tried to rub her legs together.

Elle exhaled, breath ghosting over Darcy, and then leaned in and ran her tongue up Darcy's slit, moaning softly at the way she tasted. Darcy's hips jerked, pressing closer to Elle's mouth.

Elle rocked her hips down, grinding into the rug, seeking friction, *something*, anything to take the edge off as she wrapped her arms around Darcy's thighs, holding her down, holding her open. She flicked the tip of her tongue against Darcy's swollen clit, hard and fast, before wrapping her lips around the bundle and sucking it between her lips, adding just the subtlest edge of teeth to the mix.

"Fuck." Darcy's fingers threaded through Elle's hair, tugging hard enough to make her scalp tingle. The feeling shot through her, making her wet. "More. *Please*."

Ignoring the heat between her thighs, Elle sucked harder and moved her tongue faster, sliding one hand up Darcy's thigh. A soft, satisfied mewl slipped from Darcy's lips, her heat clenching as Elle slid her fingers inside Darcy and curled them forward.

"Oh my—fuck." Darcy tossed her head to the side. The muscles in her stomach twitched as she rocked down against Elle's fingers.

Positive Darcy was close, Elle curled her fingers harder, faster, and—

Darcy's back arched, her thighs trembling against Elle's shoulders, as she clenched hot and wet around Elle's fingers. A gasp broke from between her lips followed by a low moan that set Elle's blood on fire.

She withdrew her fingers, moaning softly when Darcy continued to spasm with aftershocks. She kissed the hickey she'd left and rolled to the side, head pillowing on Darcy's thigh.

Darcy's fingers massaged Elle's head, nails raking gently against her scalp. Despite being more turned on than she could remember being, Elle savored the moment, committing it to memory. All of it, the quiet, the peace, the anticipation, the way Darcy's white decor served as the perfect backdrop for the rainbow lights shining from the naked-looking tree. How for the first time, everything in her life felt not just right, but perfect.

☆ ☆
☆

"*Margot*," Elle called out, dropping her bag by the door and leaning against the wall. After the night she'd had, she could barely feel her legs and her arms weren't much better. "You home?"

Margot popped her head out of the kitchen. "Hey. Have fun?"

"You could say that." Elle skipped around the bar, making a beeline for the kitchen. Darcy had plied her with pancakes—not from a box—but she was still hungry. Little sleep and marathon sex would do that to a girl.

She opened the refrigerator . . . the *empty* refrigerator. Save for a jar of pickles and a Tupperware container full of Taco Bell hot sauces they collected because of the funny sayings on the packets, they had nothing. "Mar, we need to go shopping."

Margot rifled through their basket of assorted K-cups and plucked out an extrabold, dark roast. The kind that made Elle jittery just from inhaling the aroma. "Want me to pick a few things up while I'm out?"

Elle shut the fridge and leaned against it, frowning. "You're going somewhere?"

"Yeah. My stupid fucking computer is practically a relic, you know? It went all *blue screen of death* on me yesterday so

Brendon offered to go shopping with me for a new one. He's busy with his mom this afternoon, but said he had some time this morning."

"Don't take this the wrong way, but I find your friendship with Brendon mildly terrifying."

"How can something be mildly terrifying?"

"Shut up. You know what I mean."

Maybe it was a consequence of this thing between her and Darcy starting out disastrously, then fake, but Elle had been wary of spending too much time with Brendon outside of their work dealings. What if she let something slip, something incriminating that might blow the whole charade? Hopefully now that she and Darcy were real, *achingly* real, she and Brendon could become closer. Like he and Margot who were suddenly best buds, their shared love of Doctor Who and rock-climbing giving them plenty to bond over in addition to the partnership.

The Keurig beeped, Margot's coffee finished brewing. She snagged her cup and lifted it to her mouth, blowing on it gently. "We *barely* talk about you and Darcy."

"But you *do* talk about us."

"Only in the sense that Brendon moons over you guys and pats himself on the back for, quote, *orchestrating the match of the decade*. I, of course, make fun of him for saying the words, *match of the decade*." Margot gulped her coffee even though it had to be scalding. "Then he gets all wistful for a relationship of his own. Let me tell you, Brendon might be more of a romantic than you are. He looked offended when I told him he needs to get laid."

"Uh, pot, kettle?"

"It's a dry spell, Elle."

Elle coughed. "*Drought.*"

Margot reached across the counter into the sink, scooping up a handful of soap bubbles and flinging them at Elle, missing by a hair when she ducked. "I hopped on Tinder and this guy legit thought that being pansexual meant I'm attracted to fucking nonstick cookware. 'Oh yeah, baby, your griddle fucking turns me on. You shake that wok. Shake it harder.'"

Elle chortled. "That's not funny."

"I joke so I won't commit fucking homicide." Margot snatched a towel and dried off her hands. "Just because I'm not looking for something serious doesn't mean I don't have standards for who I sleep with."

Elle knew how Margot felt. At least half her matches on dating apps, before she met Darcy, were couples looking for threesomes, thinking because she was bi she'd be into it. Dating, regardless of the type of relationship you were looking for, was hard.

"You keep your standards high." Elle nodded resolutely. "They make vibrators for a reason."

Margot's tongue poked into her cheek. "When in doubt, rub one out?" Margot sighed and slouched against the counter. "You think it would be awful if I hopped on OTP?"

Elle grimaced. While not *expressly* against the terms and conditions of use, OTP wasn't the app for hookups. It didn't stop people from using it for flings, but the purpose of the app was to help people find their *one true pairing*, not their one true one-night stand.

"Don't let Brendon know."

"God no." Margot laughed. "He'll give me that *I'm disappointed in you* puppy-dog frown and I'll hate myself for at least an hour."

"At least." Maybe it was because she was tired from staying up half the night doing delightfully dirty things to Darcy on her living room floor, but for the first time, Elle noticed an arrangement of pink stargazer lilies—her favorite flower. She always stopped to *ooh* and *ah* over them at the market, but paying thirty dollars for something that would die in a week—sooner probably thanks to her black thumb—felt egregious. "Where'd those come from?"

Margot shrugged, trying so hard to come across nonchalant that she seemed the opposite. "Check the card."

She plucked the fancy embossed card from the plastic pick sticking up between the lilies' velvet soft petals. "Did you read it?"

"Mm-hmm." Margot reached for her coffee. "Go on."

The way Margot was acting made her hesitate. Who was it from? She'd just been with Darcy half an hour ago; unless she had a florist on speed dial—which hey, knowing Darcy—it seemed improbable the lilies were from her. But who? Only one way to find out. Elle flipped the card open.

Elle,

~~Jane and I have both texted and you haven't responded, but you're still posting on insta so we feel~~

pretty confident you haven't died. Jane just told me that
was a shitty joke and I shouldn't have started with that
but I'm writing in pen and I spent six bucks on this
card so

Jane and I hope you're doing well. That meme about
Mercury retrograde was funny as fuck and Jane just
got mad at me for writing fuck but I thought you'd ap-
preciate

The card started over, this time in Jane's looping handwriting.

Hey Elle,

Daniel and I wanted to send you these flowers as a
belated congratulations on your deal with OTP! We're so
happy for you, little sister.

Daniel's slanted, choppy scrawl picked up.

Little sister? Could this sound more Stepford?

A smudge of ink marked the transition.

We're sorry for what happened on Thanksgiving, but
more than that, we're sorry for not realizing how you felt
sooner. You're our sister and we should have realized you
were hurting.
You've never not been good enough, Elle. We're both

amazed by how fearlessly you pursue your passions and how you don't let anyone's opinion stop you from doing what feels right. You're an inspiration and I'm so happy that Ryland and the twins will have you to look up to when it comes to always following their dreams and their hearts.

Daniel had once again stolen the pen.

~~Solid sentiment, corny execution, Jane.~~

Elle could imagine Jane standing there, hands on her hips, the perfect imitation of their mom save for the twitch at the corners of her mouth.

The next bit was cramped, Jane running out of room to write.

Daniel and I owe you dinner to celebrate, just the three of us, unless you want to bring Darcy. Who we really like by the way.

Daniel put in his two cents.

~~Definitely. Just between us, we like her better than Marcus, but don't tell Lydia we said that. Hand to God, if he mentioned his Lamborghini one more time, I was going to flip my shit at the table. His car gets eleven miles per gallon. Weird flex, but whatever.~~

Jane's exasperation shone through in the way her words were a little bolder, as if she'd pressed the pen into the card hard.

I'll give you a call and we can plan something. Answer, please!

Love you bunches,
Xoxo Jane and Daniel

P.S. I looked up my natal chart online, and apparently my moon is in Leo. That's good, yeah? You give friends and family discounts, right? –D

Oh god, someone was absolutely cutting onions in the next apartment. Elle sniffled and laughed and shrugged when Margot cocked her head.

"You gonna take them up on dinner?"

"As far as apologies go, that was basically perfect. Which kind of pisses me off because of course Daniel and Jane would make the perfect apology." Elle rolled her eyes, but was mostly kidding.

As hurt and irritated as she'd been, she hated the tension, hated not answering their texts and calls, but she'd reached her breaking point on Thanksgiving. Daniel and Jane acknowledging her feelings was a weight off her shoulders, the validation more of a relief than she could have expected. Not everything was magically resolved, but it was a start.

Margot stared over the rim of her mug. "How about your mom? Still avoiding her?"

"I'm not avoiding her." Elle pinched a velvety petal between her fingers. "I'm ignoring her calls. There's a difference."

Margot frowned. "Elle—"

"Don't *Elle* me like that, like you're disappointed." Elle tossed the card on the counter. "All Mom's messages have been *business as usual*. Asking if we're still on for brunch. If I'm coming to the next family dinner. It's like Thanksgiving never happened and I can't do it. I can't keep acting like nothing happened. Like I'm not hurt."

"You need to talk it out. Just the two of you. It's good you finally said something, but you barely scraped the surface of the issue, babe, and nothing was resolved. I'm not saying you should act like it never happened and I'm not saying you need to forgive her unless you feel so inclined, but you can't keep sending her to voice mail. What are you going to do when it's Christmas? Have another fight where nothing gets fixed? Not talk?"

She shrugged. "I don't know. I'll figure it out when the time comes."

Margot sighed. "And you don't feel like this is avoiding the situation?"

Elle didn't say anything.

"Fine." Margot set her cup in the sink. "We won't talk about that. Let's talk about this dinner with Daniel and Jane. Are you going to take Darcy?"

She didn't know. She'd just gotten the card. She hadn't thought about it, hadn't had *time* to think about it. "Maybe? If she has time."

The holidays were hectic enough; add in Darcy's mom drama and studying for her FSA exam . . . Elle didn't want to push.

It's why she'd bitten her tongue last night when she'd been

tempted to rainbow vomit her feelings all over Darcy. Caring about someone, *loving* someone, wasn't supposed to be a secret, it was meant to be shared. That was the beauty of it, the whole point, only Elle couldn't imagine a confession of that magnitude going over well this soon, not when they had yet to even define their relationship.

Not that Elle was worried. Not *really*. Darcy knew what Elle was looking for. She had told her in no uncertain terms on that first failed date—was it still a failure if it brought them together in the end?—that she was looking for *the one*. And there wasn't a doubt in Elle's mind that Darcy was it.

And she'd tell her that. Contrary to whatever Margot thought, Elle wasn't avoiding anything. All right, *maybe* she was avoiding Mom, but not this. This was good, great, *amazing*. She just didn't want the first time she told Darcy how she felt to be when Darcy was upset about her mother or stressed about her exam. There was no rush. Not when there was no longer an expiration date looming at the end of the month. Not when this was something Elle wanted to last.

Chapter Seventeen

December 13

DARCY (4:57 P.M.): <link>

ELLE (5:02 P.M.): drops of jupiter by train?

ELLE (5:02 P.M.): it's a great song

ELLE (5:02 P.M.): one of my favorites

DARCY (5:04 P.M.): Popped up on my playlist on my way to work this morning.

DARCY (5:05 P.M.): It made me think of you.

DARCY (5:05 P.M.): And I thought you should know.

ELLE (5:08 P.M.): vhjgbuinlkgydsyb

ELLE (5:08 P.M.): omg

ELLE (5:08 P.M.): you can't just say things like that

DARCY (5:15 P.M.): Sorry?

ELLE (5:16 P.M.): no it just makes me want to kiss you and you aren't here right now so i can't

ELLE (5:17 P.M.): you should absolutely say things like that

ELLE (5:18 P.M.): i like it

ELLE (5:18 P.M.): just do it when i can express my appreciation you know?

DARCY (5:22 P.M.): Ah.

ELLE (5:24 P.M.): ~ah~

ELLE (5:29 P.M.): what are you doing tonight?

DARCY (5:32 P.M.): Study group.

ELLE (5:33 P.M.): i can help you study

ELLE (5:34 P.M.): question one what is darcy doing tonight?

ELLE (5:34 P.M.): a) elle b) elle c) elle d) elle

ELLE (5:34 P.M.): see?

DARCY (5:36 P.M.): 🙄

ELLE (5:37 P.M.): bring your flashcards

ELLE (5:37 P.M.): im great with positive reinforcement

ELLE (5:38 P.M.): strip studying

ELLE (5:38 P.M.): every question you get right ill take off an article of clothing

ELLE (5:39 P.M.): if it worked for billy madison it can totally work for you

DARCY (5:44 P.M.): Fine. But you really have to help me study. And you have to feed me first. I skipped lunch.

ELLE (5:46 P.M.): pizza?

ELLE (5:46 P.M.): pineapple and jalapeño right?

DARCY (5:48 P.M.): And black olives.

ELLE (5:49 P.M.): 🙄 barf

ELLE (5:50 P.M.): but fine

DARCY (5:52 P.M.): And I'm bringing the wine.

ELLE (5:54 P.M.): hard sell but deal

ELLE (5:55 P.M.): pleasure doing business with you
DARCY (5:59 P.M.): No, but it will be.
ELLE (6:02 P.M.): 🔥 🔥 🔥

☆ ☆
☆

Physiologically improbable as it was, Darcy's heart sputtered to a stop before kick-starting when Elle stepped into the Regal Ballroom of the Bellevue Hyatt Brendon had booked for his party.

Forgoing the traditional red or green holiday attire, Elle wore a sparkling silver minidress that made her skin glow, luminescent beneath the twinkling lights of the chandeliers. She accepted a glass of champagne from a waiter and scanned the room. Their eyes met and a bright smile lit up Elle's face. Darcy tore her eyes away and stared at the bubbles rising inside her champagne flute, trying to quell the similar giddy stirring in her stomach.

"Hey." Elle stopped in front of Darcy and reached out, tracing one of the thin straps holding up Darcy's dress. Darcy fought against the resulting shiver and lost. "I like this. It's very 1930s, *let's have clandestine sex in the library.*"

Darcy coughed out a laugh and wiped champagne off her lips with the back of her hand. "I don't even know what to make of that, but thank you?"

Elle shook her head. "*Atonement*? Come on, it was the movie that made me realize you can be sad and horny at the same time."

"I'm surprised you let such a prime opportunity for alliteration slip through your fingers. Angst and arousal. You're off your game," Darcy teased, lifting her flute and taking a sip.

Elle reached out, fingers ghosting down Darcy's arm before dropping. "Your dress is distracting. I'm proud I'm even making words right now. Complete sentences. Whoops. Sentence fragment." Her eyes crinkled at the corners. "Look what you do to me."

As if Elle didn't drive Darcy to distraction, too. The majority of Darcy's dreams, both waking and sleeping, as of late, were about Elle. That terrified and elated her in equal measure.

Not knowing what to say, Darcy took another sip of champagne.

Elle spun, the light overhead catching on the multicolored glitter sprinkled down her zigzagged part, the rest of her hair left down, imperfect waves tumbling atop her shoulders. "Fancy party. I should say hi to your brother, but I haven't seen him yet."

Darcy set her glass down on the table of hors d'oeuvres behind her. "He's near the front of the room making the rounds with my mother."

"Your mom?" Elle shifted uneasily on her heels. "Do I get to meet her?"

Darcy's brows rose. "You *want* to?"

Elle reached out, resting a hand on Darcy's upper arm. "Unless you'd rather I not."

Darcy stared across the room to where Brendon was currently introducing Mom to a group of coworkers who appeared to hang on her every word. Darcy twisted the ring around her middle finger. "Later? Do you want something else to drink? More champagne?"

Elle stared at her with huge eyes rimmed with dark, smudgy liner. Glitter had fallen from her hair down onto her lids, her cheeks, her jaw. "Okay, that sounds—"

Elle broke off, cocking her head to the side. More glitter scattered around her, falling from her hair.

"This song." Elle drained her glass and set it aside with one hand, reaching for Darcy's hand with the other. "I love this song."

Dancing wasn't something Darcy usually did unless forced. But the beat was slow, had a hazy dreamy quality to it that she could probably sway to. That and Elle seemed eager, so eager Darcy didn't want to deny her. She let Elle drag her out onto the dance floor where she wrapped her arms around Darcy's waist, fingers dragging against the skin left bare by her low-cut dress. Darcy shivered and stepped closer, resting her hands lightly atop Elle's shoulders.

"Your dress." She swallowed. There was a lump in her throat that hadn't been there before, not until she caught a whiff of Elle's perfume, something sweet but not floral. Vanilla. Elle almost always smelled like cookies or some kind of baked delicacy, mouthwatering. The same scent had clung to Darcy's pillows, her sheets. She cleared her throat and tried again. "I meant to tell you I like it. You look like—"

"A disco ball?" Elle suggested, laughing. She continued to trace nonsensical patterns against Darcy's skin.

She gasped softly when Elle's fingers slipped beneath the satin of her dress. "I was going to say you look like . . . you look like the moon."

The stars, too, for that matter. Elle looked like she'd been draped in the night sky, dipped in starlight.

Rather than laugh or roll her eyes at Darcy's fumbling ineloquence, Elle pressed closer, fingers squeezing Darcy's waist. Her tongue swept against her bottom lip and Darcy couldn't help but track the movement. "Fun fact—the moon doesn't actually produce any light of its own. It reflects light from the sun, making it appear bright at night. So, if I look like the moon, I guess that means I'm reflecting the light that's around me."

Her eyes lifted, staring up at Darcy from beneath the blackest of black lashes.

"That's—"

Elle dropped her eyes, breaking their gaze. "Corny? Sorry."

No. Or, if it was, Darcy still liked it. She liked *Elle* and all her eccentricities, her quirks. Elle made her smile more in the past month and a half than Darcy could remember smiling over the course of the last two years. "No. I was going to say—" She hadn't actually known. "Interesting. It's interesting. I didn't know that."

"I taught you something?" Elle trailed a finger down the length of Darcy's spine and grinned. "Huh. Kudos to me."

"You've taught me plenty of things." Glitter from Elle's hair landed on Darcy's wrist, pink, blue, and silver freckles mingling with the rest of the moles that dotted her skin. Rather than shake it off, Darcy let the glitter linger.

Her cheeks burned when Elle stared, lips quirking curiously. Please don't let her ask what Darcy had learned.

"Teach *me* something," Elle said instead. "Preferably something that doesn't involve death statistics due to inclement weather."

Darcy cut her eyes. "It was relevant."

"It was *morbid*."

Darcy harrumphed.

"Tick tock." Elle arched a brow sprinkled with glitter.

Darcy drew a blank. Not because all her facts were boring or morose, but because staring at Elle did that to her. Zeroed Darcy's focus to figuring out what color to call the blue of her eyes. Romantic obsessions that scared her more than any death statistic.

"Um." Darcy shook her head. "I don't know. I—" Her facts *weren't* boring, but they felt inconsequential in the face of Elle's cosmic knowledge, her ability to expand Darcy's world by reducing the universe to something as finite as the fact that the moon had no light of its own, but also infinite in its ability to take her breath away. Being with Elle, around Elle, in the mere presence of Elle meant getting comfortable with constantly being out of her comfort zone. Paradoxical.

Elle's fingers dipped below the back of Darcy's dress, flirting with hidden skin, almost indecently low. Her lips twitched and Darcy *ached*. "Come on. Anything."

"I could tell you a joke."

What the hell. A joke? Where had that even come from?

Elle's head bobbed in a frenzied nod, her footsteps faltering, losing the rhythm of the song. "Yes."

"It's not funny, not *really*. Lower your expectations. It's—" Darcy sighed. Based on Elle's wide-eyed look of anticipation, Darcy had committed and now she needed to deliver. "On our first . . . our first date, you told me you weren't sure what an actuary does."

Glitter clung to Elle's lashes, making every blink sparkle. "I remember."

Here went nothing. "What I should've said was, an actuary is someone who expects everyone to be dead on time."

Elle blinked, then comprehension dawned on her. She ducked her head and snorted loudly, stumbling into Darcy. "Oh god."

"Lame, right?" Warmth flooded Darcy's chest, the knots inside her stomach loosening. Elle could've rolled her eyes or shook her head in confusion, but she'd laughed. *Snorted*. It was such a genuine sound. Real.

Elle rested her head on Darcy's shoulder and sighed. Each exhale was hot against her neck and it sent a shiver skittering down Darcy's spine. "That was worse than a dad joke. Don't get me wrong, I love it. But wow."

"You asked for it."

"I guess I did, didn't I?" Elle lifted her head, arms banding tighter around Darcy's waist as they continued to sway in time with the slow melody. "Speaking of asking for it, what do you want for Christmas?"

"You don't have to buy me something. You already got me the tree and it was perfect."

She was going to cherish that ugly little stump of a tree with its mismatched ornaments forever, keep them safe, start a new tradition like Elle had said.

"That's not what I asked."

"I have everything I want."

Time stopped when Elle looked at her, eyes soft and fond, shining beneath the light of the many chandeliers. She wasn't entirely sure if she leaned in, or if it was Elle who closed the distance between them, perhaps both. Elle's lips brushed against hers in a barely there kiss that made her sigh and sway closer, melting into Elle. When the tip of Elle's tongue darted out, dragging against her bottom lip, Darcy's toes curled inside her heels and her stomach did a riotous flip, her hands sinking into the waves at the back of Elle's neck, pulling her closer, keeping her there.

Elle drew back, champagne-sweet breath gusting softly against Darcy's swollen lips. Glitter from Elle's hair, her face, had transferred to Darcy's lashes and when she blinked, her vision went fractal, exploding in a flickering light show. Like when they'd crawled beneath her Christmas tree and she'd squinted at the lights and everything twinkled.

Elle's face shimmered before her eyes, glowing, and Darcy's chest seized, something, some tingling emotion rising up inside her too big to be constrained let alone concealed. Darcy glanced down at her chest, nearly expecting to see something there, visible just beneath the surface, pressing and clawing its way out.

Darcy cupped the back of Elle's neck and let her thumb drift, sweeping against the side of Elle's throat. "I'm happy you're here."

"Thanks for inviting me. For real," Elle whispered, but that wasn't what Darcy meant. She was happy Elle was in her life, that their paths had crossed, intertwined, even if at first it had seemed like the worst thing to happen to her. Elle had turned out to be the best, beyond Darcy's wildest expectations.

"Elle!"

Distracted, Darcy hadn't realized they'd swayed their way over to the edge of the dance floor.

Elle glanced over Darcy's shoulder, her face splitting into a grin. "Brendon, hey. Great party."

Darcy dropped her hands from around Elle's neck and took a step back, immediately lamenting the loss of Elle's arms around her. She turned to face Brendon and— Mom. She was standing beside Brendon, lips pressed into a polite smile.

Right. "Mom, this is Elle. Elle, this is my mother, Gillian."

"Of course. You're the . . . astrologer?" Mom cocked her head.

"I am. It's super nice to meet you." Elle stuck out her hand, blushing lightly when her skin caught the light and sparkled. "Sorry, this stupid glitter won't stay where it's supposed to. I guess that's what I get for using regular craft store stuff instead of splurging on the kind that's made for your hair. I figured, glitter's glitter, right? Wrong."

Elle rolled her lips together and chuckled, a little puff of air exhaled through her nose.

Mom hummed and shook Elle's hand. "Well, it's a pleasure to meet you, Elle. I wish I could say Darcy's told me so much about you, but unfortunately my daughter has remained rather tight-lipped. It's my son who's brought me up to speed."

There it was.

Beside her, Elle shifted and Darcy could *feel* the weight of her stare. Darcy's jaw ticked.

Brendon coughed into his fist. "You mind if I cut in? I know this is a party and everything, but there's something about the app I've been dying to pick your brain on, Elle."

"Sure." Elle stepped toward Brendon and shot Darcy a ghost of a smile over her shoulder.

Darcy tried to smile back and failed, dismally, the curve of her lips feeling all kinds of wrong, because Mom was watching her, eyes burning with curiosity.

"I could use another drink. How about you, Darcy?"

She sighed and followed Mom off the edge of the dance floor over to where one of the waiters—dressed like an elf, à la typical Brendon—held a tray of champagne flutes.

Plucking two glasses from the tray, Mom passed one to Darcy before clinking them together. She drained half of hers in one sip. "You and Elle looked cozy out there."

Darcy crossed her arms. "I suppose."

"I've got to say, you look a lot more serious than you made it sound last week."

Darcy shut her eyes. "We were dancing, Mom. It's a party, there's music. What do you expect?"

"I don't *expect* anything." When Darcy opened her eyes, Mom frowned. "I don't know when you got the idea in your head that I'm not on your side. I'm not your enemy, baby, I'm confused. Brendon's telling me one thing and you're telling me something else and what I see is . . . well, it's difficult for me to understand what it is I'm supposed to believe."

"Of course you're confused," Darcy whispered. "You're drunk."

Mom looked offended. "I am not."

Drunk or not, it wasn't for Mom to understand. "I already told you. It's complicated."

"Complicated." Mom's lips furrowed at the corners. "There's that word again. That word worries me for you."

"You're worried about me? That's a first."

"You're the one who made it clear that I haven't acted much like a mother to you over the years. Excuse me for doing what I can to make up for it now."

Talk about too little, too late. Her life was *her* business, not Mom's to dissect and give unwelcome advice on.

"Darcy." Mom reached out and rested a hand on Darcy's crossed forearm. "I'm not trying to be difficult. Elle's . . . sweet. But you have to admit, she seems a bit more like your brother's type, doesn't she?"

"What in god's name is *that* supposed to mean?" She didn't mean to take the bait, but that was ludicrous.

Mom made an abstract gesture in front of her. "An astrologer?"

"Like you don't spend two weeks every summer at a spiritual retreat in Ojai getting high out of your mind."

Mom rolled her eyes. "I don't mean anything by it. I'm just surprised. She doesn't seem like your type at all."

Darcy shook her head. "I don't see why it matters. Last week you were telling me I could use some fun in my life."

"That was when I thought that's all it was." Mom drained her glass. "She seems a little flighty, is all I'm saying."

Darcy scoffed. "That's rich, coming from you."

Mom drew back, looking as if Darcy had slapped her. "I know I wasn't always there, but I'm trying."

"You know nothing, Mom. And you definitely don't know her."

"And you do? How long have you known her? You thought you knew Natasha, didn't you?"

Darcy crossed her arms tighter, fists pressing into her sides, digging into her ribs. "I know Elle."

"God, I—" Mom snatched another glass of champagne and stole a quick sip.

"What, Mom? Just say it."

Mom shook her head subtly and stared out across the dance floor for a moment before finally turning her head and pinning Darcy with a bewildered stare. "If I didn't know any better, I'd say you were in love."

Chapter Eighteen

*Y*ou seriously like the addition to the chat feature?"

Brendon bobbed his head enthusiastically as he led Elle around the dance floor. "It's brilliant. Seriously. It's a bit more involved for the engineers, but the perks are undeniable. Encouraging users to continue chatting in the app for as long as possible . . . *Elle*. The projections are showing gains that are"—Brendon grinned boyishly, charming—"astronomical. The cost-benefit analysis speaks for itself."

"That's great, Brendon. I'm guessing you already told your new best friend the news? I'm feeling awfully left out."

"Hush. You're all adorably coupled up with my sister. Don't act like we left you high and dry." He raised their hands, encouraging her to twirl. She laughed and went for it. "But yeah, I did. Margot told me it was your idea."

"It was a joint effort." Elle craned her neck, peeking over his shoulder. "Have you seen her lately? Margot? We came together and she went MIA on me."

Elle was dying to get Margot's opinion on her strange introduction to Darcy's mom.

Brendon wrinkled his nose and something soft and gentle ached inside her chest, not unpleasant, *full*. Darcy wrinkled her nose the exact same way.

His eyes swept the room. "I think I saw her chatting with a few of the folks in product design before I came over here."

"I'll hunt her down later." Stumbling, Elle smiled in appreciation when he kept her from toppling over.

For a moment, they moved to the music, the silence between them comfortable, companionable.

Brendon cleared his throat. "About that with my mom."

Elle bit the inside of her cheek. "Yeah. What was that?"

Brendon shut his eyes, briefly since he was the one leading. "It's . . . nothing to worry about. Don't take it personally."

Sure, because that was easy. Elle *never* did that.

"Easier said than done, though, right?" Brendon stole the words right from her head. "I know. Don't let it get to you. Darcy knows what she feels. I'm serious. Darcy's crazy about you, you know that, right?"

"You think so?"

He looked at her like she was crazy. "Elle. Come on."

Elle bit the corner of her lip.

"I'm serious. Darcy keeps her cards close to the chest, but you'd have to be blind not to see how she looks at you."

Elle knew how it *felt* when Darcy looked at her. How it made her stomach swoop with an intensity that stole her breath, made her flush from head to toe, turned her inside out.

"How does she look at me?" she asked, out of curiosity's sake, mostly. "Humor me."

"Darcy looks at you like . . ." Brendon's lips tugged to the side, his brow furrowing. A smile inched its way across his face, both his dimples gleaming. "She looks at you like you hung the moon."

If that wasn't the greatest, most beautiful, cheesiest thing Elle had ever heard, she didn't know what was. Cheeks aching from the spectacular grin she had no hope of controlling, Elle ducked her chin. "You think?"

Brendon chuckled and when Elle lifted her head, he was staring off over her shoulder with a faraway look in his eyes. "I'd kill to have someone look at me like that, you know?"

Brendon had made his entire life about helping everyone else find their happily-ever-after and he deserved one of his own. If it could happen for her, it could totally happen for him. *Should* happen for him.

"Your dream girl is out there somewhere." She cuffed him lightly on the arm. "She probably has no idea you're out here, a total catch who's just waiting for her to stumble into your open arms."

Brendon barked out a laugh. "I'll take your word for it. Though I'm beginning to worry she lives on the opposite side of the world or something. Opposite side of the country, at least."

"That's easy. Take a road trip."

"I'd search every city if I had—" Something over her shoulder caught Brendon's attention, his eyes widening. "Shoot. One of our investors just walked in. Do you mind if I . . . ?"

She stepped back, waving him off with a smile. "Go. I should go find your sister."

Brendon looked grateful. "I think I saw her talking to Mom by the chocolate fountain."

So the chocolate fountain was where Elle headed, because *nothing* about heading in that direction sounded like a bad idea. If Darcy wasn't there, there'd still be chocolate. Win-win.

As luck would have it, Darcy was by the fondue, and so was her mother. Brushing her fingers against the edge of her dress, Elle approached. But just as she was almost close enough to announce herself, a group of three women whose giraffish height was only exaggerated by the stilettos on their feet stepped in front of her, cutting her off. She edged around them, approaching Darcy and her mom from behind instead.

"That was when I thought that's all it was." Darcy's mom finished her champagne and set the glass aside, swaying slightly. "Then Brendon's telling me you're crazy about Elle and you're telling me it's complicated. She seems a little flighty, is all I'm saying."

Darcy scoffed. "That's rich, coming from you."

"I know I wasn't always there, but I'm trying."

"You know nothing, Mom. And you definitely don't know her."

"And you do? How long have you known her? You thought you knew Natasha, didn't you?"

Darcy's shoulders curled forward. "I know Elle."

"God, I—" Her mom grabbed another glass of champagne.

"What, Mom? Just say it."

"If I didn't know any better, I'd say you were in love."

Elle's heart stopped. Eavesdropping was wrong, but she was weak.

Darcy's scoff came out strangled. "You're drunk."

"I said I'm not." Gillian teetered on her heels. "Not really."

"You're being ridiculous."

"You're saying you're not in love with her?" her mom asked.

Regret hastened through Elle's veins like poison. She should've walked away. She shouldn't have eavesdropped. She didn't want to hear anything more but she couldn't move. Anchored to the floor like cinder blocks, her feet wouldn't budge.

"We've been dating a month and a half, if you can even call it that." Darcy shook her head. "I'm just having fun. Of course I'm not in love with her. Don't . . . don't be absurd."

Elle pressed a hand to her stomach as if that gesture alone could hold her together.

Just having fun.

Darcy didn't love her.

Darcy didn't.

Because that would . . . that would be *absurd*.

Fuck, her eyes stung. She wouldn't cry, she refused. She needed fresh air, a moment alone, a moment to process, to set her world to rights and fix this dissonance, believing one thing, feeling it in her gut, feeling it down to her bones only to hear that it wasn't true.

Elle stepped back, footsteps faltering as Darcy turned. Their eyes met and Elle's chest went tight, shrink-wrap around her heart, squeezing until she couldn't breathe.

A flicker of something Elle had no name for passed over

Darcy's butterscotch brown eyes. Realization? Regret? Concern? Pity? "Elle—"

"Found you!" Elle's laugh sounded fake even to her own ears. Fake and forced and flimsy, a paper-thin front to cover what she was feeling. "I wanted to let you know I'm going to get some fresh air. I'll be back."

She turned before her face could do something terrible like crumble beneath Darcy's mother's scrutinizing stare. It made Elle want to shrink in on herself so she kept walking, kept moving in the direction of the ballroom exit, even when Darcy called out after her.

Chapter Nineteen

Darcy's lungs burned as she quickened her steps, one heel catching on a crack in the pavement in front of the hotel. Thankfully Elle drew to a stop in the middle of the sidewalk. Darcy wasn't made for running in shoes like these.

"Elle." Her breath crystalized in the air, turning to fog in front of her. "It's cold out here."

Understatement of the century. It was *freezing*, the sort of cold that cramped your muscles and made your bones ache. Darcy hugged her arms across her body, skin prickling with gooseflesh as she waited for Elle to say something.

"'m fine," Elle mumbled, back still to Darcy. Light from the streetlamp caught on the glitter that had rained down her shoulders, her arms, her bare upper back. Darcy's vision went fractal again, all that glitter turning to crushed diamonds on Elle's skin. Stardust.

Darcy's teeth chattered when she tried to speak. "At least . . . at least get your coat or something if you're going to stand out here. It's—"

"I said I'm fine," Elle bit out, voice wavering around her words, whittling them into something thin and sharp that pierced Darcy right through the chest.

She took a step forward, knees knocking as she shivered. "You don't . . . you don't sound fine."

She sounded anything but. What the hell had happened? Everything had been wonderful, *perfect*, and sure, Mom had been brusque, but that wasn't worth getting upset over. It certainly wasn't worth dashing off into the cold without a coat. Yet Darcy had followed. Chasing after Elle had been instinctive, something she hadn't thought about. Elle had looked upset, her smile forced, and she'd taken off and Darcy had been halfway out the ballroom before it had even occurred to her that she hadn't said anything to Mom. She'd left their conversation, that stupid, worthless conversation hanging and had followed Elle out into the night.

Above them, the sky was dark, not a star in sight, not even the moon. Elle was, by far, the brightest thing Darcy could see, brighter than the streetlights and the lamps, a beacon in the darkness.

Elle's shoulders curled forward, the curve of her spine enticing. Keeping one arm around herself, Darcy reached out to stroke the skin of Elle's back, to run her fingers down that arch until skin met sparkling fabric. Elle turned before Darcy could make contact and something about her hand hovering in the space between them left Darcy feeling so vulnerable that she dropped her arm like she'd been burned.

Nothing about Elle's expression looked *fine*. A furrow had formed between her brows, her eyes damp and narrowed. She'd licked the gloss from her lips, worried them red, and the cold air chapped them further, making her pout more pronounced.

"I'm . . ." With a shrug, Elle crossed her arms. One strap slipped down her shoulder and she slid it back into place absently, sniffing softly, because it was cold or because of something else, Darcy had no idea. Elle cleared her throat and lifted her chin. The look in her glossy blue eyes rooted Darcy where she stood. "I heard. What you said to your mom. I overheard."

What she'd said to her mom . . . Darcy's heart stuttered inside her chest. "What part?"

Elle scoffed gently and hugged herself tighter, elbows squeezing in, making the curl of her shoulders and the jut of her collarbone sharper, more pronounced. "All of it?"

All of it . . . okay. That was why Elle was *not* fine. Why she'd taken off, run out into the cold. Something about what she'd heard, she hadn't liked.

Nothing about that conversation had sat well with Darcy. Not Mom's prying, not her demeaning Elle, not her assumptions, and definitely not the part where she tried to force Darcy to reckon with her feelings. As if that were her place. As if Darcy needed that. Mom had no idea what Darcy needed.

Darcy shoved the heel of her hand into her breastbone and stared down the sidewalk. Empty. No one was crazy enough to be standing outside when it was this cold. No one except for her and Elle.

"Okay." She turned, facing Elle once more.

Elle shook her head, lashes fluttering as she blinked, lights catching on the glitter. "Okay? That's—" She blew out her breath, shivering softly.

"Let's . . . let's go back inside." Darcy gestured over her shoulder. It was warm in the hotel and Darcy desperately wanted to head back inside just like she desperately wanted to *not* have this conversation. She wanted to step this whole night back, return to the dance floor, back to when everything had been far less confusing, the thoughts inside her head less of a jumble. The fear of what she felt would've still been there, but it wouldn't have been so suffocating, bearing down on her with an intensity that made it difficult to do something as basic as stand there and act like she was okay. It had lingered in her periphery, but if she kept her eyes on Elle, kept looking ahead—not *too* far ahead— it was okay.

Elle's chin wobbled gently before she clenched her jaw and lifted her head, staring up at Darcy, the blue of her eyes as dark and glassy as the lake at night. "That's it? I said I overheard and you don't have anything . . . anything to say?"

Darcy bit the inside of her lip. "What do you want me to say?"

Elle stared for a heartbeat, then two, three, and Darcy's heart quickened. The air around them crackled, cold and electric and quiet. Elle's chin jerked in a barely there shake. "*Something*. I want you to say *something*." Her tongue swept out, wetting her bottom lip. "Is this— What is this to you?" she whispered.

Darcy's heart clenched, the back of her throat narrowing.

She'd told Mom that she was having fun with Elle, and that was true, but it was more than that. It was fun and frightening and more than anything Darcy had felt in a long, long time.

"It's . . . it's complicated," she admitted, feeling like that *was* the right word, the only one that could do her quagmire of feelings any justice.

Elle's jaw dropped, a little gasp tearing from between her lips before she laughed, low and dry, humorless. "That's— Could you *uncomplicate* it for me?"

If only it were that easy. "It's not that simple, Elle."

Elle stared, eyes narrowing before she pressed her lips together and gave a tiny shrug. "Isn't it? Or shouldn't it be? It is for me."

The back of Darcy's throat burned. "You wouldn't understand—"

"Why not?" Elle glared. "I might be *flighty*, but I'm not stupid, Darcy."

Darcy hugged herself tighter until her ribs ached. "I never said you were. I never called you flighty."

"Your mom did." Elle's jaw clenched tighter as she stared down and to the side where a crack in the pavement spread like branching veins all the way to the curb.

Darcy's chest went cold. "I am not my mother."

Elle was quiet and as much as Darcy didn't want to have this conversation there was something unsettling in this silence, alarming in the stillness of Elle's body, her posture. She was a force, always in movement. Twitching, shifting, vibrant. This wasn't like her, wasn't normal. It wasn't like how some of their silences were comfortable. Those contained breath in every space between their words. This was deprivation, asphyxiation in the grim absence of Elle's voice, her laugh, the sound she made when she sighed softly and she was simply *there*. Touchable.

The distance between them now felt vast and Darcy didn't have the slightest clue how to traverse it. If she could.

With another barely perceptible jerk of her chin, Elle frowned. "I'm not asking for . . . for a proposal, Darcy."

Bile crept up her esophagus, her heart tripping, flailing, faltering.

"I'm not asking you to promise me forever." Elle sniffed hard. "It's only been a few weeks, but you're all I can think about and I just want to know what this is. We were fake and now we're not, but what are we? What am I? Am I your girlfriend? Is this— How do you *feel*?"

Like she was going to throw up.

Outside of the immediate moment, Darcy had never felt like *this*, not this soon, not this fast, not this deep, not this much, none of it. Not for anyone, not even Natasha. And like Mom had said, Darcy had been ready to spend the rest of her life with Natasha, had loved her, and as a result, finding her in bed with a mutual friend had *broken* Darcy. Had shattered her heart into a million pieces and it had taken nearly two years and a cross-country move to glue herself back together and even then, until recently, she sometimes wondered if she'd put herself back together wrong.

If she was more like Mom than she wanted to believe.

What she felt for Elle was immense and it made what she'd felt for Natasha seem trivial. She'd loved Natasha but she'd never forgotten how to breathe when Natasha stared at her and remembered how when Natasha smiled. Darcy had never lost her mind over Natasha's laugh. She'd never stared at her phone waiting for Natasha to text. She'd never counted the minutes until she'd see Natasha again. She'd never felt so helpless and powerful at the same time when they kissed, like she was holding the entire magnificent, fragile universe inside her hands when they touched. Her feelings for Natasha had been . . . steady. Steady and secure with both feet firmly planted on the ground at all times. A comfortable sort of love. Sensible.

Natasha had been safe and she'd still cut Darcy to the quick.

If she felt this much for Elle, as much as she did, a scary amount, it only stood to reason that with more time, her feelings would continue to grow. Like one of those stars Elle had told her about, the ones that grew bigger and bigger and burned brighter and hotter, until one day, inevitably, they exploded, drowning out the light of all the stars around them. Like a supernova, the resulting heartbreak would drown out the memory of all those other brokenhearted moments, make them pale by comparison.

It was inevitable—sparks either fizzled or they caught fire and burned you. It had happened to Mom after twenty-five years and it had happened to Darcy, too.

No place on Earth would be far enough to run to escape that sort of pain, to start over. Not as long as there were stars in the sky and a moon over her head. She and Elle would look up at that same sky every night and no amount of distance would ever be enough to make her forget what the moon looked like reflecting off Elle's features. How it made Darcy feel like anything was possible.

Darcy curled her arms tighter around herself, going numb and not just from the cold. "I don't know. I've got my FSA exam—"

"In a couple weeks. What about after that?"

After that. Next month and the next—long-term plans. One day she'd find herself so wrapped up in Elle that when the inevitable happened, there'd be no such thing as a clean break.

When she lost Elle, she'd lose part of herself, too. Something she'd sworn never to do.

"I don't *know*, Elle. I don't . . . I didn't plan for any of this, I wasn't *looking* for this. I didn't *want* this."

Elle's expression soured, lips folding in, chin quivering before she rolled her shoulders back and stood a little straighter. "Sorry to wreck your perfect plans by having feelings."

Apparently she was not numb enough because Elle's words stung like a paper cut, not deep but unexpected. A jagged ambush that sliced open the surface of her skin, proving how easy it was for Elle to hurt her without much effort. Darcy wasn't a robot, she wasn't unfeeling, not like Elle made it sound. She felt . . . *God*, she felt and sometimes she wished she didn't. Wished she could turn it all off because she felt *too much*.

She gulped down a breath of cold air and watched as her ragged exhale fogged in front of her face. "That's not fair."

Elle's eyes squeezed shut. Her front teeth sank into her lower lip and her nails bit into the skin of her upper arms. She sniffed hard and opened her eyes. Glassy and damp, moisture clung to her lashes.

Darcy's chest panged. She'd put that look on Elle's face and it wasn't what she wanted. None of this was going the way she'd wanted.

"Not fair?" A watery laugh spilled from Elle's lips as a single tear slipped from the corner of her eyes, tracking down her cheek, and with it, glitter. One sparkling tear track. "What's not fair is that you had me going. For a minute there, I hoped"—Elle's throat bobbed and her voice cracked—"we could have something real."

Behind them, the door to the hotel opened, the soft strains of Bing Crosby's "White Christmas" spilling out onto the sidewalk. Of all the stupid songs in the world. "Elle—"

Elle gave a curt jerk of her head and scrubbed her hand over her face, wiping away her tears and smearing more glitter across her skin. "No, you know, I might be starry-eyed and I might be a little bit of a mess sometimes, and maybe I wear my heart on my sleeve." Elle took a stuttered breath in through her mouth, gasping softly. "But at least I have a heart, Darcy."

Whatever little bit of warmth remained in Darcy's body extinguished as the world spun to a stop, time slowing to a crawl. This didn't *feel* like heartbreak, this *was* heartbreak. Darcy had miscalculated; she wasn't *falling*, she'd *fallen*. She pressed a hand to her chest as if in doing so she could keep her heart from shattering entirely, but the damage was already done. Too late.

"Whoa, whoa."

Darcy turned, chin trembling and nose running, arms wrapped around her body so tight she could barely suck air in. She would not lose it. Not now, not yet. Not in front of Elle and not in front of Brendon, who'd just stepped onto the sidewalk, footsteps slowing as he approached.

He glanced between her and Elle, eyes narrowed, lingering on Elle at last. "Elle, that's not—"

A frustrated cry slipped from Elle's lips as she shook her head, walking backward, slipping away. "No offense, Brendon," she choked out, eyes wet and dull, holding none of the sparkle Darcy loved. "But you have *no idea* what this is."

Elle pivoted on her heel and in that second before she turned, their eyes met. A spark flickered in Darcy's chest, an echo of heat, of what was, what could've been. *If only.*

And then Elle was gone, turning and striding down the sidewalk impossibly fast, or it looked like that because Darcy's vision was blurred and each time she blinked she caught a staggered snapshot of Elle walking away, the distance between them growing larger and larger.

Brendon placed a hot hand on her shoulder, hissing through his teeth. "Darce, come on, you're—"

"She's right." The air was so fucking cold and it stung her scratchy throat, burned her nose. But nothing hurt as badly as her heart. Splintered and fractured, with each inhale it felt like fragmented shards scraped against her chest like daggers. Darcy could barely breathe. It was too much to bear. Darcy didn't want to hurt, didn't want to feel. "You have—you have *no idea*, Brendon."

"It'll be okay," and he sounded so sincere that what was left of her resolve crumbled.

Spine bowing forward, Darcy curled in on herself and gasped out a sob, startling herself and Brendon. "It's not. It won't. It was— *Fuck*, Brendon, it was *fake*."

Brendon looked confused. "What? Darcy—"

"Me and Elle, it started out fake." Once she started, she couldn't stop. The words tripped off her tongue as salty tears dripped from the tip of her nose, her vision obscuring until Brendon was nothing more than a tall blur beside her. "It wasn't real. It was so you'd get off my back and quit setting me up on dates because I didn't want to fall in love, Brendon. I didn't want to fall in love and *this* . . . this is why."

Darcy scrunched her eyes shut and gave a violent shiver, limbs going cold, colder than she thought was possible. It was Seattle for crying out loud, why was she *so* cold?

Arms wrapped around her, pulling her close until her forehead rested against Brendon's chest. His bow tie dug into her temple but she didn't care. She lifted her hands and fisted them in the front of his shirt.

"This doesn't look fake," he whispered, one hand stroking down the back of her head over her hair.

Too choked up to speak, Darcy hiccuped and burrowed deeper into Brendon's shoulder.

Something cold and wet landed on her bare back. Again, and again, until Darcy lifted her head and tilted back, glaring up at the black night sky.

Soft, fat snowflakes fell from the sky, dancing on the wind and landing on Darcy's arms, her exposed back, irritating her bare skin like tiny pinpricks. She shut her eyes and dropped her forehead back to Brendon's chest, muffling a sob with a bite of her lip.

Fucking snow.

Chapter Twenty

The front door banged against the wall, followed by the sound of several heavy thuds. Margot's creative cursing punctuated the ruckus, further interrupting Pat Benatar telling Elle that love was a battlefield and that she was strong.

"Motherfucking duck fucker," Margot shouted. "Ben can go fuck himself. Jerry, too. *Chunky* Monkey for goddamn sure. Christ on a shingle that fucking *hurt*." A pause. "Oh, hi, Mrs. Harrison. No, I'm good. No, no, no one's doing anything unseemly to any ducks. Nope. Monkeys, neither. Sorry. Yep, I'll get right on that. Wash my mouth out *really* well."

Oh, Margot. Their landlord was going to *love* getting a call from Mrs. Harrison complaining about them, *again*.

Margot stuck her head around the corner, peering into the living room. Elle waved weakly from her spot on the couch and Margot's face brightened. "Hey. You brushed your hair. Go, Elle."

Rude.

Elle rolled over and assumed the position she'd been in

before Margot had loudly interrupted her sulk fest. Face buried in the arm of the sofa, afghan pulled halfway over her head, one eye open so she could watch the television, which was currently on mute. Beside her, her phone was turned screen side down, Bluetooth connected to the speakers on the kitchen bar.

"Mrs. Harrison sends her love." Margot stepped farther into the living room, nose wrinkling as she stared at the coffee table.

There were a few takeout containers. Three. Okay, five. And some tissues. A lot of tissues. Elle was going to clean up after herself as soon as she scraped together the willpower to get off the couch for longer than a trip to the bathroom.

"What was with all that noise?" Elle mumbled.

Margot kicked a small pile of crumpled notebook paper with her toe. "You know, casually breaking my foot in the doorway. Speaking of, I'm going to unload the groceries I bought and then we can talk about . . . *this.*"

She frowned pointedly at the clutter before leaving.

Elle pulled the afghan the rest of the way over her head and mouthed the words to "Love Is a Battlefield."

Strong was the last thing she felt at the moment. Her chest felt like someone had punched a hole through it, ripping out her heart and shredding it into bleeding bits of confetti before stuffing it back inside her body and duct-taping the hole shut.

"I have soup," Margot shouted from the kitchen. "Your favorite. Pho Rau Cai from What the Pho."

Elle stuck her nose out from the blanket. "I'm not sick, Margot."

"You're not sick *yet*." A cabinet slammed followed by the sound of the freezer opening. "You walked all the way to Star-bucks in the snow, Elle."

Big deal. "It wasn't even a mile."

"Wearing spaghetti straps in twenty-eight-degree weather. *Snow*." Margot huffed loudly.

She sounded like—

Elle scrunched her eyes shut as another hot wave of tears flooded her ducts. *Fuck.*

"I mean, as far as dramatic exits go, that was a good one," Margot prattled on, oblivious.

A dramatic exit hadn't been Elle's intention. She hadn't meant to storm off without cash, her keys, or her phone. She hadn't meant to walk all the way from the hotel to the twenty-four-hour Starbucks several blocks over, but the need to get as far away from Darcy and her painful inability to speak had carried Elle across town on autopilot, snow and strappy heels be damned.

At least the baristas on shift had taken mercy on her, letting her use the store's phone. Then they'd gone above and beyond, embodying the real spirit of the holiday season by pouring free peppermint tea in her until she'd thawed and Margot showed up with her car, Elle thankfully having left her keys and phone in the pocket of the jacket she'd checked at the hotel.

"I don't want soup," Elle mumbled.

For a moment, Margot was quiet. The song switched from "Love Is a Battlefield" to "I Fall Apart" by Post Malone and Elle's chin wobbled.

"All right." The freezer opened again. "I bought Chunky Monkey, Half Baked, Phish Food and"—there was rustling, followed by the sound of something wet hitting the floor, then more of Margot's colorful swearing—"we've still got half a pint of Chocolate Therapy, but it's been tucked behind the frozen peas so I think it might be freezer burned."

Ah, the frozen peas. Without a doubt freezer burned, then. She and Margot only kept the frozen peas on hand in case of emergencies. They were cheaper than an icepack.

"Elle? Which do you want?"

Elle gulped in a breath of stagnant air beneath the blanket. "Both. Both is good."

"I gave you four options. Which *both*?"

"Yes."

Margot sighed and shut the freezer. A minute later, the blanket lifted, and Margot pressed something cold and hard against Elle's cheek. Elle yelped. A spoon. Margot had pressed a spoon to her hot, puffy face.

With a flourish of her fingers, Margot gestured to the coffee table where she'd shoved some of the takeout containers aside, making room for the four pints of Ben and Jerry's she'd lined up. "Ice cream therapy. Dig in."

Elle adjusted the blanket around her shoulders like a cape and jabbed her spoon into the pint of Half Baked. Spoon laden with cookie dough goodness, Elle collapsed back against the couch and nibbled. That was enough energy expended.

"Okay, now that you have ice cream, you want to tell me about *this*?" Margot gestured to the table and surrounding area.

"It's not that bad," Elle mumbled around her spoon. "I'm gonna clean it up."

Margot sighed and dipped her own spoon into the Chunky Monkey. "Elle, it's a mess."

It *wasn't*. It was some takeout and some tissues. And paper. A cup. Socks. Elle's eyes burned.

"You're right." It was a mess. *She* was a mess. "My mom's right. Darcy's right. I'm a mess."

Margot's eyes widened. "What? No. I didn't say that. Darcy's not right about anything. Fuck Darcy." Margot set the ice cream down and crawled her way across the floor, heaving herself onto the couch and wrapping her arms around Elle, squeezing until Elle could barely breathe. "Say it with me. Fuck. Darcy."

Elle shook her head. She couldn't do it. Rendered mute, she sniffed instead.

"Elle, you're not—" Margot sighed. "Okay, right now, you're a little bit of a mess. But it's temporary. You'll clean this up and you'll stop being a mess, yeah? Eat your ice cream."

Elle shoved her spoon in her mouth and closed her eyes.

If only it were that easy. Clean up the mess and be okay. Problems solved. "'m not a Virgo, Mar."

Margot leaned back, dropping her arms. "You're right. It's— Shit, Elle. Just . . . tell me what you did today. You've obviously been busy with"—she reached over the edge of the couch and grabbed a handful of crumpled paper off the floor—"lists! You've been making lists. Oh My Stars lists?"

Elle nodded.

Focus on work. That's what she had planned to do after that awful first date with Darcy. Her plan had been waylaid, but she could pick it up now. Who says heartbreak had to ruin her focus?

Margot stared down at the crinkled paper in her hand. "Asphyxiation, decapitation by elevator, burned alive in a tanning booth . . ." Margot looked up at her with startled eyes. "What the actual fuck, Elle? This is morbid."

She pointed her spoon at the television. "Horror movie marathon. How would you die in *Final Destination* based on your eighth house?"

"That's . . . I don't know what to say." Margot scrunched the piece of paper back up and threw it across the room. "Moving on. What"—she tilted the paper to the side and furrowed her brow—"I can't read this. It's all smeared. What does this say?"

She shoved the paper in Elle's face. Once Elle had uncrossed her eyes and pulled the paper back, she grimaced both because of what it said and because the paper was blotted with tears . . . snot, too. "This one's dumb."

"Does it involve death and dismemberment?" Margot grabbed the pint of Chunky Monkey off the table and cradled it in her lap.

"No," Elle admitted. Not in the literal sense. "It's the zodiac signs as breakup songs."

Maybe heartbreak was screwing with her focus. But only a little.

Understanding passed over Margot's face as she tilted her head and lifted a finger in the air. "Hence the music."

Other way around. Bless Spotify. The playlist *I Should Be*

a Sad Bitch had pulled double duty, letting Elle sit in her feels while providing inspiration. Multitasking at its most depressing.

"Give it back." Margot snatched the paper and brought it closer to her face, squinting. "This is good. Except . . . *Elle*."

What Breakup Song Should You Listen to Based on Your Zodiac Sign?

Aries— "Survivor" by Destiny's Child
Taurus—"No Scrubs" by TLC
Gemini—"We Are Never Ever Getting Back Together" by Taylor Swift
Cancer—"Bleeding Love" by Leona Lewis
Leo—"Irreplaceable" by Beyoncé
Virgo—"Happier" by Marshmello
Libra—"Thank U, Next" by Ariana Grande
Scorpio—"Before He Cheats" by Carrie Underwood
Sagittarius—"Truth Hurts" by Lizzo
Capricorn—"I Am a Rock" by Simon and Garfunkel
Aquarius—"I Will Survive" by Gloria Gaynor
Pisces—"Total Eclipse of the Heart" by Bonnie Tyler

Elle snagged the pint of Half Baked off the coffee table and shoved another bite in her mouth, studiously ignoring Margot's exasperated stare.

"'I Am a Rock'?" Margot demanded. "Elizabeth Marie."

"What?" Elle sighed around her spoon. "It's fitting. It's— Darcy's a Capricorn."

And clearly, she was a rock, an island who had no need for feelings. At least not any feelings that had anything to do with Elle.

Elle stabbed at her ice cream. Maybe it wasn't Darcy. Maybe it was her. Elle *was* the common denominator in her love life or lack thereof, after all.

"Here." Margot grabbed a pen and crossed out the song, scribbling something neatly in its place.

Elle licked her spoon, then shoved it back in the pint before setting it on the coffee table. She wasn't hungry. "What did you put?"

With a nonchalance Elle couldn't muster if she tried, Margot tossed the pen and paper on the table. "'Too Good at Goodbyes' by Sam Smith."

The back of Elle's eyelids burned, her vision blurring with tears. She wasn't going to cry. She wasn't. She was going to keep staring at the coffee table until she became dehydrated and her body reabsorbed her tears. They wouldn't fall. They wouldn't. She wasn't—

A hot tear slid down her face, trailing sideways on the curve of her cheek and catching on the side of her nostril, salt burning her chapped skin. Damn it.

"*Elle*." Margot grabbed her by the shoulders and hauled her across the couch until Elle was halfway lying in Margot's lap. She petted the back of Elle's head and that did it.

Composure completely kaput, Elle buried her nose in Margot's stomach and clenched her eyes shut. Fat, slippery tears leaked from the corners of her eyes, making her face wet and sticky, her nose beginning to run. She gasped in a broken breath and clenched her fingers in Margot's sweater. "What's *wrong* with me?"

Gently, Margot brushed back the baby-fine hair from around Elle's temples. "Nothing. Nothing at all, Elle."

"Obviously, something." There had to be. There must've been something about her that made it so easy for Darcy to walk away. Metaphorically. Elle had done the actual walking but Darcy hadn't stopped her, hadn't even tried.

Elle had bared her heart for Darcy, her soul. From day one, she'd been clear with Darcy on what she wanted, what she craved. Darcy had given her hope that she could have that, that *they* could have that together. False hope or no hope, Elle wasn't sure which was worse. From where she was sitting, both made her ache, made her feel like there was something critical missing inside her. That spark, the little voice that kept her going when everything else was grim and dark and bearing down on her. Hope didn't spring eternal in Elle after all.

She couldn't even sleep in her own room, couldn't stand the sight of the stars on her ceiling because now all they reminded her of was the night that Darcy had stayed, their night beneath the stars.

Darcy Lowell had ruined the fucking stars for Elle. Of all the things. Elle had given Darcy *everything* and now she had nothing.

"Darcy has fucking problems, okay? And those are on her, not on you. You did nothing wrong. Do you hear me?"

Elle lifted her head and stared up at Margot through clumpy lashes. She bit the inside of her cheek and had to drop her voice to a whisper to get her question out without choking. "But why doesn't she want me?"

That was the question that had kept her up last night, awake and staring at the ceiling of the living room until her puffy eyelids grew too heavy and she eventually drifted off into a fitful sleep plagued by dreams of happier times. Like last week when Darcy had made her pancakes for the second time and had kissed the inside of Elle's wrist when she'd stopped Elle from stealing one off the plate. Or when they'd been up on the astronomy tower at UW and Darcy had looked at her, ambient light from the stars and the moon turning her hair into spun sunlight, all reds and golds, fire in the night, and Elle had felt seen. Like Darcy had taken a peek at Elle's soul, had heard the tempo of her heart, and decided she liked it. Liked it enough to stay.

But only for a little while, apparently. Temporarily. Not long enough.

"Elle—"

"Am I not enough?"

Margot shook her head, eyes fierce, the clench of her jaw vehement. "No. You are absolutely enough."

Of the wrong things. Her chin wobbled, a fresh batch of tears sluicing down her cheeks. She didn't have the energy to try to stop them. "Then am I too much, Margot? Be honest."

Her family certainly thought so. Darcy, too.

"You're just right, Elle." Margot pushed back Elle's bangs and rubbed her thumb over Elle's temple, wiping away tears. "*No one* is worth feeling like you're not good enough, that you're not amazing exactly as you are. If Darcy can't see that,

that means she isn't right for you, okay? It means she's not *your* perfect person."

Elle bit down on the side of her tongue until she could speak without fear of sobbing out her words. "I don't think I have one of those. A perfect person."

This was the antithesis of who she was—full of fear, doubt, hopeless. But she didn't feel like herself, not at all. Maybe a sanitized version, scrubbed down to all bones, no heart. *Elle minus.*

Margot grabbed the sides of Elle's face, forcing Elle to meet her stare. Margot's throat jerked and she blinked fast. "You do. You absolutely do, you hear me? And honestly, you probably have lots of perfect people. Look at us. You're one of my perfect people. You're my best friend, Elle. You're my *family*."

Shit.

"Margot." Elle's nose stuffed, her throat burning like she swallowed sandpaper.

"And you don't need to change a single thing about yourself for anyone, okay?" Margot cocked her head, black hair curling against her neck. "Okay, you need to shower and, like, open a window to air the apartment out because it smells rank in here, but other than that, you don't need to change a damn thing."

Elle coughed out a weak laugh.

"You deserve someone great, Elle. Someone who loves you for exactly who you are, as you are." Margot stretched, snagging a fistful of tissues from the table. She pressed the whole bunch into Elle's face, making her laugh a little stronger.

Wiping the tears from her face, Elle scooted to sitting. "I get it." She touched the side of her head with the pads of her fingers before tapping her chest. "But when am I gonna *believe* it?"

She wanted to feel that certainty she was so used to. Positivity, that unerring ability to *believe* everything was going to be all right. Optimism. She missed that. She wanted it back.

Margot frowned and shook her head slowly. "I don't know, babe. But I'll keep telling you until you do, okay?"

"It could take years, Mar."

Margot arched a dark brow, expression shrewd. "Are you going anywhere? Because I'm sure as shit not."

Elle sucked in a shuddering breath and nodded. "Thanks."

"That's what friends are for, right?" Margot stood and reached for the ice cream that was beginning to go soupy. "You know what else friends are for?"

Elle shook her head. She could come up with plenty of things friends were for, but it was easier to ask when Margot made it sound like she had something specific in mind.

Margot headed into the kitchen and put the ice cream back in the freezer. Then she grabbed a paper bag from beneath the counter hefting it into the air. Stamped across the paper was the logo from the liquor store on the corner.

She grinned. "Tequila."

☆ ☆
☆

Elle rolled over, trying to get comfortable, but the couch was so hard. Something dug into her side and something under her gave off a terrible, shrill squeak. She shifted away, smacking her funny bone on something even harder. A frisson of pain shot down to her wrist all the way up to her shoulder, her fingers tingling. *Ow.*

Cracking open an eye—*ah*, bad idea. Elle burrowed her head into— Styrofoam?

She tried again, cracking open her eyes slowly. Beneath her face was one of the many takeout containers. And she was using it as a pillow because . . . she was on the floor. "What the hell?"

Ew. Her tongue was gummy and her teeth needed to be scrubbed. Twice. For good measure.

Sitting up slowly, Elle squinted around her. The coffee table was still littered with all the same junk, plus a bottle of tequila . . . missing most of the tequila. Oh. She pressed a hand to her forehead. No wonder she felt like hell and had slept on the floor. *Fucking tequila.*

"Oh, hey. You're up." Margot bounced into the living room looking bright-eyed and bushy-tailed and not at all hungover. Not one bit. She was wearing real people clothing, black jeans and a lace bodysuit. And makeup.

"Mar," she croaked. "What the fuck? Please tell me there's not a tiger in the bathroom."

"There's not a tiger in the bathroom and I promise you still have all your teeth." Margot winced, eyes darting over to the tequila. "Yeah. You had a lot of that."

"What about you?"

"Me?" Margot set the glass of water she was holding on the table in front of Elle. "I drank a little, but I wanted to keep an eye on you."

Elle tilted the glass and let the cool water run down her

parched throat, soothing the burn. She was so thirsty she felt the water run down through her chest and into her churning stomach. Now all she needed was some ibuprofen and—

"What the heck is that?" Elle pointed at the floor beside the couch where a strange doll-shaped bundle sat.

Margot followed her gaze, eyes widening and lips rolling together. "I meant to get rid of that before you woke up. You . . . how much do you remember?"

There'd been ice cream. And crying. Then tequila. She and Margot had made a list of all Darcy's most annoying attributes and . . . her memory went fuzzy. "We made a list?"

"Good, yeah." Margot chewed on her thumbnail. "We made a list and you kind of lost the plot and started saying things you liked about Darcy so I tried to get you back on track. Which worked. You got pretty amped up and you decided to . . ."

"To what?" Between the alcohol and Margot's reluctance to give Elle a straight answer, Elle's stomach churned and her mind flitted from one worst-case scenario to the next, her panic escalating. She had decided to call Darcy? FaceTime her? Elle brought her glass to her lips and took a slow sip to soothe her tummy.

Margot winced. "You made a Darcy voodoo doll."

Elle choked, sputtering water down her chin. "What?"

"You know, a Darcy effigy—"

"I know what a voodoo doll is, Margot." Elle set her glass down roughly, water sloshing on the table. She scrambled across the carpet on her hands and knees and grabbed the human-shaped doll off the floor. In reality, it was a T-shirt stuffed with what looked like pillow fluff made humanoid by tying off limbs with hair ties at the joints. Thankfully, it looked like she hadn't gotten to the point of doing something crazy—*crazier*—and poking pins in the damn thing. "What the hell was I thinking?"

Margot bared her teeth in a grimace. "Tequila. You weren't doing much thinking."

"Did I . . . did I realize how stupid this was?" Elle shook the doll in the air. She'd even attached those twisty-ties they kept in the junk drawer, the red ones from bread loaves, to the doll's head like hair. It looked terrifying, like some rustic doll of olden time possessed with the spirit of a vengeful child. Elle was creeped out that *she* had made it. "Please tell me I came to my senses."

Margot's head seesawed side to side. "Uh. Honestly? You started crying that you couldn't get the freckles right and then you passed out beside the coffee table."

She stared at the doll with wide eyes. Sure enough, there were scribbled splotches, smudged dots that had bled into the cotton fabric. Freckles. Elle slammed her eyes shut and clutched the doll to her chest. *Fuck.*

She hadn't had enough time to commit the constellations those freckles and moles connected into memory. Not nearly enough. She was never going to see those freckles again.

A hand landed on Elle's shoulder making her jolt. Margot tugged the Darcy doll from Elle's hands, setting it aside. In its place, she pressed Elle's phone. "You might want to check that."

Elle's heart crawled into her throat. "I didn't call anybody, right?"

Margot set her hands on her hips, an affronted frown on her face. "I'd never let you do that. You have another missed call from your mom." Her mouth pinched. "And you have a text."

"Did you . . . did you look?"

Margot bit her lip and nodded.

"Is it—" She stared at Margot, eyes wide and heart pounding inside her chest, pulse leaping painfully in her neck.

One little jerk of Margot's head was all it took to send her spirits plummeting. "It's Brendon."

�§ �§
✧

Inside her pocket, her phone buzzed. Brendon, maybe? She wasn't running late.

No. *Mom.*

If she didn't answer, Mom would just keep calling. The calls had escalated in frequency over the past two weeks, word no doubt getting back to Mom that Elle was no longer avoiding Jane and Daniel, just her. Better to bite the bullet than prolong the inevitable. "Hello."

"Elle, you answered. Good." She sounded relieved.

Elle shut her eyes and leaned against the stop-walk sign. "Look, Mom, now's not a good time."

"I've called half a dozen times. I left you messages."

Something about the way she said it, as if *Elle* owed *her* an explanation made Elle grit her teeth.

"I didn't have anything to say." No, that wasn't right. "Or I did, but it didn't feel like you were ready to listen."

Silence filled the line, until the clearing of Mom's throat broke it. "Elle, I'm . . . I'm sorry. It was never my intention to belittle what you do."

"But you did. You called it a pseudoscientific fad. Do you not realize how badly that hurt?"

It *still* hurt, the sting of her words fresher than ever after Elle's falling-out with Darcy.

"I didn't. I just . . ." Mom sighed. "I'm just worried. It's my job to worry about you, Elle-belle. I want what's best for you. That's all I've ever wanted."

What about what she wanted? They'd been having some variation of this conversation for years, tiptoeing around it and Elle was *tired*. "I'm happy. Why can't that be good enough?"

"I've gone about it all wrong. I know that now."

"Let me guess. Jane said something? Daniel?"

"It was Lydia, actually." At Elle's stunned silence, Mom laughed. "She confessed that she agrees with a lot of what you said. That I put too much pressure on you, *all* of you, Lydia included. I had . . . I had no idea, Elle. But Lydia, she told me that she and Marcus are thinking about eloping, can you believe that? She doesn't want to plan a wedding with me. Apparently, I have *impossible* standards and not just when it comes to color schemes and venues. Which makes me feel great, let me tell you." Mom's laughter took on a frantic edge. "I just want what's best for all of you. The best, Elle. I read all these stories about no one being able to retire, that no one can buy a house, and there might be another recession, and it makes me nervous."

"Look on the bright side, I might not be able to retire but

at least I love what I do. I'll be super happy working until the day I die."

Elle cringed until Mom chuckled. "I don't know if that's supposed to be funny."

"I don't know either." The light turned green and Elle hustled across the street.

"Maybe"—Mom coughed—"at our next brunch, you can tell me more about this consulting you're doing for OTP. I promise to actually listen this time."

Elle chewed on the side of her thumbnail, frowning at the brick building but not yet going inside. Brendon was waiting for her, waiting to talk. About what, Elle wasn't sure, but she'd been having flashes of that stress dream, the one where Brendon ripped up their negotiations.

Contracts had been signed; there'd have to be some massive breach to void them, or else OTP would have to pay her and Margot out. Regardless of the legalities, Brendon wouldn't be spiteful like that. Then again, what did Elle know? Nothing. Her gut was all wrong, miscalibrated.

Hopefully when this was all said and done there would still be a deal to tell Mom about. "Sure. But right now, I need to go. I'm meeting a friend for coffee."

"Darcy?"

The sound of her name put a lump in Elle's throat. "Brendon, actually. I'll talk to you later, okay?"

"You'll be home for Christmas, won't you?"

"Of course. I'll drive over on the twenty-fourth, okay?"

One phone call didn't automatically undo years of damage, and she'd bet Mom still wouldn't *approve*, but maybe she wouldn't be so antagonistic. It was a start, a tiny weight lifted off Elle's shoulders. She'd take it.

Shoving her phone back into her pocket, Elle stepped through the door, the warm, nutty aroma of coffee hitting her like a wave. In the back corner of the coffee shop, Brendon sat, frowning at his cup.

Elle's chest throbbed at the sight of him. The resemblance was obvious, painfully so.

Rather than dawdle in the doorway, Elle skirted the ordering counter and headed straight for Brendon's table. Her stomach was too unsettled for caffeine and the acid in the coffee would only amplify the burn in her chest. The sooner she got this over with, the sooner she could head home and— Well, then she'd figure out what came next. This—whatever urgent matter Brendon had requested they meet to discuss—was eating up all her focus, all her energy, her attention.

Brendon looked up from staring morosely into his cup, his brown eyes widening as he caught sight of Elle. Unfolding his long legs from beneath the table, Brendon stood and took a half step toward her before awkwardly freezing like he didn't know how to greet her. "Elle. Hey. You made it."

Elle rested her hands on the back of the chair across from him. "I said I would."

"Right." He nodded, too quick. Frenetic. Jerky. "You did." He cleared his throat and gestured to the chair with a silly little sweep of his hand. "Sorry. Sit. Please."

Elle lowered herself into the chair on wobbling knees. She set her hands on the edge of the table, fingers curling around the wood. Ugh, that made her look nervous. Which she was.

But Brendon didn't need to know that. She dropped her hands into her lap and clasped them tightly before finally shoving them between her knees. "So."

Brendon collapsed into the chair with a heavy sigh, raking his fingers through his hair and messing up the strands. "So."

So. This was awkward, more so because Brendon was *acting* awkward, exacerbating an inherently thorny situation. It set her teeth on edge, wondering what *exactly* it was that had Brendon all in knots. "Is . . . is everything all right with the partnership. OTP and Oh My Stars?"

She held her breath, shoulders tensing.

Brendon's jaw dropped. "What?"

"Is—"

"No, I heard you." Brendon ran a hand over his face, eyes shutting for a second before opening and looking tired. He looked . . . exhausted. Not as rough as she felt, but not well rested, that was for sure. He met her eyes, lips curling in a weak smile. "Everything's fine with the partnership, Elle. Of course, it is. It's . . . it's perfect."

Her shoulders relaxed infinitesimally. "Good. That's good."

"I didn't ask you to meet me here because of work," Brendon said, shifting forward in his seat. He pushed his tea aside and rested his arms on the table. "This doesn't have anything to do with OTP."

Elle bit the corner of her lip, too nervous to ask what he *had* asked her here to discuss.

Brendon dropped his chin, staring at his hands. "Darcy."

Even knowing, realistically, what was coming, hearing Brendon say his sister's name made Elle's heart stutter pathetically. "Hmm."

"Elle." Brendon stared at her, with wide eyes the *exact* same color as Darcy's. "I need you to be honest with me."

She blinked, trying hard not to take offense. "Excuse me?"

Brendon licked his lips. "I said—"

"I *heard* you." Elle shook her head, knees pressing hard in on her hands. "When exactly have I ever been anything other than totally honest?"

"I didn't say you weren't, I—"

"Implied it," she said, shoving down her rapidly rising hackles. Now wasn't the time to lose her chill. "I've always been honest. With you and with your sister, too, for that matter. And I'm sorry, but I don't exactly appreciate you implying otherwise."

Brendon lifted his hands in supplication. "Sorry. Sorry. I'm . . ." He raked one of his hands through his hair again. "Out of my depth, yeah? I'm trying."

Trying to what, exactly? She shook her head. "Why'd you ask me here, Brendon?"

"I'm saying this all wrong." Brendon dropped his head into his hands and groaned. "Darcy is a wreck, Elle."

Darcy was a wreck? Why? She wasn't the one who'd gotten her heart broken. Her life hadn't been upended, her whole world turned upside down.

"Darcy told me. She told me how this started and she also told me how it changed," Brendon said. "She told me . . . she told me everything."

A chilling sense of understanding settled in Elle's upset

stomach, cooling her anger into frosty irritation. "Well, sorry I ruined her ruse. Wasn't my intention."

Just like falling in love with Darcy hadn't been Elle's plan. It had just . . . happened. Hindsight being what it was, Elle should've known better than to think she wouldn't fall ass over head for someone like Darcy.

Brendon groaned softly. "That's still not— *Fuck*, Elle."

Elle stared. Had she ever heard Brendon swear?

"What you said on the street. You were wrong, Elle. Darcy's not heartless, okay?"

Elle pried her hands out from between her knees and crossed her arms, shielding herself from the intensity of Brendon's stare. "Did you ask me here to tell me off, or something? Because to be honest, I'm a little hungover and a lot miserable, and I'm not in the mood to be scolded—"

"No." Brendon shook his head quickly. "Look, Darcy keeps her cards close to the chest."

He kept saying that, but this wasn't a game of poker and she and Darcy weren't supposed to be playing against each other.

"I don't think that's an excuse at this—"

"Darcy was engaged," Brendon blurted.

Elle's jaw dropped. "What?"

"I shouldn't be telling you this," Brendon admitted.

A spike of irritation shot through her. Wasn't that what got her into this entire mess to begin with? Brendon revealing state secrets. Well, and Darcy lying. "Maybe you *shouldn't* then."

Even though a part of her was desperate for him to keep talking.

Brendon shrugged and gave a weak little laugh. "In for a penny, in for a pound, yeah? I'm trying to fix this."

She worried her lip and waited.

He took a sip of his tea. "Natasha. Her name was Natasha. They met in college, dated, moved in together. Darcy proposed. She was happy."

Elle's chest threatened to cave in on itself.

"A month before the wedding, Darcy came home early from work. She . . ." Brendon puffed out his cheeks, eyes dropping to the table. "She, um, found Natasha in bed with a friend. Darcy's friend. A mutual friend. Ex-friend, now. But yeah. She broke things off."

Sympathy spread throughout her chest, hot and achy. "Brendon. You shouldn't—"

"Too late." He lifted his head and blinked fast. "It was bad, Elle. It was"—he coughed—"bad. Darcy tried to make things work in Philadelphia, but it was too rough. She packed up and moved to Seattle."

That's why Darcy had moved. She'd mentioned a breakup and how she'd wanted a fresh start, but she'd never said *that*, nothing that communicated that ugly or painful of an end.

God. "That sucks."

Brendon's lips quirked wryly. "Understatement."

None of this explained why Brendon was telling her this. "Why are you telling me this?"

He stared. "It's not obvious?"

She could fill in the blanks, but that was all she ever did. Fill in other people's blanks. Darcy's blanks. "Spell it out for me."

"My sister has trouble letting people in. She's scared, Elle.

She doesn't think I know. Darcy does everything she can to keep me in the dark because she's got it in her head that she's got to be strong all the time, but I know her better than she realizes. I've been pushing her to put herself out there because if I didn't, she wasn't ever going to. Because she thinks it's easier to be alone than risk falling in love and getting hurt again."

Elle shook her head. "I understand. I get it. But your sister doesn't love me, okay? She's not—we're not anything, okay?"

Brendon cut his eyes. "Nothing? You don't feel anything for her? Nothing."

That's not what she said. "Look, Brendon. I love that you care about your sister. You're a great brother, clearly. And I like you and I like working with you. You're a good friend. But it's not fair for you to try to turn this around and make it about what I feel, okay? Because I've been up-front about what I'm looking for since day one. Since day one I told Darcy what I wanted. I never stopped wanting to find someone to fall in love with. My soul mate. And Darcy knows that." Her next inhale was shaky. "I understand that your sister has baggage, but we all have baggage, Brendon. We've all got shit and I'm—" She sniffed, stupid eyes watering. "I'm tired of having to constantly put myself out there and not be met halfway. That's not fair."

Elle wasn't so naïve as to believe life was fair, definitely not *love*, or at least the pursuit of it, but she wished she didn't have to keep stripping her skin off and showing the whole world her tender heart to get her point across.

Brendon bit his knuckle and nodded.

Elle's head ached, her eyes burning with tears unshed. She

stood, arms dropping to her side. "And no offense, but next time, if Darcy has something to say to me, she can say it herself. I . . . I deserve that."

Margot would be so proud. But Elle would celebrate that tiny victory later. Right now, she felt like she was going to either cry or be sick and doing either in the middle of Starbucks sounded like a recipe for humiliation.

Brendon covered his mouth with his hand and nodded, eyes full of despair yet nowhere close to what Elle felt. "Yeah. That's . . . you're right."

She was. She didn't need Brendon to keep acting as Darcy's emotional intermediary, constantly translating.

Elle clenched her back teeth until her jaw creaked. She needed to get out of here. "I'm gonna . . . I'll see you around, okay?"

She didn't wait for Brendon to reply. Turning on her heel, Elle booked it out of the coffee shop, stepping out into the cool, gloomy afternoon light. Gray skies and low-hanging clouds promised rain.

Elle stopped at the crosswalk and stared hard at the red light until she saw spots, the glow burned into her glassy eyes.

I deserve that.

Maybe if she kept saying it, she'd start to believe it. Not in her head, but in her heart, where for her, it mattered most.

Chapter Twenty-One

Darcy's apartment was quiet in a way that had nothing to do with noise.

She'd always appreciated that her neighbors were considerate and the noises from traffic never penetrated the serene little neighborhood pocketed in downtown. This was different. Never before had the loudest sound inside her apartment been the ever-persistent thud of her heart.

Darcy cradled her coffee cup against her chest and spun in a slow circle. Perhaps the loudest sound wasn't the thud of her heart, but the echoes of Elle that lingered in the kitchen and on the couch, the floor, the shelves, the Christmas tree beside the window. The curious hum Elle had made when running her fingers down the spines of Darcy's books. The sweet chime of her laughter in the kitchen when she'd dunked her finger in the pancake batter and dotted a dollop on Darcy's cheek. How that laughter had evolved into the prettiest moan that had resulted in burned pancakes and a blaring smoke alarm and sheepish smiles and Darcy whispering the words *fuck it* against Elle's neck.

The longer she stood studying her apartment, the less quiet it seemed.

How the hell was Darcy supposed to get rid of an *echo*? A sage smudge stick? Even that sounded like something Elle would say, and she would've gotten a kick out of the look on Darcy's face when she suggested it.

Darcy glared at her bookshelf and chewed on the inside of her cheek. No, she'd do things her way. Erasing all traces of Elle would be her first step, a sound one. She'd scrub her apartment from top to bottom, bust out the Ajax, then she'd spackle over the void with all new furnishings if that's what it took.

Erase all traces.

Darcy inhaled deeply and set her coffee cup on the table. She could do this.

She'd alphabetized the shelves by author's last name. An hour later, they were now alphabetized by title, books lined neatly in a row, nary a one sticking out farther than the rest. Darcy had double-checked, taken a goddamn ruler to the shelves to make sure. Elle might've touched those spines, but not in that order. And she'd never touch them again. Darcy bit the inside of her cheek and nodded.

Don't think about it.

Next, Darcy hauled the box of rosé over to the sink and twisted the nozzle, pink wine swirling down the drain. The wine bladder went into the trash and the box into recycling. Kitchen back to normal, Darcy moved back to the living room, checking off items from her mental to-do list, spring cleaning in the middle of winter.

She got down on her hands and knees and fished out the gel

pen that had rolled beneath her television stand. *Indigo Sky*. Darcy frowned at the pen. It was a close match to the shade of Elle's eyes.

Don't think about it.

Darcy stared at the tree, chest burning. She couldn't bring herself to tear it down, not yet. She'd just try not to look at it. Christmas was tomorrow, anyway. She'd take it down right after.

Don't think about it.

Darcy moved into her bedroom. Stark white sheets and a matching duvet covered her bed. Nothing was remiss save for the speckled composition notebook full of facts about Elle lying on the nightstand. Her birth date. Her favorite gummy bear flavor. All her planets . . . placements . . . houses . . . something like that. Elle in a nutshell. Darcy smoothed her hand across the cover, thumb brushing the pages at the bottom.

Not true. Elle couldn't be contained in pages, constrained to paper. She was larger than life, but these pages held an imprint, the closest Darcy would ever again get.

Recycle, it belonged in the recycle. All she had to do was chuck it and her apartment would be an Elle-free zone once more. Neat, tidy, everything where it belonged. *Quiet.*

Darcy clutched the notebook to her chest and left the room. She opened the cabinet beneath her sink where the trash and recycling resided, and paused. *Drop it.* It was only a notebook, only paper. It wasn't Elle. So would it really matter if she kept it? She'd only used a few of the pages, it would be a waste to toss it. She could rip out the front pages and repurpose the rest. And she'd do that later. But for now, she'd tuck it in the back of her closet behind her shoeboxes. Out of sight, out of mind. She'd ignore it, just like the tree.

Darcy shut off the light to her closet and stood in the middle of her bedroom, arms crossed. There was nothing left to do, nothing left to fill her time, nothing to drive away the silence she was desperate to fill with action and noise.

Sitting still wasn't an option. If she sat down, she might not get back up. Like an object in motion, Darcy needed to keep moving or else the feelings inside her chest that had taken root would branch out. Like some invasive species they'd wrap around her, choking her until she couldn't breathe, couldn't—

Darcy pressed the heels of her hands into her eyes. Keep moving. She'd shower, then— *No.* One step at a time. Minute by minute. Like sands through an hourglass, so were the days of her life.

A desperate, broken chuckle splintered the silence. Darcy clapped a hand over her mouth and breathed in through her nose.

Don't think about it.

Stepping into the bathroom, Darcy flipped the light switch, then reached for the hem of her shirt, pulling it over her head. Her eyes caught on her reflection, something out of place on her face. She dropped her shirt and leaned closer, tilting her head. That wasn't there earlier, that was—

Glitter.

A speck of glitter stuck to her cheek, beneath her eye where the skin was puffy and swollen, so puffy no eye mask or cold compress could combat it.

Darcy rubbed at her skin with her fingers. No dice. She

rubbed harder, scraping with the edge of her nail. It wouldn't budge. It was adhered to her skin like glue, going nowhere. She turned on the faucet and splashed her face, gasping a little at the shock of ice-cold water against her flushed skin.

Jesus, was it embedded? Was it stuck beneath the surface? It was *glitter*, of course it wasn't going anywhere. Glitter never went anywhere other than exactly where you didn't want it, where it didn't belong.

Turning off the water, she hung her head, sucking in air through her mouth because her nose wasn't working. Was suddenly stuffed. She couldn't breathe through it, why couldn't she—

"Darce?"

She shrieked and jumped back, nearly slipping on her discarded shirt atop the tile floor. Hands grasping the counter, Darcy caught herself, then ducked and grabbed her shirt, tugging it over her head. The tag brushed her chin, her shirt backward.

Brendon.

"What the fuck? Don't you knock?" Blood pumped adrenaline to her extremities, making her fingers twitch.

Brendon stared at her with wide, frazzled eyes, the crests of his cheeks pink. "I did? I knocked. I called. I texted. You didn't answer so I used the key—"

"The key I gave you in case of *emergencies*, Brendon. Christ. This isn't . . . this isn't an emergency. It's *not*. You don't get to come in here, just waltz in my apartment like you own the place. An emergency is if I don't pick up for hours or a day or two days. This isn't an emergency."

Brendon guppied like a goldfish. "I was worried. I didn't—"

"That's not your job." Darcy pressed a hand to her chest over her racing heart. "*You* are not supposed to worry about *me*. I worry about *you*, got it? That's *my* job."

"Darce—"

"*No.* I'm mad. I am mad at you. Do you hear me? I'm *so* mad." Darcy sucked in a gasp and bit the inside of her cheek. Her vision blurred so she shut her eyes. "God, what's wrong with me?"

Hands grasped her arms tight, held her as she sunk down to the bathroom floor. She tucked her knees against her body and leaned into Brendon who shushed her with empty words meant to make her feel better. *I'm sorry. There's nothing wrong with you. You're okay. It's going to be okay.*

"It's not." She gasped. "It's not going to be okay."

She could scrub the apartment from top to bottom. She could rearrange her books and get rid of all Elle's things, everything Elle had touched. Darcy could burn her whole apartment to the ground, salt the earth, and move halfway across the world but there'd be no escaping the memories, the *glitter*. Virtual fingerprints she'd never get rid of.

There wasn't a part of Darcy Elle hadn't touched, her skin, her hips, her hair, her lips, her heart. She'd be finding glitter from now until eternity.

Brendon cupped the back of her neck with fingers that felt cool against her flushed skin. "You've got to believe that it's going to be okay. *I* believe it's going to be okay."

God. He sounded like Elle.

Darcy pushed at Brendon's shoulders and lifted her head.

"Elle wanted to know how I felt. I told her I didn't know. I was—"

Scared. Like Brendon had accused her of being.

And now he knew. It was hard to pretend to be some pillar of strength when he'd watched her fall apart.

He leaned back, staring. "All right. Then tell *me* how you feel. Tell me something about Elle."

Seriously? "Brendon—"

"Come on." He nudged her with his knee.

"*Why?*" Anger sparked, never having gone away, instead drifting into the background, pain pervading. Why did Brendon care? When was he going to stop making her do things she didn't want? Things it was so hard for her to say no to?

He took her outburst in stride, shrugging congenially. "Why? Because I care about you and you're wrong. It's not your job to take care of me."

"It *is*—"

"No." Brendon shook his head. "It's not. You're not Mom, and it was never supposed to be your job to take care of me. You did more than you needed to, more than I probably know about, but you don't have to do it by yourself anymore. It's our job to take care of each other, okay?"

"I don't need you to take care of me," she whispered.

"Needing help, *wanting* help, it doesn't make you weak, Darce. Let me in. Let me help you."

This was Brendon. And apparently, he knew more, was far more perceptive, than she'd given him credit for. He'd already seen her at rock bottom; how much worse could it be opening up? "You want me to tell you about Elle?"

He nudged her again. "Humor me."

Fine. Darcy licked her lips. "She tastes like strawberries."

Brendon wrinkled his nose, face scrunching up in disgust. "Oh, come on."

Darcy kicked him in the foot and laughed, swiping beneath her eyes. "I meant her lip gloss. She tastes like the strawberry jam Grandma used to make. Remember?"

Brendon leaned his head back against the bathroom wall and smiled. "Yeah?"

She twisted the ring on her hand and nodded.

"What else?"

The easier question wasn't what she liked about Elle, but what she didn't. Because Elle wasn't perfect, there were things about her that drove Darcy up the wall, like how she never wore a jacket and would sometimes drop off in the middle of a sentence when a new thought flitted through her mind, but listing the things she loved about Elle was like asking her to count the stars in the sky. They'd be there all night and even then, it wouldn't be enough time.

"Her eyes are my new favorite color and if you make fun of me for saying that I'll—"

"Issue an empty threat?" Brendon nodded. "Not laughing, but got it. Go on."

Darcy sighed and leaned back against the bathroom cabinet. "I can talk to her, trust her with things I don't tell everyone. Like how I watch soap operas and used to write *Days* fanfic—*don't* say anything—and she didn't laugh. She told me I should do whatever makes me happy." Darcy rested her hand over her throat. "She makes me happy. *Made* me happy."

Brendon reached out, resting a hand on the top of her foot. "Sounds like you love her."

Darcy shut her eyes and bit her tongue.

He hadn't said it the way Mom had, intrusive and anxious. Brendon made it sound simple. The sky is gray. It's raining out. You love Elle. As if it were easy. But there was nothing simple about how she felt.

"Brendon." She choked. "I can't. I can't love her. I can't do it."

He squeezed the top of her shin and made a soft sound in the back of his throat, half hum and half cough. "I don't think it's a matter of can or can't. You either do or you don't, and I think we both know you do. There's— If I make a Yoda joke, will you kill me?"

"Yes."

He smiled. "You feel how you feel and that's not going to change just because you didn't tell her, because you didn't say the words. I mean, you didn't stop loving her after the party the other night, did you? How you feel . . . that's not really the question, is it? It's whether you're going to let Elle in. Whether you're going to let her love you the way you deserve to be loved, Darce."

Would Elle even want to hear how she felt, or was it too late? What if Elle turned her away? Or worse, what if everything went perfect, only to go wrong again in a month, six months, two years?

There was no accounting for anything when it came to love and that was terrifying.

"Come on," Brendon said. "What's the worst that could happen?"

Darcy swallowed. "I'm scared."

Brendon's brow furrowed like he wasn't expecting her to admit it, to finally say it. But it was about time she finally owned up to the fact that she was constantly terrified. That her fears had come true and the hope of fixing this only to fail all over again was almost enough to make her throw in the towel and never put herself out there again.

"That's normal, Darce. Everyone's scared. You wouldn't be human if you weren't."

But not everyone was afraid of *this*. "I don't want to be like Mom. She built her entire life around Dad and . . . look how that turned out."

Maybe Darcy hadn't built her life *around* Natasha, but she'd built a life *with* her and when that life had come crashing down, there was no clean break, no easy way to separate out the parts of that life that belonged to her alone. There was too much overlap, too much muddying of the waters. She'd lost her apartment and her friends, save for Annie. Darcy still had her job, so no, it wasn't exactly the same as Mom, but the fear of everything else crumbling around her again, the thought of having to rebuild her life all over again, after having already done it once, was suffocating enough to make the differences in their situations feel nominal. It was the whole reason why she'd sworn off dating and buried herself in her work and exam prep in the first place.

"I'm not trying to take anything away from you or downplay what happened with Natasha—you went through a breakup, a really bad breakup granted, but it's not the same. That's not the type of person you are." Brendon took a deep breath. "Running at the first sign of something serious because you're afraid someone's going to hurt you isn't any better. You're just going to hurt yourself like you're hurting right now. And you're going to keep hurting until you do something to fix it. Try. Be honest with her. Trust her."

Darcy had a choice. Not whether to love Elle, because Brendon was right. There was no choice in that. What she was going to do about it was a different matter. Because maybe she couldn't control what happened in a month or six months or a year or twenty years, but she could do something about this. Here and now.

Brendon's lips quirked as if he knew what was going through her head.

Darcy scrunched the hem of her shirt in her hands, wringing the fabric. "What if I'm too late?"

"You love her?"

Darcy screwed up her face. *Obviously* or she wouldn't be in this pathetic state on her bathroom floor crying over glitter. Not that she didn't appreciate the wake-up call, but why did it have to be *glitter*?

Brendon laughed at her expression and kicked her gently. "Then it's not too late. It's never too late if you love someone."

"Wow," Darcy teased. "You sound like a Hallmark card."

"What occasion would that be? Belated anniversary? Birthday? Just because?"

"It's going to be *sympathy* if you don't get out of my apartment." Darcy smiled, softening the threat. She grabbed the counter and used it to heave herself to standing. "I have to clean myself up and figure out what I'm going to say." Her heart raced frantically. No matter what Brendon said, this was going to be no small undertaking.

"I'm good with grand gestures if you need help." He cracked his knuckles and hopped to standing. "My favorite movies have prepared me for this."

Darcy was less concerned with what to *do* and more concerned with what to *say*. "I'm going to have to tell her . . . everything."

Darcy gritted her teeth. Fun.

"About that." Brendon raked his fingers through his hair, wincing sharply. "Don't hate me, but I, uh, might've meddled." He held up his hand, thumb and index finger nearly touching. "A little."

✩ ✩
✩

Darcy shifted the potted plant in her arms and grimaced.

Too late to ask Brendon for advice on grand gestures now. Standing in front of the door to Elle's apartment was it. Showtime.

Darcy knocked just below the shiny silver wreath hanging lopsided from a Command Strip hook. Then she waited. And waited. And—

The lock flipped, the door opening. The beautiful, haunting voice of Joni Mitchell singing "River" poured out into the hall as an arm rested against the doorframe, blocking her view into the apartment.

Margot.

A decidedly pissed-off-looking Margot. Darcy gulped and

stood up straighter, smoothing her expression into a mask of disaffection no doubt undermined by the terra-cotta planter cradled in her arms.

"Margot." Darcy dipped her chin in a polite greeting.

Margot glared. *Hard.*

Fuck. The air was stifling, the building's heat turning the hall into a sauna. Darcy shifted the plant again and swept her hair over one shoulder.

"Elle's not here." Margot began to shut the door.

She had not hiked all the way to the market to buy this stupid, precious plant and then all the way up to Elle's apartment only to get turned away. No. This was not her dead end. All she needed was a chance. Needed to try, needed Elle to know how she felt.

Darcy clenched her back teeth and shoved the boot of her toe in between the door and frame, wincing a bit when the door bounced off her foot. "Then where is she?"

"Alexa, stop." The music cut off midverse. "In case you hadn't noticed, it's Christmas Eve. I have an hour-long drive ahead of me *if* traffic's clear, which it won't be. All I want is to finish packing, hit the road, make it home before my dad eats all the gingerbread cookies, and then I want to drink several strong glasses of eggnog. Talking to you doesn't rank very high on my to-do list. In fact, it doesn't even warrant a spot. So, piss off, Darcy."

"I just want to know where Elle is and then I'll leave you alone."

Margot narrowed her eyes. "Why do you care?"

"Look—"

"No, you look." Margot let go of the door and leaned against the frame, crossing her arms over her chest and thrusting out her chin. "You don't get to come here, demanding to see my best friend if you can't even tell me why you want to see her."

Darcy bit the side of her tongue. Not that she'd ever thought for a second Elle hadn't told Margot about what had happened between them, but there was the confirmation. Confirmation that Darcy had fucked up.

She met Margot's eyes so she'd see how sincere Darcy was. "I fucked up."

Margot pursed her lips. "Huh. Something we agree on."

Darcy huffed. "Well. Can you help me *un*-fuck up?"

"I could." Margot's way of making it painfully clear Darcy's fate partially rested in her hands.

Between the nerves and the hike to Pike Place and her difficulty finding this plant, the *right* plant, Darcy was at her wits' end. "Are you *going* to help me?"

Margot cocked her head, one slender brow arching sharply above the frames of her glasses. "Depends."

"On?"

"Do you love her?"

That question. A flicker of fear lit up her brain, the part that signaled to her legs to flee the danger. Darcy planted her feet and gripped the plant in her arms tighter.

"I think I should tell that to Elle."

Margot shoved her thumb under the ridge of her brow bone. "Shockingly, something else we agree on. Question is, *are* you going to say something or are you gonna fuck up all over again?"

"Aiming to not fuck up. Hence the reason I'm here."

Margot dropped her hand, eyes lowering to stare at the plant in Darcy's arms. "What the fuck is that?"

Darcy cleared her throat, heat creeping up the back of her neck. "It doesn't matter. Could you please just tell me where Elle is?"

Margot sighed. "Look. I told Elle I wasn't a fan of this, this *fake dating* shit you sprang on her. I told her from the beginning not to expend emotional labor you didn't deserve. Quite frankly, I'm still not sure you deserve Elle because she's my best friend and the greatest person I know. I will *always* think she deserves the absolute best and I don't like you right now so in my book, you're the worst. But who's best for her isn't up to me to decide. I pour the drinks and feed her ice cream and hold her hand when she cries and yeah, I give my opinion and plenty of advice, but Elle can make her own decisions. For whatever reason, she wants you. But so help me god, if you break her heart again, I will slash your tires, Darcy Lowell."

"I sold my car when I moved here," Darcy admitted.

Margot rolled her eyes. "Then I'll break into your apartment and move everything three inches to the left and fuck with your flow, okay?"

Darcy stared because, *shit*, that actually sounded awful.

The sentiment, however, was nice. Nice that Elle had someone who had her back, who loved her enough to make those kinds of eerily unsettling threats. Good thing Darcy wasn't planning on ever breaking Elle's heart. Not if she had her way.

"Got it. Loud and clear. Now, can you please tell me where to find Elle so I can try to fix this?"

A slow smirk tugged at Margot's lips, easily as unsettling as that threat to induce paranoia by subtly altering Darcy's surroundings. "How do you feel about metaphysical book-stores?"

✩ ✩
✩

A bell above the door chimed loudly as Darcy stepped into the bookstore. Patchouli and sandalwood tickled her nose, nearly making her sneeze. She coughed lightly and gripped the plant tighter in her arms, glancing around the hole-in-the-wall bookstore.

A dizzying maze of wall-to-wall, floor-to-ceiling shelves were crammed inside the store, the aisles between them narrow, a fire hazard. Near the front of the tiny shop was a wide rectangular table wrapped in silver garland and covered in colorful, translucent crystals and nonfiction paperbacks. *How to Awaken Your Third Eye. Tantric Sex 101. You and Your Yoni.*

"Can I help you find something?"

Darcy jumped, nerves getting the best of her. Behind the counter stood a man in a red-and-green caftan and a woman decked out in a black corset, leather pants, and an ear full of piercings. Darcy glanced down at her wool trousers and sensible green sweater, plant cradled against her chest. Out of her comfort zone was putting it lightly.

They were both watching her expectantly. Darcy pasted on a smile. "Yes, actually. I'm looking for Elle Jones."

The woman with the many silver piercings in her cartilage grabbed a binder from under the desk and ran her coffin-shaped candy-cane-striped nail down the page. "She should be finishing up with a client in the next few minutes if you—"

Beside the counter, a purple beaded curtain parted. Out stepped a woman who looked to be in her midfifties wearing a smile as she spoke in hushed tones over her shoulder.

Elle stepped through the curtain, batting the beads out of her face and Darcy's heart seized.

Gently patting her client on the shoulder, Elle then waved good-bye. She performed a quick double take before staring at Darcy.

Darcy shoved down the nerves threatening to choke her, render her mute. That was the opposite of what she needed. "Hey."

Elle sucked her lower lip between her teeth, eyes dropping to the floor in front of Darcy's feet. Her shoulders rose and she lifted her eyes, pinning Darcy with a merciless glare. "Darcy."

The look in Elle's eyes turned Darcy's stomach, weakening her resolve. *No.* She'd come this far. Hunted down this plant, faced Margot. She could do this. "Can we talk?"

Elle crossed her arms over her chest. "Not gonna have Brendon run interference?"

Ow. She deserved that but it didn't make the jab sting any less.

Darcy squared her shoulders and shook her head. "No. I'm not. I'd like to talk to you."

A flicker of interest passed over Elle's face, her eyes narrowing briefly before her expression smoothed into a mask of indifference. Darcy knew that look. She'd perfected that look. "I'm busy. Working, in case you didn't notice."

Darcy hadn't come all this way to have the door metaphorically slammed in her face. "How much for a . . . reading?"

"What?" Elle's eyes bugged.

Darcy juggled the plant in her arms, shifting until she could reach inside her crossbody purse and grab her wallet.

A soft noise of distress slipped from Elle's lips. "You don't . . . you don't believe in astrology. It's a waste of time. Yours and mine."

"You accept cards, I assume?" Darcy slid her Visa across the glass counter.

Elle made a tiny choked sound in the back of her throat, half shriek and part huff. "*Darcy.*"

Darcy took her card back from the woman and signed the receipt with a flourish, turning back to Elle with wide, pleading eyes. "Please, Elle."

She held her breath as Elle deliberated, chewing on the side of her lip, eyes locked on Darcy's face. After a gut-wrenching moment wherein Darcy tried to mentally and facially communicate how sincere she was—likely looking crazed or worse, constipated—Elle finally sighed, tossing her hands in the air before stepping back through the beaded curtain. "Fine. You want a reading? I'll give you a reading."

Chapter Twenty-Two

*E*lle threw herself into the velvet wingback chair behind the slightly wobbly round table and watched as Darcy's nose occasionally wrinkled, no doubt having all sorts of opinions about the Nag Champa wafting from the incense burner in the corner of the room.

She tucked her right leg beneath her and crossed her arms over her stomach. This was fine. Darcy wanted a reading? Elle would read her to filth.

"Have a seat." She reached for her phone and pulled up the chart she'd saved weeks ago. She set her phone on the table, eyes staring shrewdly at Darcy's houses and alignments. "Let's see, you want to start with your Capricorn stellium? Maybe dig into your seventh house Pluto? Hmm, we could spend a whole hour talking about your south node in Virgo."

Darcy shifted that stupid-looking plant—*why* in the world was she carrying a fucking *shrub?*—on her lap and nodded quickly. "Okay. Sure."

Just like that, Elle deflated.

She couldn't do this. She couldn't take Darcy's chart and use it against her. Astrology was a tool for empathy, not one to exact payback. She wasn't going to twist something beautiful into something ugly, make it malicious, because her feelings were hurt. Understatement. But still. This wasn't how Elle operated and she wasn't going to change that, no matter how heartbroken she was. She wasn't cruel and she didn't want to hurt Darcy with barbed words, tear her down. Hurting Darcy wouldn't mend Elle's broken heart.

Elle flipped her phone over. "I can't do this."

Darcy pursed her lips, sitting up straighter. "I paid."

"Go ask Sheila for a refund, then. I'm not going to waste my time giving you a reading when you don't even believe in this. Especially not on Christmas Eve, Darcy."

Darcy's hands hugged that ugly terra-cotta planter, knuckles turning white from her grip. Her nail polish, that same boring pink shade she always wore, was chipped, peeling away from her thumbnail. All her nails were bitten down to the quick. "You're right. I don't believe in astrology."

Despite having given Darcy the out, Elle's throat narrowed, her chest tightening.

What hurt the most in that moment was that she'd thought Darcy had understood. That it wasn't whether it was real, but it was about understanding each other. Connecting. Feeling less alone. "Cool. Like I said, ask Sheila for a refund."

Darcy didn't move, didn't get up, didn't leave the room. She barely shook her head. "But you do. You believe in it."

Duh.

"It's been a long time since I believed in something, any-thing," Darcy whispered. She opened her mouth and a little hiccup of a gasp slipped out. "You make me want to believe in something, Elle. And I do. I don't believe in astrology, but I believe in you and I believe in this, in what I feel. And I know you're mad and it's probably too late, but could you let me ex-plain? Please."

Elle's heart went haywire. Stuttering, speeding, *stopping* be-fore clawing its way up her chest. Speaking wasn't something she could do with her heart lodged inside her throat. She nod-ded instead.

"Yes, I never planned for this. I didn't want to fall in love, not again, not after—" Darcy broke off, air stuttering from between her lips, lips that quivered gently before she swallowed and got ahold of herself. She met Elle's eyes across the table, didn't so much as flinch at the contact. Her brown eyes were wide and vulnerable, brow lightly pinched, but the rest of her face was lax. "Brendon told me he already told you about Nata-sha. I'll spare you the dirty details but putting myself out there again was the last thing I wanted. Then you came along."

Elle snorted. Ah, yes. She came crashing into Darcy's life, uninvited. How could she forget? Spilled wine and butting heads. Charming.

"You were the exact opposite of what I wanted," Darcy said.

Elle clenched her hands into fists. She'd asked for sincerity, but she hadn't asked for *this*. Hearing her worst fears con-firmed. "That's—"

"Please," Darcy whispered, shaking her head. "I'm not . . .

you were the opposite of what I thought I wanted but it turned out you were exactly what I needed and somewhere along the way you became the one thing I wanted more than anything. What I said to my mother, it wasn't true, Elle. I lied to her and I lied to myself. This is so much more than me just having fun."

Elle took the deepest breath she could with her arms crossed snug over her stomach. "I know I'm not the most punctual person and I can't tell the difference between a cabernet sauv— whatever and a pinot to save my life. I believe in astrology and I follow my gut more than I follow my head. And all of that? It's who I am." Her stupid eyes had to go and water. Elle blinked fast and shrugged. "I like who I am. A lot. What I do, who I am, it makes me happy. And I . . . I deserve someone who likes me exactly the way I am, mess and all. I need to be able to know that. I need to hear that. I need to believe it. I deserve someone who can say it."

Each time she said it, she believed it a little more, and a little more. This time, she believed it all the way, believed it the way she believed in the stars, and the moon. Elle believed in herself, and no matter how much she wanted Darcy—which was an absurd amount—loving herself was no mere consolation prize.

Darcy's throat worked through several convulsions, and she nodded. "You do. You do deserve that, Elle."

Elle sniffed and jerked her chin, curiosity finally getting the best of her. "And by the way, I can't take care of plants. I have the opposite of a green thumb. So . . ."

Might as well be totally honest. What else did she have to lose that she hadn't already lost?

Darcy stared down at the plant, laughing wryly. "I should've asked Brendon for his advice after all. Grand gestures aren't exactly my forte. And I'm bad at saying something. But it doesn't have anything to do with you. It's me. I was scared." Darcy shut her eyes and rolled her lips together. A pink flush worked its way up her face, turning her nose and the skin beneath her eyes red. When she opened her eyes and lifted her head, the bloodshot look of desperation in her glassy eyes snatched Elle's breath.

"I was *terrified*. I'd gotten my heart broken once before and it scared me because I'd watched my mom fall apart and suddenly, *I* was the one falling apart and I never wanted to put myself in a position where that would happen again. I moved to Seattle and promised I wouldn't let that happen. Falling in love was the last thing I wanted, but then you came into my life and somewhere along the way what I felt for you was more, *so much* bigger than I'd ever felt for anyone else. Bigger than I felt for the person I thought I was going to spend the rest of my life with. One month, Elle. One month and I was—" Darcy pressed the back of her hand against her mouth. "I fell for you and it scared me because, what if I lost you? What if something happened? What if you broke my heart?" Darcy turned her head to the side and blinked fast, lashes fluttering like butterfly wings. "I was scared of losing you and I was equally as afraid of getting to keep you, because how much worse would it hurt if I lost you later? I said nothing and I lost you anyway."

Darcy lifted the potted plant in front of her. "It's cilantro. Because I've liked you for longer than I knew how to say, before I could say it. Before I could say it the way you deserve to hear it. But I have and I do. I like you exactly the way you are, Elle. Boxed wine and glitter and astrology and most of all"— Darcy sucked in a gasping breath—"I love the way you make me hope. You make me hope and you make me happy. You make me *so* happy, Elle."

Astrology involved a certain balance between prediction and manifestation, preparation and action. This though, Elle never could've seen this coming. This was too good to be true, even better because it was.

"Yeah?" she whispered, eyes wide and unblinking because if she blinked, she'd cry and she wanted to be able to see Darcy's face, watch her, drink her in. Memorize this moment, a picture-perfect snapshot she'd cherish for the rest of her life, for as long as she could remember.

"I told you I didn't know how I felt." Darcy set the cilantro plant on the table between them and stood. She brushed her palms on her thighs, shoulders rising with her inhale. "I lied. I know how I feel and I'm five hundred percent certain that on a scale of one to ten, I want to be with you, exactly as you are, infinity."

Elle pressed her fingers to her lips, both trembling. "Infinity? That's . . . that's a big number."

And Darcy saying it was an even bigger deal.

Darcy rounded the table and reached out, grabbing Elle's hand in hers. Darcy's hand shook and something about that little tremor made Elle flush with warmth from the top of her head to the tips of her toes. Darcy cared enough that she was shaking, shaking like Elle. "Technically, infinity isn't a real number. But what I feel for you? That's real. It's the realest thing I've ever felt, Elle."

Thumb stroking the back of Elle's hand, Darcy met her eyes. A spark. A connection, the kind that couldn't be faked.

Elle pressed up on her toes and wrapped her free hand around the back of Darcy's neck, smiling into the kiss. Champagne fizzing and shooting stars, fireworks and late nights riding in the back of a too-fast car, lights of the city whizzing past, the bridge of her favorite song blaring. None of it held a candle to this moment, this feeling burning in her veins and warming her chest, bubbling in her stomach and erupting goose bumps along her skin. *Magic.*

For the first time, Elle didn't need a *maybe*, didn't need to *hope* because she *knew.*

This was it.

Boom.

End game.

A lifetime of butterflies.

Acknowledgments

I count my lucky stars that I have so many amazing people in my life to thank. In this, words can't do my appreciation justice, but I'll give it my best.

Sarah Younger, *oh my gosh*, thank you for seeing something in my writing worth taking a chance on. I'm so beyond grateful to have you in my corner during this roller coaster of a journey. You are a rock star and the best agent anyone could dream of having and I am so thankful for everything you do. To my amazing editor, Nicole Fischer, and the entire team at Avon, thank you for taking a chance on this quirky, queer romcom that is so near and dear to my heart. Thank you, thank you, *thank you* for believing in this book and helping make this dream of mine a reality.

I absolutely would not be where I am without the other amazing writers who have helped me along this journey. To the Pitch Wars class of 2017 and the Golden Heart class of 2018, the Persisters, thank you for showing me what it means to be a part of a writing community. This business has the propensity to be solitary, but you all have made me feel like I'm not alone. Your knowledge, commiseration, and support mean the world to me.

Brighton Walsh, I very well might've given up on writing had it not been for you seeing a kernel of *something* in my writing worth encouraging. You taught me so much and I honestly can't do justice to how much I appreciate you reading—and rereading—an earlier manuscript of mine and for telling me to not give up. I will never forget your kindness and your willingness to help other writers. From the bottom of my heart, thank you.

To Layla Reyne and Victoria De La O, I am so appreciative that you chose me as your mentee in Pitch Wars 2017. Thank you for choosing me out of countless submissions and helping me strengthen that manuscript. Without you both, I'm confident I wouldn't be the writer I am today.

Brenda Drake, thank you a million times for creating Pitch Wars. You've helped so many writers in their journeys to publication, myself included. I can't possibly thank you enough for building this community and giving it your all without asking for anything in return.

Rompire. Oh god, I don't even know how to begin to express my gratitude for all of you. I'm so honored to call you all not just my writing pals, but true friends. Amy Jones, Lisa Leoni, Megan McGee, Julia Miller, Em Shotwell, Lana Sloan, and Anna Collins, thank you for listening to me rant, make cheesy jokes, and for not laughing when my hair is a hot mess on Marco Polo. You've kept me sane over these past few months—and for some of you, much longer—and you all inspire me more than I can say. Because of you, I strive to be a better writer and I'm in awe of the amazing women that you all are. Thank you. And a special shout-out to Amy for reading so many of my words, even when I had no idea what I was doing. Your feedback has been invaluable.

I've been blessed to have many amazing teachers who changed my life for the better. To David Kline, my high school creative writing and theater teacher, I can't possibly thank you enough for encouraging my passion for storytelling and creating. You made me believe that a life dedicated to art is never a life wasted. On the flip side, thank you to the creative writing professor I had in college who laughed at my interest in genre fiction. I'm just stubborn enough that telling me I shouldn't do something is a surefire way to make me want to throw myself into it, heart, body, and soul.

To my fur baby, Samantha, thank you for being the best alpha reader a girl could ask for. And by that, I mean thank you for listening to me talk to myself and for only looking at me like I've lost my mind a *little*. Each time you fall asleep on my notebooks and stomp across my keyboard, you remind me that stepping away from the computer and focusing on the world around me is important. You are my ultimate cuddle buddy and I love you to the moon and back, Sam.

Last but not least, I would not be here—quite literally—without my mom. Mom, thank you for always encouraging me to pursue my passions and supporting me no matter how many times I changed my mind about what I wanted to do with my life or how many times I failed. From the very beginning, when I was a little kid telling wild stories about my imaginary husband, Rodger, a green dragon whose mother hated me, you supported the quirky storyteller inside of me. You are my best friend and I love you to the stop sign and back.

Keep an eye out for Brendon's story . . .

HANG THE MOON

Coming Summer 2021

About the Author

Alexandria Bellefleur is an author of swoony contemporary romance often featuring lovable grumps and the sunshine characters who bring them to their knees. A Pacific Northwesterner at heart, Alexandria has a weakness for good coffee, Pike Place IPA, and Voodoo Doughnuts. Her special skills include finding the best pad Thai in every city she visits, remembering faces but not names, falling asleep in movie theaters, and keeping cool while reading smutty books in public. She was a 2018 Romance Writers of America Golden Heart finalist. You can find her at www.alexandriabellefleur.com or on Twitter at @ambellefleur.